head
start

Cedar Tree series #7

FREYA BARKER

Cover Design:

RE&D - Margreet Asselbergs

Editing:

PREMA - Vanessa Leret-Bridges

DEDICATION

To my son, Stijn, who has not (and likely never will) read one single book I've written, but is nevertheless one of my biggest supporters.

He is the perfect example of an empathetic, sensitive Alpha. A man's man, a hunter, a fisherman, who knows what he wants and works with his hands, but who is at the same time a nurturer. A man, able to whip up a gourmet meal as easily as he can build a beautiful barn wood table from scratch. Who despises too much attention but can't help smile when his fiancé basks in the centre of it with her cute antics. A man who doesn't like talking, but has no problem letting his girl (and his mom!) know how much he loves her. Both in word and in action.

I'm so proud of the adult my son has become. Not because of fancy degrees, economic accomplishments or material things, but because he is an amazing man and a fantastic human being.

TABLE OF CONTENTS

"Later!" she calls out as she leaves the locker room.

"Have fun, and be careful." This from Jeanne, her supervisor, who is lingering by the nurse's station.

"Stop worrying. He was great when we met for coffee. Tonight is just gonna be dinner. I'll take it slow, I promise." She smiles at the older woman, who only has her best interests at heart. She knows that.

Jeanne's face softens at her words. "Okay, honey. Enjoy yourself and I'll see you tomorrow."

With a last wave, she almost skips to her car in the staff parking lot of Mercy Regional Medical Center, where she's just entered her tenth year. She'd started working there straight out of nursing school. Eager to escape the oppressive, small Nebraska town she grew up in, she had jumped at the chance when she saw the job postings for the brand new hospital. The first time she'd flown into Durango, Colorado, for her interview, she'd been immediately sold. Everything she'd dreamed of, right there at her fingertips. The only thing missing was the right man to start a family with. Thirty-three years old, and aside from a few attempts at something more serious, she'd never come close. Until now.

Starting up her aging clunker, a smile steals over her face as she recalls the first e-mail she received from him. So polite, almost shy in his approach, just like he'd been when they finally met for coffee last week. He had blushed when he asked her out for another date, and seemed almost embarrassed to suggest a picnic.

His car was already waiting when she pulled into the parking lot at Smelter Mountain. He'd told her to wear hiking gear for the short, but steep trek up the trail to the lookout point, from where they'd be able to see the lights come on in Durango below. So romantic.

"Hey." He smiles sheepishly and she notices again how very handsome he is when he does that. Perfect white teeth and a strong chin. She can't stop the little shiver of anxious anticipation rolling down her back.

"Hi. I brought the blanket." She holds up the quilt she remembered to grab this morning before leaving for work.

"And I brought dinner," he says, holding up a sizable backpack before slipping the straps over his shoulders. He turns to her and holds out his hand. "You ready?"

Tentatively, she grabs his hand, the blanket tucked under her arm, and follows behind him up the trail. They encounter a few fellow hikers, who are on their way down to the parking lot. Each time she slips behind him to allow them to pass, she can't help but notice that his grip on her hand tightens more. She does find the way he seems to duck his head a little bizarre, but she blames that on his timid nature. Not everyone is comfortable looking strangers in the eye.

A little winded from the ascent, she's glad when they finally reach the ridge. In the mountains, the sun often appears to set earlier, and already the light is getting more diffused. The view is beautiful. Looking down, she notices some of the lights along Main Street are coming on and the picturesque town seems cozy, nestled in between the mountains.

A sharp tug at her hand has her turn her head. He is looking at her instead of the view, and suddenly she feels a little unsettled. At some point he has taken off his glasses, and what had appeared to be warm, dark brown eyes now look hard and cold. She instinctively tries to pull her hand free, but he holds on. With a twist, she manages to free her hand, immediately rubbing it with the other to restore blood flow.

"I'm sorry, was I squeezing to hard? I was worried you were getting too close to the edge," he says, the now familiar shy smile on his face, but it doesn't reach his eyes.

"No…I'm… It's okay. I'm not feeling too well," she mutters, not entirely lying. "Maybe I should head back."

The next moment, he has her face pressed to his chest and an arm holding her tight against his body. She's shocked to feel his prominent arousal pressing into her stomach and tries to pull back, but his unforgiving hold prevents that from being at all possible.

"Don't worry, lamb. I'll take care of you." His lips brush her hair as he whispers to her.

The small sting to her neck is barely noticeable. If not for the rapidly spreading heat that seems to sap the strength right out of her, she might have simply dismissed it.

This was a mistake, is the last thought she has.

CHAPTER ONE

Kendra

"No, Karly, I'm not going on a singles' cruise with you."

I roll my eyes at Naomi who is chuckling as she walks by the front desk. Naomi is Doc Waters, technically Dr. Morris since she married Joe Morris last year, but everyone still knows her as Doc Waters. We opened this clinic in Cedar Tree over a year ago. Already Naomi is near capacity with her patient load, and I'm at a point where I'm here on an almost full-time basis. Just two shifts a week left for me at Southwest Memorial in Cortez. Most of my regular physical therapy patients have already followed me here to Cedar Tree.

Two weeks from now, I'll be moving out of my beloved apartment in Cortez and into a cute rental here in town. Actually, the house belongs to a friend, who prefers renting it out over selling. The rent is actually slightly less than what I pay for my apartment so it wasn't a particularly difficult decision. Not to mention, I will have a backyard, a great L-shaped living/dining room, two good-sized bedrooms and a bath. The place even has a swing on the porch. I'm looking forward to drinking my morning coffee there. And the best part about it? I can walk to work every day. I love walking.

The grating high-pitched sound of my sister's lament drags me back to the conversation.

"Why not? It's half-price, one of those short notice deals." My sister resorts to the pre-adolescent whine that gets our mom to cave every single time. Unfortunately, Karly hasn't yet figured out that it does the opposite for me.

"Because those things are like floating sausage fests."

"You're such a stick-in-the-mud. Mom said she'd come too."

Oh my God. Like that is any sort of enticement. I have to swallow hard to shove the contents of my stomach back down where they belong. I automatically turn my back to the waiting room when I hear the tell-tale ding of the door opening. "Not helping your case, Karly. Just sayin'… I'm not into quick, convenient fucks. Especially when most of the guys on those trips are looking to score as much and with as many as they can manage in the shortest possible time frame. Not keen on being the dessert buffet for a bunch of young idiots, hopped up on Viagra. Besides, as I told you a month ago, I'll be moving house in two weeks, so I can't come. End of story. You and Mom have fun, but count me out."

By the time I get my nympho sister off the phone, my eyes have rolled heavenward a few more times. I should have spared one eye-roll to confirm it actually was my next patient coming in. It wasn't. A familiar face with a toothy grin is leaning on the damn counter, right behind me. Instantly, my German ancestry betrays me with the robust blush I feel burning on my cheeks. Fabulous.

"What can I do for you, Neil?" I say none too kindly. One of his heavy eyebrows lifts all the way up, and the grin slips into a smirk.

"That, is a loaded question," he teases, "especially given the tantalizing conversation I just overheard." The heat on my face has now reached my hairline while I curse myself six ways to Sunday. "By the way, I like that color on you," he mumbles, tapping me on the cheek.

"Neil—that was fast. I just called like twenty minutes ago." Naomi smiles as she walks in and leans in for a peck on his cheek. I release a sigh of relief at her timely interruption.

"I much prefer that kind of greeting," he rumbles in that raspy dark voice of his, giving me a pointed look. A sound inconsistent with his youthful surfer boy looks and bright blue eyes, yet unfortunately has me steady myself on the edge of the counter.

"Maybe I should introduce you to my sister then, she's about your age," I snap back and grab the file for my next patient, but not before I see the flash of anger in his baby blues. Deciding to ignore it, I make my way around the desk only to be held up by Naomi.

"Have you been on your computer yet? I had problems this morning logging on," she asks.

"Haven't had a chance. Why?"

"Well, if Neil is here anyway to fix whatever's wrong with mine, he might as well have a look at yours; make sure all the upgrades are up to date and stuff."

I shrug my shoulders. "Be my guest, here is my next patient," I say with a chin nod toward the reception area. "I'll be busy for the next hour anyway." With that I motion to Mrs. Winkler, who I've been treating for a frozen shoulder. "Come on in. The needles are waiting for you." With a small smile for Naomi and Neil, she follows me into my treatment room.

"How have you been?" I ask her once I've closed the door behind us. "Are you noticing any improvement?" I have treated her with acupuncture twice a week for the past three weeks and I'm hoping to see some loosening in the joint. She was so seized up by the time she came to see me, there was no movement whatsoever in that arm.

"I'm still having trouble with the kitchen cupboards and getting dressed in the morning isn't much fun, but I do believe I have a bit more movement," she says as she sheds her blouse and lays on the bed in just her undershirt.

"That's great. Let's have a look."

For the next twenty minutes, I manipulate her shoulder joint. Finding her mobility is indeed a bit improved, I start preparing the needles. With the TENS machine hooked up to the needles and doing its work, I slip out of the room to quickly grab some coffee. Just as I pass by my office, Neil sticks his head out the door, causing me to almost drop my mug. "Holy shit."

"Sorry," he mumbles a bit sheepishly. "I just wanted to have a quick word if you have a minute."

"I do if you follow me to the kitchen. I need more caffeine."

I can barely hear him behind me. For a large man, he is surprisingly light on his feet. I pull my one indulgence, hazelnut-flavored creamer, from the fridge and wave it in his face. "You want one?" The look of disgust on his face is comical, and I can't stop the snicker. "Guessing that's a no?"

"I'll have my coffee plain, thanks," he says, opening a cupboard for a mug.

I'm still smiling as I pour our coffees and almost burst out laughing again when I see him watch me pour enough creamer in my mug to turn my coffee a delicious beige. "So what's up?" I ask, closing my eyes automatically as the taste of hazelnut with a hint of coffee hits my taste buds.

"Two things actually," he clarifies. "First, do you need any help moving? I have my old truck which can haul a shitload of stuff."

I look at his youthful face with his far-too-serious eyes that seem ancient. Sure, most of the time, they shine with a teasing glint, but there's a darkness hiding behind them too. "Sure," I accept, because really—when a young guy built like a tank offers to help you move, especially after your family ditched you for an aquatic meat market, you don't pass it up.

"Great. Just let me know when and where, and I'll make sure my schedule's clear." His smile is genuine, and I'm struck once again by how tempting it can be to get lost to his charms. Even though I know he'd get bored with me soon enough in favor of something "fresher."

"Sounds good," I say quietly.

"Oh, and secondly, I was cleaning your drive when I noticed your cache file is pretty full," he says, receiving a blank look from me, since I have no clue what he's talking about. I can work a computer, but I don't understand it. "Are you getting a lot of pop ups when you're online? Those little screens with shit you don't wanna see that suddenly cover your monitor?" he clarifies, thankfully, and I now understand exactly what he's talking about. I shiver thinking about the vile, sadistic porn sites that have started popping up on my screen.

"Actually, I do. Disgusting. How did they get there?" I half expect Neil to make fun of me, but he instead looks concerned.

"One of the sites you've visited has left something behind on your computer. An imprint that generates these links popping up. I want to have a look to see where it comes from."

"Go right ahead. I've gotta get back to Mrs. Winkler." I wave my hand in his general direction, not even half understanding what he just told me.

It isn't until much later, when I'm lost in thought with my hands working the tension from my patient's shoulder, that I realize Neil is going through my history with a fine-tooth comb.

Holy schnikes.

Neil

Oh, I'm pissed.

No sooner had my hopes flared when Kendra agreed to let me help her move, that they deflated instantly upon finding the links to the MatureDatingOnly website in her Internet history. She'd been busy. Fuck me. Here I am thinking I might finally be making some headway with her, convincing her that the age difference between us means fuck-all, when reality hits me in the face. I know I'm crossing a line when I check her e-mails for evidence of some douche nozzle trying to hook up with her, but I figure the end justifies the means. Nothing. Not a damn thing. Which probably means she didn't sign up with her clinic e-mail, because as beautiful, and fucking funny as she is, there's no way she wouldn't have had any interest. Christ.

I just finished clearing all the crap from her history, as well as cleaning up her drive, when my phone buzzes in my pocket. I pull it out and see Gus's number, and swear softly at the sight of my boss's name on the screen. I was about to go talk to Kendra about accessing questionable websites. Frustrated, I slide my thumb across the screen.

"Yeah?"

"Neil, you almost done? Meeting in my office in twenty."

"On my way."

Slipping the phone back in my jeans, I quickly finish installing the upgraded firewall and log off. With one look back at the still closed door of her treatment room, I pull her office door shut and head for the front desk, where Naomi is just showing her patient out.

"You done?"

"Didn't take much," I tell her. "Yours is up and running, was just a glitch with the automatic updates, and Kendra's is cleaned up. She's still in with Mrs. Winkler so I'll catch up with her later."

"Thanks, Neil." She smiles at me and it hits me again how fucking lucky my colleagues at GFI are. Every last one of them has found their match and are building a future. Fuck, how I want that. I'll admit, I've had fun sowing my wild oats, but I'm long since done with that. Left that part of my life behind when I came here from Grand Junction, but every good woman who has crossed my path has been snatched up from under my nose before I had a chance to make a move. And the one I've wanted most since meeting her is determined to keep me at a distance. Fuck, I almost lost a good friend to this stupid hang up of hers.

I shake my head to clear the frustration and bend down to kiss Naomi's cheek. "No problem, Doc. I've gotta run, though, duty calls." With a two-fingered wave, I step out of the clinic and into the warm spring sunshine. Damn, it's going to be good being able to get out again. The Cedar Tree winters can be brutal and make the terrain traitorous but with this warmer weather, I can't wait for a chance to try out my new ATV on the trails.

I'm at Gus and Emma's place, also the GFI main office, five minutes later. It takes that long to get from one end of town to the other. I used to think I'd need a larger place to keep me busy, but since my first trip to Cedar Tree, it has never been boring. For a small town like this, they sure see a lot of action, which is why Gus—after our fist case here—moved the office from Grand Junction to here. Of course the fact that that first case netted him his wife, Emma, helped make that decision. During the first years, I stayed mostly in Grand Junction to run the office there with Dana, our office manager and resident mother. But she has since retired and Gus decided to close down that office. I started out in the guesthouse behind their house, but have recently moved into the apartment above the local diner, Arlene's. She and her husband Seb have become good friends, as have all the other members of the GFI team. Two more members have been added since the office opened. Joe Morris, Naomi's husband and the former sheriff of Montezuma County, and Mal Whitetail, Caleb's brother. Of course Caleb and his wife, Katie, have both been operatives longer than I have.

By the looks of the cars assembled in the driveway, everyone has been called in. When I walk in the door, the unmistakable smell of something baking greets me. Emma, Gus's wife, is our resident baker and will use any damn excuse to shove a pie or some pastries in the oven, even an emergency GFI meet.

She leans against the counter, wiping her hands on her apron and wearing a big ass smile. "Hey handsome."

"Hey." I smile back. "I swear, if Gus didn't force us to hit the gym at least twice a week to stay in shape, you'd have all of us sporting guts with your need to feed."

Emma flaps her hand. "Whatever, it's just a few cinnamon rolls. Looks like you guys might be in there for a while and I didn't have time to make soup for lunch. Gus just got the call forty-five minutes ago. You better get in there."

I wrap an arm around her neck and pull her close, planting a kiss on her fiery mop of auburn curls. "You're the best, Ems."

"Coffee in the boardroom," she yells after me when I turn into the hallway attaching the kitchen to the addition in the back which holds the GFI offices.

"Neil, good. Sit. FBI is gonna be here in fifteen and I want to get you guys up to speed." Gus sits at the head of the massive boardroom table with my partners seated along the sides. I slip into a vacant chair beside Katie, giving her a wink as I sit down.

"Damian Gomez, as you know, is now leading the field office for La Plata County. He called in asking for our help. He's short on staff, been working almost single-handedly on the disappearance of a number of women from this general area."

"How general?" Joe pipes up. He's the one with all the law-enforcement connections and I can hear the wheels turning. Gus turns to him.

"For now, limited to La Plata County, but with feelers out further. Once he brings in copies of what he has, we can talk about what it is we're looking for in terms of matching cases up with other jurisdictions. I can confirm that there are five women missing. All are between twenty-five and forty years of age. Four were single, one married. As of this morning, three bodies have been found. Two had been there for a while. One was fresh, which makes number six. A hiker who was out early this morning stumbled on the bodies when he tripped and slid off the trail and down a twelve-foot ridge. He found them at the bottom, between a pile of sizable boulders. According to Damian, they looked to have been dumped there. The latest victim appears to have been there only a few days at most. Police is looking at getting her identified. All appear to be women." Gus stands up, turns to the window and runs his hand through his hair. "We've had our share of trouble in this region, but if Damian is correct, this could be the first serial killer of this caliber since fucking Ted Bundy and Gary Ridgeway made Colorado unsafe."

"Have mercy," Mal breathes from the other side of the table.

"No shit. We'll need it," his brother Caleb adds.

The door opens and Emma pushes her walker in, a tray of sandwiches and the freshly baked cinnamon buns balancing on top. Behind her, FBI Special Agent Damian Gomez walks in, toting a case of bottled water and a stack of files.

"She got you working?" Gus smirks, looking at his wife appreciatively. He and Damian go back a ways, and not all of it very good, but in recent months, since Damian's taken over the Durango office, things between them have been more amicable.

Damian's grudging smile and raised eyebrow is his only response. Mal takes the tray from Emma and sets it on the table, while Damian adds the case of water.

"Thanks, Damian." Emma smiles up at him, leaning in to give him a kiss on the cheek, something that obviously surprises him and stirs up Gus, whose low guttural growl can be heard clearly. "Oh geeze, Gus." She turns on her husband, one hand on her walker for balance, the other resting on her hip. "Put your balls away, will ya? We all know they are exceptionally large. Now eat!" With that, she shuffles out of the room.

Gus shakes his head, unable to keep the smirk off his face. "Well. Now that that's been established, grab something to eat and let's get this show on the road. I'll just be one minute," Gus says, as he stalks out the door behind Emma. Most of us have a knowing grin on our faces, except for Damian, who looks a bit confused.

"Just go with it," Katie tells him with a wink as she offers him a bottle of water. By the time Damian is done giving everyone a file folder, Gus comes walking back in, a satisfied look on his face.

"All right," Damian starts. "Six missing women, three bodies recovered this morning. The latest one, Cora Jennings, was a nurse at Mercy General in Durango. The report on her was only filed this morning by her supervisor at Mercy. She apparently had a date two days ago, didn't show up the next day and when her supervisor couldn't get a hold of her, she went to check her apartment. The woman's car was gone and no one answered the door. Durango PD is over there now waiting for the landlord to show up with the key so they can get in. We suspect the third body found on Smelter Mountain was that of Cora. It hadn't been out there long. All bodies were partially dressed. Looks like their clothes were neatly cut open along the front. They look to have been violated and the cause of death appears to be strangulation. The coroner will make a report, hopefully by the end of today, on the latest victim. He'll also be able to confirm her identity, but we're pretty sure it's Cora." He sits back and gives us time to scan over the pages in the file.

"Jesus," Joe says. "Are we sure, aside from the bodies of course, that all six of them fell victim to the same perp? Better yet, are we sure six is all there is?"

"That's where I'm hoping you guys can help out. Other than the three bodies, I don't even know for sure the others, still technically listed as missing, are connected. I need someone to run a ViCAP search, see if any similar cases might be linked, and then follow up with whatever police department. Then I need sharp eyes on patterns, similarities, anything in the victims' profiles that overlaps. Anything that may give us a starting point on this guy." Damian gets up and checks his watch. "I have to run. Autopsy scheduled in an hour and a half and I want to be there. I'll be in touch." With that he's gone.

"Have a bad feeling about this one." Mal is the first to speak.

"Right," Gus breaks in. "Neil, you run ViCAP."

"I'm on it," I tell him, my laptop already open to the sign in page.

"The rest of you, run through the files you have and start digging for similarities."

Katie is shifting in her seat beside me. "I may have found one," she says, flipping back and forth between the profiles of the six women. "All of them appear to work in the medical field in one capacity or another."

I grab the file and shift through the papers. Sure enough, a pharmaceutical rep, two nurses, a medical secretary at a private clinic, an anesthesiologist and an ultra-sound technician.

Gus gets up, walks to the dry erase board on the far wall and starts writing. "Neil, add that to your search and include all of the Four Corners region. Joe, make a note of all the reporting officers on each of these profiles and find out as much as you can about each of these victims. Mal, I want you to follow Gomez back to Durango. Get any information that comes out of that autopsy and keep us up to date. I want you to be our eyes and ears there. The rest of you, keep going through these files with a fine-tooth comb. Going just by what we have, this guy has been at it for over a year. God knows how many are out there. Let's stop that fucker now."

CHAPTER TWO

Kendra

I almost drop my groceries on the doorstep, trying to balance the paper bags on one arm, while digging frantically through my purse to find my keys. The phone I forgot on the counter when I left to get some groceries is insistently ringing on the other side of the door.

"Hang on, dagnabit," I mumble under my breath, as I finally pull free my key ring and wiggle the quirky lock on my door. Stumbling over a few packing boxes, I manage only to lose the containers of yogurt that were balancing precariously on top of my bag of veggies before I make it to the counter where I dump the bags and snatch up my phone.

"Hello?"

Dead air. I almost hang up when I hear a deep sigh on the other side.

"Am I interrupting something?" Neil's all too familiar voice has my heart suddenly racing for another reason altogether.

"I should be so lucky," flies from my mouth before I can slap on a filter. I'm so glad he can't see the pained look on my face as I literally bite my tongue—hard. The soft chuckle does nothing to settle my sudden nerves.

"You know that can easily be resolved, right?" he coos, immediately sending a tingle down to my toes.

"Ha!" is the only intelligible word I can form before shaking my head and determinedly changing the subject. "I just walked in with groceries and had forgotten my phone at home. What's up?"

All I hear on the other side is a sharp hiss.

"You know it's becoming more and more difficult not to find double meaning in everything you say." Before I can give that a response, he continues, "I just wanted to check in with you about the move. You were supposed to call me with a place and time?"

Shit. I know I was and I'd been postponing, having reconsidered the wisdom of letting him help me move. I mean, it's not like I have a lot of stuff. It would only take me three or four trips in my little SUV. The couch and the bed would be a bit of a problem, though. "I know. I'm sorry, it's been a bit of a hectic week. It's this coming Saturday, but you know what? I can probably manage." And I would. Somehow.

"Yeah, I've been busy too. Would've called you earlier but this case… Let's just say it's intense. So give me the address and what time do you want me there?" He totally disregards my last remark and I figure it'll probably be less of a headache to let him help than it would be to try and deter him.

"I can make sure I have everything packed up, and the bed dissembled the night before. So let's say nine o'clock?"

"Where are you gonna sleep?"

"Not sure what you mean."

"If you're taking apart your bed Friday night, then where are you gonna sleep?" he asks, and I can hear the smile in his voice.

"Oh. On the mattress on the floor."

"Right," he chuckles. "You know I can help with that too."

"I'll have you know I've been able to sleep by myself for forty years, I think I'll manage," I blurt out a little irritated. The guy is relentless.

"Kendra? I meant disassembling the bed."

"Oh." I need to get off the phone before I make an even bigger ass of myself. "No need. I've done it before. So, is nine okay for you?"

"I'll bring coffee," he says simply before hanging up.

I drop the phone on the counter and bang my head a few times. Why is that man so persistent? I can't seem to get through to him that I am probably ten years older than he is; way too old for him. More importantly, he's way too young for me. I've seen up close and personal how these *May-December* relationships work. Always explosive in nature, and short in duration.

My mother was an expert. The first five years after my father passed away when I was only twelve, Mom never dated. A beautiful woman, she didn't lack for suitors but she would swear high and low that my father had been her one true love and she wasn't interested in anyone else. It was the commitment she had an issue with. Most men her age were looking for a wife, and she was not on the market.

I was in my senior year in high school when she overheard one of my male friends call her a MILF. I about gagged. When Mom asked what it meant, I was going to make something up, but my then ten-year-old sister was all too eager to explain. Finding out she was attractive to younger men opened up a new world for her. One where marriage and building a long-term future were not expected, but in fact avoided as much as possible. I hit college and it was like my mother was given new life. She used every excuse in the book to come visit me, just so she could check out the male college population. Needless to say, she developed a reputation fairly quickly, to my absolute horror. I didn't date through college, the risks of going out with someone my mother had already slept with was too big. Besides, my sister was fast following in my mother's footsteps, and at fourteen had had more boyfriends than me at twenty-two.

Don't get me wrong, I love my mom *and* my sister, but there is a reason I no longer live in Durango. I'm happy they're having such fun, embarrassing as it might be. But the moment people started calling me *One of those Schmitt girls,* I was out of there.

Now that I think about it, I should probably give Mom a call. Find out from her whether she is actually going on this cruise or whether it was a ploy by Karly to get me to come. But when I spot a small puddle forming under the bag that holds my one indulgence, frozen yogurt, I quickly tend to my priorities first. Yes, the frozen yogurt.

"Hello?"

"Is this Kendra?"

He sounds almost wary on the phone. Lars is his name, a man I met about four months ago on the dating site I'd signed up for. Well I never actually *met* him, but we'd been e-mailing back and forth occasionally. After a week on the dating site, I'd taken down my profile. Too many creeps out there. A lot of them plain sleazy in their approach, and I swear some of them were married, looking for an affair on the side. Not my cup of tea. The only decent guy who'd approached me tentatively was Lars.

We'd exchanged a couple of e-mails before I'd decided to take down my name and when I warned him, he'd asked if we could continue to just talk over regular e-mail. He's a high school teacher in Gallup, New Mexico, and the moment he mentioned that, I'd looked him up. There hadn't been any pictures for the teachers on the online staff directory for Miyamura High School, but the description fit him to a T.

I had seen a picture on his profile on the dating site where he was hiking the Grand Canyon—one of the main reasons he'd peaked my attention. Rather studious looking, but handsome. Forty-three years old and never been married, according to his description, but looking for someone who shared his main passion: nature hikes. It seemed like a good place to start.

Over the past months, he'd proven himself to be witty, regaling me with some funny teaching stories that would put a smile on my face. So when I spotted his e-mail, right after hanging up with Mom, who confirmed she'd be leaving with Karly over the weekend, I read it eagerly. To my surprise, he's asking to meet. We'd never really talked about that possibility. Although in hindsight, it seems only natural things would progress to that at some point.

Coffee in Cortez. He's apparently on his way to a conference in Grand Junction and since it wouldn't be out of his way to stop in Cortez, he thought I might like to meet. That's when he asked for my number, which I freely give him. Four months of talking, surely if he was after something more nefarious than a bit of companionship, he'd have grown tired of me by now. I'd barely hit send on the e-mail with my phone number and the damn thing rings.

"Hi, Lars?" I respond, a little out of breath. It's a bit unnerving to suddenly be talking to someone who's been more of an abstract figure behind the computer so far. A gentle chuckle sounds over the line.

"That's me," he says. "A bit weird, isn't it? Hearing a voice to go with the words we've been exchanging for the past months? I mean, you sound great. I mean, nice." He seems a little flustered and for some reason that puts my mind at ease. "I've got to admit, I'm a little nervous. I've never actually gotten this far."

"What do you mean?" I ask, a little confused.

"I mean, I've talked to a few people before, but never actually moved beyond e-mails."

"Oh, well, if it makes you feel any better, I've never really done the online thing at all before. So all of this is new. Not sure what the rules or expectations are, but you mentioned coffee and that seems harmless enough."

"Good. That's good. Yes, so I'll be driving to Grand Junction on Friday, and I was hoping maybe you'd be willing to meet me in Cortez. You did say you lived in Cortez, right?" He sounds like he's smiling, not a bad sound at all.

"Yes, I do." I don't feel the need to tell him that Friday will actually be the last day I effectively live here. There is plenty of time for that.

"Okay, so maybe you know a place? Somewhere you feel comfortable meeting a middle-aged teacher from Gallup," he chuckles in self-deprecation.

"Hardly middle-aged yet, Lars."

"Hmmm, I like that. You saying my name." The sudden shift from shy and hesitant to blatant flirting sends a bit of a shock to my system. I'm not quite sure what to do with that. Neil says stuff like that all the time, but it's never given me a cold chill, like a sudden draft against my neck. Not entirely pleasant.

"So coffee?" I say rather curtly. He must pick up on it because when he speaks next, the shy teacher is back.

"If you're sure, that would be great, yes. I'd love a chance to talk to you about those hiking trails in Mesa Verde you mentioned."

Back on safer ground, I remind him I have several maps of the national park that I can bring for him to look over and he seems very receptive.

"So where and when is good for you?" He wants to know. "I'm leaving probably around five. Classes end at three o'clock and I'll swing home to pick up my stuff and grab a bite, so I should be there around seven? Maybe seven thirty?"

I don't have to think hard for a place to meet. Mal's wife Kim and her friend Kerry introduced me to a great coffee shop a few months ago. "The Spruce Tree Espresso House. I'll e-mail you directions. That's probably easiest. And seven thirty sounds great, but won't it be too much of a delay? If you still have to get to Grand Junction?"

"It's probably four hours driving from Cortez, and the conference doesn't start until the afternoon so I can sleep in."

"Okay, if you're sure. Then seven thirty it is."

"Looking forward to it," he says before I hear the distinct click of a hang up.

A little abrupt. I didn't get a chance to match the sentiment or say goodbye. I shrug it off, making myself a note to find those Mesa Verde hiking maps before Friday.

Oddly enough, I don't feel any nerves about meeting him. No nerves, no butterflies. Not excitement either. Just a tiny seed of discomfort at the slight personality shifts. That never really came across when we would talk via e-mail. It's just coffee. If I don't get a good vibe, I'll say goodbye and leave it at that.

Neil

I smile when I hang up the phone. Kendra may think she's keeping a safe distance, but the way she is easily flustered when I tease her shows me she has more than a passing interest.

I'm not stupid. I know she has a massive hang up over our age difference, and she's wielded that like a sword for the past year since I made my interest pretty clear.

My interest runs back a lot further than that, almost since the first time I saw her, but for a while I thought she had her sights set on Mal. When he met Kim on a case he was working last year, though, it became obvious that whatever was between them had simply been friendship, because Mal fell like a brick for Kimeo. Even encouraged me to go after Kendra at some point, having picked up on my feelings for her. It's not like I haven't tried. I've just not been very aggressive, and Kendra has been extremely dismissive. Still, I see the way her eyes flit at me when she thinks I'm not looking. I can hear the hitch in her breathing when I get too close for her comfort. And I've let her get away with it, hoping that at some point she'll see beyond the difference in years, and see *me*. Not the guy she thinks I am, but the one I'm proving to be.

Seeing the links to the dating site on her work computer has thrown a switch for me. She's obviously looking for something, and still fucking refuses to look for that something with me. That's going to change. I'm done waiting for her to get on the ball. I'm going to run the play from here on in. Keep her off-balance and create my own opportunities.

This case has me rather tied up, though. When the reports from the coroner came back and showed the mutilations on each of the victims, the investigation FBI agent Gomez had drawn us into went full swing. Intricate carvings in the skin of each of the three victim's backs depicting angel wings along with the word *Mercy* had been inflicted while the women had still been alive. At least that was the opinion of the coroner based on his findings. He suspected the use of succinylcholine, or a similar drug used to paralyze the muscles, when he noticed the imprint of a breathing mask on the latest victim's face. Sux, the commonly used name for the drug, paralyzes the muscles needed for breathing so artificial respiration is needed to keep someone alive until the drug wears off. Otherwise, it is a slow, agonizing death. The victim would have been fully aware of everything done to them, but completely unable to help themselves. Unfortunately, it leaves very little evidence behind in the body, so it is difficult to detect. According to the coroner, the mask used might have been attached to a relatively simple CPAP-machine, providing the positive air pressure needed to keep the victim breathing and alive, but barely.

The last victim showed evidence of violent sexual interference resulting in tissue damage and the cause of death is listed as asphyxiation. Over the last few days, he has been able to confirm similar findings on the other victims. We now also know their names.

The ViCAP searches turned up four more possible cases in Utah and another three in New Mexico. All missing women, all between twenty-five and forty, although the majority are over thirty, and all of them worked in some capacity of the medical field. According to the last count, thirteen potential victims, three accounted for, spread over three states. All of this within the past two years. It's a very disturbing trend.

An hour ago, Gus called us in to the office where only a week ago we first got wind of this crazy fucker. As I pull my truck up to the house, I let my mind wander back to Kendra and the unofficial *date* we have for Saturday. Doesn't matter that she won't look at it that way, I'm just happy to have some time with her. I'll be keeping my eyes and ears peeled for any space she'll give me and jump all over it. My endless patience, one of my better qualities, is starting to run short where she is concerned.

This time, when we're all seated, Gus wastes no time to announce that FBI brass has swooped in, putting a lid on any information shared for fear of mass panic. They want no word of the case to leak, so GFI has effectively been eliminated from the investigation.

"Seems Damian suddenly has more sets of hands than I'm sure is welcome," Gus tells us. "He's not too happy with the way this investigation is shaping up. That's why he's asked us, unofficially, to keep our eyes open." Gus looks around the table at each of us. "That means we fly under the radar. I'm not letting it interfere with our other cases, but let's keep plugging at whatever leads we can get our hands on."

"Maybe this is a good time to let you know that I've managed to get into Cora Jennings's e-mail account and discovered an interesting chain of e-mails." All eyes turn to me, but Gus speaks up.

"The Feds will have their own IT techs on it now, so unless there's a way to get in and out undetected, I suggest you cease and desist any further attempts at hacking. Don't want to get us in hot water by way of interfering with an ongoing investigation. Having said that, you wouldn't happen to have print outs of those e-mails, would you?"

I open my laptop, click a few buttons, and the large printer in the corner of the boardroom whirrs to life. With my signature cocky smile, I look back at Gus. "Printing out as we speak. I managed to back up her entire e-mail folder before I got out."

"Who says brains aren't sexy?" Katie winks at me from across the table, causing Caleb to pull her close by the neck.

"Quit flirting with the boy," he growls, immediately setting me on edge and earning one of Katie's sharp little elbows in the ribs.

"Hardly a boy, Caleb, and keep your shorts on."

Perhaps a bit louder than necessary, I slap my laptop closed. "Anything else, boss?" I ask Gus, pointedly not looking at anyone else at the table. Gus calmly looks back, the only evidence he's picking up on my irritation being the slight twitch of his eyebrow.

"Nope. I'll hand out the prints. Good work, Neil. Check in with me end of the day, and if you do decide to do some more digging, try to stay invisible."

"Sure thing." And without acknowledging anyone else, I get me and my sudden bad mood out of there, feeling the strange looks from my colleagues burning holes in my back. I don't give a fuck. But if I thought I was getting out of there fast, Emma has other ideas.

"Where are you storming off to?" she asks, blocking my way to the front door, her hands on her hips. "You're not staying for lunch?"

"Not this time." I try to control my temper, but as expected, Emma hears the bite to my voice.

"What happened in there?"

I try to shake my head and leave it at that, but there is no escaping her soft and slightly accusatory "Neil."

"I'm just tired, Ems. Tired of being treated like an irresponsible adolescent instead of a fucking grown man. I'll be thirty-two in a month and I still feel like I have to prove my worth like someone wet behind the ears."

"Hmmm," she mumbles as she tilts her head to the side. "Honestly? I don't think there's anyone who knows you who would mistake you for irresponsible or wet behind the ears. You may look young, but you have an old soul. A wise soul." The soft hand she lays on my cheek feels nice. Comforting. Still, I can't hold back the deriding snort.

"Ha. I wish that were true," I blurt out before I snap my mouth shut.

Emma gives her head a slight shake. "She'll figure it out," she says, proving once again to be more perceptive than most.

Very little escapes Emma.

CHAPTER THREE

Kendra

"Hey, girl!"

Arlene is standing behind the counter of the diner when I walk in. Arlene's Diner, named after its owner, has become a favorite hangout in the past year. Arlene runs the place, and her husband Seb is Cedar Tree's own culinary wiz. The daily specials he adds to the standard diner fare on the menu since taking over the kitchen a few years ago, have not just drawn in the locals, but diners from Cortez and even Dolores. I first met Seb and Arlene when they brought Seb's sister, Faith, to the area. A devastating childhood brain injury had left her stuck in time. They had moved her into a full-time care facility in Cortez where I'd been working at the time.

"Hi there, Arlene. Guess who I saw yesterday?"

Arlene chuckles. "Already heard. Seb heard all about it when he called her last night. You'd think Santa came early with the way she carried on."

I'd popped in to visit Faith after my shift at Cortez Memorial. These last months have been so busy with the clinic, my two remaining days at the Cortez hospital and the upcoming move, I hadn't been in to see her. "She seems to be doing well. I was glad to see she got over that bout of pneumonia."

"Yeah, that was scary for a bit. Seb was over there every day. So what can I get you? A bit early for dinner, no?"

"Actually, I was hoping for an early bite. I have to head back to Cortez to pack up the last of my things tonight. Tomorrow I'll officially be a resident of Cedar Tree. That reminds me, did Beth leave her key?" The cute house I'm moving into belongs to Beth, one of Arlene's good friends. She's hung on to the place since her marriage to Clint Mason, another fairly new import in Cedar Tree, and has been renting it out. My luck that it was available when I started looking for a place. One of these days I hope to buy something, but for now I'm happy renting.

"Dropped it off this morning. Here you go." Arlene opens the cash register and pulls out a ring with two keys. "She says to tell you that the one key will open both the front and backdoors, as well as the gate to the backyard. Second one is a spare. Neil installed that brand new security system last year so you'll have numeric keypads on the front and backdoor as back up." She hands me a little card with a four-number combination. "Says if you want another code, Neil can help you set it up."

At the mention of Neil's name, I look up from the card I was studying. Arlene's eyes study me intently, making me feel slightly uncomfortable.

"So when are you gonna put that boy out of his misery?"

And there it is. It seems the more I try to keep my distance from him, the harder the universe conspires—with a little help from my friends—to hook us up.

"Arlene," I start, but she won't have it.

"He's a good man, Kendra. A real good man. And from what I can tell, he's got it bad for you." She leans over the counter conspiratorially. "Haven't seen him with anyone in over a year. Not once. Not since he moved into the apartment upstairs."

An odd feeling presses under my breastbone, and I lift my hand to my chest. Fiddlesticks. Why is this so hard? I shouldn't care if he sees half the female population in the Four Corners area. I shouldn't. Despite the undeniable attraction I feel for him, I've not allowed myself to even consider going there. Hell, I even tried dating Malachi at one point, before Kim came on the scene, but that had been weird. The one kiss we'd shared had felt…off. Flat. It did less for me than a single touch of Neil's eyes on me. Why can't I just turn off this stupid reaction I have to even the mention of his name? I know he isn'　t the one for me. It would never work. Yet…

"You gonna stand there with that dreamy look on your face, or are you interested in hearing today's special?" Arlene cuts into my thoughts, a knowing smirk on her face.

With a slight shake of my head to clear it, I turn my eyes to the big blackboard behind the counter. "I'll have the spinach and goat cheese stuffed meatloaf. That sounds good. Oh, and some unsweetened ice tea, please."

"Grab a seat. Coming right up," she says as she disappears into the kitchen. I take stool at the counter and turn to scan the diner. It's only a little after four in the afternoon and only one booth is occupied. I'm sure over the next half hour the place will start filling up. Friday nights are generally busy at the diner and Arlene usually has two extra servers coming in over the weekend.

A ding on my phone shows a message from my mom, but the chime of the door has me turning toward the entrance, as the one person I should be trying to avoid walks in and straight toward me. A big smile on his handsome face.

"Bonus," he says cryptically as he pulls up a stool beside me.

"What does that mean?" I tuck away my phone and try not to notice the brush of his shoulder against me as he settles in.

"Thought I would have to wait until tomorrow to see you but here you are. Bonus." The slight nudge of his arm against my side has me looking up from the counter, where I've tried to keep my focus. I immediately feel my resolve melting under the warm fire in his baby blues.

"You have to stop flirting with me," I whisper softly, unable to pull my eyes from his. "You're making this so hard."

Bending his head down, he leans in closer. "Can't help myself around you, and it doesn't have to be hard at all." The puff of his breath against my skin causes a little shiver to run over me. Danger signals are shooting off in my brain while my body instantly responds to him, ignoring the warnings. His scent, so uniquely him, surrounds me and I just want to snuggle up to him. Breathe him in.

"Neil!"

My eyes, which had slipped shut, pop open to see his face just inches from mine, staring at me intently. With a small twitch of his mouth, he lifts his head to acknowledge Arlene, who just walked over with my ice tea in hand.

"Hey there, boss lady. What's on the menu?"

"On the blackboard, smartass. That's why I hung it up there, so I don't have to repeat myself all damn day."

Arlene is all bark and no bite. It's one of the things I love about her. She definitely takes no prisoners. A good person through and through, she has a gruff exterior that protects the giant, but fragile, heart she owns. She doesn't take any nonsense and doesn't give it either.

Neil, of course, smiles his signature big smile at her snarkiness. He loves teasing her. Loves teasing everyone, especially the women around town. Charms each and every one of them. Of us. A deep sigh escapes my lips before I can check it. To camouflage it, I take a quick sip of my tea, ignoring the two pairs of eyes I can feel trained on me.

"Do me today's special, honey," I hear Neil say.

"Coming up." I hear her footsteps retreating but keep my gaze on the glass in my hand.

"Relax."

I hear the rumble of his voice at the same time his large, warm hand finds my jeans-clad knee and gives it a squeeze. The brief contact leaves his palm print burned on my skin.

"Work still busy?" I ask, trying to distract him, and myself.

"Nah," he says, but there's something about the tone of his voice that has me look up. He is staring straight ahead, and suddenly he looks much older with evidence of strain on his face. Without thinking, I put my hand on his arm. Big mistake. I feel the muscles of his forearm shifting under my hand as he clenches his fist on the counter.

"You okay?" I prod, watching him as he slowly turns his eyes to me.

"Promise you'll be careful out there?"

The question catches me off-guard. Actually, it's the intensity in his eyes that throws me. "Of course I'm careful. What's going on?"

"Just…fuck." Neil clasps his hands around the back of his neck. "I can't talk about it, but please trust me when I say I need you to be careful."

"I promise," I say softly, a little unnerved. It doesn't help when he covers the hand I still have resting on his arm with his.

"Can I ask you something? Don't get mad. When I cleaned out your computer last week, I couldn't help but notice you'd been on this dating site."

Okay, that's embarrassing. I'd figured he probably would have seen that, and I did my best to pretend otherwise. I try to pull my hand back, but he just folds his big fingers around it and holds on.

"Don't. Don't be upset, just listen. For the foreseeable future, please don't plan to meet up with someone you met online. I can't tell you more and it drives me fucking insane, but trust me when I say it's important."

My mouth opens to object, to tell him it's no business of his who I date, but the serious look on his face shuts me up. For a second, I consider telling him about my coffee date tonight, but decide not to. I've done my due diligence on Lars and from what I can gather, he is everything he claims to be. A single forty-something-year-old teacher from Gallup, New Mexico. Besides, it's just a coffee.

"Okay," I lie, a little niggle of doubt messing with my stomach. Neil gives my hand a little squeeze before releasing it. Before either of us can say anything else, Arlene is back with two steaming plates of meatloaf and potatoes. Good country fare if not for the slightly exotic twist of spinach and goat cheese stuffing.

Neil

A sight for sore eyes; the familiar shapely silhouette and signature ponytail sitting at the counter.

I'd just spent a stressful afternoon in the GFI office, reporting some of the things I'd discovered over the past day or two.

Cora Jenning's e-mails showed her conversations with a man she'd originally met through an online personal ad, by the name of Alan Cymars. There was no mention of a specific website, just some reference to the descriptions in the ad early on in their e-mail exchange. Two months of e-mails before Alan had sent her his phone number to call. No e-mails after that which would support that she, in fact, contacted him by phone after. Gomez promises to check her phone records for his number.

Sitting with Gus and Katie in the conference room, and Gomez on speakerphone, we outlined our findings to him. Katie was also able to tell him that the number Alan Cymars had listed in his e-mail had since been disconnected. Another red flag. In his e-mails, this guy had been the one to ask the questions, but said little about himself, other than that he worked for a bank in Farmington and his hobby was hiking. From what Damian told us, a colleague of

Cora＇s had voiced some concerns when she'd mentioned meeting this guy. Apparently, the night she disappeared had been her second time meeting him. The first time had been for coffee, but the night of her disappearance, they were supposed to go out for a hike and dinner. Alan Cymars's name was at the top of the list. Except there's been no trace of him. He doesn't exist, therefore there is no way to connect him with the other possible victims.

It's not until I sit down beside her at the counter, that I think about the website link I'd discovered on Kendra's computer and a niggle of worry takes form. Stroke of luck, I decided to stop in for a quick bite before retreating to my apartment upstairs and the stack of files waiting for my attention. I'm well aware that lives are at stake. Still, I'm unable to resist the draw of the woman who has been the main focus of my fantasies.

I can't help teasing her a little when I sit down. Seeing her reaction each time I push her a little out of her comfort zone gives me hope that one of these days, she'll forget to slam the door in my face. Again. I take the liberty of touching her leg when I notice her tensing up beside me. I don't want her tense. I want her at ease with me. But then she turns those gray eyes on me, and the concern I see there when she asks me about work brings my worries back to the forefront. Her embarrassment is obvious when I voice my concerns about the dating site I found on her computer, and I'm frustrated as fuck that I can't explain to her why. But her promise to be careful puts my mind at ease. I don't have the right to ask more of her. Not yet anyway.

Seb's special is amazing, as usual. I don't think I've ever had a meal here I didn't like. Kendra and I eat in silence, except for the little sounds of appreciation she makes with every bite of her dinner. Torture. Her little moans are like nails scraping down my spine and I have to shift around my seat to get comfortable. When she puts down her fork, wipes her mouth and groans deeply with her hands rubbing her stomach, I push my stool back. I'm this close to throwing caution to the wind, yanking her off her stool and kissing the breath out of her until she moans like that for me.

"Be right back," I mumble as I walk, a bit uncomfortably, to the men's room. By the time I've done my business, wash my hands and splash some cold water on my face, I walk out to find the counter empty. Fucking hell. My head whips around, just in time to see her take off in her green Toyota RAV4. She took off on me.

Arlene stands by the cash with a big smirk on her face. "She had to go. Had some last boxes to pack before she had to meet someone for coffee. Paid for your meal, though. Says to consider it payment for your help with her move tomorrow."

My jaw clenches. My mind gets stuck on her meeting someone for coffee. Could be anyone, I guess. A friend, a neighbor...but for some reason, I don't think so.

"Did you hear what I said?" Arlene nudges my shoulder as I lean on the counter, staring out at the now vacant parking spot outside.

"Sorry?" I turn to face her.

"I said you might wanna gear it up a notch before it's too late. Going for coffee sounds like a first step." Her eyebrow is raised to her hairline.

"Did she say who with?" I lean over the counter.

"Nah, but there was something about the way she said it. Dang, that girl is proving to be a tougher nut to crack than Beth was." Her knowing eyes smile at me. "Good thing we've all got your back on this."

"Don't know what you're talking about," is my futile response. Because I know by now that everyone sees the situation much clearer than either Kendra or I do.

A bit disappointed, but even more determined to make good use of my time with her tomorrow, I push off from the counter and head out the door. Arlene's cackle following me all the way outside.

Kendra

I should probably be nervous, but if I'm honest, the anxiety over tomorrow's move overshadows anything else I might feel. Particularly, meeting this man I've been talking to for months. He seems like the perfect guy for me. The right age, a respectable job, many similar interests, not the least of which is hiking.

The moment I pull the door open to the Espresso House, the mouth-watering scent of freshly brewed coffee wafts out. I know I'll have to go with a decaf, or I'll be up all night, but they make it so good here, you don't even notice the difference. I lift my hand in greeting to one of the baristas I've become friendly with since discovering the place, and let my eyes roam around. I know it's him the moment my eyes settle on the tall, rather lanky but undoubtedly handsome man. Dark hair neatly trimmed, pale eyes behind the studious glasses and a tentative lop-sided smile as he looks at me. I smile in response as I walk over. He pushes up from the chair and rounds the table, stumbling over a backpack by his feet before righting himself.

"Hi, Kendra?" His voice is soft. Softer than it sounded on the phone. I reach out and grab his proffered hand.

"Hi. Yes, and you must be Lars."

"Right. Nice to finally meet you face to face." The smile he shows me seems a little uncertain. In fact, he seems a little awkward. Maybe nerves, or maybe he's just shy. "Can I get you something?" he asks as he pulls out a chair for me.

"Please. I'd love a decaf café latte." I sit down and watch as Lars makes his way over to the counter, placing our order, but I quickly turn my head when he walks back my way.

"I forgot to ask if you wanted something to eat. Hope you don't mind, I ordered us a slice of pecan pie. It's my favorite."

I look up to find him staring down at me, a little too intense, so I lean back in my chair to create a bit more distance. This whole situation may well be a waste of time. I can already tell there is no real connection and I don't feel any kind of spark. Besides, there is something about the way he seems to scrutinize me that feels a bit uncomfortable. In fact, I regret not canceling the way I've wanted to do in the last few hours. Lars is a very handsome man, but he seems a little socially inept which doesn't give me good vibes. In fact, he puts me on edge a little.

I rummage through my tote and pull out the stack of trail maps I managed to find earlier. "I promised you Mesa Verde maps," I explain when I see the blank look on his face. Instantly, his face warms with a smile.

"Right. Yes, you did mention that. Wonderful, can I have a look?" He immediately starts unfolding the first map, spreading it out over the table.

For the next twenty minutes, we talk about the best trails, favorite places we've been, and spots we hope to visit in the future. I spend some time boasting the beauty of Mesa Verde, a place I've enjoyed since I was young, and Lars seems quite interested. By the time we finish our coffees and the pie, I've almost forgotten the uncomfortable start. I fold up the maps we've been looking at and hand them over to him.

"Here, you take them. I can always pick up new ones."

He looks at me strangely before accepting them and examining the covers. "These are older. Had them for a while?" he asks, tapping his finger on the date stamped in the corner.

"I have, some of them I've had since I was a teen. Like I said, I'll pick up some new ones next time I go. It's not an issue." At least I hope it's not. Lord, he's a strange duck. Suddenly that slightly creepy feeling is back.

"No. Not an issue, I just thought…" He doesn't finish his thought, and I know I should let it go but I can't help myself.

"What?" I prompt.

His eyes flick up to my face as he pushes his glasses up on his nose. "Oh, I was hoping we'd be able to hike these trails together. I'll be back on Monday. I can leave Grand Junction early and be back here in the morning. We could pack a lunch or something?"

Oh boy. What now? One look at his face tells me this is not going to be easy.

"Look," I start and immediately his expression changes. His eyes go hard and his mouth sets in a stark line. He knows what's coming. "I really have enjoyed talking to you and hope the maps will bring you as much enjoyment as they've brought

me over the years, but I'm afraid I'll have to decline. I'm
moving this we—"

"You're moving?" He cuts me off mid-sentence and
suddenly I'm so relieved I never told him about my place in
Cedar Tree. I don't think I made mention of the clinic there
either. At least I hope I didn't.

Grabbing my bag in one hand, I stand up from my chair.
"Actually I am."

"Where to?" he inquires, standing up as well and
towering over me.

"Right. I'd better head out. I have packing to do. Good to
meet you and again. I hope you enjoy Mesa Verde." Before he
has a chance to react, I turn on my heels and beeline it out the
door. By the time I get to my car, my keys are already in my
hand, and only when I'm inside with the doors firmly locked do
I allow myself a deep breath.

Holy schnikes. What a head case.

Looking through the windshield, I see him standing at
the edge of the parking lot. His hands on his hips and staring at
me through the glass. In just seconds, I have the car started and
drive past him without sparing a glance his way. My heart is
pounding in my chest. I'm cursing myself for having wasted
time on this guy. He'd seemed like a nice enough guy on paper,
but obviously a bit creepy and intense in real life.

Just in case, I circle through a few side roads before
driving home. By the time I pull into my parking spot, I'm pretty
sure no one could have followed me. For a moment I am
tempted to call Neil, but quickly dismiss that thought. I don't
need to encourage him even more.

I quickly get to work on the empty boxes that are waiting
for me, packing up my kitchen and loose odds and ends
throughout my apartment. By the time I'm done, I'm dead on my

feet. It doesn't take me long to clean up in the bathroom before slipping on my oversized T-shirt and crawling under the covers of my mattress on the floor, exhausted.

Still, it isn't until I can hear the faint chirping of birds announcing the onset of dawn, that my mind finally lets me drift off.

CHAPTER FOUR

Neil

"One americano, one latte, please," I tell the woman at the Silver Bean. It's a quaint aluminum Twinkie trailer, converted into a coffee shop, sitting at the start of Main Street in Cortez. "Oh, and add a couple of breakfast burritos and two cinnamon rolls, please."

I turn my back on the trailer and look out on the road. It's surprisingly busy for an early Saturday morning. I'm lost in thought, wondering how to capitalize on the time I'll be spending with Kendra today. Breakfast seemed like a good place to start, which is why I pulled in here. I'm hoping to score points with the Latte, her favored way to drink coffee. I pay attention, making it a point to know as much about her as I can. Too bad all she wants to see is the joking, gaming, young buck. I've been trying to eradicate those preconceived ideas for a long fucking time. Of course I worked hard myself in establishing that carefree impression to cover up memories of dark nights on desert hills. Most of the guys at GFI know I served overseas, but they never asked and I never told. Gus is the only one who knows I was a sniper with one of the Special Ops units. It's not something I advertise. My technical skills weren't the only thing Gus was interested in when he hired me, but I was happy to play the techie nerd for everyone else. It also worked in my favor that I look younger than I am. The guys know my birthday but not the year, except for Gus, and I never volunteered the information. I made my own bed, regarding Kendra, who has some serious hang up about age, and despite the fact that the difference isn't as big as she thinks, she *is* still older, and it's the one thing I cannot change about myself for her.

"Two breakfast burritos, two cinnamon rolls, an Americano and a Latte."

I turn around, grab the two brown paper bags and slap a twenty on the counter before picking up the tray with the coffees. Hope she's hungry.

Her apartment is close by. I pull into a parking spot closest to the front lobby and, armed with breakfast, make my way to her front door. I have to knock on the door a few times before I hear the click of a lock being turned on the other side.

"Hey," she says, her eyes swollen with sleep and hair a mess, barely stifling a yawn. She's wearing nothing but a large shirt which she tugs down to cover as much of her legs as she can. The pillow creases on her face show me she just woke up. She looks cute, cuddly, like a wrinkly little puppy.

"Let me guess," I wink at her as I slip by her into the apartment. "The mattress on the floor didn't quite cut it." Turning back to her, I see she is still standing with the door partially opened in her hand, looking out over the parking lot below. "Kendra?"

Her head whips around and she quickly closes, *and locks*, the door. What the fuck?

"What's going on?" I snap, instantly wincing at the loss of my carefully honed control. Kendra gives me a long look before turning down the short hallway toward what I assume is her bedroom. Even though her behavior concerns me, I can't help but appreciate the sway of her round ass and the shape of her toned, althletic legs.

"So what did you bring?" She comes out a minute later, having put on a pair of worn jeans, likely in an effort to cover up. Her hands are working to pull her hair into her standard ponytail as she throws an inquiring look my way.

"Breakfast. And don't think for one second you can distract me. Something's going on and you *will* tell me."

She frowns and presses her lips together, while looking over my shoulder at nothing.

"Kendra." I use my most threatening voice, which sounds more like a growl. Her eyes snap to mine immediately. "What has you spooked? You open the door in a sleep shirt, looking like you've barely slept at all. It's obvious something has you shaken. What is it?" I pull the lid off her Latte and shove it toward her. It was that or pull her in my arms, which I'm not sure would go over well.

"I didn't sleep well," she mumbles, her lips around the rim of the coffee cup, her hair falling from the haphazard ponytail to cover her face.

"I can see that, babe. Talk to me." This time I don't hold back, I reach out, wipe her hair off her face and tuck it behind her ear. Her eyes come up and I can see a hint of surprise there.

"It's nothing, I'm just tired," she says, and I know right away that she's not telling me everything. I observe her as she sips on her coffee and distractedly picks at the bun I handed her.

"Kendra." I make every effort to keep my voice soft. "Did anything happen?"

The question startles her, and I can see her visibly shake off whatever is on her mind before she turns to me with a smile. "I'm fine, I just really need a quick shower."

And just like that, I'm distracted. I try to keep my breathing steady as I imagine Kendra, naked, a stream of water cascading down her body. The thought causes my body to react, and I step sideways behind the counter to hide the evidence.

"After," I tell her. "First finish your breakfast. Then I'll start loading up while you get ready. We'll get you into your new place in no time." And close by in Cedar Tree, within easy reach, but I don't add that. I'll keep those thoughts to myself for now.

"Sorry I wasn't ready." Her words are muffled by a mouthful of burrito. She looks at me with an apologetic smile on her face.

"Don't worry, Pup, I'm in no rush." I allow myself to lean in and kiss her forehead. She smells like sleep and Kendra. A scent I wouldn't mind waking up to every fucking day.

"Pup?" she questions when I turn my attention back on my burrito.

"Breakfast is getting cold. Eat," I tell her, hoping to distract her.

I'm thinking it's probably not a good time to tell her a pup is what she reminds me of, with those sleep-swollen eyes and lines still creasing her face. Not a good idea.

Kendra

"Are you hungry?"

We've just finished unloading the bed and couch at my new place. A couple of beautiful baskets hanging on hooks off the porch welcomed us when we pulled into the driveway earlier. Beth had also left a nice welcome-home card on the kitchen counter with a friendly message and a bottle of champagne in the fridge. The rest of the fridge is empty, though, and the cooler with food I brought over won't be enough. I'll need to make a grocery run. Neil looks over my shoulder into the empty fridge.

"I don't have much in the way of actual food. I should head back to pick up the last of the boxes and stop in at Safeway." I try to duck underneath Neil's arm which he has casually draped over my shoulder, but he moves right along with me. Both his hands end up on my shoulders and he slowly turns me around until the small of my back is wedged against the counter. His hands drop down to brace on either side of me and his face is mere inches from mine.

"I can wait," he says in a low voice, keeping me trapped with his eyes.

"Neil, I…" I barely get the words out before his mouth is suddenly on mine. Soft, gentle, pulling my bottom lip between his. With a languid stroke of his tongue, he traces the contour of my lip before letting it slowly slide from his mouth. *Oh boy.* Somehow my hands have fisted in the front of his shirt, and time has ceased to exist. *I'm in trouble.* "We can't…"

"Hush," he says, leaning in for a soft brush against my mouth. "I'm going to hook up your Internet and put together your bed while you get your groceries. Take that time to wrap your head around what just happened here, because the way you just responded to that kiss tells me a much clearer story than the crap you've been feeding me for the past year. Not gonna let you push me away after that, Pup."

I can barely think. The deep timbre of his voice and the way his nose rubs against my cheek as he talks has me mesmerized. That's why, when he steps back, I almost lose my balance. My eyes fly to his face and I see he has a hard time not smiling.

"I tripped," I lamely say. Naturally, now he chuckles. *I'm an idiot.*

"Of course you did," he teases before touching the tip of his finger to my nose and walking out of the kitchen, leaving me wondering what the hell I'm supposed to do now.

Groceries, that's what. I dig in the cupboard under the sink where I stuffed some grocery bags, grab my purse and head out the door. I'm about to get in the RAV when I hear Neil calling.

"Kendra, can you bring back some True Blonde Ale? Those yellow cans. I think Safeway carries it." Neil is hanging out of the window of my bedroom toward the back of the house.

"Sure." With one last look at his ear-to-ear grin, I slip behind the wheel. I'm in trouble, all right.

All the way back to my apartment, I practice what I will say when I get back. It's not original. I've said all of it before and he's made it clear he doesn't consider those good enough reasons. Not anymore. Regardless, there's no way I can start anything with him, however tempting he is. I know in my heart I don't have it in me to recover if he breaks me. And I have no doubt he will. Before long, the hot fling with the older woman will lose its shine, and I'll just be alone again.

Walking down the hall to my apartment, I'm so wrapped up in my thoughts, I don't notice something leaning against the front door. Not until I pull out my keys and look down. A beautiful field bouquet, in yellow and purple. Wrapped in clear foil, I can see the edge of a card stuck between the tulips and heather. I pick up the bouquet, unlock the door, walk in and drop it on the counter.

I don't like this. The card is printed on one side with the word *Sorry*, and I carefully peel back the wrap to pull it free. On the inside, written in tidy small letters is a note:

It was wonderful meeting you, and I hope you'll forgive my enthusiasm.

Immediately, my eyes scan the hallway. That's a little freaky. I don't remember telling him where I live and I don't think he could've followed me home last night. Closing the door, I notice my heart is beating a little fast. I toss the flowers on top of a box by the door and do one last walk through of the apartment. Confident I've got everything, I load the remaining boxes in my SUV and go back to pick up the last one. The flowers are still on the last box by the door and, on impulse, I tuck the little card in my purse, before dumping the bouquet in the garbage can in the lobby. The whole thing leaves me a little rattled and I have no intention of hanging on to them.

Luckily, Safeway is around the corner from my building, and I'm in and out of there within twenty minutes with my bags stuffed. I even remembered to pick up Neil's beer. But I notice myself checking the rear-view mirror the entire drive back to Cedar Tree.

I find myself feeling relieved when I pull in behind Neil's truck. I turn off the engine and rest my head on the steering wheel, letting go of the tension caused by last night's fiasco and this morning's flowers. Done with that. Done with blind dates. It's not worth the stress. A loud knock on the window right beside me has me jump clear across the console. Before I can even get my bearings, Neil yanks open the door and leans in.

"What happened, Kendra?" His brows are drawn together and his eyes express concern. "What happened?"

I close my eyes and lean my head back, blowing out a deep breath in relief. His hand comes up to stroke my cheek with the back of his fingers.

"You're fucking shaking," he mutters, grabbing my hand and pulling me from the car straight into his arms.

"Because you scared the crap out of me. I'm fine. Just a little jumpy." I gently push back on his firm chest, trying not to get too comfortable in his arms. Reluctantly, he loosens his hold on me. "Really." I plaster a reassuring smile on my face. " Let's just get this stuff inside." Although still showing concern, Neil lets me step out of his arms.

Once the last of the boxes are inside, I start putting away the groceries, leaving the makings for sandwiches on the counter. It's damn near two-thirty and I'm hungry as all get out.

"Grilled ham and cheese okay for you?" I ask Neil when he walks into the kitchen and leans against the counter.

"Sounds good. You want a drink?" He pulls open the fridge and comes out waving a beer.

"I'll just have some juice, thanks."

I'm surprised how easily we move around each other in the kitchen. It's a rarity. I usually get irritated when people get in my way while I'm cooking, but Neil seems to be able to anticipate my moves before I make them. And vice versa. Therefore, it doesn't take long before we're sitting at the dining room table, with croque-monsieurs on plates in front of us. The smell of melted cheese makes my stomach rumble and I don't hesitate taking a huge bite from my sandwich.

"This is good," Neil mumbles around a mouthful of grilled cheese. "Better than a regular grilled cheese."

"That because I put three different cheeses and shoulder ham in there. It's called a croque-monsieur. My mom used to make these all the time. It's *the* best comfort food." I watch as he easily devours the first one and I'm glad I had the foresight to make him two. Aside from his looks, smarts and his technical savvy, Neil is known for his bottomless appetite.

This feels nice—too nice—sharing a meal. Not that we've never shared a meal before, but that was usually in a group or at a gathering. It's never been just the two of us. It feels…intimate, and oddly comfortable, which in itself is a little bit disconcerting.

"As if there weren't quite a few things to discuss already, I would love to know what thoughts were going through your mind just now." Neil's voice cuts into my drifting thoughts.

"They were visible on your face," he says as he pushes back his chair, collects our dishes and sets them on the kitchen counter. Turning back to me, he pulls me up from my chair and leads me to the couch, where he sits and tugs me down beside him. "Tell me what had you so jumpy."

I shift to create some space between us, but with his hand still clasping mine, he doesn't let me go far. "Just a guy who doesn't know how to take no for an answer," I finally concede.

I feel the slight jerk of his hand around mine and his body seems to go on alert beside me. "Go on," he says in a deceptively calm tone, but when I chance a glance at his face, I can see the dark intensity in his eyes.

With a sigh, I continue, "He left flowers at the apartment. They were there when I went back for the boxes, sitting in the hallway propped up against my door." Pulling my hand free, I reach for my purse on the coffee table and pull out the card and hand it over. "It was just a coffee date. We talked about hiking. I'd brought some maps for him to look at. He didn't seem happy when I told him I wasn't up for going hiking with him. I went home thinking that was the end of that until I found the flowers."

"This guy, how did he know where you lived? Lars…" He studies the card intently, before dropping it back to the table and twisting sideways to face me. "That his name? How did you meet him?"

"Seriously, I think you're overreacting," I tell him, afraid to admit I ignored his caution last night at dinner. "Look, even if the guy was a bit...*off*, and he managed to get his hands on my address, it won't do him any good now, will it? I officially don't live there anymore." Perhaps I'm trying to convince myself of this as much as I'm trying to convince Neil. I don't want to admit to the hint of uncertainty lingering. I've lived forty years, and aside from my mother's penchant for young boys and my sister's borderline nymphomaniac behavior, I've never had reason to feel unsafe. So it's not a surprise this has me unsettled.

Neil is not easily convinced, however.

"Kendra," he growls impatiently. "Talk."

I shoot an irritated look his way, which leaves him annoyingly unmoved.

"Fine." I lift my hands in surrender. "I met him on MatureDatingOnly at the beginning of the year. I'd put a profile up before Christmas and never looked at it until the day after New Year's. There were a bunch of messages from total sleezeballs, which I immediately deleted, but there was one that stood out from the rest. It was a very polite note from a guy who had similar interests to mine and I ended up responding to it. He seemed nice, but the other, less savory messages kept on coming and I'd already had enough of the whole scene. When I told him I was going to shut down my profile, he sent me his regular e-mail and left it up to me to contact him." I lower my eyes and look at my hands, a tad embarrassed. "I kept his e-mail, and ended up sending him a message. Like I told you earlier, we were just talking this whole time. Mostly about the outdoors: good hiking trails, beautiful spots to see, that kind of stuff. Although, he also told me stories about his students. He's a teacher in Gallup, and I shared a little about my work. Never was there anything more to it, I swear." I don't know why it's so important for me to impress that on Neil, it just is. He simply nods encouragingly. I continue telling him about how we ended up meeting for coffee, a bit ashamed I had so easily given out my telephone number.

I'm wringing my hands in my lap during the prolonged silence that follows, until one of Neil's large ones covers both of mine, stilling them. "Could your address have been on the maps?" he asks calmly.

I think back. Like I'd told the guy, most of those maps date back decades, but I had picked up some newer ones not that long ago. A thought occurs to me. "I actually think I may have had one sent to me a few years back. I'd bought an annual pass, and I think they sent me a map as a thank you. Maybe that had my address on it?"

"That's probably it. But if he contacts you again in any way, I need you to tell me," he gently insists, and I lift my eyes. His face is close enough so that even the slightest movement from either of us will likely result in a touch. Or another kiss. His crystal clear blue eyes are mesmerizing and I respond with a breathy "Okay," instantly regretting my easy compliance.

What is wrong with me?

CHAPTER FIVE

Neil

"What's up?" Mal answers his phone immediately.

"Have you heard anything from Damian on those telephone records? He was going to check if Cora Jennings had actually called this Alan Cymars guy the day she disappeared."

"Yes. A few calls actually. Damian's pretty convinced he's the guy she was planning to meet for dinner. Unfortunately they're coming up empty. No one by that name at any bank in Farmington, and there was only the phone number which was likely a burner. No longer active. They're working on tracking his e-mails, but each one was sent from a different IP address, most of which from unsecured wireless routers in residential areas all over the Four Corners region."

I swear under my breath. "He fucking just drove down neighborhoods trolling for signals. It means he's got a tablet or laptop in his car, and he's at the very least computer savvy if he knows how to avoid IP tracking."

"What's got you wired?" Mal, perceptive as always, inquires.

"It's Kendra."

After a rocky start, Mal and I have forged a pretty solid friendship since his marriage to Kim. During the months prior to that we'd spent some intense times together, which is why I don't have to think twice talking about Kendra with him.

"What's going on?" he prompts me.

I tell him about this Lars guy Kendra met online, and about the weird vibe she was getting off him. I tell him about the flowers and the card. By the time I'm done, the silence on the other side is deafening.

"Look," Mal finally says. "I get that you're protective of her. Hell, you know I am too. But from where I'm sitting, it could just be what it looks like: the guy's more interested in Kendra than she is in him, and he's giving it one last go with the flowers. Can you blame him? Not sure you need to make more out of it."

"I don't know. I mean, Kendra says she checked out his profile up on the high school website where he works. The guy spent four months e-mailing back and forth with her. You're right, he could just be an asshole who doesn't know when to give up."

Mal's point of view helps put things in perspective. My reaction is likely more out of jealousy than common sense. It doesn't completely settle my gut—I'm just not a believer in coincidence.

"It always pays to be cautious, though. Keep an eye on Kendra, not that you need any encouragement." Mal chuckles. "You can always look into the guy for yourself. I just wouldn't advertise that to her. She may not thank you for butting in."

"I should just lock Kendra up until this fucker is caught," I say, thinking out loud.

Malachi bursts out laughing. "I hear you, and good luck with that. You're gonna have to catch her first. Maybe consider letting her in on why you are up in her business."

"I'll think about it." I can't help consider that telling her might scare the shit out of her unnecessarily. "Hey Mal, you think we should put a bug in Damian's ear about this guy? Even just make a footnote on the files? Couldn't hurt. I'm going to have a quiet look into a high school teacher from Gallup with the name Lars. Can't be many of those around."

"Sounds good," Mal says. "I'm gonna have a chat with Damian, if you'll make sure Gus is up to date. And keep an eye on our girl."

"I'll stick as close as she'll let me."

I can still hear Mal's laughter as I hang up the phone.

With my feet up on the railing of the porch, I lean back and fold my hands behind my neck, enjoying the afternoon sun.

"Everything all right?" Kendra walks around the corner of the house and sits beside me on the swing.

"Did you get your stuff squared away?" I reply.

"Are you answering my question with a question of your own?" She comes right back, apparently onto my sad attempt at evasion. She squeals in protest when I hook my arm around her neck and pull her to my side.

"Talked to Mal. That case we've been working on—the one I wasn't able to talk about? I'm still technically not able to talk about it but I'm gonna." Just like that, I've made up my mind to tell her enough to take this seriously.

She pushes back from my side and turns to look at me. "Am I going to freak out?"

"Possibly." I chuckle at her attempt to look threatening before I turn serious again. "Remember I told you it might not be a good idea to go on dates with guys you meet on the Internet?" At her affirming nod, I continue, making sure I have her settled back under my arm. "I had good reason. Remember Damian Gomez? He's the FBI agent who's been involved in some of our cases in the past. He asked GFI for help on a case. A number of women have been reported missing from La Plata County over the past few months. There may be even more disappearances that are connected across state borders. Last week three of the women were found near Durango, deceased." I feel Kendra stiffen under my touch, but she doesn't say anything. "From information we got on the latest victim, there might be a link to dating sites. It's possible the singles scene is what's being used to connect with these women." Before I have a chance to hold her back, Kendra is off the swing and pacing up and down the porch, pulling the elastic from her hair and running her hands through the loose strands. Seeing her this flustered, I decide I've told her enough. No need to get into details that might keep her awake at night.

"No way. No fucking way. *Son of a fucknugget.*" She is mumbling under her breath, obviously agitated. On her next pass, I manage to snag her wrist and pull her back down beside me.

"Relax," I try, but her head snaps around and her eyes shoot sparks.

"Relax? Don't tell me to relax—I have to call my sister. She's got profiles up on more than one site." Her gaze meets mine and something in my eyes must alarm her. "That's why you warned me yesterday. You think…is he…?"

"He's likely just a legitimate asshole." I tell her the same thing I told Mal. "I don't think there's anything to worry about, but let's not take any chances. I'll make sure a note is added to our file, and in the meantime, we're going to have to let Gomez know about the website. We'll leave it to the FBI to decide what to do with the information. And like I said earlier, you need to let me know should the guy try to contact you again."

"Ahhhh, I can't believe this is happening," she moans with her face in her hands. "It's embarrassing enough, you finding out I'd resorted to dating sites, but now everyone's gonna know."

I grab her by the shoulders and lightly shake her. "Knock it off. No one's gonna care. Everyone's much more concerned about stopping whoever is taking these women." That quiets her down.

"You're right," she whispers, her fingers pressed against her lips. "I wasn't thinking."

The moment I see tears forming in her eyes, I stand up, taking her with me, and walk us inside. In the kitchen, I reach for a towel and wet it under the tap. Tears are now rolling freely down her face, and I quietly wipe them away, waiting for her to compose herself. I think things may have just gotten a bit too real.

"Better?" I ask as the flow of tears seems to slow down. She's not looking at me but gives me a sharp nod in response.

"I'm an idiot," she mumbles against my chest when I pull her in my arms. For once, she doesn't resist me.

"You're not an idiot. This is not a *normal* situation." I notice with great satisfaction when she slips her arms around my waist, fisting the shirt on my back. "We may well be over vigilant, but better safe than sorry. And even contemplating the possibility of something like this touching your life is a shock to the system. Most of us don't ever have to deal with ugly realities like this in our lives."

"How did you get so wise?" she asks, leaning back to look at me in surprise. It almost makes me laugh.

"You forget this is my work. Spending years overseas in the military helped. I have seen and still see enough human aberration and cruelty to last me a few lifetimes." I know I've let too much of myself show when she looks at me strangely. Her hand comes up to rest in the middle of my chest.

"What happened to you?" she asks softly.

I can't answer that. I wish I could. "Life, Pup. Life happened." It's the best I can do.

She slightly tilts her head when she asks, "How old are you exactly?"

I instantly release her and step away. *Fucking seriously? We're back here again?* My frustration must be visible because she reaches to stop me with her hand on my arm.

"Why the fuck does a bloody number matter so much to you? Every time I think we're getting somewhere, you throw my age in my face, like it's some kind of blemish. What the fuck am I supposed to do about that, huh? The one thing I can't change."

I pull my arm from her grip, turn around and walk right out of there. This whole screwed-up situation is too high octane for my blood right now and I need to cool off. But I don't get very far.

"Wait!" Kendra comes running out of the house after me just as I'm getting into my truck. "Please, don't go. I…I didn't mean anything by it. Can I please explain?"

Goddammit. She's hanging on to my door, her face pale and biting her bottom lip with a vengeance. I reach out and pull her lip free with my thumb. "Don't do that," I tell her softly, already regretting my outburst. I know people are lulled into thinking I'm a laid back guy—I work hard at it—but when it comes to things that are important to me, I can have an explosive temper. Yet another piece of myself I'd rather keep from her. I'm fucking up.

"Please come inside." Her voice is soft, pleading, and it pulls at me.

I drop my head and hit it on the steering wheel a few times before sliding back out of the truck and following her inside.

⸻⬥⬥⸻

Kendra

I'm so relieved when I hear his footsteps behind me. I hadn't expected that kind of reaction to the question that simply popped out. Listening to him, realizing there was so much more to him than the person I'd made him out to be, had prompted me to ask about his age. The moment I hear the door close, I swing around to face him.

I watch him linger just inside the door and take a few steps closer. "You surprised me, just now. I know it's my own fault, never wanting to look beyond the surface. I've been too hung up on my own…issues to look any closer." I shake my head to clear it, hoping to find the words to explain. "There's more to you than I've given you credit for. Oh," I add quickly, seeing the clench of his jaw. "I think I've always known, which is a big reason why it seemed safer not to look too deep."

He's been quietly watching me struggle through my words, and I'm not sure I'm making any sense, but something must have stirred him, because he takes a step toward me.

"I've purposely kept you at a distance. Because of our age difference, I let the red flag fly high. Honestly? I think it's the only thing that I can make into enough of a reason to push you away." At my words, Neil moves in even closer, only a step away. The look on his face is intense, but no longer angry, and I decide to open up a little more. Before I have a chance to open my mouth, he beats me to it.

"I'll be thirty-two next month."

Eight years. Not as bad as the twelve years I thought separated us. Still, eight years.

"I'm forty," I tell him stupidly.

"I know, and I don't give a flying fuck," he says fiercely before adding, "and neither should you."

"You don't understand," I try to explain. "I…my mother…she…" Neil closes the distance between us and cups my face in his hands.

"I. Don't. Care."

I don't have a chance to say anything before his mouth hits mine, effectively cutting off any other communication. One of his hands slides in my hair, cupping the back of my head, while the other runs down over my shoulder and around to the small of my back where he presses me to his body. *Holy fudgesticks*. His body leaves me with no doubt as to his desire for me. The prominent evidence is pressing in my stomach. There's also no way I can deny what he does to my own body. Heat tingles over my skin from wherever we are touching, converging in a needy throb between my legs. His mouth— Jesus, his mouth. Soft in touch but hard in demand, with his tongue claiming my own dominantly while his gentle lips slip over mine. Bliss.

"I'm not gonna fuck this up," he mumbles as he slowly pulls his mouth from mine. I can't stop the little moan that escapes me at the loss of his lips. "As you can well tell, I want nothing more than to throw you over my shoulder, take you upstairs to that big ass bed I spent an hour putting together, and feast on you. But I'm not going to push."

All I can think is *push, please push,* but I don't say a word when he presses those freaking fantastic lips against my forehead and walks to the door.

"I'll be back later. I have to head over to the office to pick up a few things and get some information to Gus. I also need a clear head, and right now there's not enough blood left up here for that." The little smile tilting his mouth slightly is cocky, and combined with his words, hot as heck. "Call me if you need me. I won't be more than a couple of hours." With that, he walks out the door.

Okay. What just happened here? I'm still trying to process that kiss, and the fact that kisses from Neil seem to carry more punch than a lifetime of half-assed sexual experiences. He's coming back? I don't know what that means, what to expect.

Over the next hour or so, I do my best not to think too much as I put away my clothes, make the bed and finish emptying a few boxes. When I unwrap my favorite family picture—Karly, Mom and I with our arms wrapped around each other, smiling at the camera—I suddenly remember they're leaving tonight. I grab my phone off the kitchen counter where I'd left it to charge and check the time. I quickly dial my sister's number, hoping I'll be able to catch them before they're off on their cruise. The phone rings and rings, until her message comes on. *Dagnabbit.* I dial my mom's next. Same result. After trying Karly's phone again without success, I leave her a brief message for either of them to call me if they haven't left yet.

I know I'm being paranoid, but I want to warn my sister in particular to stay off her favored dating and chat sites for a while. It was she who suggested I set up a profile in the first place. I curse myself that I didn't immediately call to give her a heads up. They must have just left. They were supposed to fly to Fort Lauderdale tonight and were scheduled to embark early tomorrow. Although it does settle my nerves to know that they will be safely away on a ship.

Regardless, I'm restless. I've put away most of my stuff—all that remains is to hang up some frames and pictures— but plan to work on those tomorrow. I realize I'm fretting. About what is happening with Neil. About some maniac out there who is harming women. And about a bouquet of flowers. I'm suddenly in need of some air.

With just my old jean jacket on to ward off that spring evening chill that sets in when the sun starts to drop, I snag my keys and lock up behind me. A walk is what I need so I take off to explore the neighborhood. As opposed to Cortez, all the houses in Cedar Tree have a decent amount of property around them. The town is not on a major thoroughfare like Cortez is, and therefore there is plenty of space. With a population of about six hundred people, and no major industries, it's not likely it will grow by much, although from what Naomi tells me, what used to be an aging population is slowly being replaced with younger families. At the end of the street, a trail leads into the hills to the south. I'm heading that way when my phone starts ringing. I almost jump out of my shoes before pulling it from my pocket.

"Hello?"

"I'm at the house and you're not here."

"Observant," I smart off, trying to hide my jumpiness.

Neil's response is more like a growl. "Kendra."

"Oh fine. I needed to get out, and was on that trail at the end of the street. I'm turning back now. Happy?"

"Very." That's the only thing he says before hanging up. How *very* irritating. I start back down the trail at a brisk pace, tucking my phone back in my pocket.

Before I even get back to the street, a tall figure is turning onto the trail, long strides eating up the distance.

"Christ, you test me," Neil says when he reaches me, grabs my elbow and starts walking back.

Wait. What?

"Sorry? You call, I come straight back. How is that testing you? And who the fuzzbuckets do you think you are anyway?" I'm working up a head of steam, being half dragged down the trail and onto the sidewalk. Neil makes no signs of stopping, so I stop for him, planting both my feet and simultaneously pulling back on the arm he still has in his grip. It doesn't quite work out the way I hoped.

"Fuck, Ken. What the hell?" He barely has time to swing around and catch me as my face heads straight for the pavement. I'd stupidly locked my knees and Neil's forward momentum pulled me right off my feet. The guy is a freaking tree.

"Everything all right over there?" A concerned voice belonging to an elderly neighbor comes from across the street.

"It's all good," I hasten to answer, as Neil yanks me upright with his hands under my arms. "I just tripped!" I yell across the street, worried she'll have the sheriff out here in a heartbeat if I don't diffuse the situation. To hammer my point home, I slip my arm around Neil's waist and with a saucy wave at the white-haired lady, start walking the rest of the way home.

By the time we walk up my driveway, Neil is chuckling and I'm laughing out loud. I felt the woman's eyes burning holes in my back the entire way.

"Do me a favor," Neil says, opening my door with the code I didn't realize he had. "Next time, let me know before you feel the need to take a walk."

"Really?" I huff out, pushing past him into the house, but I don't get far because his hand snakes out and swings me around by my arm. With both hands on my shoulders, he leans down, touching his nose to mine.

"Please?" Lingering amusement sparkles in his baby blues. "Otherwise you're gonna turn me old before my time, and your neighbor will never survive."

With some added drama, I roll my eyes, but I can't contain the snort bursting through.

CHAPTER SIX

Neil

"I'm stuffed."

Kendra flops back in her seat, folding her hands on her stomach. "I think I ate too much."

I don't know how a single damn burger and fries can fill her up, but then I've always had a *healthy* appetite. Mom still jokes I ate my way through my college fund before I was even enrolled. The truth is that I had some seriously naive and idealistic dreams about saving the world and college didn't fit into that picture. I enlisted instead. Barely nineteen when I joined. I learned a lot, always was better at applied learning than I was at academics. Not for lack of smarts, but the abstract way of learning never suited me. How ironic that I ended up discovering I had a knack for information technology. It's about as abstract as you can get. I was always big and bulky and the combo of brains and brawn had made me attractive in the field. Especially when it turned out I had a pretty sharp eye too. That one surprised me. I'd never shot a gun in my life; my devout parents would never allow it. Yet, the first time I was on the gun range in training, I managed to impress myself—and my sergeant. As excited as I was when I managed to eliminate target after target on the range, the shine disappeared quickly the first time I had a living, breathing target in my sights.

"Holy schnikes. What's gotten into you?" Kendra's voice pulls me out of my thoughts and her hand covers mine on the table. "I hope it wasn't me you were thinking about," she says quietly as she turns my hand palm up. I'm surprised to see I'm bleeding. Glass is scattered over the table. I slowly become aware of the noise in the diner. A quick look around establishes that whatever just happened, no one seems to have taken much notice. Even Julie, our waitress, has her back turned. Only Arlene, who stands behind the counter on the far end has her worried eyes fixed on me. A tug on my hand has me turn back to Kendra.

"Let's go clean you up," she says calmly, wrapping her napkin around my hand, which seems to be bleeding quite a bit now. I don't feel a thing, though.

I let her lead me through the diner past Arlene, who is waving us through to the kitchen.

"Grab the private restroom beside my office. I'll fetch the first aid kit."

Seb turns around from the grill. "Hey. How's it going?"

Still a bit dazed, I don't answer immediately, but Kendra jumps in. "We had a little accident with a glass. Just gonna use your bathroom."

"Sure, sure," he says, waving us through.

In the small room, Kendra holds my hand over the sink and turns on the tap. I've still not said a word. It's like my tongue is stuck to the roof of my mouth. She doesn't push, just calmly rinses away the blood from a nasty gash right across the palm of my hand. A soft *tsssk* sound comes from behind me as Arlene pushes into the confined space.

"Impressive." She winks at me while taking some gauze and a bottle of something out of the kit she brought in and handing them to Kendra. "I'll be up front if you need me." The soft click of the door behind her leaves Kendra and me steeped in silence.

Kendra pushes me to sit down on the toilet and examines the cut, after pouring on some kind of disinfectant. That, I can feel. It starts with a stinging and slowly turns into a steady, deep throb. *Fuck.*

"You'll need some stitches," she says, taking great care as she stacks squares of sterile gauze on the wound before wrapping it up tight with a bandage.

I still haven't uttered a word.

Her hand comes up to cup my jaw and she leans down to get in my face. "What's going on?"

Instead of answering, I wrap my other hand around the back of her neck and pull her down farther so I can kiss her. I can taste the salt from the fries on her lips, licking them slowly before sliding my tongue in her mouth and filling myself with just the taste of her. With her hands landing on my shoulders to balance herself, her body instinctively moves in between my legs.

"I like kissing you," is what I end up mumbling against her mouth. I can feel her lips forming a smile against mine.

"You're relentless," she whispers back. "But we really should get you stitched up. Give me your keys, I'll drive."

After our little spat on the sidewalk this afternoon, I managed to convince her to come grab a bite at Arlene's. I figured being with her in the familiar surroundings might help her start seeing me in a different way. This was obviously not part of my plan. "I'll drive. It's a manual."

"So?" she snaps, rising to her full height, which, given that I'm still sitting on the can, allows her to look down on me. "Any rules I should be aware of that state women can't drive standard?"

I chuckle at her vehemence. "No. But I noticed you're driving an automatic yourself, so I wasn't sure."

"I'll have you know that my previous car was a Mustang and it certainly was not an automatic."

"A Mustang, huh? What happened?" I'm intrigued. Not that I can't see Kendra driving one, because I sure as fuck can. Nothing wrong with my imagination. It's just that there is a world of difference between that and the little utilitarian SUV she drives now.

"It would appear that a sporty convertible is not exactly a handy car to have when living in Durango," she admits rather sheepishly. Cute. "It was a post-graduation phase of mine that passed as quickly as the coming of first snow. By the time I moved to Cortez, I was making better choices." She looks a little melancholy, and I make a note to myself that given the opportunity, I'd get her behind the wheel of a Mustang again. "Come on." She pulls me up. "Let's see if Naomi is around to do some stitching, unless you want to drive to Cortez?"

"Nope," I tell her, handing over my truck keys. A little smile twitching the corner of her mouth is my reward.

With a quick word with Seb to let Arlene know we're off, we slip out the backdoor.

"I'd forgotten you live here now," Kendra says as she adjusts the seat and the mirrors in my truck. "I still think of this apartment as Mal's."

"A year now, Kendra," I snap, suddenly irritated. From the corner of my eye, I can see Kendra's hands still on the steering wheel and I feel her eyes on me. Now I'm pissed at myself.

"I didn't mean anything by it," she says softly as she starts up the truck. "It's just that I haven' t been up there since you moved in."

The reminder that she so easily befriended Malachi, while keeping me at bay the entire time stings, but I know I overreacted. Reaching over with my left hand, I cover hers on the steering wheel. "Sorry I snapped," I apologize a bit weakly.

"No worries." She briefly turns her hand to give mine a squeeze before releasing it and grabbing the stick shift. Easily slipping the truck into first, she pulls smoothly out of the parking lot. "*Dagnabit*," I hear her mumble under her breath.

"What?"

"I forgot Naomi and Joe are in Durango this weekend, packing up Fox's room."

Naomi's son, Fox, started attending Fort Lewis in Durango a few years ago. Majoring in anthropology. Although he'd always shown a keen interest in the archeological digs around the area, spending a few months each summer volunteering on a variety of digs, his aim is medical anthropology. When I first met the kid, he was just sixteen years old but seemed far older and wiser than his years. He'd encountered some problems when first moving to the area with his mom, and ended up losing his father, so we'd ended up spending quite a bit of time together. I like the kid, although at almost twenty, and almost as tall as his stepfather, Joe, he could hardly be considered a kid anymore.

"I forgot about that. This will be the end of his second year, right?"

Kendra smiles when she turns to me. "Sure is, and he's doing really well. I had him on the phone last week and he mentioned hooking up with you for some *ass-kicking*, as he called it."

It makes me laugh. Fox had a hard-on about beating me at a game I helped develop. We'd hung out gaming quite a bit, and I have to admit, the kid is good. Almost had me a time or two. "He wishes," I tell her with a smile, glad some of the tension is gone from the truck cab.

"Okay, so I'll just head for Southwest in Cortez. I'll make sure you're in and out of there quickly."

The mention of the hospital turns my focus on my hand, which is still throbbing steadily in my lap. Damn.

"Are you ready to tell me what happened?"

My eyes take in Kendra's profile as she keeps her gaze steady on the road. So damn pretty. Her hair is back from her face in its signature ponytail, a few strands having slipped from the elastic band holding it back, drifting around her face. Her clear and observant eyes are framed with thick, dark lashes and ringed with fine laugh lines. Evidence of the weather is smattered across the skin of her nose and forehead, with a sprinkling of freckles that seem to get darker and more spread out as spring progresses. She really does look like the prime example of a *girl-next-door*. Pretty, fresh, and outdoorsy looking. A face I've become intimately familiar with over the past few years. But that mouth…holy fuck…those lips. That's the stuff dreams are made of. And that's what I focus on when I take a deep breath in and try to answer as honestly as I can.

Kendra

I can feel his eyes tracing my features and I can't help but wonder what it is he sees exactly. I know I'm pushing, but something happened back there at the diner and it worries me. Before I have a chance to prompt him again, I hear his sharp intake of breath as if he's preparing himself, so I wait him out. It doesn't take long until I'm rewarded with his words.

"It's funny actually. The food got me thinking about my mother—my family—and the reasons I enlisted in the army."

The derisive chuckle emitting from him is quite obviously self-directed, and I try not to react. "I was so full of myself then. Thinking I would be able to make an impact. What a joke. I was just a cog in a very large war machine." His gaze finds mine before he quickly turns back to look outside once more. But not before I catch a hint of torment behind his eyes. *Yowza.* Carefully keeping my expression level, I direct my focus back to the road. "Sometimes when I let my thoughts go, when I think about some of the shit… Whatever…" he shakes his head before he continues. "I sometimes lose track of where I am."

He doesn't look at me, but I can sense him waiting for a reaction. Rather than give him a verbal one, I slip my hand off the gearshift and find his resting on his thigh. Quietly, I slide my hand under his palm and lace my fingers with his. I never take my eyes off the road. The only response is the slight tightening of his hand on mine.

The entire rest of the trip to Cortez is traveled in silence, each of us with our thoughts. Whenever I pull my hand from his to change gears, he just as quickly places it back on his thigh, interlacing our fingers every time. Maybe that's why, once we park the truck in the hospital parking lot and start walking toward the emergency entrance, it seems natural for our hands to find each other's.

Walking into the lobby, holding hands with Neil should have me worried, but I'm not thinking about what it means. I just know it feels right in this moment, so I hang on.

It doesn't take long for Neil to be led into one of the treatment rooms, where a second bed is already occupied by a little boy, his mom sitting beside him, doing her best to silence his crying.

"I'm so sorry," she says immediately when she sees us come in.

Without hesitation, Neil walks over to where the five or six year old boy is, with his hand wrapped up in a kitchen towel, fighting his mother's hold, protesting loudly. "May I?" Neil asks the mother, indicating the edge of the boy's bed. She nods her head with a tremulous smile. The little guy is suddenly still, watching Neil sit down with suspicious eyes. With a broad smile Neil points at the boy's makeshift bandage. "What did you do? I cut my hand on a glass," he says, showing off his own bound hand. "It was silly, I wasn't being very careful."

The boy's eyes look from Neil's bandaged hand to his own, and with tears still tracking down his cheeks, he softly giggles. "Helping Mommy cook." His words are almost whispered as he looks from under his eyelashes at Neil.

"I see." Neil settles in comfortably on the boy's bed, his back against the headboard and his feet crossed on top of the blanket, looking for all intents and purposes to be completely at ease. "Guess we were both a little silly then, right? Did you cut yourself too?"

The kid nods, his face serious as he moves out of his mother's hold and settles back against the headboard as well, mimicking Neil's pose. His mother looks at me and tries to hide her smile, as do I.

"My name is Neil, what's yours?"

"Brandon. And I'm five." He helpfully holds up his good hand, fingers spread wide.

"You go to school yet, Brandon?"

"After the summer, Mommy says."

"Hmmmm," Neil hums deep in his throat, and despite the odd situation, the sound gives me inappropriate goose bumps. "By that time your cut will probably be healed already. It won't hurt anymore, but you'll probably have a scar. Scars are cool."

I only manage to swallow half the snort that wants to escape me when I see Brandon's eyes go big. Neil turns his head and gives me a little wink before turning back to his pint-sized admirer.

When the attending comes in a little while later, Brandon is chattering away, his tears and his injury almost completely forgotten. But when he sees the white coat of the doctor, his bottom lip begins to wobble. Once again, Neil takes control. "Have you met my friend yet?" Big teary eyes look up at him. "This is my buddy, Doctor…"

Quickly cluing in on the game, the young physician chimes up. "Ross. Doctor Ross, but call me Jeff. Everyone does."

"My buddy, Jeff. He's gonna fix us right up, Brandon. He'll give us both a cool scar."

Carefully, Neil tries to make room for the doc to get in, but Brandon starts shaking his head when Jeff reaches for his hand. "Him first," he says, pointing at Neil's hand.

"How about I look at you guys at the same time?" Jeff suggests.

While he carefully unwraps Neil's hand and then Brandon's, I take a seat next to the empty bed. Listening with half an ear to the conversation taking place, I try to analyze the warm and fuzzy feels I'm getting. Yet another aspect of Neil I would never have credited him with. I'm thinking I may not have been fair to him and I suddenly understand a little better why he might have gotten upset at my remark earlier. I'd been so focused on the fact he is younger, I stuck him into a box he doesn't belong in. Never bothering—or daring—to look any further. What I've seen of him, especially this past year, in no way justifies the *irresponsible* label I somehow affixed him with. And after what he skimmed over on the drive here and the way he handles his new little buddy, I have a newfound respect for the man he is. Respect he deserved a long time ago and I've been too stubborn to grant him. *Fiddlesticks*. Now I feel guilty.

I sit there, staring at the floor, full of self-recrimination, when I see the toes of his boots step into my view. "Are you okay?" he asks, tucking some of my flyaway hair behind my ear as I look up. I obviously wasn't paying much attention, too lost in my thoughts, because the room is empty except for the two of us.

"Where did everyone go?" I ask, feeling confused.

"We're done. Brandon and his mom went home. He watched me get my stitches and was a trooper when it was time to have his hand stitched up. I thought you were sleeping. You've been quietly sitting here for over half an hour."

"No. I mean, I wasn't sleeping, I was thinking." I push out of the chair to stand, but Neil isn't budging. He just smiles down at me as my body brushes lightly against his. "Guess I lost track of time."

"Guess you did." Neil swings his good arm around my shoulders and walks me out. Unthinking, I slip my arm around his waist. It seems like the natural thing to do.

Walking up to his truck, he lets his arm fall away and I'm instantly hit with chills, despite the jean jacket I'm still wearing. I start walking around the front of the truck when a sound like shifting gravel has me look to the edge of the parking lot. Neil's voice right behind me has me turn my eyes to him.

"Give me the keys and I'll get her started up." Neil holds up his hand.

"But you're hurt. I'll drive," I protest.

"I'm good. I promise. I can shift the gears on this thing with two fingers and the local anaesthetic hasn't worn off yet."

Reluctantly, I pull his keys from my pocket and hand them over. In no time, the engine is running and heat is flooding the cab. Once again, the drive is silent and this time, because I'm sitting on the side of his injured hand, there is no handholding.

It's not until he pulls into my driveway that I remember I wanted to try calling my sister again, but they've probably already hit the sack. It's a little past eleven and they are scheduled to embark at eight o'clock tomorrow morning. Not going to call them now. At this time of night, it'll only freak them out and I don't want them to have a bad sleep their last night on terra firma. As long as she's out on a cruise, there isn't much trouble she can get into. Right?

"I'm gonna head home," Neil says as he pushes open my front door. "Been a long day, and I'm beat. Besides," he mutters as he backs me against the wall beside the front door, bracing my head with an elbow on either side. "The plans I had for tonight will have to wait a little longer now that I don't have full use of my hands. I'm gonna need them both for what I have in mind."

How a smell that is part hospital antiseptic can be so appealing, I don't know, but on Neil it most definitely is. Of course his proximity and the soft lull of his voice have something to do with that. Not to mention his message. There's that.

Before I have a chance to string together a few coherent words, he rattles my brain even further with a soul-scorching kiss. By the time he pulls back, I'm literally gasping for air. The man can kiss, and with each one I feel myself slipping further and further under his spell.

Holy tater tits.

CHAPTER SEVEN

Neil

"H'lo…"

"You up?"

I run my hand over my face, immediately pulling back when the odd texture and biting sting in my palm hit me. Right. I forgot about that. I carefully peel back my eyelids. Damn, it's bright outside. A quick glance to the alarm clock on my nightstand tells me I slept a hole in the day. Not surprising, given that I didn't fall asleep until well past three this morning. I'd come home after dropping Kendra off, a feat that cost me a considerable amount of discomfort, since I was hard as a fucking post. Ever try to drive straight when you have a fully torqued NASA rocket trying to poke a damn hole in your jeans because it wouldn't bend? Not fucking easy.

Still, I made it home in one piece and figuring I wouldn't sleep, I flipped open my laptop. I'd spoken briefly with Gus earlier yesterday to put a bug in his ear about the douchebag Kendra had found online. Of course, Gus had felt the need to remind me to keep an eye on Kendra, as if I wouldn't. After hanging up, I snooped around Facebook a little and managed to find two of the three unaccounted for Durango area missing women. When I found a link through their accounts with some of the popular dating sites, I was surprised at how easy it was to hack into their profiles. Neither woman had protected their Facebook account very well, and once there, it wasn't hard to figure out how to access all their information. By that time, my eyes were hard to keep open and I finally rolled into bed. Painful hard-on long forgotten.

"I'm up, I'm up," I finally answer Gus.

"Good. Get yourself ready and come down to the diner. We're having a breakfast meeting. Gomez is here."

I'm in and out of the shower in a matter of minutes despite the plastic bag I had to duct tape over my hand. About ten minutes after my call with Gus, I walk through the kitchen into the diner. A glance at the large station clock shows almost ten o'clock. Seb is just serving plates of eggs and bacon to Gus, Damian Gomez, Joe and Mal, who are sitting at the large round table in the corner. The rest of the diner is empty, the Closed sign still on the door.

"Sit," Seb says, indicating an empty chair. "I'll be right back with yours."

"Coffee?" Gus asks, holding up a large thermos that was sitting in the middle of the table. I turn over one of the clean mugs in response. "What the hell happened to your hand?" Gus points at the bandage.

"Broke a glass. Had to get some stitches. Nothing a solid dose of caffeine won't fix." I wave the still empty mug.

"Good. You'll need it. They just found another body early this morning. The twenty-nine-year-old pharmaceutical rep. Damian came straight from the scene," he says as he pours the hot black liquid.

I take a decent-sized gulp of the coffee, barely noticing it burn my mouth. I have a feeling I'm going to need all the help I can get to stay sharp today. That's why, when Seb shows up with my bacon and eggs, I dig in while listening to Damian's briefing.

"She was found in a ditch off the road about a mile up from the Mesa Verde park gate by an early morning road crew checking for wildlife carcasses. Coroner arrived at the same time I did and did a preliminary examination of the body right there. Same carvings on the back, signs of asphyxiation, but also some evidence of injuries inflicted over time. There wasn't much more he could give us without a proper autopsy, except for a general time frame. She'd likely been there between forty-eight to seventy-two hours. A slight difference with this one from the other three victims is that she went missing two weeks ago, while the other three were killed shortly after their disappearances. It looks like our unsub kept this woman alive for two weeks before he killed her. He kept her somewhere." Obviously stressed, Damian runs a shaking hand through his hair.

"What's her name?" I put my fork down a little too loudly, but it always irks me how victims of crime seem to lose their identity along with their life. She was a person. Someone's child, or perhaps even someone's parent. People missed her.

"Sorry?" Damian looks up a little confused.

"Our victim, the woman you found, what was her name?" From the corner of my eye I spot Mal lowering his head, a smile tugging at his mouth, as Damian rummages through his papers.

"Tracy Poole, she was reported missing by her sister when she didn't show up for a baby shower she had organized. Was last seen at Walgreens."

"Thanks," I simply say, having made my point. I understand that for people like Damian, sometimes the only way to get through the day is to maintain an emotional distance. We don't have the kind of constant exposure to violent crime like he does. A name and person behind the victim motivates me to work harder, look further and dig deeper.

While I turn back to my breakfast, Damian continues to catch us up on the investigation, taking care to mention the known victims by their first names. I look up at the mention of my name.

"Sorry?"

"I was checking if there was any way you could link up with my office from here. Agent Greene—Jasper—is working on the victims' social network and Internet histories, but with the possible number of victims we have, he can barely keep up." Damian turns to Gus to further explain. "I've cleared it with the head office. We're thin on technical support as it is, so convincing the powers that be to put together a task force was an easy one. Contract and conditions same as before." With that, he shoves a thick document over to Gus.

I guess we're officially on the job.

Kendra

The fresh, crisp, morning air smells like spring.

It hits me as soon as I open the door to the back patio. A gorgeous stark blue sky greets me and the sounds of the neighborhood slowly coming alive on a Sunday morning put a smile on my face. After living in an apartment building in the middle of a relatively noisy town for years, the thought of enjoying my morning cup of coffee surrounded by the sounds and sights of nature was very appealing.

I scoot back in to don a sweater to ward off the morning chill and the moment the coffeemaker stops its gurgling, I arm myself with the largest mug I can find, a book and my cellphone and head out. The patio holds a large wooden lounger, which will be fantastic once the weather warms up, as well as a utilitarian picnic table. I chose the last. With a sip of the hot coffee, tugging the sweater a little tighter around me, I sit and breathe in deep.

I slept surprisingly well. After Neil left me hot and bothered in the hallway last night, I thought for sure I'd have another sleepless night ahead. Amazing what a hot shower and an orgasm can do for relaxation. I feel only a little guilty for having used him to visualize while aiming the showerhead in a pulsing stream to my clit. With my eyes closed, his taste still on my lips and his head imagined between my legs, I was groaning out my release almost instantly.

A harsh ringing has me jump and slosh hot coffee over my hand. *Darn.* That hurts. I wipe my hand on my yoga pants while snatching up my phone with the other.

"What are you up to?"

I was half expecting Neil, so it takes me a minute to place the voice and the instant I do, I feel the hair on my neck stand up.

"Lars? Look, I thought I'd been cle—"

"I left you flowers. Did you not like them?" The question sounds almost like a dare. There is an edge to his voice I don't like.

I stand up from the table, with my heart racing in my chest. "They made me feel uncomfortable," I admit honestly. "How did you know where to find me?" I try to keep my voice steady as I scan the brush and trees around me, as if he could jump out at any minute.

"Not that hard to figure out. You left the address for me to find on one of your maps. I was hoping to surprise you." His tone becomes a bit petulant, like a child caught with their hand in the cookie jar.

"I assure you that was unintentional. I'm sorry if it gave you the wrong impression. I'd prefer if you didn't call me again."

"Don't hang up, please! I'm sorry if I overstepped. I thought I was doing something nice. I was hoping I could change your mind about maybe going for a hike." His voice is now smooth and cajoling, but I'm not having any of it.

"I don't think so. I'm sorry." With that I end the call, quickly gather my things and head inside, closing and locking the door behind me.

"Everything all right?" Neil answers his phone on the third ring. "Kendra?"

"Yes, well…maybe. I just got a call from Lars, and—"

"Lock up," Neil barks, cutting me off mid-sentence. "I'm on my way." Without another word, the connection is broken.

Immediately, the phone starts ringing again with an unlisted number. Without answering, I turn off the sound and lay it upside down on the counter. On an impulse, I yank down the blinds in the kitchen and stand there, clutching my coffee until I hear the beep of the touch lock on the front door and Neil stalks in. It had taken him less than five minutes to get here.

"Kendra!" His voice booms through the house.

"In here," I offer, peeking around the doorway to find not only Neil, but Malachi and the FBI agent in the small hallway as well. The moment Neil spots me, he bridges the distance and draws me in his arms, tucking my head under his chin.

"Are you okay?" he asks.

From the corner of my eye, I watch both of the other men walk around my space. "Yes," I tell him, self-consciously taking a step back from him. "Hey," I say to Mal, when he throws a smile my way.

"Talk to them," he says, indicating Neil and the other man with a chin lift. "I'm going to check outside." And he disappears out the back door.

"Where's your phone?" the dark-haired, olive-skinned and intimidating third man asks.

"Pup," Neil draws my eyes back to him. "This is FBI Special Agent Damian Gomez. I think I mentioned him before. And Damian," his tone is much sharper when he addresses the guy, "please meet Kendra Schmitt."

I almost smile at the stare-down taking place in my hallway between the two. I have to admit, it's more than just a little flattering that Neil should throw down as my protector. Even from bad manners. Apparently Agent Gomez knows it too, since he's the first one to lower his gaze.

"I apologize," he says, his voice much softer than his initial bark, and something tells me this man could be devastatingly charming if he tried. "It's no excuse, but it's been a long day already. Please call me Damian."

I take his words to mean something more than just the passing of time, since it is only now coming up on eleven in the morning. The stress is evident on his face, so I'm guessing that despite the fact that the day is only a few hours old, they have been unpleasant ones for him. That causes a chill to run down my spine. I reach out my hand, which he shakes with a polite little head nod.

"Phone's on the kitchen counter." I point in the right direction when he lets go of my hand. "I turned off the sound." As Agent Gomez—Damian—walks into the kitchen for my phone, Neil's arm comes around my chest and pulls me back into his.

"You didn't answer my question," he whispers in my hair.

I lift my hand to hold on to his forearm, the feeling of vulnerability quickly disappearing. "Okay. I'm okay … now," I add, with a little squeeze of my hand. "But isn't this a bit much?" I point in the general direction of the kitchen. "I mean, he gave me the heebie-jeebies but you come running like he had a knife against my throat." I try to joke away my discomfort, but Neil doesn't seem to think it's funny.

"Don't fucking joke about that," he lectures, making me feel about a foot high.

"Sorry," I mumble, feeling duly chided. "Wasn't thinking."

With his arm still holding me, he starts moving me toward the living room, where he gestures for me to sit on the couch. He takes a seat on the edge of the coffee table and leans forward with his elbows on his knees and his face just inches from mine. "Tell me about the conversation."

Ignoring Damian who has followed us into the room, I start talking. I seem to be able to recall the conversation almost verbatim. Neil asks me a few questions; did I hear any noises in the background, could I tell whether he was somewhere indoors or outside. That kind of thing. Not much I can add, except that the quick shifts in his personality during that short phone call had made me very uncomfortable.

The sound of a muted conversation draws my attention away from Neil's large hands, which have found their way onto my knees while I've been recounting the conversation. Damian is by the dining table, on his phone, while thumbing through mine with his other hand. I can only make out the odd word but from what little I catch, he's relaying some of the information I just gave to someone on the other end.

"He's probably just checking out the phone number." Neil's steady voice breaks my concentration.

"Are we overreacting?" I hear the uncertainty in my own voice but seem unable to mask it. Mal walks in and catches my words. He's the one who answers.

"It's possible," he tells me honestly. "But the one thing you learn in this business is that coincidences are rare. Let us check it out. If anything to rule out any connections."

"Is his last name Cayman?" Damian speaks up, his phone still at his ear. "My colleague found a Lars Cayman teaching at Miyamura High School in Gallup. He's supposed to be at some conference. We're working on confirming his whereabouts now."

"He mentioned that," I affirm. "He said it was a two-day conference in Grand Junction."

"That's the one." Damian turns his back, says something in the phone and after briefly listening, ends the call.

"Agent Greene is putting a call in to the field office in Grand Junction. He's going to ask them to check the hotel." He places my phone on the coffee table and takes a seat in one of the chairs. Mal takes the other one and Neil chooses to sit beside me on the couch instead of on the table. The three men appear to exchange some unspoken communication before Damian continues. "Looks like he's tried calling you three more times and then finally sent a text." The instant he mentions that, I reach out to check my phone, but Neil beats me to it, placing it screen down on his leg and covering it with his hand.

"Hold on," he says calmly as I try to pry his hand off my phone.

"Kendra," Damian gets my attention. "It's not very nice."

A feeling of dread begins to set in as I look past the worried expression on Neil's face and try to snatch my phone from his firm hold once again. This time, he lets me pull the phone from under his hand, while he puts his other arm around me and pulls me against his side. I don't even protest—I'm focused on reading the text.

Four-month investment. You think you can just walk away?

You're nothing but a cockteasing CUNT.

Whoa. Quite the change of tune. Someone doesn't like rejection. I have to admit, it's not so much the name-calling that gives me the chills as it is the implication he's not done with me, even though I'm *so* done with him. I look up and see all eyes on me. "That twatwaffle has a potty-mouth *and* a temper. Think I'll pass on a second date, and change my phone number."

Damian's eyes pop open in surprise and Mal bursts out laughing. Neil just tucks me closer and whispers with his lips skimming the shell of my ear. "Atta girl."

"Good to see you have a sense of humor." Damian is smiling. "It'll come in handy over the next little while, 'cause you're gonna be stuck with some uninvited guests. At least until we can check this guy out. You'll have to wait to change your number until we find him. For now it would help if you leave the number as is, so we can monitor any calls."

My mind is racing over the implications of what he just said. "Wait. So what you're saying is that someone is going to babysit me until … until what exactly? I mean, I get you want to check him out, seeing as three women have died already, but I just can't believe—"

"Four women," Neil says quietly beside me. I swing around to face him, but I already have a good idea what he's telling me from the serious look on his face.

"What?"

"Fourth known victim was found this morning just inside Mesa Verde. Same MO. She was one of the missing women," Neil fills me in gravely. "And, Pup? We just got a call on our way here. Coroner found a piece of paper clutched in her fist. A piece torn from a map. A map with your name written on it."

In a rush, the single coffee sloshing around in my stomach, comes surging up. I slap my hand over my mouth and take off running for the bathroom.

I'm dry heaving over the bowl, having already emptied my stomach when the bathroom door pushes open. I don't need to look up to know that it's Neil. I can see the scuffed noses of his boots from the corner of my eye. I briefly hear water running and then I feel his hand on my head, pulling the hair that is stuck to my face. A cold washcloth is pressed on my neck and it feels wonderful.

"Better?"

"Mmm-hmm." I make sure not to open my mouth. I likely reek. Bad enough tossing my cookies in front of him, I don't need to add insult to injury by blowing puke breath in his face. *Eewww.* Dropping from my knees to my ass, I rest my back against the tub, gingerly eyeing Neil, who is crouched on the other side of the toilet bowl. *Lovely.* "Let me just—" I lean forward to flush, but Neil is faster. He drops down the lid and pushes the lever.

"Got it. Look, I'm sorry. I should have been a bit more careful—" he starts, when there's a loud knock on the bathroom door.

"Neil?" It's Mal on the other side. "I've got Gus on the line, he's bringing over your laptop. Anything else you need?"

Neil looks at me, lifting one finger to ask for a moment. Standing quickly, he pulls open the door a crack, while I bury my embarrassed face in the washcloth. I don't even bother trying to hear what else is being said; my mind has slipped back to where an innocent woman was found murdered in my favorite park, clutching my name in her hand. The thought that Lars, a man I'd talked to, shared stories with, went on a freaking date with, might be responsible has my guts in a twist. A new wave of nausea has me resume my position over the toilet, retching.

"Shit," I hear Neil say. "Gotta go."

The door shuts with a click, and for a moment, I think he stepped out. Until his large hand scoops my hair back, holding it away from my face. *Jeepers*, how much more embarrassing can this get?

"Just go," I mumble when I finally manage to catch a breath.

"Not a chance in hell," he replies, turning the tap back on to rinse the washcloth I'd dropped on the floor. "Get used to it."

CHAPTER EIGHT

Neil

"What's up?"

I'm surrounded by the case files Gus dropped off with my computer, taking up half the dining room table. I'd just left Kendra in the bathroom to take a quick shower when he showed up. After setting up tracking on Kendra's phone, connecting it with my laptop and the FBI computers in Durango in case the guy tried calling again, Damian ended up leaving with Gus, promising to be in touch.

A quick glance at my phone screen before I answered showed Damian's name.

"Just got a call from the field agent who went to check out the conference. Lars Cayman left around noon, citing a family emergency. But get this: he was seen around all weekend, even participated in a few workshops. Theoretically, he could've been responsible for Tracy Poole's murder, but something about this seems off. The timeline is pretty tight, especially if we consider the possibility she was held somewhere for the weeks since she'd been missing. She would've had to have been pretty damn close by for him to be able to have coffee with Kendra, fetch Tracy from wherever she was and drive her into the park. Neil, whoever it is, took his time with her. She was raped and sodomized. The coroner doesn't think it was the first time; there was evidence of prior damage done. The carving on her back was done intricately, artfully. It would've taken hours. Hours he didn't have, because the hotel in Grand Junction confirmed him checking in just prior to midnight."

And just like that, the case we thought we had deflates like a balloon.

"Fuck. Back to square one," I swear, doing my best to keep my voice down so Kendra, who's puttering around in the kitchen, can't hear. But Mal does. He's sitting across from me with a concerned look on his face.

"Perhaps," Damian concedes. "But don't forget the piece of the map they found on her body. Cayman may have been in Grand Junction, but how the hell did a piece of one of the maps Kendra gave him end up clutched in the hands of the victim? Like I said, something is seriously off here. The office in Grand Junction has a few people going over pictures taken at the conference to see if they can pick him out. The DMV photo of him they pulled is a few years old, but I'll email it to you to see if Kendra recognizes him. I also have them pulling her telephone records, see if that helps us any."

"What about the school he works at? Anyone on that?" I ask, sharing the uneasy feeling Damian seems to have.

"First thing tomorrow I'll have someone in Gallup with an eye on Cayman. But in the meantime, if you could do a bit more *creative surfing* into whatever online accounts Tracy Poole had, I'd be much obliged. I'll be in touch later."

"Damian?" Mal asks under his breath as I put down my phone.

"Cayman seems unlikely at this time." I tell him the rest of what Gomez just relayed. About halfway through, I can sense Kendra standing behind me and Mal gives me a raised eyebrow in confirmation, but I keep talking. Nothing gets a woman riled up more than keeping her out of the loop. Besides, news that Cayman may not have been the guy would probably be a relief. I don't even look up when she finally pulls out a chair and sits next to me. I just put my hand on her knee and give it a squeeze. The ping on my laptop indicates an email and I quickly open the file attached.

"Have a look at this. Is this Cayman?" I ask Kendra, turning the screen to face her. She leans in close and squints her eyes.

"I think so. I mean he seems much younger and isn't wearing glasses, but I can see the resemblance."

I turn the screen back and close the lid. "Good. They're using this picture of him to confirm his presence at the conference."

"So does that mean he's not the one?" she asks, the hopeful note in her voice unmistakable. "I mean, I know he sent me that vile text, and is creepy as shit, but if he's been in Grand Junction this whole time…" She lets the sentence trail off, and looks at me to reassure her. Before I have the chance, Mal jumps in.

"It looks that way, but don't celebrate just yet," he tells her solemnly. "We still have a few unexplained things on the table. Like your map? Somehow that ended up from Cayman's hand, who got it from you, into Tracy Poole's. We shouldn't let down our guards until we have a bead on the guy."

She takes a minute to consider that and then nods her head firmly. "Okay, so what are we looking for?" she says, grabbing for one of the file folders.

"Whoa." I stop her, covering her hand with mine. "What are you doing?"

"Well, I can't go anywhere, I've already unpacked, I've just about had my fill of meal prep for the week, and I don't like sitting idle, so tell me how I can help."

With a smirk and a dismissive wave of his hand, Mal dives back into the file he was working, leaving me to deal with Kendra. *Nice.*

The afternoon passes slowly. No calls coming in and I've managed to compile a list for the four victims, and so far two other missing women who all had a profile up on some dating site at some point. Kendra has turned out to be a great help. Something about the way the female mind works when coming up with passwords. Some of the accounts were easy to get into but there'd been the two I was stuck on. After giving those files to her, she started shooting off possible combinations to try. Damned if I wasn't able to gain entry to each of their profiles within half an hour. Now it was a matter of finding commonalities other than the ones we're already aware of that might shed some light.

That's what we are doing—pulling e-mails from their online suitors, looking for similarities in name, or writing— when someone starts banging on the front door. Kendra's out of her chair and halfway to the door by the time I catch up with her. I manage to stop her with my arm around her waist.

"What the fuck do you think you're doing?" I hiss in her ear, as she struggles against my hold. "You don't just go to open the door."

Mal passes us with his weapon drawn but hidden behind his back as he carefully pulls the door open a crack. Only to have it pushed open all the way from the other side, throwing him off-balance. I don't hesitate to pull Kendra behind me. A cloud of floral perfume assaults me as an immaculately decked out, but extremely agitated older woman comes barging in.

"Who are all you people? And where is my daughter?"

I can feel Kendra freeze behind me. "Mom?" With her hands holding on to my waist, she pokes her head under my arm.

"What's going on here, Kenny?"

While her mother and Kendra move in for a hug, Mal quickly tucks the gun back in his ankle holster. When I look back at the women, Kendra's mom has her arm around her shoulders and is looking back and forth between Mal and I. "Kenny? Introductions?" she says with a hint of seduction now in her voice. Kendra rolls her eyes heavenward in response.

"Mom! What are you doing here? Why aren't you on the cruise with Karly?"

"Honey, didn't you get my message? I sent it on Thursday … or maybe it was Friday, I can't recall. Anyway, I came down with a bug. Had to cancel last minute. Karly was only a little disappointed," she chuckles. "When I reminded her I just bettered her odds by me staying home, she happily went off on her own. Luckily the bug didn't last. Now," she says pointedly, checking Mal out before turning to me. "I think introductions are in order?"

"Fine," Kendra grumbles ungraciously. "Mom, this is Malachi Whitetail, he's a friend … and just had the cutest little baby with his *wife* Kim," she adds with emphasis, forcing me to swallow a chuckle. "And this is Neil James, he's … also a friend. They work together with Naomi's husband, Joe. You remember Joe? Guys this is my mother, Elsa."

With Mal clearly declared off-limits, her mom turns a full-wattage smile on me, eliciting a groan from Kendra. "Well hello," Elsa purrs. She's holding out her hand for me to take, which I do, but only for a quick squeeze, trying to ignore the suggestive stroke she gives the back of my hand with her thumb. *Fuck no*. Her hand lingers on my arm, so I quickly throw my arm around Kendra's shoulders and press my lips to her hair. "What a surprise. Isn't it, love?" I return a slightly panicked look in response to the slightly irritated one Kendra gives me. Malachi just chuckles and grabs for the door handle.

"Well, it was nice meeting you Elsa, but as Kendra explained, I have a wife and little baby boy at home I need to get back to. I'll leave you to your family reunion. Give me a call later, Neil."

Traitor. I manage to throw him a deadly glare before he pulls the door shut, but not before he shoots me an amused smirk. He will *so* pay for that.

⸺◆⸺

Kendra

All right. What had already been a pretty crappy Sunday just turned crappier.

Don't get me wrong. I love my Mom, but right now I wish she were anywhere else. It's embarrassing, the way she is ogling Neil.

"Mom!" I hiss at her. "Can you stop?"

With a fake look of innocence, she finally turns to me. "As I mentioned in my text, if I felt better, I would pop in to see how the move was coming along. I assume these guys were helping?"

Right, the text. I vaguely remember one coming in from her but I never went back to read it. "Yes, actually Neil was helping yesterday, today I'm helping him sort through some paperwork." Mom may be sixty-five, but she has sharp eyes, and I can see the wheels turning when she spots the paperwork on the table. I figure I'll give her something, if not a full explanation. If she had any idea of what was going on, she'd demand to move in. Or worse, have me move back home with her. Life is confusing as it is right now, having Mom underfoot would constitute chaos and the added joy of migraines.

"Well then, I guess you're both due for a break. Why don't I take you both out for dinner at that lovely restaurant you've been telling me about? Gives me a chance to check out the town. I've never been here." Somehow my mother wedges herself between myself and Neil, who's been alarmingly quiet. A quick look at his face still shows a trace of panic, but also the beginnings of a smirk as he catches me looking. "Grab your bag," she motions with her free hand waving in the air, the other one already tucked in the crook of Neil's elbow. Her doing, not his. "This handsome fellah can give me a quick tour of the house in the meantime."

I hustle for my purse, knowing my mother won't take no for an answer, from either of us. A quick turn around the kitchen to make sure the back door is locked and the coffee maker is turned off. Best thing to do is just go with the flow. *Her* flow, which seems stuck in overdrive all the time. That's why I'm not surprised to find them coming down the stairs already. Mom has no real interest in the place. Generally, she's happy with the knowledge I have a roof over my head, but by the sound of their voices, she *is* interested what Neil is to me.

"So how long have you known my daughter?"

"A few years," he mumbles uncomfortably as they come down the last step.

"Really?" Mom's eyes flit between Neil and me until I put an end to it.

"Yes, Mom. We've known each other, but only as friends. Now…" I realize I've just blocked myself in and to my chagrin both my mother *and* Neil's eyebrows are raised, waiting for me to finish my thought. Damn Neil is looking way too smug. "Now that seems to have shifted a bit."

"You'll have to forgive her, Elsa," Neil jumps in. "She still can't quite believe we're together now." I could easily slap the look of triumph off his face when he meets my eyes. With a chuckle, he grabs me by the neck, pulls me forward and drops his head for a brief brush of his lips against mine. And just like that, I forgot why I was irritated to begin with.

Dagnabbit.

"Oh my," is Mom's reaction when we walk into Arlene's. It would appear everyone is out for an early dinner tonight.

I'm already scanning the diner for an empty spot when a loud squeal stops me in my tracks.

"Neil!"

A tall dark-haired beauty comes barreling through the restaurant, straight for our little group. Or more specifically, Neil, whose face lights up like a Christmas tree when he spots the girl. I barely manage to step aside when she throws herself in his arms, planting a big kiss right on his lips. My stomach instantly turns sour and any appetite I might have had is instantly gone. I've never seen Neil with a woman, other than my friends. How's that for irony? I just basically told my mother that Neil and I are a *thing*, something I'm sure has given me instant gray hair, and right in front of me is evidence of all the reasons I was steering clear in the first place.

"Jesus, Kara." Neil sets the girl back a little. "When did you get here? You look fantastic."

Okay, someone shoot me now? This is Emma's elusive daughter? I've heard her name enough and even saw pictures at Emma's, but I've never actually met her, and I have to say, she puts her pictures to shame. I feel my Mom sidling up to me, slipping her arm through mine.

"Let's find a seat, Kenny," she whispers in my ear, and I realize I've been staring. I turn away and blink a few times to clear away the stinging in my eyes that accompanies the sick feeling in my stomach. Neil is blissfully ignorant about all of this, his focus on the chattering woman still in his arms.

"Okay," I tell my mom, but my voice comes out hoarse. She leads me to a booth by the table and we pass a booth where Gus is seated, who is watching his stepdaughter with a big smile on his face, and Emma, who is smiling at me. The smile doesn't mask the look of concern in her eyes. "Hi," I say stupidly when she slides out of the booth.

"Hey sweetie, who's this?" Emma gestures at my Mom.

"Oh, right. This is my mother, Elsa Schmitt. She just popped in to see my new digs and wanted to grab a bite before heading home." My not so subtle way of letting Mom know I need to be alone tonight. "Mom," I turn to her, trying to ignore the injured look she gives me. "This is Emma Flemming, and her husband, Gus. You'll have to make sure you try some of the pie tonight. Emma is a phenomenal cook; she bakes all the pies and pastries for the diner."

"Nonsense," Emma says, shaking my mom's hand. "But the food *is* excellent here. It's a pleasure to meet you."

"Likewise," Mom says, also shaking Gus's hand who is now standing as well.

"Kendra," he says simply, pulling me in for a hug. "You hanging in?" he asks softly enough so only I hear him.

"I'm okay," I tell him, with a smile I don't feel. Mom is chattering away with Emma instantly. So weird to see one of my friends connect with my mother. They're not even that far apart age-wise. I think Emma is closer to Mom than I am to Emma. Funny how those years between us never seem to have had an impact on *our* relationship.

Before I realize what's going on, Emma is sliding back in the booth, pulling Mom to sit beside her. Gus motions for me to move in across from Emma before he too sits down. *Trapped.* The sound of laughter has me lift my head, only to see a laughing Kara and smiling Neil walk toward the booth. His arm hanging loosely around her shoulder. I quickly bend my head and feign interest in the menu that stands propped up against the condiment rack. From under my lashes, I see Neil take a seat next to my mother and Kara scoots in across from him, wedging Gus in the middle.

"Well, damn, will ya look at that?" Arlene walks up to the table with a tray of drinks. "Faces I see too much of," she says, purposely looking at Gus and then Neil. "Faces I don't see enough of." This she directs at Kara with a smile before turning to Emma and me. "Friendly faces I see regularly and one unfamiliar one." With those last words she turns to Mom, who appears a little dumbstruck. A miracle.

"Arlene, this is my mom, Elsa. Mom, this is *the* Arlene."

Understanding takes over her expression. "Ohh, Arlene's Diner. Got it. Nice to meet you."

"Kendra?" Emma speaks up. "Since we're doing introductions, I don't believe you've met my daughter Kara yet?"

These moments I can do without. It's been hard enough trying to avoid looking at either Neil or her, but now I'm forced to look at her. Her long brown hair falls in waves around her gorgeous heart-shaped face. Sparkling hazel eyes that look like gemstones, and the widest white smile I've seen since the last Colgate commercial. I hate her on sight.

"Hi," I nevertheless say, leaning across Gus to offer her my hand which she eagerly grabs.

"Oh my God. I'm so excited to finally meet you. I thought it was you when I saw you come in with Neil. I've heard so much about you! And is this your mom?" With an equally big smile, she turns to my mother, who is looking a bit uncertain when she shakes the proffered hand. "I'm Kara," she says, and I'm suddenly finding it difficult to hang on to my dislike for her.

She seems nice. Really freaking nice. My eyes catch Neil's and he's looking a tad confused. *What?* I ask silently with my eyes bulging. All he does is raise one eyebrow, which I ignore as I turn my attention back to the menu.

"Well," Arlene says, breaking an awkward silence, her pen poised on her notepad. "Now that that's been taken care of, are you folks ready to order? Let's start with drinks for the latecomers." When everyone has put in their preferences, she tucks away her notepad and as she walks away, slaps the back of Neil's head.

"Hey!" He turns around, and I see Arlene mouth something to him over her shoulder. Looks like "smarten up."

Dinner is torture. If not for Emma and Mom discussing everything from raising daughters—who are both right there, by the way—to swapping recipes, and Neil and Kara talking about her work in Boston, with Gus dropping a question every so often, this meal would be excruciatingly painful. As it is, my silence is barely noticed. I've just been pushing food around on my plate, trying to ignore the inquiring looks sent both by Mom and Neil.

Arlene walks up and starts clearing the table. "So are you staying a while?" she asks my mother, who shoots a quick glance my way before answering.

"Actually, I'm driving back to Durango after dinner. I just came for a quick visit."

"Oh, you have to get back to Durango tonight? Not sure if that's possible," Arlene says, looking a bit concerned. "Seb just heard over the scanner that the road is flooded just a few miles east of town. McElmo's Creek apparently breached its banks right before the turn off for the Inn."

"What about the west side: County Road J?" Gus asks.

"From what I hear the creek is cresting there too. Right at the junction with G," Arlene says. "Just a matter of time before that side of town is closed off too. Best stick around," she addresses Mom. "It won't be resolved tonight. That's for sure."

Well, son of a monkey. I mentally sort through the boxes with linen I stuffed in the spare bedroom, trying to think of sheets that might fit that twin bed. I can feel a migraine setting in. Right now I just can't get my head around the things that are being thrown at me. Creepy blind date, dead women, Neil's persistent interest that seems to have evaporated the moment Kara came on the scene, and now to top it off, an unexpected overnight guest. Too much. I try to close my eyes against the light that suddenly is overwhelming and nudge Gus beside me.

"You okay, girl?" he asks as he nudges Kara from the booth, following out after her.

"Fine," I manage to grind out between my teeth as I slip past him. Bathroom or fresh air? With my eyes squinted, I make a beeline for the outside door. Don't want to end up hanging over another toilet bowl today, so fresh air will have to do. The air outside is nice. Mild with a bit of a cool breeze.

I stumble around the side of the building, trying to find a quiet spot where I can lean with my forehead against the siding. With a sharp tug, I pull the elastic from my ponytail letting my hair fall free. Even my hair hurts and with my fingers, I try to massage the tension from my scalp. Hands land on my shoulders and gently start working the rock hard muscles there and into my neck. Even if I couldn't tell by his hands, Neil's scent is distinctive enough to recognize him. No way I would mistake the woodsy musk of his soap, mixed with the honest scent of man, from anyone else. Not anymore. Not since my nose has been dipped in that scent up close and personal a few times now.

"You should get back to your friend," I tell him, my voice croaking with the effort. "I'll be fine." Okay, so maybe I'm being a bit bitchy, but how much more fucked can my day get?

"I'm taking you home." Is all he says, and I'm sucked down too deep in my own misery right now to even care about anyone else.

CHAPTER NINE

Neil

"So Gus tells me you might be staying with Kendra?"

I just managed to get Kendra home and in bed. I hope to God those pills she took will take the edge off, because she looked like death warmed over. Was barely coherent when I was pulling off her shoes, and she didn't even react when I unbuttoned and stripped her jeans down her legs before tucking her in. I wasn't going to touch the rest of her clothes. Not like that.

"I am," I tell Arlene. My phone started ringing when I walked out of the bedroom, and I was half expecting someone to call, since I never bothered going back into the diner to let anyone know we were leaving. I would've called myself, but Arlene beat me to it.

"What happened?" Her concern is genuine.

"Migraine I suspect. She was gray by the time I got outside. I got her into the truck and home right away. She has medication, so I'm assuming she has these often."

"That's what Elsa guessed it was. You do know you left her mother stranded here, right?"

Fuck. Hadn't even thought about that. Not even when I pulled around her car in the driveway. Too focused on Kendra. "Shit. Now I do," I tell Arlene, running my hand through my hair. "Would it be possible for someone to drop her off here?"

"Actually," Arlene's voice drops to a whisper. "I was thinking I'd offer her your bed upstairs. Emma doesn't have room, because Kara has the guest house, and she's welcome to stay with us in the spare room, but I thought she might be more comfortable in your apartment, since she doesn't really know us from Adam."

"Christ, what fucked-up timing for a road closure."

"Is something going on? Something that has Gus standing outside the door urgently talking on his phone, and you watching over Kendra like a hawk? Is she in any danger?" Should've known Arlene would be suspicious. The woman has a keen eye and a nose for drama.

"It's under control, Arlene. And if you're worried, talk to Gus. He'd have my balls if I spoke out of turn."

I hear her low chuckle on the other side. "Ha. I'll talk to Emma and let her squeeze her man for info. She'll get it out of him."

I smile. She sure will. Emma may look the cuddly, warm-hearted softy, but when push comes to shove, that woman is someone to reckon with. And she absolutely has a firm grip on Gus's balls. "To answer your earlier question, yes, by all means, give Elsa my bed. Do me a favor, though? Check the linen closet for clean sheets and make sure I haven't left a disaster. I don't think so, but I can't rightly remember anything more than stumbling out of bed this morning with my eyes still closed."

"No problem. And I'll run her over there tomorrow morning before the breakfast rush."

"Thanks Arlene, I owe you one."

"No worries, I've got your back. Just look after my girl," she says before hanging up.

It's only seven thirty, but it feels like a full forty-eight hours have passed since the phone woke me up this morning.

Still, there's no way in hell I'm going to bed now. Not when there's a crazy bastard out there picking off women. With a cold beer from the fridge, I sit down at the table and boot up my computer.

I've just finished spreading out the notes I made on the dining room table, any possible parallels between the files highlighted. All six women from La Plata county except for one, were single, between the ages of twenty-five and forty, working in a medically related field and all, at some point in time in the last year, had had a profile up on one of three dating websites. I don't have access to the files from the possibly related cases from other counties that had been flagged, but I assume Agent Jasper Greene will be able to get a hand on those, if he doesn't already have them. For each of the six women, I made a list of profile names for people they were approached by or had contact with through the dating sites, and I've been looking for the same or a similar name on each of them. I could do a background on every profile they've connected with but that would take me forever. If I could narrow it down to one profile, it would speed things up. Nothing stands out at first glance until I spot a few that seem oddly familiar. I'm about to pop them into Google to see if there's any significance when there's a knock. With half an ear to the upstairs listing for any movement, I quickly open the door.

"Hey," I greet Gus, joining him on the porch. I don't want to chance waking up Kendra, so leave the front door open only a crack. "Something happen?"

"Got a call from Gomez," Gus says as he leans up against the railing, crossing his arms over his chest. "They picked up Cayman half an hour ago in Gallup, pulling into his driveway. He'll be driving out there sometime tomorrow with plans to take on Cayman's questioning himself."

"That's great news. Fucking fantastic news," I tell him. It is great news, but it doesn't explain why Gus came to tell me in person when a phone call would've done the trick. "But why do I get the feeling that's not why you're here?" The slight tick of his jaw tells me my guess is on the money.

"Kendra," he says, squinting at me. "What are you up to with her?"

Instantly my defensive hackles go up. "Not sure if that's any of your business, Boss." The last I say with a bit of an edge, enough for Gus to raise one eyebrow into his hairline.

"I also consider you a friend," he says, calmly deflating my indignant balloon. "Kendra as well. Which is why I'm asking." He slowly uncrosses his arms and reaches back to grab the top of the railing, effectively using his body language to show a little less confrontation. "Maybe the better question would be what are you up to with Kara?"

Now I'm confused. Kara? We're good friends, he knows that. Hell, everyone knows that. But then I think of the odd look I was catching from Kendra across the table and there was that remark she made outside of the diner. I hadn't thought much of it at the time, although she did sound a bit off. In fact, she'd been off most of the evening.

"I don't understand. I haven't seen Kara in over a year. We've been friends for years, Gus. What the hell? Everyone knows that. I know there was a period where some people thought there might have been more, but friends is all we've ever been." Of course I don't tell him that Kara has even less interest in me than I might have in her, but that's not for me to share.

"Sure most of us know that, but not necessarily everyone, bud. Would Kendra have reason to know that? She'd never met Kara before tonight. Look," he urges when I make a move to object, "I'm not blind. I know you've had a thing for Kendra since she first came to town, but I don't know where you're at with her. Or where she's at, for that matter. All I know is that seeing you and Kara together did something to her. Don't know what, but I know she was shaking beside me almost the entire meal."

Son of a mother-fucking-bitch.

I drop my head back against the house and blow out a lungful of air through my tightened lips. Dammit. It never occurred to me how it may have come across. I never even fucking stopped to introduce them. Frankly, I didn't even know they'd never met. To me, Kara is synonymous with Cedar Tree, and so is Kendra. The one difference is that I'm probably the only one in Cedar Tree who knows everything about Kara. Which is part of the reason we're so easy with each other. She's like my sister. But to Kendra … Jesus. I'm an ass.

"I see I made my point," Gus says with a grin. "Better clear that up ASAP, boyo."

Kendra

I feel like I've slept a year.

My head is heavy, but the migraine is gone, thank God. Carefully cracking open an eye against the sunlight streaming in, I take a peek at my alarm clock. Six forty-five. Shit. Already fifteen minutes behind. It only took me ten minutes to get to the hospital for my shift from the apartment. Now, I'd need at least another fifteen minutes. My internal clock apparently hadn't received that message and I'd been too out of it last night to set my alarm.

Last night…shit. The whole day yesterday had been one stressful thing on top of another. I thought at the time, my mother's arrival would be the cherry on the cake but it managed to get worse. No wonder I ended up with the migraine to end all migraines. Did I puke? Can't remember. I do remember Neil following me outside and taking me home, but very little after that. Before my mind has a chance to drag me places I don't want to go, I swing my legs out of bed and rub my hands over my face. Thinking can come later. Time to hustle.

It's not until I see myself in the bathroom mirror that I notice I'm still wearing yesterday's clothes. At least the top half of them. My legs are bare. Neil must've undressed me. A hint of panic is almost instantly quelled when I realize he stopped there, and I blow out a deep breath in relief. With quick movements and with my back to the mirror, as always, I whip off the rest of my clothes. Once under the hot shower, I feel the lingering tension drain from my body. After quickly washing my hair, I squirt some shower gel in my hand and soap up my body, shaving the stubbly bits as I encounter them. My fingers slide over the ugly ridges on my skin. Scars I don't think I'll ever get used to.

My migraines started when I was maybe fourteen. Just about the time I started ballooning out of my training bras. By fifteen, I had a chest that seemed to be everyone's envy. Or focus. I hated it. It wasn't until I was twenty-six that I started thinking those two might be connected—my boob size and the migraines. But it wasn't until about six years ago that I worked up the courage to do something about it. At first it had been worth it as it seemed my migraines were gone.

They weren't, so now I had scars and migraines to contend with. Big ugly scars from complications after the surgery. Scars I couldn't even bear to look at, let alone expect someone else to.

Wiping briskly with a towel, I finish drying myself off, and will the negative thoughts from my head. I still have my back to the mirror, though.

Twenty minutes later, I'm dressed—my hair blown out and up in a ponytail—and am coming down the stairs. It's not until I'm halfway down that I realize I'm smelling coffee. Neil never left.

"Hey," I say in greeting as I walk into the kitchen and see him at the counter, doing something with a bowl of eggs. Relaxed in a T-shirt and jeans, he looks unfairly gorgeous as usual.

He turns around and throws me a smile. "Morning. How's the head?"

"Better," I mumble as I edge up to the counter to see what he's doing. A cutting board with diced peppers and onion is sitting beside the stove, and in a pan he has some chopped up bacon sizzling. "What are you making?"

"Omelet. Thought I'd do a mushroom omelet, but you don't have mushrooms."

I wrinkle my nose at the thought. Mom tried to feed me mushrooms every so often when I was younger but I never could stand them. I'm a bit better now and can stomach them if they are chopped up small enough and hidden in a bunch of other ingredients. A mushroom omelet sounds disgusting, though.

Neil chuckles when he sees my expression. "I'm guessing mushrooms … not a favorite?" I simply shake my head in response.

"What are you still doing here?" I ask as I watch him deftly sauté the vegetables with the bacon.

"Had planned on staying anyway, Pup. Sure wasn't gonna leave with you not feeling well." He pours the eggs right on top of the contents of the pan and shoves it in the oven.

There it is again— Pup. Irritating me and making me feel warm inside at the same time. But before I can voice an objection, he has swung around. Tagging me behind the neck, he pulls me close and takes my mouth in a firm kiss. "Morning," he mumbles against my lips.

"You already said that," I point out, my brains about as scrambled as those eggs.

"I needed to do it right. Especially since I fucked up."

I push back on his chest and take him in. "How's that? What did you do?"

Grabbing my hand, he pulls me into the living room.

"Hey, your eggs."

"Twenty minutes in the oven. We need to talk," he says, pulling me down on the couch with him.

It's never good, when someone tells you they need to talk. Those words lead to disappointment and pain. Which is why I scoot to the other side of the couch and pull my legs up to create some distance.

"I fucked up yesterday and I didn't realize it. Kara and I—"

I immediately hold up my hand to stop him. I don't want to do this right now. I don't want to hear it. I've had a fudged-up weekend and I'm done. "Please, no need. I get it, we're good. You two obviously go way back and you seem perfect together. I wasn't really—"

"Shut up," he growls. Growls. At me.

I'm already on the move, prepared to pick up breakfast on the way and forfeit that delicious looking omelet in the oven, when I'm stopped in my tracks, his hand on my wrist. With one tug, he has me sitting on his lap. "Neil, I—"

"Quiet. You're gonna have to let me explain." His words are clipped.

"Really, it's not necessary." I slide off his lap and laugh. Even to my own ears it sounds fake. "You don't owe me anything."

"Christ, you are exasperating, would you be quiet and let me talk?" The eye-roll to the ceiling was a bit over the top if you ask me. But I press my lips together, figuring that it'll be over much faster if I let him have his say.

"As I was saying, Kara and I met years ago when Gus first met Emma. We've always been friends, good friends, even though we don't see each other that much. Seeing her last night was a surprise. It didn't even occur to me that you two had never met." He slips his arm around me and pulls me right back on his lap again. Ignoring my struggles, he wraps both arms tight around me and stuffs his face in my neck. "Should've introduced you. I screwed up."

I sit motionless, not sure what to say.

"Kendra," his low voice urges. "There is nothing between Kara and I. Nothing but friendship. There never was anything more."

"But why? I don't understand. You seem perfect together." I've finally found my voice and I hate that insecurity sounds through. Since I've known Neil, I've fought tooth and nail against any attraction I may have felt for him. Have been able to convince myself this was not something that was in the cards for me. So why, after all this time, can I suddenly not shut myself down? The small tastes of him I've had over the past days have weakened the resolve I've held on to for so long. Defenses are down and already he has the power to hurt me. Dagnabit.

"You're wrong, babe." He shifts me on his lap so I'm sideways and lifts a hand to turn my head so I'm facing him. "You're using this to try building that wall up again. The one I just managed to start knocking down. Don't bother, I'll just bring a bigger sledgehammer." He strokes his long fingers along my jaw, his index finger rubbing along my bottom lip until my tongue slips out to lick along the tingle he leaves behind. He sounds genuine. He feels genuine too, if the state of his lap is anything to go by. There's no denying the hard ridge pressing against my butt cheek.

Taking a giant leap, I lean forward and softly brush my lips against his. A risk, but one that is quickly forgotten when his arm tightens around my back and one hand slides up my back and tangles in my hair, pulling my head back to expose my throat where his open mouth latches.

"God," his voice rumbles. "You taste amazing."

"It's my body lotion," I offer, a bit out of breath.

"Bullshit. It's you. This … I've wanted this for so fucking long, I'm aching with it."

"Neil," I breathe, finally allowing my hands to explore him. My fingers kneading the muscles of his defined back and shoulders, my other hand cupped on the back of his head to hold him to me. Just as the previous few times his mouth has been on me, my brain becomes one big blank. Nothing registers except the slightly rough texture of his tongue stroking down my neck and teasing my clavicle. Down the sensitive skin that dips between my breasts where he nudges the edge of my T-shirt. I can't stop the needy, senseless whimpers escaping me, pressing my chest out in offering. It's not until his hand leaves my hair and starts tugging my shirt down that sanity returns and I manage to still his hand with mine. Even keeping it trapped against my breast, his fingers don't stop moving. The gentle abrasion of his calloused fingertips over the bared strip of skin, edges closer to my nipple, already tightly puckered.

"Let me have a taste." The deep vibration of his voice against my chest only intensifies the erotic sensation. When he scrapes a single fingernail over my areola, I experience a full body shiver.

Suddenly his mouth is back over mine and I eagerly open up to allow his tongue entry. With his entire hand now covering my breast, kneading gently, my body is buzzing. Buzzing loudly, because I don't hear the door opening until my mother is standing in the doorway, clearing her throat loudly to announce her presence.

"That's my girl," she says with a big, proud smile.

And just like that, my body turns frigid. "Mom…" I scramble off Neil's lap, trying to straighten my top at the same time. "I'm late for work. I'd better go." A quick glance at Neil shows him squinting his eyes at me.

"Can't," Mom informs me. "The road is still closed." Calmly she drops her purse beside the chair and sits down.

Fudge. Totally forgot about that. I immediately walk into the hallway to get my phone from my bag. By the time I've explained to the hospital I won't make in today and why, both Neil and my mother have disappeared into the kitchen. When I poke my head in Neil is taking his omelet from the oven and Mom is pulling plates down from the cupboard.

"Breakfast," she announces casually over her shoulder. She's always had a knack for knowing whenever my sister or I are around. When we were younger, we truly believed she had eyes in the back of her head, like she used to claim. "And then you can explain to me what is going on here."

Neil's head shoots up and he looks at me, eyebrows raised in question. I shrug my shoulders; I'm used to Mom's uncanny extra-sensory abilities.

The omelet is delicious. I'm surprised I'm able to eat any of it, but I end up digging in after tasting the first bite. Another checkmark on the plus side of my Neil list. If my mother hadn't dumped a bucket of water on my weakening resolve where Neil is concerned, this might have tipped the scales in his favor.

Mom leans back in her chair and takes a sip from her coffee. "Are you gonna talk or am I going to need to pull it out of one of you?" she challenges, looking from one to the other.

"I'm working on an investigation that may involve your daughter. Not…" he says with his hands up when Mom starts to protest. "Not that she is directly involved. But she may have unwittingly been in contact with someone who could be related to the case. So until we can make sure it will have no negative effect on her, we're going to make sure she stays safe."

A very eloquent, and extremely evasive explanation that doesn't seem to impress Mom much. Then again, she's fierce when it comes to the protection of her girls.

"And feeling my daughter up is part of your job description?" she asks in a biting tone.

"Mom!" I jump in, not quite able to hide the smile at seeing Neil put on the spot. Yet, he stays surprisingly calm.

"No, it isn't. Your daughter is stubborn. I'm simply taking advantage of the fact she can't avoid me like she has done her best to this past year." He looks my mother straight in the eye, and she meets his gaze squarely.

"And how old are you?"

There we are. My misery is complete. I drop my head on the table, narrowly missing my empty plate and my mother starts chuckling.

"Why? Did you think I didn't notice you have a few years on him?" She directs at me. "It's not as if I don't know how you feel about dating younger men. God knows you lectured me enough about the dangers when you were barely out of your teens."

I groan loudly. "Barely, Mom? I was in college."

"You were judgmental … and rigid. Always were, because you couldn't understand my motivations. But Kenny, you are not me. I hope you never have to face losing the love of your life and struggling to find ways to keep living. And I certainly hope you don't dismiss the promise of a good man by merit of something as insignificant as a few years."

"How do you know he's a good man?" I counter weakly, lifting my head slowly.

"A year, Kenny? He's been waiting for an opportunity for a year?" As if that is answer enough, she gets up, collects the plates and disappears into the kitchen.

Neil leans over, places his hand under my ponytail on my neck and whispers in my ear, "I think I like your mother."

CHAPTER TEN

Neil

"Any news on the road closure?"

I left Kendra and her mom on the back patio. We'd gone out there to enjoy the warm morning sun with a fresh coffee, where I was subjected to more intense questioning from Elsa. Exactly what kind of work do I do? Do I have family? How often do I see them? I had no problem answering her about my job and the company I work for. The family questions were a bit more challenging, since I grew up the single child of Mormon parents. A restrictive household where personal exploration had been virtually impossible when I was younger. One of the reasons I willingly enlisted and still a reason why other than the occasional phone call, I don't see my parents. They don't approve of my chosen life. Kendra was quiet, but intently listening. When Elsa started asking questions about my years in the military, though, I evaded the inquiries. Kendra appeared to pick up on my reluctance and steered the conversation in a different direction, giving me an opportunity to excuse myself. I had a stack of files to sort through and some phone calls to make. I'd fallen asleep on the couch last night. It's been a while since I've slept more soundly. Well rested and with my head clear, I need to get going on that list of names, but first I should touch base with the team.

First person to call is Malachi, who is likely still stuck on the other side of the road closure. He and his wife Kim live in a small house just on the north side of Cortez, with phenomenal views of the mesa. He answers on the first ring.

"Water is slow to go down from what I hear. Drew says it's too soon for the road crews to go in. Looks like part of the road is actually washed away, so this is not going to be a quick clean up. Even if the water goes down over the next twenty-four hours, it will take time to make the necessary repairs." Drew Carmel is Montezuma County's sheriff, and we've worked with him on many cases over the years. Doesn't surprise me Mal got his information from him, since Drew makes sure he keeps his finger on the pulse.

"Looks like we're stuck here. I bet you're glad you managed to get home just in time."

"Sure am. And how are things going over there?" I can hear the smile in his voice. *Bastard*, bailing on me last night. "Nice visit with Kendra's mom?"

"You owe me," I warn him. "Long story short, she ended up in my apartment when we discovered the roads were closed. Arlene dropped her back here early this morning."

"I see." There was a heavy implication in those two words.

"Not that it's any of your business but Kendra wasn't feeling well, so I crashed on the couch," I justify, mildly irritated that I even needed to. "I guess Elsa will be staying here now." I'm determined to get this call back to business, so I shift topics. "I may have found something last night I'm looking into further today. I'm e-mailing you a file with some of my notes. If you could take a look at it, it'd be great if I could bounce some things off you later."

"No problem," he says, but the sound of a baby crying almost drowns him out. I hear some rustling and a brief muted conversation before he comes back on the line. "Sorry about that. Asher is grumpy this morning. He doesn't like his mom taking even five minutes for herself. Demanding already at only five weeks old," he sighs dramatically, making me chuckle. He's full of shit. He dotes on his son, and I have to admit, the little critter is kind of cute. "Look," he says in a more serious tone. "I'll give you a call as soon as I hear anything about the road and we'll hook up, whether over the phone or in person."

"Sounds good. Give that delicious wife of yours a kiss for me." I hear Mal's colorful word choices for me as I hang up the phone, laughing.

Next is Gus and he tells me he hasn't heard anything from Gomez yet. We briefly discuss the case and he tells me to keep digging. He'll be giving Damian a call this morning to see what the status is on Cayman. He should've arrived last night in Gallup, but we don't know whether he's had a chance to interview Cayman yet. In the meantime, I'll send an e-mail to Jasper Greene. Give him a head's up on the odd names. Perhaps he's noticed something similar in the out of state cases he's working on.

A quick peek out the kitchen window shows the two women talking. Perfect time for me to grab a quick shower.

❖

Kendra

"You shouldn't encourage him," I look at my Mom after watching Neil's back disappear inside.

"Didn't raise you to be a fool, honey," Mom immediately fires back.

"I just don't think it's the smart thing to do; getting involved with him. Whatever shine he thinks he sees on me now will wear off before long and then where am I?" I turn to her, grabbing her hand. "Tell me it didn't hurt each time one of your boyfriends left you."

I couldn't be more surprised when Mom throws her head back and laughs heartily. When she turns her eyes on me, they dance with a hint of glee. "Oh, my sweet girl. Wherever did you get that idea? I wasn't *left* by anyone. I was doing all the *leaving*." Seeing the confusion on my face, she goes on to explain. "My choice. Each and every one of them were my choice to get involved with, just as it was my choice to leave them behind. I prefer no complications. When your Dad passed away, I wasn't looking for anything more complicated than a light-hearted fling. I had two girls to raise and had my hands full with complications. I like my life the way it is. I'm free of responsibilities now and simply don't feel like taking any new ones on. Being alone suits me." She brings up her hand to cup my face. "But honey, I *am* sorry if my choices have made you uncomfortable. And it would be an absolute tragedy to let *my* choices dictate *your* life."

I think this may well be the first time Mom and I have had a conversation like this. As adults. We sit silently for a while, each with our own thoughts. Mine revolve mainly around how openly I view the world, but how incredibly narrow my mind becomes when it concerns me. I have no problem with people stepping out of their box, but I feel more secure inside mine. I'm avoiding risk. And isn't that exactly what opening your heart to someone is? A huge risk? Age has nothing to do with that … but fear does.

"I'm thinking of getting a dog."

Mom turns to me, surprised. "A dog? Why would you want a dog? Dogs are work. They tie you down."

It's true—they do. Somehow that knowledge doesn't make the idea any less attractive. I'm not exactly sure what precipitated that train of thought, but an idea popped into my head just seconds ago. This house, this yard, it needs a dog. It'd be nice to have a four-legged companion on my hikes.

I stand up to go inside. "Come on," I tell Mom. "Let's find out where the closest shelter is." She just shakes her head, but she doesn't quite manage to hide the smile tugging at her lips.

"A damn dog," she grumbles under her breath as she pushes out of the chair and follows me inside.

Time to step out of that box.

"Look at this guy! He's so cute." I point at the picture of the large black mutt. "It says he's a retired working dog. What does that even mean?" Mom is not paying much attention anymore. She lost interest when I stopped looking at the pint-sized poodles she was pointing out, more interested in a larger dog. One I could envision along side me for a day-long hike. The little fluffy creatures Mom pulls up don't exactly seem the hardy type.

I look up to see her rifling through the papers Neil left on the dining room table. "Mom! Don't touch his stuff." When we came in Neil wasn't in sight, but I could hear the water in the bathroom running. That is up until a couple of minutes ago when the shower turned off. "Mom, that's confidential," I try one last time without avail. She doesn't seem to hear me, doesn't even look up. Her eyebrows are drawn together as she intently studies his files. I set my laptop down on the coffee table, ready to physically take those papers from her when the sound of steps on the stairs announce Neil.

"Archangels," she says before I have a chance to warn her. "All of them. They're archangels."

"What did you say?" Neil's voice booms from the doorway and his legs eat up the distance to the table, where he takes the note Mom hands him.

"Those names you jotted down—Sariel, Gabriel, Uriel, Remiel—they're all archangels. And that's not all. You missed a few." Mom picks up another piece of paper and points at it. "Look, there are more: Raguel and Mikhael. Six of the seven archangels."

Neil takes the papers from her hands and lays them down on the table. "Son of a bitch," he curses. "I couldn't quite put my finger on it before." Suddenly he turns to Mom and gives her a resounding kiss on the cheek. "Elsa? You are a treasure."

Her face lights up with the compliment.

Neil

Son of a bitch.

Archangels. Don't know why I didn't put that together right away.

I boot up my laptop and pump in the names Elsa spotted. Six of the seven archangels. Messengers of God. Angels of mercy. *Jesus*—the wings. Each of the four confirmed victims had wings carved into their back. I pick up my phone; it's faster than waiting for e-mail.

"Jasper Greene, please," I say when a woman answers the phone at the Durango field office.

"Greene."

"Jasper. It's Neil. Neil James with GFI. Did you get my e-mail?"

"I did and I was just about to send you one back. I have some of those same names appearing. Uriel and Remiel are names on two of the New Mexico cases and then I have Sariel, Gabriel and Remiel again in the Utah files."

"There are more cases out there," I say, the pieces slowly starting to come together. "These are names of archangels. There are seven in total." I give him the seven names. "All of the six women here were approached at some point by someone who used the name of an archangel as their profile handle. Where is the seventh? Maybe he hasn't had a chance to grab her yet. What if he's going down a list? Seven victims in each of the areas he's been active in?"

"Motherfucker," Jasper swears under his breath. "That would potentially make twenty-one victims. But why?"

"Another thing. The carvings on the backs of the victims, were any pictures taken at autopsy?"

"Wings," he says softly, the connections probably snapping together as fast as they had for me. "I'll get the coroner's office to send you copies." He's turned all business now. "I'm also going to start digging through the known dating sites for more of those angel names."

"Any word from Agent Gomez?"

"He's just left for his interview with Cayman. I'll try to get word to him. Let him know to see how Cayman reacts to these names. As soon as I know something I'll let you know."

I'm glad to note the FBI agent's mind is running along similar tracks as my own.

I've barely hung up with Greene when a steaming mug of coffee appears on the table beside me and a cool, soft hand on my neck has me turn my head.

"Thought you could use some," Kendra says with a soft smile on her face looking down at me. I slip my arm around her waist and note that instead of pulling away, she leans her hips into me.

"I'm sorry I'm preoccupied," I tell her. "But your mother may well have provided the break we needed."

"I'm glad," she says. "I didn't want to interrupt earlier, but did you ever check Lars Cayman's profile? He was first known to me as Raphael."

My hand on her hip flexes. The seventh archangel. He had Kendra pegged as his next victim.

Son of a fucking bitch.

With a tug, I pull Kendra down on my lap and I take her worried face in my hands. "He won't get near you. He's being held for questioning and I'll make sure they don't let him go."

"Okay," she replies.

I lean in and softly kiss her lips. "I promise," I mumble against her mouth.

"Okay," she says again. "I'm getting a dog."

It takes me a minute to switch tracks with her. "Sorry? A dog?" She nods her head.

"Yes, as soon as the road is passable, I'm taking Mom to the shelter in Cortez. I want a dog."

With Cayman still safely held at the Gallup police station, there's no reason she can't do whatever she wants. "Okay, baby. You get yourself a dog. But tell me, what brought this on?" I'm pleased when she leans into my body a little farther.

"I was talking about it earlier with Mom. I like the idea of having a companion. Someone to come home to and go for walks with. Plus, this house seems perfect for a dog."

It's on my lips to tell her I'd be happy to walk anywhere with her, or be her companion. That I happen to love this house where I've spent quite a bit of time over the years. But I hold my tongue. I don't even tell her that the timing may not be the best to go out and get a pet.

"I just want something *normal* today," she admits, and I can understand that.

It's a little after one when Mal calls again. Kendra and her mom are on the patio, eating lunch. Elsa made sandwiches and brought me a stack before they headed outside. It's a gorgeous day. Too bad I'm spending it inside.

Mal tells me he looked at the names and started making notes on the Cora Jennings file.

"What have you got?" I ask him.

"I think Alan Cymars, the guy Cora was e-mailing with, is the same guy as this *Sariel* profile. *Sariel*'s messages stopped when Alan Cymars's e-mails started. And the tone is very similar."

"Okay. I think we may need a few more eyes on this. I'm calling Gus."

Gus tells me to meet him in the GFI offices in half an hour. He proposes a conference call set up for those who can't make it into the office, and maybe Damian, if he is able to. He's going to contact the rest of the team and leaves it to me to call Mal and Jasper with a heads up.

I'm just sorting my notes and packing up my computer when Kendra and her mom come inside. I look up to find Kendra leaning against the doorway, watching me, while in the background I can hear Elsa running water in the kitchen.

"Have you heard anything about the roads?" she asks.

"Nothing good," I tell her, seeing disappointment settle on her face. "Mal says the floodwaters did some damage to the asphalt and they have to wait for them to recede before they can fix it. Looks like your mom will be here at least another night."

"Oh," she says softly, worrying her bottom lip with her teeth and making me think of other things I'd like her to be doing with that mouth. When I lift my eyes, I see a little of the heat I'm feeling smoldering in hers. She's already moving toward me when I reach her and bend my head to lick at her mouth. She tastes of fresh air and a hint of sunshine as she opens to let me in. All too soon, I hear a throat clearing. I lift my head to find a smiling Elsa standing behind her daughter.

"Sorry to disturb," she says. "I was just curious about the roads. If they're still closed, I'll have to call my work."

I reluctantly let Kendra go, as she repeats to her mother what I just told her while I finish packing my things.

"Where are you going?" Elsa has spoken, but both women are looking at me expectantly.

"I have to go into the office," I answer Elsa, but my eyes are on Kendra. I don't think I'm imagining the flash of disappointment in her eyes. "We have a lot of stuff to cover. It may be late." I'm not quite sure why I felt the need to add the last, but I hate the idea of disappointing Kendra if I end up not coming back. In fact, while her Mom is still here, I want to use that time to get as much digging done as I can. The sooner this psycho is caught, the sooner I'll be able to focus on Kendra.

Ignoring her mother, I tag her around the neck and touch my forehead to hers. "Promise me you'll call if you go out?" A slight nod seems to be the only answer I get. "Okay, Pup. I'll check in with you later."

With a smile for Elsa, I grab my things and head out. As I'm pulling out of the driveway, I'm already making a mental checklist of things that need looking at. Pulling names to match the profile handles is one, but we'll have to run through the task force for that. They'll likely want us to wait for a warrant to get that information. We'll occasionally straddle the thin line of what is considered *by the book* and don't shy away from time to time obtaining information by less legal means. However, in an official investigation, especially a federal one, any information will have to be obtained and confirmed according to proper procedure. Another thing I want to look at is the carvings in the skin of the victims. The coroner reports it is intricate, and Damian confirms it, but I'd like to see it. Another lead to explore. There's the significance of the archangels, the victim's medical associations, the nature hikes. Where is the connection?

And of course, we need to hear back from Damian, because who knows, we may already have the bastard. So why do I still have this little niggle of doubt?

"So what are you saying?"

Joe, who had been at the office with Gus when I got there, is pacing on the other side of the conference room. "Are you suggesting that this whole business with the archangel names, the carvings on the victim's backs and their connections to medicine somehow all link in? Because frankly, although I see the connections in all of those three areas, I'm not getting how the areas are connected."

I know he's frustrated. *Fuck.* So am I, because what he says is true. There are three areas of connection between all the victims, but it doesn't exactly tell us how it ties in with him. He's also frustrated because Jasper, who's on conference call, reports that Damian was only able to see Cayman for half an hour when his lawyer showed up. Not enough to get anything usable from Cayman, who was now holed up with his legal counsel. We all know that unless Damian can find something to hold him on, they're going to have to let him go at some point.

"One thing Damian mentioned earlier," Jasper's voice comes over the speaker. "He wants us to double check some of the physical descriptions. How did Kendra describe the guy again? Something about pale eyes?"

I rifle through my notes trying to find her description. "Here it is, tall but on the slim side, dark hair and pale gray or blue eyes. Also, he wears glasses."

"Okay, that's what Gomez said, but he mentioned the guy moves with a slight limp. According to him, Cayman fits the description, but there was no mention of a limp in Kendra's description.

"Maybe he just twisted it," Gus suggests.

"No. Guy was in a car crash twelve years ago. Crushed his ankle. He's apparently got a bunch of pins keeping everything in place. Possible she missed it. There could have been dim lighting in the coffee shop, but just for the record, check with her, it may just be something she forgot to mention."

"I'll double check with her," I offer calmly, but inside that niggle starts getting a bit more pronounced.

"You do that, and in the meantime, I just sent those files you requested. I'm out. If there's anything new let me know and I'll keep you up to date on any news from Gallup." With that, we hear the click of Jasper hanging up.

I turn to Joe, who is facing the large whiteboard set up along the far wall of the conference room. On it are listed the names of the four victims, the two women still missing and added to the bottom is Kendra's name, slightly set apart. Beside them are the corresponding archangel names and beside those are names associated with those archangel accounts. Katie has been busy, digging up one more name and one partial one for the aliases. The other three accounts we have yet to sort through.

Tracy Poole †	- *Raguel*	- Marc Salany
Cora Jennings †	- *Sariel*	- Alan Cymars
Lise Carbonneau †	- *Mikhael*	- Carl M.
Alison Kewen †	- *Uriel*	

Shirley Haig	- *Gabriel*	
Jenny Weber	- *Remiel*	
Kendra Schmitt	- *Raphael*	- *Lars Cayman*

A ping from my laptop alerts me to the arrival of Jasper's e-mail with the promised images. I wince when I open the first attachment. The mottled expanse of a woman's back, with what looked to be two slim wings starting on either side of the spine, curving up and across the shoulder blades before dipping down as far as the curve of the woman's buttocks. Zooming in I can see individual feathers carved in the flesh, feathering the outside of either wing. If I didn't know I was looking at the work of a knife, I'd think it was a massive tattoo. As it is, it must have taken hours upon hours to accomplish. On each of the feathers carved out, a thin layer of skin was lifted back from the subcutaneous flesh, curling up at the tips and resulting in the appearance and texture of real feathers. Intricate and macabre. Artistic and grotesque.

"Holy hell," Gus voices behind me. "Forward that to Mal."

"Sending you the files right now, Mal," I announce, knowing that he is still conferenced in. Joe has closed in behind me, looking at the screen over my shoulder at the gruesome images. As I flick through the files, I note that the wings on each of the victims are almost identical in appearance, as if it was done by rote. Someone with artistic ability who clearly has drawn or painted, or maybe even carved these wings over and over again.

"He's an artist," I throw out there and the responding hums and grunts tell me I'm not alone in thinking that. "Mal, are you seeing this?"

"I sure fucking am." There is no mistaking the sound of disgust in his voice. "Had to close the door to make sure Kim doesn't happen to walk in on this sick crap."

"Okay," Gus takes his seat at the head of the table again. "Mal, you're the resident artist: start looking for artists anywhere in the Four Corners region, who have a thing for wings. And use a print out of the best of these pictures to make a sketch. Something you can use to show people. We can't use these damn photos. Google it, talk to galleries, art departments at colleges. Any kind of connection you can think up. This kind of talent can't have gone unnoticed." Then he turns his attention to Joe. "Joe, can you add the artist bit to the board?"

Joe takes up his position by the white board again and adds to the list of traits we have so far ascribed to the unsub. His picture is getting a little clearer, but it seems the more we uncover, the more questions arise.

CHAPTER ELEVEN

Kendra

It's been three days since I last saw Neil.

He's called a few times every day, and I could tell he's been preoccupied, but I still feel out of the loop. Or maybe I just miss him. *Ridiculous.* A handful of kisses and nothing else, and already I managed to get hooked.

When he called this morning to let us know the road had just opened, I was so disappointed. Not that the road is open, because once again my food supply is getting low, and I really need to hit the grocery store. But that he didn't come by. Not like he lives very far.

I'd worked a few shifts at the Cedar Tree clinic, but a lot of my regulars normally drive in from Cortez or even Mancos, and no one was able to get in. I managed to use some of the freed up slots for locals who were waiting for appointments. I was still left with holes in my workday and too much time to think. Luckily, the same was true for Naomi, so we were able to catch up a bit. She already heard about the missing women from Joe and was worried when I told her about my slightly disastrous foray into the world of online dating. Fortunately, the timely arrival of Fox killed that discussion quickly. I love that kid. Even though he can hardly be called a kid anymore.

Mom had kept busy during the days spring-cleaning the yard. Something I had no idea was needed and happily left to her. This morning she'd just finished planting a vegetable garden. Perfect timing, because the moment Neil called to say the road was passable, she started gathering what little stuff she had—she'd been dressing in my clothes—and was ready to get out of town. And I have to admit, as much as I loved spending some good time with her, I'm ready for my life to get back to normal too. Sort of.

"Isn't he a little big?"

Mom is standing at a safe distance, even though the lanky, large black dog I'm crouching next to, is as docile as a baby. I managed to convince her to come with me to the animal shelter before she left.

The young man who showed us to the dog's cage chuckles in the background.

"He really is a very sweet and gentle dog," he tries to assure my mother, but from the look on her face, I can tell she's not convinced. She's stuck on his size, and he *is* big. With short black hair, gangly legs that make him look like a young calf, the slightly elongated muzzle and his soulful brown eyes, he's already captured my heart. How could I not fall in love with this four-legged creature whose first move was to walk straight into me, butting his head into my thighs and staying there? Chaos, the nametag on his cage says.

"How old is he?" I ask the volunteer.

"From what we can gather, he's around six years old. He's up to date on his shots, has been neutered and is otherwise healthy. He spent some time with a foster family when he was turned over to us. We had to make sure he was suitable as a family pet."

The big galoot, his tongue lolling as I scratch him behind his ears, is certainly friendly enough. "I assume he is, or he wouldn't be up for adoption. Now it said in the description that he's a retired working dog? What does that mean?"

"He was a sniffer dog for the DEA, but he failed his last two field tests and was retired. His handler couldn't keep him due to family circumstances and so he ended up here."

Poor rejected baby.

"Okay, so what would I have to do if I wanted to adopt him?" I ask, ignoring Mom, who is looking at me with her eyes bulging.

"Fill out an application, but I would suggest you take it with you. There are some specific questions on there regarding your home, experience and work schedule that might trigger some questions on your part." From there, the man goes into what sounds to be his standard listing of things to consider when adopting. I listen, a little disappointed I can't just bring him home today, and trying not to get too distracted by the big warm body of Chaos pressed against my side.

By the time we walk out of the building, I already know that, unless the shelter finds some kind of fault with me, Chaos will be coming home with me. As soon as possible.

"Shall we grab a quick coffee before I get on the road?" Mom suggests, and I give her directions to the Spruce Tree Espresso House. Once there we settle in at a table for two at the window, and I'm suddenly reminded that just three days ago, I met Lars here for coffee. Scary to think that so much can happen in such a short period of time.

Mom interrupts my thoughts when she starts talking. "You know, I'm thinking maybe I should stay a bit longer. At least until this situation is resolved. I can call the hospice. I'm pretty sure they'll understand if I change my plans again."

"No, Mom. Really. It'll be fine. You've met the GFI guys now. Do you seriously think they'd let anything happen to me? Besides, you can't disappoint your residents again. They love you."

Mom works a few days a week at Mariposa Hospice in Durango. She started working there about five years after my father passed away. The residents of Mariposa are mostly palliative care patients, and they are offered a home-like setting to spend their last months, weeks and sometimes even days with around the clock care. Mom has a love-hate relationship with her work, but still love wins out. It's important work, guiding people gently into an inevitable death. I know I couldn't do it.

"Can I be honest with you?" she says with a smile.

"Of course."

"I was a little bit relieved when I got that stomach bug. As much as I would probably have enjoyed myself on the cruise, I'm glad I stayed home. It feels good to be needed here, and it was an unexpected treat to spend some time with you."

We sip our coffee, with Mom mostly asking questions about the clinic, how am I liking the new place, am I sure a dog is a good idea and last but not least she tries to probe me about my feelings for Neil. Something I try not to think about too much.

"Just don't waste too much time, okay honey?" Mom says as we say goodbye in the parking lot. She promised to call me in a few days to see how things are and made me promise to let her know if anything happens. My mother still gives the best hugs, and for a minute, I close my eyes and let the feeling wash over me. I'll never get too old for that.

Once she gets in the car, I lean in to give her a kiss on the cheek, but she catches my face in her hands. "Dare to be happy, Kenny. There's no payoff without a little risk, and regrets are so much harder to carry to your grave than mistakes are."

"Do you need a hand with anything?"

I turn to the sales clerk at the Pet Pad who walks up beside me.

I'd been about to turn right out of the parking lot of the coffee house to head back to Cedar Tree when I remembered there's a pet store around the corner. On impulse I turned left, figuring I'd put my mother's last words into action. Taking a little risk.

Well, the risk right now is picking the right dog food. Good grief, I never realized how many different kinds there are.

"I'm a little overwhelmed with the choice," I admit with a little smile to the young woman. She instantly smiles back.

"Oh I know, right? I can barely keep it straight. So what do you usually feed your dog?" she asks. A perfectly valid question, but one I have no good answer to.

"I don't know," I mutter, but seeing the confused expression on the girl's face, I quickly elaborate. "You see, I'm about to adopt a dog"—Of course I'm not a hundred percent sure yet, but I'm rolling with it—"so I haven't actually had a chance to feed him anything yet."

The clerk looks in my cart, which holds the largest dog bed I could find, two large metal bowls with this handy little stand, a handy-dandy leash that can clip around my waist for hiking, a bulk bag of chew bones and six different kinds of doggie treats, just in case. I can tell the girl is barely able to suppress a giggle.

"Fine, I admit, I'm totally new at this." I throw up my hands when she finally bursts out laughing. "Tell me what I need."

A smile still on her face, she asks me about the dog, and I tell her what I know, which turns out to be not a whole lot. She briefly pauses to look at me with her eyebrow lifted when I tell her I haven't even filled out the adoption form yet. We manage to whittle down the treats to one bag of natural little chews—great for training, according to my new friend. She also tosses the bulk bag back on the shelf and hands me a giant single rawhide bone with big knots at either end.

"A big dog can choke on those small bones. The big ones are better."

Right. Don't want to choke my dog the first time I give him a bone.

Instead, she adds a rubber thing she calls a Kong, and explains that if you put some all-natural peanut butter in that thing, a dog will be happy all day. I'll just take her word for it.

A mere $236.17 later, I have my SUV loaded with dog stuff I may or may not need. Lissy, the girl at the pet store, almost sold me a dog crate too. The sad part is, if the thing hadn't been big enough to fill the entire living room, I might've bought it. I really want to be a good dog parent.

Since I've got my car turned the wrong way anyway, it probably wouldn't hurt to make a stop at Safeway to stock up a bit. And while I'm there *anyway* I might as well pick up some of that beer Neil likes so much. Just in case he were to come by. Anyway, beer doesn't spoil.

Just needing to stock up on the basics, it doesn't take me long before I'm walking out of the store with a couple of bags in my hand. The sound of brakes screeching has me whip my head around to where a woman with a shopping cart barely manages to jump out of the way of an older station wagon. Dark green and with rust holes the size that would fit a man's fist, the car looks oddly familiar. With the woman yelling at whoever is driving, the car accelerates and speeds by me, allowing me only a brief look at the person behind the wheel.

Impossible.

For a moment there, I could've sworn I saw Lars's pale eyes behind those dark-rimmed glasses looking back at me. It initially startles me but I soon come to the conclusion it can't have been him. Last I heard he's being held for questioning in Gallup. There's no way he could have been the one behind the wheel.

The woman is already moving again, pushing her cart toward her car. She seems to be okay. The bags are getting heavy in my hands, so I make my way over to the RAV. I lift the last bag in the backseat and have my body leaning in the door, when a heavy hand lands on my shoulder and the air rushes from my lungs.

Neil

It's late afternoon by the time I leave the GFI offices. My plan is to drive home, grab a couple of things just in case and go check in on Kendra and her mom.

For the last two nights, I've been holed up either in the GFI boardroom or in the guest house with a crying Kara whose partner of two years just broke up with her over the phone. Not really my cup of tea—heartbreak—but given that I'm the only one who even knows there is a partner in the picture, there was no one else for her to turn to. So long hours of talking—well, Kara talking and me listening—and then finally, later last night, there was a bit of a break through. I only heard Kara's half of the conversation, but from the teary smile on her face, I could tell the news was good. Thank God. I don't think I can *do* this understanding bit much longer. Not when I have a slightly relationship resistant woman of my own to contend with. One who I'd much prefer spending some time with. Good thing Elsa's been around.

When I pull into the street, I can see from a distance that her car isn't in the driveway. Right away I get that uneasy feeling in my gut. As soon as I exit the truck, I lift my hand at the old lady across the street, who once again is peeking over her fence, before leaning back in the cab to grab my gear. I leave the overnight bag I quickly packed in the truck. It's good to have it just in case, but with Elsa still around, the likelihood is slim that anything will happen. I key in the number to unlock the front door and walk straight through to the dining room table, where I dump my stuff. There is no evidence of either woman in the house, so out of curiosity I head up the stairs to the bedrooms. The spare bedroom is exactly as I last saw it, and when I push open the door to the bathroom, I see only one toothbrush in the holder. Looks like Elsa may be on her way home.

Over the last few days, we've been able to narrow down a profile of sorts on the unsub, which is helpful if you know where to look. Cayman was released on Tuesday with nothing to hold him on, but he had volunteered to cooperate fully with the investigation despite the objections of his lawyer. He apparently claimed he had his car broken into and indeed had filed a report with the Grand Junction PD on Saturday afternoon that his door had been forced open. He claims his briefcase, with the maps Kendra gave him, as well as his laptop and stereo were taken from the car. He'd ended up having to rent a car to get home. I haven't had a chance yet to speak with Gomez face to face, but I hope he is smart enough to keep an eye on the guy regardless. In the meantime, I have no intention of leaving Kendra on her own until this guy is caught. I just haven't had a chance to discuss it with her yet.

The sound of the front door opening, a loud crash and then what sounds like muttered swearing, announces Kendra is home. A deep sigh of relief releases tension I wasn't aware I was feeling.

The moment I step down the last step, Kendra's hunched figure startles and backs up, stumbling into the wall with a thud. "Ohmigod, Neil," she gasps with one hand covering her mouth and the other clutching her shirt to her chest. "*Fudge.* You startled me."

"It's okay to say *fuck*, Kendra," I point out, just now noticing the pile of bags littering the floor just inside the door.

Her lips pinched, she glares at me, her hands now propped on her hips. "I can say *fuck* just fine, thank you. I just prefer to find more creative ways to express myself."

Her snarky tone and defiant pose work on my sense of humor and I bark out a laugh. "So noted," I concur, quickly getting myself under control under Kendra's disapproving eye. "Where's your mother?" Kendra appears to be the only one who came in, Elsa notably absent.

"What are you doing here?" she answers with a question of her own, and I can't help but smile. "And for your information," she adds. "Mom's on her way home."

It takes a lot of effort not to throw a fist pump. "What all did you buy?" I swiftly change direction in hopes of distracting her. It works.

Kendra's face lights up with a smile before bending down and picking up her treasures.

"I realized I didn't have anything to provide a good home for Chaos, so I ended up buying a few necessities. Of course, I'm not a hundred percent sure I'll get to bring him home—first I have to fill out this package of paperwork—but I'm hopeful." She continues to chatter as she walks over to the couch and dumps the armload of plastic bags on the couch. I listen with half an ear while picking what looks like a large pillow and a six-pack of my favorite brew off the floor. "Yeah," Kendra says, watching me walk in. "I would wait a bit before cracking one of those," she says, pointing at the six-pack dangling from my hand. Right. The crash I heard earlier. "I almost forgot them too. The check out kid caught me in the parking or I would've come home without. Damn near stroked out when he put his hand on my shoulder."

"Hey! Where is your bandage?" She changes direction as she looks at me with her eyebrows raised. "Your stitches."

"They were bothering me. I took 'em out."

She's beside me in a flash, taking the beer from my hand and examining my palm. "But it hasn't been a week yet."

"I heal fast," I tell her with a shrug. "It's fine." The cut on my hand is healing nicely and the edges have stayed closed. Kendra shakes her head at me but says nothing as she drops my hand and carries the beer to the fridge.

"What's the pillow for?" I follow her into the kitchen.

"That's the bed for Chaos," she says, as if that is supposed to explain everything. I must look as confused as I feel, because she rolls her eyes and explains. "Chaos is my dog. Well, technically he's not my dog yet, but he will be. Weren't you listening at all?"

This. This right here is a prime example of being damned if you do and damned if you don't. There's no winning. No right answer, and no way out. So I do the only thing that comes to mind when I look at her pretty face. Some of her hair has escaped the elastic of her ponytail and is framing her face, softening it. Her gray eyes are sharp on mine and her mouth is slightly pursed. That's where my focus is. With one big step, I brush up against her body, wrap one arm around the small of her back, and with the other hand, I tug her head back. Perfect. My mouth fits tightly over hers as I kiss the fight right out of her.

The instant my tongue touches hers, her body melts against me and I know I not only escaped the firing squad, I won the whole damn battle.

"A dog, huh?" I mumble against her lips.

Her body is tucked underneath mine on the couch where we ended up. My hips are wedged between her thighs and I can feel her heat through the two layers of denim separating us. I try to pull back when I find myself grinding and rutting against her like the *young buck* she believes me to be, but the strong muscles in the legs she has wrapped around me hold me in place. I want to show her control and reverence, not mindless, hard fucking. Hence my attempt at distraction.

"He's *so* sweet," she responds immediately, and I have to bite my lip not to smile. "He snuggled up against me the entire time. He's a bit gangly and looks clumsy, but you should see him run. Just beautiful." In all her excitement about the dog, she doesn't even notice when I sit up and pull her with me. Her eyes are sparkling and she uses her hands to help her talk. On impulse, I tug her toward me and give her a hard, closemouthed kiss. It's fucking amazing to see her eyes glaze over and her focus gone. Powerful fodder for my ego.

"I have those forms to fill out," she suddenly announces before she jumps up and starts digging through her purse. "The sooner I get that done, the sooner I can bring him home."

Okay, so maybe I didn't shake her focus entirely, but for a minute there, I bet she didn't know where she was. *Fuck. I* barely remembered. That is one potent set of lips.

"What do you feel like eating?" I ask as I get up and move into the kitchen. I don't get an answer and when I peek into the dining room, she's sitting at the table flipping through some document, completely lost to me.

Smiling at her single-minded concentration, I pull open the fridge to see what can be done about dinner.

145

CHAPTER TWELVE

Kendra

"Look at me."

I have a hard time lifting my eyes. I don't want to see what I know I will find in his.

It was inevitable, really. I knew from the instant I found him in my house this afternoon, that this moment was coming. Oh, I'd grabbed on to every excuse that seemed reasonable to evade it, but every time he'd touch me, or kiss me, any resolve I had melted. His controlled restraint, when I could feel his body's need to burn, was an added aphrodisiac. He toyed with me and I was putty in his hands. He fed me grilled chicken and pineapple smothered in a spicy peanut sauce, and it was so good, I almost had an orgasm on the spot.

No, I had no doubt we'd end up right here. In my bedroom.

"You're thinking too hard, Pup. I can hear the wheels turning over here. It's simple, all you have to do is trust me enough to look at me." His voice is gravelly, deep with a veiled need.

It's not that I'm unsure of his want for me, his interest in me. It's that once we take this further, there is no going back. No way back to the casual friendship, the occasional flirts, the delicious fantasies that inevitably followed. And no way to erase the look of recoil when I'm bared before him.

"*Look* at me," he urges, and I slowly lift my head.

He's sitting on the edge of my bed, his hands holding my hips as I stand between his legs. All I see in his eyes is faint amusement and heat … so much heat. His hand reaches up and with only his index finger, he strokes my cheek, follows the contour of my lips and skims along my jaw. My body responds to that simple touch with the lightest of shivers. With his eyes boring into mine and a little smile tugging at his mouth, he drags his finger down my neck, over the flushed skin of my upper chest and across the smooth tops of my breasts.

"Lift your arms," he says softly and I don't think, I simply raise my arms and allow him to remove my tank top. His eyes are like an anchor, never losing their connection with mine. He carelessly tosses it aside, his finger instantly back where it left off. My breath hitches when the calloused pad of his finger reaches my nipple, the slight abrasion sending tingles over my sensitized skin. When he leans forward and wraps his lips around the tight bud, I'm the one to break eye contact when my head falls back and my mouth opens at the sensation. Warm, wet heat, pulling all the way down to my core. The low vibration against my skin as he moans around my flesh. I'm mesmerized, seduced and virtually blind to all but the impression he leaves on my body. His hands, fingers wide, spread across my back, pressing me tight to the suction of his mouth. I don't notice one hand sliding around to my front, molding my breast until his mouth suddenly releases my nipple and fingers start tracing the raised, puckered skin underneath.

I stop breathing.

I can sense him leaning back, examining the deep divots left behind by the skin necrosis that resulted from my surgery many years ago. Behind my closed eyes, every last insecurity freshly surges in my head, making it impossible to take a breath. I knew once I gave myself to him, Neil would have the power to break me. No one else has, because no one really mattered. Not until him.

"Breathe," his breath strokes over my skin, just before his lips touch. The small kisses he presses under my breast cause my breath to release in a sob. In an instant, I'm on my back in the bed, Neil hovering over me, his forehead resting on mine and our noses touching. "Listen," he whispers, his eyes staring into my blurred ones. "I've never tasted skin more beautiful than yours. Or softer. Even without ever touching or tasting it before, I knew the effect it would have on me. Just like I knew all of you would be as magnificent as what little you allowed me to see before now. There are no parts to you, there's only all of you."

There is no room to process his words, because the moment he stops talking, his body shows me in the clearest language. Skimming, stroking, brushing, licking, biting: each touch setting me further on fire.

"Neil…please," I plead when I feel his weight leave me. A rustle of fabric and the distinct crinkle of a condom wrapper registers faintly, before the brush of his clothes against my body is replaced with the heat of his skin. On instinct, my legs open to make room for his hips. *Yes.* A few deceptively lazy strokes of his long, deft fingers along my crease before they slip between my folds and into the wetness gathered there. "Fuck me," I manage, as my hips start moving against the fierce rhythm he's building. "Please…I need your cock."

"You'll get my fingers, you'll get my mouth, and when I've heard you scream my name, you'll get my cock. Because Pup, once I slide inside you, I'll be fucking you hard."

The sound of his coarse voice wrapped around those words has me writhing against his hand, reaching for the release building inside. Before I can even protest the loss of his fingers, his lips and agile tongue replace them, sending me soaring again. One arm braced over my hips to hold me in place, his mouth eats at me like a starving man. When I'm teetering on the edge, he slows his pace, keeping the climax just out of my reach.

"Let me come. *Please*, Neil, I need…"

In one swift move, his body is over mine, our lips almost touching. "Taste yourself on me," he growls before claiming my mouth, the tang of my arousal mixed with Neil is heady. I can feel the crown of his cock probing at my opening, slick with my juices.

Neil's head comes up, his eyes focused on mine and his hand slides down to my leg, lifting it in the crook of his elbow. "I can't hold back," he grinds out through clenched teeth.

"Then don't," I whisper, followed by a deep groan as his long, hard length fills me. *So good.*

Our bodies become a blur; a growling, clawing, furious frenzy of passion. I forget where I end and he begins. It doesn't take long for me to reach that precipice again, trembling briefly on the edge before falling into a blinding orgasm with his name on my lips. My body is still convulsing around him when he lifts my other leg, spreads me wide and with deep thrusts, hammers his release inside me on a groan.

"Pure beauty." His lips whisper against my skin as his body collapses on me.

Neil

Long after Kendra's warm, soft and sated body stills with sleep, I simply hold her. My eyes are fixed on the ceiling, determined not to close despite the deep level of relaxation my body has reached. There's a reason I prefer sleeping alone. But tonight, still savoring the feel and the scent of her body, I don't want to leave her side. Instead, I hold her and think about the case.

Gus asked me to pull together what we have so far and join him for a full task force meeting with both the FBI and local law enforcement in Durango tomorrow morning. I'm pretty organized, but could stand to have a quick look over the file.

A little sigh from her lips brushes against my skin. Fuck, how she twists me up. You'd think after at least a year's worth of anticipation, the actual sex might pale in comparison. Not likely. It was as close to perfect as one might ever expect to come. More would've made it perfect; I could've easily spent the entire night losing myself in her, but she drifted to sleep so peacefully, I didn't have the heart to wake her. I still don't. I've worked too hard to prove to her I'm not a wild stud, looking just to sow his oats. I'm not about to wake her so I can have another go at her now.

With that thought, I carefully untangle myself from her limbs. She's like an octopus, twisted around my body. When I lift her arm away from my chest, where she was resting it, she twitches and murmurs in her sleep. I tuck my pillow to her front, and she immediately wraps herself around it, making me smile. One last look over my shoulder at the bed, making sure she's still sleeping, before I leave the room.

I spend some time working on the file, but at some point my eyes get so heavy, I can barely see the computer screen. Shutting everything down, I head upstairs. The twin bed in the spare room is cold and unwelcoming, but still so much better than some of the conditions I've slept under. It's not a wonder that shortly after my head hits the pillow, I finally allow the draw of sleep to take me.

When I wake up to the dim light of morning, on the floor, with my knees curled up to my chest, I'm glad I'm alone. *Son-of-a-bitch.* That was a doozy. Not my worst, I'd woken up to the remnants of a motel room that time, with Gus holding me down to prevent me from doing more damage to the room and to myself. His face was bloodied, and I'd needed stitches after that one. My body had seen its fair share of those. That's why I hardly ever go back to a clinic to get them removed. It would just be a waste of time. It's just as easy to do it myself.

Still lying on my side, I quickly check my hands and face for any bleeding. I'm clean. Relieved I roll on my back, and my eyes wander to the door, where a sleep-tousled Kendra is quietly leaning against the doorframe. Her arms are crossed under her breasts, which are regrettably covered with the shirt I was wearing yesterday. She must've put it on just now. Her head is slightly tilted to the side, but her soft gray eyes are warm on me.

"Hey," I croak out, my throat dry from sleep.

"Comfy?"

"Hmmm. Not really." I push myself up off the floor at the same time as Kendra walks in the room. When I sit down on the side of the bed and rub the sleep from my face, she sits down beside me.

"How often do you get them?" she asks, putting a cool hand in the middle of my sweaty back. I lift my head from my hands and turn my head to the side so I can see her. There's only warm concern in her eyes. No judgement, no pity. No fear.

My normal reaction would be to deny, to evade. Other than Gus, no one knows about my crazy nightmares. Or should I say, the nightmares that *make* me crazy. But this is Kendra, and she's just seen the aftermath of one. Not as bad as it can get, but still. Before I can make the conscious decision, my mouth is already answering her. Honestly.

"As many as three times a week, but usually maybe once a month. It depends." My voice sounds hoarse. "It can get bad." At that, those expressive eyebrows of hers lift back up.

"You mean to say this wasn't bad? You were yelling so hard, I thought I heard the windows rattle in their frames."

"I was? Christ, I'm sorry." That explains my rough throat. My eyes do another scan of the room to make sure other than the bedding, nothing is out of place.

"That the reason you snuck out of bed in the middle of the night?" she asks calmly, and I just nod my response. "You're afraid you'll hurt me." It's not so much a question as it is a conclusion. One she has come to by herself without having me explain. Or at least try. "Do you know what triggers them? Is it anything I did?" The hint of uncertainty in her voice kills me. This has nothing to do with her.

I twist my torso, grab her by the waist and pull her on my lap. "Not at all." Her eyes slide away to the side, but I take hold of her chin and lift her face back to mine. "You did nothing," I tell her more firmly. "Sometimes…stress or excitement or any other kind of strong emotion can be a trigger." This time it's me turning away, but Kendra's hand on my cheek draws my eyes back.

"Okay," she simply says, kissing my lips softly as she gets up and walks to the door.

"Wait. That's it?" I'm confused. Or maybe shocked is a better word. I thought she'd have a million and one questions, would want to push the issue, but instead she just says *okay*.

"Look," she says turning back, one hand leaning on the doorpost. "I'm a smart girl. You're ex-military, you've been stationed overseas. You've seen and done things. Post Traumatic Stress Disorder is no longer a dirty word, Neil. Not something to hang your head in shame over. Certainly not with me. And you don't need me to prod and pry, I'm sure you've had enough of that. So yeah, that's it—okay. Sure, I hope to be able to wake up, still in your arms, at some point. Especially after what you gave me last night. The way you reminded me it's about the whole and not the parts, the way you didn't pry and just simply accepted my scars. When you're ready, I'd like to show you I feel the same."

I'm struck silent. I don't quite know how to respond to that.

"Go have a shower. I'm gonna put some breakfast on." With a wink she's gone.

A bit numb, I sit for a few minutes trying to process her words, until I hear sounds of pots and pans from the kitchen. Then I get up and head for the shower, feeling lighter than I did yesterday.

◆

Kendra

It wasn't hard to figure out.

When he left the bed in the middle of the night, I thought about going after him, but I fell back asleep before I had my mind made up. The cries from the spare bedroom this morning had me shooting up straight in my bed. It sounded like an animal in pain. I wasn't sure what I was going to find when I pushed the door open but the sight of that big, healthy man curled up in a ball on the floor was enough to stop me in my tracks. I wasn't sure how happy he would be if I saw him in this state. I almost backed out of the room when I noticed him waking, but something kept me rooted in the spot. Those normally penetrating eyes looked dull with pain when they found me, and it almost felt like I was invading.

If he hadn't said anything, I would've left at that moment, but he did. And opened the door for a few simple questions that quickly confirmed my suspicions. The fact he opened up even a little felt like a major vow of trust. And just like he rewarded my trust in him last night, I want to honor his trust in me. That's why I didn't push for more. If he wants to tell me, he can.

The gurgling of the coffee machine announces my first hit of caffeine is near. I need it. A lot has happened since last night, and I've barely had a chance to process.

I toss some bacon in a pan before pouring coffee in my favorite mug. I'm thinking cheesy scrambled eggs or banana-stuffed French toast. It takes me two sips of coffee to decide I'm craving sweet. French toast it is. I grab two bananas from the wire basket on the counter and the Italian loaf I picked up yesterday. I cut the bread in extra thick slices and with a paring knife, make a slit in the crust on the bottom, creating a little pocket for the sliced banana. Two eggs go in a bowl with a little almond milk and a bit of cinnamon. And then a quick stir with a fork to loosen the yolks. A piece of butter goes in the big second pan to melt and the bacon is flipped. When the butter is hot enough, I dip the four stuffed slices one by one in the egg mixture and arrange them in the pan.

I'm leaning against the counter, sipping my coffee and inhaling the mouth-watering scents of bacon and cinnamon when Neil walks in, shirtless. I freeze with my mug halfway to my mouth at the sight of his chest. *Holy schnikes*!

I'd been so overwhelmed with sensation last night, I never took the time to check out his body. Not that I hadn't done that already, but he was always dressed. Mostly it consisted of sneaking peeks and inconspicuously wiping the drool off my chin. Neil with clothes on is a sight to behold. Neil shirtless is awe-inspiring. I don't even want to think what Neil naked would be. Heart-stopping?

A deep chuckle draws my eyes to his face, which is sporting a cocky grin. "Babe," he points out. "Your mouth is open."

With a snap I close it, biting my tongue in the process, which in turn causes me to slosh hot coffee over my hand. *"Fuck!"*

"Shit!" Neil is immediately there, taking the mug from my hand and dragging me to the sink. With his body behind me, he turns on the tap an holds my hand under the cold water.

"You said *fuck,"* his low voice sounds right by my ear.

"Well, it hurts!" I bite off. Then add with a heavy dose of sarcasm, "Forgive me if that offends you."

"Not offended in the least. In fact, it's kinda hot."

With his head leaning over my shoulder and his front butted up against my back, it's hard to ignore his physical response, which is pretty prominent.

"I have to flip my French toast," I announce in a feeble attempt to break the heated atmosphere that hangs thick in the kitchen. With another of his chuckles, he lets me go.

"And you might wanna put on a shirt," I suggest as I quickly dry my hand, which is numb from the cold water, and tend to breakfast with my back to him.

"You're wearing it," he points out before I hear his footsteps retreat. Moments later, the front door closes and I finally turn around, wondering if he's taken off. But just as I'm sliding breakfast on a couple of plates, the door opens back up and Neil comes back in, wearing a shirt and carrying a bag.

"Better?" he asks with a smirk.

"Much," I fire back, putting breakfast on the dining table while he's going through cupboards in the kitchen. I'm just pouring the real Canadian maple syrup I found at Safeway on my toast when he walks in carrying two mugs of steaming coffee. The kitchen clock catches my eye, and I see it's only six thirty. Early yet.

"Dayum," Neil mumbles with his mouthful. "This is great."

I look over to his plate and it's already half empty. In the time it takes me to eat one of mine, he's done. I'm already pretty full so I slide my second one on his plate. "I'm full," I explain when he looks like he might object.

I watch him eat while I sip my coffee. Nice. Weird. Oddly comfortable. Neil looks like he's totally at ease. No remnants of his rough night visible. My mind drifts to what happened before that and I feel my body's thermostat rise instantly. The memory of that same mouth currently folding itself around the forkful of dripping French toast being between my legs last night. The way he licks the sweet maple syrup off his lips too much like the way he looked hanging over me, mouth shining with my arousal, demanding I taste myself on him… My gaze trails up his face to find his eyes staring at me from under his eyebrows, burning with hot hunger. *Oh my.*

"I'm ehh… I'll just take these…" I mutter, quickly collecting the dirty dishes and taking them to the kitchen. There, I stack them in the sink and start running the warm water to wash them. Anything to get my hormones under control.

"What were you thinking just now?"

I don't need to turn around to know that Neil is right behind me. When I look up, I can see his reflection behind me in the kitchen window. I don't answer. He obviously has a good idea what was on my mind because he takes a step closer, puts his hands on my hips and slowly slides the shirt up before wrapping his arms around my front. In the window, I can see one hand sliding up underneath my top, cupping my breast, while the other sneaks under the elastic of my panties.

A deep hum rumbles in his chest when his fingers find me slick. With one hand caressing my breast and the long fingers of the other stroking lightly through my folds, my knees turn to rubber. Keeping my eyes on the image we make in the window, I drop my head back and give myself over.

"That's it, Pup." Neil's voice is rough with need, when another, much louder, voice rings out from the front hall.

"Mornin', got any coffee left?"

CHAPTER THIRTEEN

Neil

Son of a bitch.

I manage to square my body to block Kendra from view the moment I hear Gus's voice. Two minutes later and I would've had her bent over the sink, her panties around her ankles and my tongue or my cock buried in her pussy.

The bark of laughter behind me, as Gus walks into the kitchen sets my teeth on edge, and I fight to hang on to my temper when I slowly turn my head. "A minute," I bite off between clenched teeth at the man who is standing in the doorway, grinning ear to ear. Gus doesn't seem affected at all by the angry scowl I throw his way. He just throws up his hands in a defensive gesture and backs out.

"Ohmigod, ohmigod…" Kendra's whispered mantra reaches my ears as I slowly withdraw my fingers from where they'd been playing with her.

"It's okay," I mumble in her hair, pulling her shirt back down to cover her. "He's gone."

No sooner have I said that and she whips around, punching me in the arm.

"What was that for?"

"You," she spits out. "Making me forget myself. In the bloody kitchen, of all places." I'm hanging on to my straight face, because even a hint of the smug smile I feel tugging at my mouth, and the spitting mad—and supremely adorable—woman in front of me would not hesitate to castrate me. Instead, I wrap my arms around her and bury my face in her neck.

"You make me forget myself wherever I am, Pup. And you don't even have to try."

Apparently that was the right thing to say, because with a little sigh, she slips her arms around my waist. "I should get dressed," she mumbles.

"You do that. I'll get some fresh coffee going and find out why Gus is here." I give her a quick kiss on the lips and a pat on her luscious ass. That earns me an irritated glare over her shoulder as she scurries out of the kitchen and straight up the stairs. I use the time it takes to prepare a fresh pot of coffee, to bring my body back down from its primed condition.

"See you've discovered the draw of the kitchen," Gus says as I walk in with a mug for him and a fresh coffee for myself.

"Shut it."

He doesn't. He just starts chuckling again. "Only fair, seeing as I think you've caught every last one of us in a similar position at some point during the past couple of years."

"Whatever," I mutter, but I do it smiling. He's right. I've been in the unlucky position of walking in on too many of my friends going at it on the kitchen counter or against the fridge. Never could figure out what the deal was with the kitchen. Now I can. Shit, I'll never live this down. "How'd you know I was here anyway? I thought I was supposed to meet you at the diner?" I change tracks.

"Emma is a bit under the weather, so I left her in bed and grabbed a quick breakfast at Arlene's. Saw your truck was gone and took a guess. Thought I'd save you backtracking to the diner." With a gulp he throws back his coffee and walks with his mug to the kitchen. "By the way," he calls out, "we're leaving in five, so if you need to say goodbye, I suggest you get to it. Just don't finish what I walked in on just now—it'll have to wait."

I rub my face, hearing him clearly. I'd better get to it like he says, because for all I know, Kendra heard him too and will only add it to her lists of reasons not to get involved with me. Too late, she's already there.

I find her in the bathroom, pulling her hair back into a ponytail. Dressed and ready for work in a pair of scrubs, I already miss seeing my shirt on her. Her eyes watch me in the mirror as I step in behind her, sliding my hands to her stomach where she stops any progress by putting hers over mine.

"That can't happen again," she says with determination, but I can feel the give in her body as I lean my chin on her shoulder.

"Can't guarantee that, Pup. You're irresistible. Get used to having my hands on you at every damn opportunity."

"Neil, please…"

I band my arms around her when she pleads. "Babe," I groan. "Don't say please after you say my name—not unless it's followed by fuck me. Because that's all I can think about when I hear those words."

In an unexpected—but welcome—move, Kendra turns her head to the side while wrapping her hand around my neck, pulling me in for a kiss. Another bit of resistance melting away. I pull away much sooner than I'd like to, but I don't need a repeat of what happened in the kitchen. If Gus says five minutes, then Gus means five minutes, and four of them are gone.

"Baby, be careful today. You've got my number and Joe's gonna stick around town, so if anything is the matter, you call Joe first and then me. Okay?" I wait for her to nod her understanding before I go on. "I'm not sure how long we'll be, but I'll call you when I'm heading back."

"I'm working in Cortez today," she reminds me. "I'll probably have my phone on silent in the hospital."

Right. "Okay, then I'll text you. Just check regularly."

Gus is waiting with his foot on the bottom step. "Cut that close, my friend," he says with a smirk.

"Quit busting my balls."

We've just picked up some more coffee at the Silver Bean and are leaving Cortez behind us when Gus suddenly pipes up.

"Do you know what's going on with Kara? She was moping around the house earlier this week and now all of a sudden she's all bubbly again. She's got Emma literally worried sick. She pregnant or something?"

I almost choke on my coffee. God—they think she's pregnant? I feel guilty keeping something I've known about for a few years from them, but it's not my secret to tell.

"I don't think she's pregnant, Gus. She would've told me," I offer, hoping it will satisfy him.

"Well, then what the hell has her going all hormonal on us?" he asks, frustration clear in his voice before he turns to me. "She keeps saying everything is fine, but it's clear she's not fine, Neil. She shows up out of the blue for an indefinite vacation, leaving her job and life in Boston behind. It's clear something is eating at her. Is she sick? I know you and her are just friends, but I also know you've spent some time with her this past week. Anything you can give us?"

Fuck.

"Look," I scramble to find the right thing to say. "I can tell you safely that she's healthy as a horse. As far as I know she's not hiding any detrimental illnesses from you."

"But she's hiding something?" he asks, his eyes boring into me.

"Dammit, Gus. You're asking me to betray a trust I don't want to betray," I swear, pissed to be stuck in the middle. "You're an investigator. You were trained to ask the right questions. Ask her the right things. Don't ask if she's all right, or feeling okay or any other vague questions that are easy to evade. Look, listen and when you do ask her, make sure there's no way for her to answer with a simple yes, no or fine. Be specific. Fuck."

The rest of the drive to Durango is as quiet as it started. Except now I could almost hear the gears turning inside Gus's head. Good. Time for this shit to come out into the open. Kara is stubborn—but then so is Gus.

And that reminds me, I forgot to mention to Kendra I'd spent some time with Kara. First chance I get, I'm going to take care of that.

⚔

Kendra

I smile at myself when I walk from the far end of the parking lot where I parked to the hospital's entrance. I can feel every step. He warned me he was going to fuck me hard and he did. The rub of my tender flesh and the slight ache in my joints and muscles not only a reminder that it's been a while, but also that I'm not getting any younger. Something I'm finally starting to believe makes absolutely no difference to Neil. I don't think I've ever had my body worshipped like that before. And then this morning… I feel a blush burn up my cheeks as I think of Gus walking in.

"I missed you on Monday."

I turn to the familiar voice of Mrs. Henderson who is dropped off by her husband twice a week for hip-replacement rehabilitation.

"I'm sorry Mrs. Henderson, I just moved to Cedar Tree and the roads were washed out," I tell her as I hook my arm in hers and walk her into the hospital, waving at her husband driving away.

"I heard about that, County Road G, right?"

"Yes, ma'am. I was lucky I'd just done a big grocery run to fill up my new cupboards."

"I'll say. Is that country diner still there on Main Street? Been years since Buck took me there for a meal."

Every time Mrs. Henderson calls her husband Buck, I have to fight not to burst out laughing. Mr. Henderson is no more than five foot six, if he even makes that, and so thin, a stiff wind would blow him off. To hear her talk about him, you'd think she was married to a big strapping lumberjack type, but I guess it really is all in the eye of the beholder, and Mrs. Henderson adores her husband. I'm sure to her he is all that and more. And just like that, my mind slips back to Neil.

"All done for today," I tell the seventeen-year-old kid. Star receiver for the high school football team, Tom blew out his knee at the end of last season. The orthopedic surgeon had questioned if he'd play football again, but Tom was adamant he'd be ready to play the next season—his last year. Over the past few months, he's shown more grit at his young age, than many grown-ups that come in here. He kind of reminds me of Neil. Young, smart, focused and very determined. Several colleges were interested in him before the end of last year, and he'd been assured of some interesting scholarship offers before his injury. Coming from a low-income family with four kids,

Tom is well aware those scholarships were perhaps his only chance at getting an education. That's why the kid has been working his ass off in here every chance he gets, and why I almost have to force him to stop his exercises.

"I'll see you on Monday," he calls out over his shoulder as he walks out.

"Three o'clock," I remind him. "Later, Tom!"

Last patient of the day, and all that's left is cleaning up the exercise equipment and writing up my notes. I'll miss this place once the Cedar Tree clinic gets too busy for just the three and a half days I'm there. I'd have to give up my shift-and-a-half here. It would be nice in the winter, not to have to go that far to get to work. I had to go the opposite way this past winter, from Cortez to Cedar Tree instead of the other way around, and there were days I'd wished I could just stay in. The roads were that traitorous.

With everything wiped down and clean for the weekend shifts and all my notes up to date, I head out into the warm late afternoon sun. I see Tom still hanging around his old pick-up truck, chatting with a friend, when I walk across the parking lot. I lift my hand in greeting as I think about what to make for dinner with the ground beef I pulled from the freezer this morning. A slight movement in the low brush at the edge of the pavement draws my attention. But when a sudden burst of wind, blowing the hair around my face, also makes the brush rustle, my thoughts turn back to dinner.

I unlock my RAV and climb in behind the wheel when I remember I'd promised Neil to check messages. I didn't look once all day. Fudgesticks. A quick glance at my phone shows two voicemails and a bunch of texts. Mom, Naomi and Neil all texted at some point during the day, but both messages came from Neil's number. I decide to listen to those first. When I hear his voice asking something about Lars limping, I catch the little stumble as he signs off. Not quite sure what that was, but I know it leaves my heart beating just a little faster. The second message from him is a bit more urgent, asking me to call him back right away. When I look at the time stamp, I see that it came in while I was saying goodbye to Tom.

I'm just about to call him back when suddenly the driver's side door is yanked open. I let out a startled cry, which is almost immediately cut off when a bag is pulled over my head and a large hand clamps over my mouth. Before I have a chance to react, I'm hoisted from my car with an arm around my waist.

"Quiet," his voice hisses in my ear. "One fucking peep out of you and I'll break your neck. Wouldn't be the first time."

With my faculties returning, I let my body go heavy, so my feet can touch the ground. I can't do anything to defend myself if he holds me suspended and he's moving away from my vehicle. But it's too late. I hear the distinct slide of a door and am hoisted up once again and tossed in the back of a van. I scramble away as fast as I can, but the moment the door is slammed shut behind me, I instantly yank the bag off my head. Complete darkness. No windows, no light, except for a tiny crack of what probably is the back door. On hands and knees, I crawl around the space trying to find a door latch, as I hear the engine start up and feel the van start moving. My movements become more frantic, because the farther away he gets, the harder it will be to find my way back. Or for someone to find me.

A crackling noise like static sounds from the ceiling, followed by a click, and then I hear his tinny voice coming over some kind of intercom, freezing me on the spot.

"You owe me, bitch! Told you I wasn't gonna let my investment go to waste."

Another click and then silence, except for the steady drone of the engine carrying me farther away. My heart hammers in my throat and I frantically try to swallow the fear that threatens to paralyze me.

Time. I have no time. Panic almost overwhelms me when I belatedly realize my phone has to be in here somewhere. I still had it in my hand when he tossed me in the van. With renewed effort, but this time with a specific goal, I crawl on my knees while running my hands over the floor in front of me. At the same time, I'm trying to keep track of the stops and the turns he makes. I hear a squeal of tires sound from right behind us before the van turns sharply to the right, tossing me against the far wall. The van is veering from side to side and with nothing to hold on to, I'm tossed around. Trying to find something to grab, my fingers touch a familiar surface and my hand closes over my phone, right before I'm thrown across the cargo-hold with a sharp left this time. More tires squealing and suddenly I'm hurled back as something hits the side of the van. I realize the screams I'm hearing are my own when the van tilts sharply. An instant later, I find myself airborne when it tips over. I'm bounced around, not knowing which way is up or down. The last thing I hear is the screeching sound of metal tearing.

CHAPTER FOURTEEN

Neil

"Hey Neil," Jasper, or Jas as he was called by his colleagues, calls on me. "Did you ever get a chance to check with Ms. Schmitt to see if she recalls Cayman limping?"

Shit. That totally slipped my mind, but before I can make my excuses, Gus jumps in. "Probably not. Neil seems to have had his hands full," he says, the corner of his mouth twitching.

"Fuck off," I tell him before turning to the FBI agent. "I'll get that done today."

The meeting at the FBI Rock Point offices is taking up most of the day. We don't break for lunch, which is a tray of sandwiches ordered in and the coffee keeps coming. Thank Christ the coffee is not the crap grade you'd normally expect in a place like this. It's actually really fucking good, so I've been sucking down cup after cup.

"In fact, I'll get it done right now," I say to Jasper as I get up. Stepping into the hallway, I first find the restroom. Damn coffee. Then I step outside for some fresh air and dial Kendra's number.

"Hi, it's Kendra. I'm sorry I can't take your call right now, but leave a message and I'll get back to you as soon as I can."

Crap. Forgot she turns her sound off in the hospital. A quick glance at the time shows it's close to three o'clock. She'll be done with her shift in another hour. Instead of trying for a text, I leave her a message.

"Babe, it's me. I'm still in the meeting, but there's something I wanna run by you. Do you remember Cayman limping at all? Let me know when you get this. Lo…later," I finish lamely. I fucking hate talking to recordings. Inevitably, two seconds after you leave a message, you realize you should've worded one thing or another differently, or in this case, shut up altogether. I almost blurted out something on a goddamn message that has no business coming out of my mouth. Yet. And definitely not in a message.

When I get back to the large conference room, Montezuma County Sheriff, Drew Carmel has joined the party. It's a virtual who's who of law enforcement in here with the FBI agents, Durango PD Operations Commander, Keith Blackfoot, lead investigator Boris Parnak from the La Plata County Criminal Investigations Unit, Gus and myself, and now Drew. Getting pretty crowded.

I'm quickly sucked back into the minutia of the case, with everyone contributing bits and pieces of information that Luna Roosberg, the newly assigned field agent, carefully records on the massive white board. The case outline on this board is massive compared to what we have in our offices.

"Has Mal had any luck with the wings?" Damian directs at Gus.

"He's hitting an art gallery in Farmington called In Cahoots. Found the name on a Facebook page he was checking out. They showed a picture of the interior of the gallery and he thinks he spotted something that looked similar. He's taking his drawing with him."

"When's he going? I'd like to send Agent Roosberg with him."

"Probably there already," Gus answers. "Let me give him a call."

While Gus gets in touch with Mal, I check my phone for any word from Kendra. Nothing. I slip out of the room and call her number. Again, no answer, so I leave another message, this one a bit more urgent. When I get back, Gus is furiously writing notes and everyone else is watching him closely.

"Got something," he says when he ends the call, checking his notes. "The gallery has a series of prints with what looks to be the same style of wings as left behind on the victims' backs. Similar detail on the feathers. It's from a collection called *Angels of Mercy* and the artist's name is Casal Maryn."

I immediately put the name in my search engine and across the room, I hear Jasper typing furiously on his laptop. "You got ViCap?" I call across the table.

"Yup."

"Hang on, guys," Gus jumps in. "Focus on Cortez and surrounding areas. Looks like he's got a postal box in town!"

Luna is frantically scribbling on the whiteboard. Damian is barking in his phone and the rest are either on their phones or jotting down notes.

"Okay." Damian slaps his hand on the table to get everyone's attention. "Gus, you've got that post box number?" On the responding nod, the agent turns to Jasper. "Vicap search up and running?" A thumbs up there. "What's everyone else doing?" he wants to know, turning to each of us.

When he gets to me, I quickly look at the screen to see if anything has popped up yet and I'm surprised when it has. "I've got all the information we have so far loaded into a program that looks for parallels, similarities, patterns—anything that might signify a connection. I just popped in Casal Maryn and it's throwing out that it has the same letters as the two full names we found connected to the victims' e-mail accounts as well as Lars

Cayman's. The bastard used anagrams as aliases." My eyes whip to Damian. "Where is Cayman now?"He grabs his phone and starts punching in numbers.

"It's Gomez. Tell me you've got eyes on Cayman." I watch the color drain from the other man's face as he wipes a stack of papers off the table. "Son of a—"

The ringing of my phone drowns out the rest of Damian's swearing. A quick glance shows Kendra's number and without hesitation I take the call.

"Kendra?"

"Uhhh, no this is Tom Bridges. I already called the ambulance, but there was an accident."

"Where? Where is she?" I stand up, kicking my chair over in the process, bolting in the direction of the door.

"County Road D."

I must've heard him wrong. She would've been on her way home on County Road G. "Country Road G?" I ask to clarify.

"No D as in Delta. He grabbed her from the hospital parking lot. She's…she's my PT," he says, his voice shaking. "I was talking to a buddy in the parking lot and I saw this guy pull up beside her in a van. She never even saw him coming. He—"

"Hang on," I tell him, turning around and bumping into Gus who is right behind me. "Kendra was grabbed from the hospital parking lot. There was an accident on County Road D. She's hurt. I've gotta go." I don't get a chance to go two steps when I feel Gus's hand on my shoulder.

"Hold up. I'm driving." Punching numbers on his own phone, he follows right behind me out the door.

"Tom?" I prompt the kid as I rush toward the car. "Who was it?"

"I don't know him. As I was saying, I saw him pull a bag over her head and pull her from her SUV and toss her into the back of a cargo van. I started running, but my knee…I wasn't fast enough. He took off. I got back to my truck and followed them. When he turned off the highway, I panicked. I'm sorry, I didn't know what else to do. I'm sure he spotted me because he started weaving all over the road. When he turned onto a dirt road, I tried to stop them. They ended up in the ditch, and by the time I got to the van, it was upside down and he was gone." The boy is whispering by the time he gets that far and I dread asking the next question as I climb into the cab of Gus's Yukon.

I swallow hard before I can bring myself to speak. "And Kendra?" My voice cracks on her name. *Please God, let her be alive.* Don't finally let me get this close to her and then yank her away.

"She had blood on her. I…I found her phone clutched in her hand when I was trying to find a pulse. She's unconscious but she's breathing. I can see a cut on her head." The boy starts sniffling.

"You did good, kid," I manage.

"I hope I didn't do anything wrong. I don't have minutes left on my phone and needed to call 911. Otherwise I wouldn't have touched her phone."

"It's fine. You did the right thing. Are you near her?"

"I'm standing next to her. The van is on its side but the backdoors must've opened when it rolled because she's lying half out of the van. Maybe I should move her?"

"Don't touch her," I bark into the phone and immediately feel Gus's steadying hand on my shoulder. "Don't move her. Let the EMTs take care of her when they get there."

"Okay." He lets out a shuddering breath. "I won't leave her. Even if the guy comes back, I promise I won't leave her."

"I'm staying right here with you, buddy. They're on their way, just hang tight."

I cast a glance at Gus who's still on his own phone. Sensing my gaze he turns to me. "Joe's already on his way. It's possible he'll beat the first responders. He was on his way home from Cortez. I called Drew, who is en route behind us, and was gonna get ahold of his guys. Hang tight."

I barely notice the landscape whipping by as we're barreling down the highway. "Hey Tom? Can you hold her hand?"

"I already am," the boy whispers.

"Good man." I struggle to hold on to my own emotions as fear, frustration and anger swirl in my gut. "Listen, a friend of ours might get there before the ambulance does. He drives a black SUV, a big Chevy Tahoe. You may know him. Joe Morris? He used to be the county sheriff a few years back." I'm babbling and I know it.

"Joe wants to know east or west of the 491," Gus asks, and I pass the question on to Tom who says west.

"West," I repeat to Gus.

"I see headlights. Oh, and I can hear sirens farther up the road now." Relief is evident in his voice.

"That'll be Joe with rescue apparently right behind him," I reassure him. Once he confirms Joe and rescue have arrived, I let him go, leaning back against the headrest. Gus briefly squeezes my arm.

"I'll get you there. Just breathe, have faith, and I'll get you there as soon as possible."

Kendra

My head is pounding.

I try to reach up with my left hand, but a pinch on my arm has me drop it again, only to try with my other hand. This time a hand closes around my wrist, stopping me.

"Don't touch your head, honey," I hear Joe's voice say.

Joe?

I can tell we are in a moving vehicle and panic washes over me. Joe's in the van with me? I struggle against the hold on my arm and my heart races in my chest.

"Kendra—you're fine. Stop struggling. You're in an ambulance and we're on our way to the hospital in Cortez. You've been in an accident."

An accident? I try to open my eyes against the bright lights that are a shock to my system. Steadily, my recollection of events starts surfacing. The bag over my head, the man... "The man." My voice sounds weak and I clear my throat before trying again. "Someone put a bag over my head and threw me in a van. I didn't see... I heard his voice. Sounded familiar but I'm not sure. He said I owed him a hike. Same words Lars Cayman had used, but something... something was off. He sounded...different."

"Don't strain yourself," Joe says, and I squint against the light to see his face. "You were out for quite a stretch. I'm no doctor, but from the goose egg on your head and that nasty cut, I'd say you took a significant hit to the noggin. Let's get you looked after first and then we'll worry about what happened."

"Neil..."

There is no mistaking the broad smile on Joe's face. "He's meeting us at the hospital. Boy was right upset by the sounds of it. Naomi owes me." My confusion must show because Joe goes on to explain, "Last Sunday, after you called

Neil about Cayman's phone call, I said to Naomi that from the look on his face, I could tell he wasn't gonna let you keep your distance much longer. I told her no more than a week. She was sceptical and challenged me to a bet."

"You bet on me?"

"Sure did," Joe chuckles unapologetically. "You forget, Neil's my friend. I've worked with him for a long time. I know how he can get when he's determined. Everyone sees him as this easy going kid, but that's just his outside."

I avert my eyes, recognizing I was one of those who didn't look further than what met the eye. I think I've always known there was more to him. "So what did you win?" I ask Joe, turning back just in time to see a blush hit his cheeks.

"Certain sexual favors." He sheepishly smirks.

The ambulance makes a sharp turn and slows down, but before it comes to a full stop, the doors at the back are pulled open.

"Jesus, Neil. Wait for the damn thing to come to a stop first, will ya?" I hear Gus's voice from the back of the ambulance.

A familiar EMT I hadn't really noticed before stands up to block the doors. "Please sir, let us do our job."

"I need to see her." Even though I can't see him, I can hear by the sound of Neil's voice that he's close to losing it.

"Joe?" I plead, and he immediately gets up and whispers something to the medic who reluctantly steps to the side. Joe climbs down and a few muted words are exchanged that I can't quite catch.

The medic disappears as well and then I feel the gurney I'm on moving. The moment my body clears the open door, Neil's face is over me. "How are you doing, Pup?" is all he says, but it's not the words that have the tears pooling in my eyes, it's the dark anguish in his eyes.

"I'm all right, honey. I'm good." I put my hand on his cheek and he turns his face into my palm, his hand covering mine. "I promise," I whisper when he bends and softly touches his lips to mine.

"Kendra?"

I'd just closed my eyes for a minute after finally convincing Neil to grab something from the hospital cafeteria before they close for the night. He refuses to go home tonight, even though they've told us I'll have to stay at least until tomorrow. I have a concussion and a nasty cut along my hairline from my forehead almost to my ear. I was lucky, apparently. I haven't looked in the mirror yet, but I'm thinking it doesn't look pretty, judging from Emma and Naomi's faces when they'd peeked in earlier. Gus and Mal had both come in about an hour ago, after I was stitched up, and I told them what I remembered. Neil had kicked them out at some point, saying they'd have to wait until tomorrow. A hushed conversation had taken place by the door before those two left, leaving Neil and I alone in the room. Finally, a quiet moment to call my mother. Neil had already spoken to her earlier and assured her I was fine. He promised her I would call her as soon as I could. She was full of apology that she hadn't shown up yet, but one of her patients had slipped into a coma and is not expected to make it through the night. I have to admit, I was a little relieved.

I'm tired to the bone when I hear my name. Opening my eyes, I see Tom Bridges standing in the door opening.

"Hey, buddy. Come in." I watch him limping as he approaches my bed and I pat on the mattress beside me. "Come sit. I understand I owe you big time."

He gingerly sits down beside me on the mattress, not looking at me. "I don't know about that," he says quietly.

"How is that? If you hadn't followed us, I might've been…" Realizing I was about to let on more than perhaps was wise, I shut my mouth and instead grab his hand in mine.

"I'm the reason you got hurt," he says, his voice cracking on the last word. "I ran you off the road."

"I'm grateful, Tom. So very grateful you did exactly that." I squeeze his hand when I see him furiously blink against tears.

"But—"

"No buts." Neil's voice sounds from the door. "No ifs or ands either." Both Tom and I turn toward Neil, standing just inside the door, a brown bag and a coffee in his hand. Slowly he walks toward the bed, and Tom instantly stands up, wincing a little when he does. Neil puts his stuff on the nightstand, turns to the young man and holds his hand out. "It's not only Kendra who owes you gratitude, my man. I do too. Having you on the phone, knowing my girl was looked after—meant the world. Not to mention, you having the presence of mind to follow and stop the guy when you did. I don't know many guys your age with that kind of courage."

Obviously taken aback and a little hesitant, Tom places his hand in Neil's. "Thanks," he says hoarsely. "My dad just picked me up from the police station and I said I wanted to quickly come and apologize."

"No reason to apologize, son. You did exactly what I would've done in your shoes," Neil says, clapping the boy on the shoulder. I have to work hard not to snort at his use of the term *son.* He would've been a very young father at fourteen.

"Thanks for checking on me, Tom. I should be right as rain in no time. But you hurt yourself, didn't you?" I put him on spot.

"Not so bad," he mumbles, but I can see he's worried. He's downplaying it.

"Please see your orthopedic surgeon as soon as possible, honey. If you damaged it again…"

"I will," he blurts. "I'd better get going. Hope you feel better." With an awkward hug for me and a nod for Neil, he walks out the room.

Neil turns to me. "I'm just gonna see him off. It's dark out. I'll be right back." With a quick kiss, he disappears as well.

I'm just dozing when Neil comes back in a little later. I hear him pull up a chair and crinkle the brown paper bag. An odd sense of wellbeing comes over me as I listen to him sip his coffee and eat his food.

"I'm not sleeping," I admit after a few minutes, slowly lifting one eyelid. "I'm just resting my eyes. But if you're done eating, I wouldn't mind a hug." The words haven't left my mouth before he's out of the chair, his cup and bag discarded and he's toeing off his boots. When he approaches the bed, I scoot over as far as I can, making room. It's a bit tight, but when he carefully rolls me on my side, and curls around me from behind, we fit perfectly. "Is everything all right with Tom?" I ask.

"Yeah. Just wanted to make sure his dad knew that if not for his son, I might've…" He stops mid-sentence, but I know what he was going to say. He lets out a deep sigh. "I was so scared," he admits softly, his face in my hair. I close my arms over his, wrapped around me. "I asked the kid to hold your hand, because I couldn't, and he said he already was. I'll be forever grateful for that."

"I'm all right," I tell him again, but it's not until after I hear his breathing deepen with sleep, that I manage to drift off myself.

CHAPTER FIFTEEN

Neil

It's been only three days, but it feels like a month.

After I was able to bring Kendra home on Saturday morning, the house has had a revolving door. People in and out non-stop, even though I'd tried to limit the visitors so she could have some rest. That was our first run in. Damian and Luna, who'd set up shop in Cortez while Maryn's lead was hot, had come to take Kendra's statement. Cayman was in the wind and that in itself put him right back at the top of the list of suspects, although no concrete connection had been found between the two other than their name. Well, and their connection to the case. Not five minutes prior, Emma, accompanied by Arlene and Kara, had left. They came loaded with food, as per usual. It seems to be a habit here in Cedar Tree that whenever something happens, first thing people think of is food. Kara's presence was a bit tense. Especially since Emma made some references to my visits with her last week. I could feel the cool breeze coming from Kendra's direction and cursed myself for not telling her earlier. Probably doesn't look too good that for those few days, I barely had time to even talk to her, yet I obviously managed to see Kara. Worst part is, I wouldn't have been able to explain without betraying Kara's trust. It's fucked up.

The moment the three left, leaving us with enough food to last the week, Kendra turned to me. "You don't have to stay," she said in a cool voice. "I can manage, thank you." Before I had a chance to respond, she disappeared into the bathroom. Yup, I fucked up.

It was minutes later, while I was waiting for her to reappear, that the two FBI agents announced themselves. I wanted to tell them to come back later so I could fix things with Kendra first, but with Casal Maryn, or whoever the hell he is, still out there, I had no choice. Seating them in the living room, I went to get Kendra. The bathroom door was still closed, so I knocked softly.

"Kendra? The FBI is here," I tried. The only response I could hear was the flushing of the toilet. I gave her a minute before trying again. "Kendra?'

With a soft click, the bathroom door was unlocked and opened. Kendra, her face swollen and head bandaged stepped out, her eyes downcast. She tried to slip by me but I stopped her by the shoulders.

"Are you okay to do this?"

Slowly her face came up and the moment I saw her eyes, I suspected she'd been close to crying. Still, she lifted her chin and her mouth was pressed into a tight line. "I'm fine."

"Look," I started, wanting to smooth things over. "I can explain."

Don't know what I was expecting but it sure wasn't the derisive snort.

"I'm sure you can, but I believe I have guests," she said before pulling from my grip and turning to the stairs. I wasn't about to create a scene with Damian and his agent sitting downstairs so I reluctantly let her go, following closely behind.

She spent at least an hour going over the whole ordeal when Luna asked her to describe Lars Cayman again. I knew what she wanted to know. I'd still not asked Kendra about the limping. It took her a minute to think before responding. She indicated perhaps he was favoring one leg, but explained it could have just been because she'd watched him maneuver through the tables of the coffee shop.

The agents left shortly after that and while I was showing them out, Kendra had disappeared upstairs. When I went to check, she'd been curled up in bed, her back to the door. Knowing she was probably exhausted, I figured it probably wasn't a good time to address Kara, so I left her to sleep.

Since then we'd barely been alone, especially when her mother showed up Saturday night, and stayed. Her patient had sadly passed away that morning and she'd been busy with the family. The moment she could, she'd hopped in the car to come here. There'd been an awkward moment when sleeping arrangements were discussed because Elsa of course would take the spare bedroom, which was fine, because I'd intended to sleep with Kendra anyway. That is, until Kendra pushed a pile of blankets in my hands, relegating me to the couch.

That's where I've been every fucking night since. With Elsa taking care of Kendra, I've been keeping busy going over all of the victims' records, to see if I could find any ties with Maryn/Cayman. I'd simply used an online anagram creator to come up with as many versions of names possible with that set of letters. There were quite a few of them and I was able to connect him that way to four more victims. Each time he'd set up an entirely new online identity. Jasper is working on it from his end and together we've generated quite a few leads for the task force to run down.

But now with Elsa heading back to Durango after breakfast, it's time to clear the air with Kendra. She's frozen me out long enough. I find her in the kitchen putting dishes in the sink and without pause, I take the plate from her hand and pull her to the living room.

"What the hell, Neil?" she snaps instantly, trying to yank her hand from mine, but I don't let go. Instead of the couch, I push her to sit in the chair where she is boxed in with armrests and me crouching in front of her. "Is it necessary to manhandle me?"

"Unfortunately—yes. Seems to be only way for me to get some face time with you." I'm hanging on to my patience by a thread, so I take a few deep breaths before I launch in. "Kara is a *friend,* nothing more. I know I've said it before but it bears repeating."

"It doesn't matter," she mutters, looking at her hands. "This was all just a bad idea to begin with."

"Jesus Christ, Kendra. Are we seriously back there again? Please don't tell me that after I fucking laid myself bare to you, after barely keeping it together when you got hurt, you're gonna use this to push me away?" My voice steadily rising, I take another breath to calm down before continuing. "I get it's not the simplest thing to wrap your head around, believe me I know that. I still get a little itchy when you talk about Mal. The difference is I *trust* you when you tell me he's just a good friend. Maybe it's because I can't see anything but good in you and yet you seem determined to find the bad in me." Exasperated, I run my hand through my hair at the lack of response. It fucking stings. I drop my head while at the same time pushing up from my uncomfortable position on the floor. At this point, it feels like anything I say will fall on deaf ears and I can only hope a few of my words will eventually filter through.

Dejected, I sit back down at the dining room table and start working on the property searches I'm running in Montezuma County in the name of Casal Maryn, Lars Cayman, or any of the other aliases we've found. I'm trying hard not to listen for sounds coming from the living room and instead make an effort to focus on my screen.

A soft hand is placed in the center of my back, and without her needing to say anything, I drop my head in my hands in relief.

"I'm sorry," she says quietly. "You're right. I'm ashamed that you're so very right. You've given me no reason to doubt your honesty. It's been a crazy roller coaster of a week—not that I'm trying to offer excuses," she quickly adds, "but even though these extreme circumstances seem par for the course for you, they're not for me. I'm a little overwhelmed at it all and went into protective mode." I can feel her resting her cheek on my head, and when she faintly whispers, "I'm scared," I know she's talking about more than the serial killer we have on the loose. She's talking about us. I turn and immediately pull her down on my lap, my arms holding her tight.

"It's all good, Pup."

Kendra

I hate being wrong.

The moment Neil tells me I'm determined to see him in a negative light, I know he's right. Eating crow tastes like a freaking mouthful of ball sacks. But as soon he goes to sit at his computer, I know I'll have to choke it down and own it.

So that's what I do. I walk up and own it and surprisingly, he ends up being his usual comforting self again. Sitting in his lap, with his arms around me, I feel as safe as can be. His words are simple, but as always, they hit the mark. Right here and now I decide, perhaps not for the first time, but certainly the last, that I will stop finding ways to undermine what we have. Or could have.

"Now, lets get this shit aired out for once and for all. And I'm gonna break my promise to her to make sure there can never be any misunderstanding again." I open my mouth to tell him it's not necessary but he silences me with a quick, hard kiss. "Hush. Let me finish. Last week, Kara was going through some shit. She knew I was in the GFI offices late, so she waited and caught me coming out. I know she has no one else here who she can talk with about certain things, so I spent some time with her that night and the next, mainly to listen. You see, Kara is—"

Before he has a chance to betray his friendship, I grab the back of his head and slam my mouth against his, forcing my tongue between his lips. I can't be responsible for ruining his friendship, because like he said, what goes for the goose should go for the gander and like it or not, his relationship with Kara is part of his life. To accept the man, you have to accept his friends. Like Pavlov's dog, he responds immediately, his tongue tangling with mine while his hands knead my flesh. In seconds, I can feel his cock harden under my butt and an intriguing method of distraction comes to mind. I slide my hand between our bodies and start teasing his hard length through the rough denim of his jeans. Rubbing with the palm of my hand and slightly scraping with my nails over the distinguishable rims and ridges. When his deep moans tell me he's forgotten what he was talking about, I slip down between his legs, losing his mouth in the process.

"Pup…"

The endearment sends a shiver down my spine, as I quickly take care of the buttons of his fly to release his swollen member in all its formidable glory. On my knees, with one hand fisting him at the base, I run my nose along his length, breathing him in. I never thought the scent of a man could turn me on, but Neil's does. A mix of his shower gel with his own unique musk—a heady combination, and I don't hesitate to open my mouth and let my open lips slide along the thick vein running along his cock.

"Baby, you're hurt," he tries, his voice hitching on the words as I run my tongue around the crown. I taste the tang of his arousal as the tip of my tongue probes the tiny slit, making him hiss between his teeth. His hand comes up to fist in my hair, holding it away from my face, and as I look up in his heavy-lidded gaze, I slowly but purposely slide my mouth over him.

"Ahhh, *Christ,* you're killing me," he groans, his hips flexing on the seat and his hand tightening in my hair. With every slide up his length, I press the mushroom against the roof of my mouth with my tongue, earning a deep guttural moan of satisfaction. Never considering myself particularly talented in the field of fellatio, his response to being inside my mouth does something to me. Gives me a sense of power and a feeling of immense gratification that I could have this impact on a man. Especially one like Neil. Bolstered with renewed confidence, I start working him in earnest, bobbing my head up and down him, while pumping my fist around his root. His hips lift inadvertently each time I suck him in until the tip of his cock hits the back of my throat and I instinctively swallow down.

"*Fuck me,* " he exclaims, trying to pull my head up. "I'm too close, I'm gonna let go in your mouth if you keep this up."

"Let me," I plead, looking at him and reveling at the dark blush high on his cheekbones. His lush lips are slightly open and I see in the rapid rise and fall of his chest that he's struggling to control himself. Determined to make him lose it, and more turned on than I could've imagined, I shift my bottom so my heel is pressed against my pussy. As I suck him back inside, I swivel my hips and rock myself on its hard surface.

"That's the sexiest goddamn thing I've ever seen," he says, fucking my mouth.

Already soaked and primed, it doesn't take me long to start humming my impending climax around his cock, which has Neil bucking twice before coming all over my tongue. I barely manage to swallow him down while chasing my own climax, when I'm suddenly up with my pants around my ankles. He bends me forward over the table, spreading my legs wide in the process. His hands slide down from my ass to the backs of my knees before trailing back up to the inside of my thighs. When I feel him spread me from behind, an involuntary groan escapes.

"Neil... Please, hon— Ahhh..."

The moment his mouth closes greedily over my wet core, all ability to consciously communicate ceases. The contrast of his tongue teasing along my folds before his lips suck lightly at my clit is enough to have me frantically grab on to the opposite edge of the table. Both his hands are molding the cheeks of my ass, before his fingers start playing along my crease. Spreading me wide, he slips digits from each hand alternately in my wet channel, creating an entire new set of sensations. With his mouth working my clit and fingers pumping in my pussy, he slides the finger of his other hand up and around my thus far closed-to-business back door. Alive with sensation, coherent thought isn't possible. So when his digit, slick with my own juices, is pushed through the tight ring of muscle, the trifecta of pleasure pushes me over the edge, tearing a raw scream from my throat.

"Christ, you're magnificent," Neil mumbles, kissing his way up my spine until he's draped over my back on the table his face burrowing in my neck. "Are you okay, Pup?"

"Mmmmm," I hum, sated, and immediately follow up with a little whimper when I feel the heat of Neil's body disappear.

"Just going to clean up," he says, first stopping to pull up my underwear and yoga pants. Seconds later, I hear the water run in the kitchen.

With my faculties slowly returning, I crack open my eyes and freeze instantly when I notice the front window. Luckily, with the porch wrapping around the house, it's impossible to look in. Unless of course it's dark outside and all the lights are on in here. Movement catches my eye and I suck in a sharp breath as I straighten up. Through the window, I spot the edge of the swing moving in and out of my line of vision.

"What is it?" Neil asks, walking up behind me and giving me one last kiss on my shoulder.

"Someone's outside," I whisper, unable to take my eyes off the swing. Immediately, Neil shoves me behind him. He stills when he sees the same thing I did.

"Stay put. Do not move a muscle," he says as he pushes me back into the kitchen. I watch him pull a gun from his ankle-holster and make his way out the other door into the hallway.

"Neil!" I whisper-shout, scared out of my gourd.

"It's okay, just stay right where you are," he throws me a tight smile over his shoulder and then he's gone from sight. I don't hear the front door open, but I can feel the cool morning air streaming into the house. With my hands pressed against my mouth to keep from making a sound, I slowly sink down, my back against the wall.

"Son of a bitch!" I hear Neil yell and then nothing.

Crazy thoughts whirl through my mind but I can't bring myself to move. And I'm still not moving when I hear heavy footsteps walking into my house.

CHAPTER SIXTEEN

Neil

My gun in hand, I manage to open the door without making a sound.

The thought that someone was out on that porch, watching me with Kendra, is enough to make rage boil in my veins. But years of training kick in as I manage to narrow my focus. Keeping my steps rolling from toe to heel, and as close to the wall as possible, I'm able to move silently, despite the aging wood of the porch beneath my feet. A quick glance around the corner and I can see the silently swaying porch swing. Empty. Immediately my eyes snap up, taking in the surroundings. There is nothing—no sound of a car taking off, no movement anywhere. Except… Looking across the road, I see the white-haired, old lady peek out from behind the curtains in her front window.

My eyes drift back to the swing and now I see what I missed earlier. A newspaper? I step around the corner to take a better look. A map.

"Son of a bitch!" I yell, when I spot the corner missing. I carefully pick up the map by a corner and with one last look, I turn to walk back into the house. To the terrified woman inside.

I find her in the kitchen on the floor. Her knees pulled up to her chest, her head buried in her arms and her back pressed into the corner. "Babe…"

Her head whips up and immediately tears pool in her eyes. "Oh my God—Neil. I thought…" Her voice trails off when she sees what I have in my hand. "What is that? Is that…?" Her eyes are big and fixed on the map I have to take care of without destroying any possible evidence.

"Nothing I want more than to put my arms around you now, babe, but I have to make sure I don't mess any possible prints on this thing. Do you have any wax or parchment paper?" She nods, looking a touch confused, as she scrambles to her feet and roots through one of the drawers, coming up with a roll of wax paper. "Good. Now if you could cut off a good length and lay it on the counter?" Her hands still shaking, she does exactly as I ask. Carefully, I place the map in the center of the paper and fold the end over, before turning and pulling Kendra against me. Her arms immediately close around my waist, fisting in the back of my shirt. Her body trembles in my arms and I mumble some nonsense in her hair. "It's okay, Pup. There's no one outside. Whoever was there is gone," I tell her, knowing full well that whoever is out there somehow has found out where she lives. And that is not fucking good.

"How did he find me?" Her voice is soft but not weak. I can hear fear but also anger simmering under the surface. Good, it will make what I have to say next go down a bit easier, I hope.

"Not sure, but we'll find out. You can't stay here, Kendra." Her head tilts back the moment the words leave my mouth, anger in her eyes.

"Like hell! I'm staying here. Where am I supposed to go? Not letting this creepy chucklefuck scare me out of my house. It's my house!" Her hands that were clutching me seconds ago are now shoving at my chest angrily. Probably because I couldn't hold back the snicker at her colorful verbiage. Her choice of swearwords is different, to say the least, but different is damn cute on her. "Don't laugh at me," she admonishes. "This isn't funny." And just like that, cold reality settles back in. No, it's not funny at all.

Leaning down, I first kiss her tightly pursed mouth before taking her angry face in my hands. "You're absolutely right, which is why you're coming with me."

"Coming where?"

"My apartment. It only has one entrance and is as secure as this place is, if not more so. Start packing whatever you think you'll need." I already start turning away to grab my phone when a tug on my arm turns me back around.

"I can't. I have to be at the clinic this afternoon. I have patients."

Is she for real? "Kendra, you're not going to work," I tell her, holding up my hand right away when I see her gearing up for battle. "All you would do is draw whoever this is out there to Joe and Naomi's place. You might even be putting your patients at risk. Do you want that?" I'm not playing fair, but I'll do whatever it takes to make her understand how dangerous this situation is.

"No," she says sharply in a deceptively soft voice, and I feel a pang of guilt. "I don't want that." With a hefty shove, she manages to slip from my arms and takes off upstairs. She's pissed. I can work with that.

Ten minutes later, I have given both Gus and Damian a call. On Gus's suggestion, we're going to stop at the GFI offices first, where Damian is going to meet us to pick up the map. It'll give Kendra a chance to let off some steam with Emma.

I'd forgotten about Kara.

The moment I walk in with my arm around Kendra's angry shoulders, I feel her stiffen even more when Kara's bright smile greets us from the kitchen. "Hey guys! I'm just pulling some fresh lemon scones from the oven. Want some?"

The warm, slightly sweet citrus tang in the air makes my mouth water, but Gus is standing behind her in the hallway, tipping his head toward the office behind him. Guess no scones for me. "Not for me, duty calls." I indicate Gus, who's already walking down the hall. "I leave you in good hands," I tell Kendra, earning a ball-shriveling look in return. Ouch. I open my mouth to try and dislodge my foot, but Kara beats me to it.

"Awesome," she directs at Kendra. "I'll finally have a chance to chat with you." Kendra's smile is as fake as a two-dollar bill and suddenly I'm not so sure this is a good idea.

"Where's Emma?" I ask Kara, hoping she's around to help.

"She's out dropping off pies at the diner and picking up a few groceries. Only reason I have a chance at the oven." She smiles with the tiny lift of one eyebrow. Kara noticed my girl's reluctance. She would, she's sharp as a tack and reading folks is part of her job as a social worker. Which is probably why she steps up, throws an arm around Kendra's shoulders and marches her into the kitchen, chattering away. The last thing I see before walking down the hall is the slightly panicked look Kendra throws over her shoulder. I cross my fingers Kara can put her at ease, but I have to admit, I'm pretty fucking pleased at Kendra's response. She wouldn't react that way if she didn't care about me.

So when I walk into the boardroom with the evidence in a Ziploc bag, I have a big-ass smile on my face.

Half an hour later, I'm not smiling anymore. The FBI was able to get a credit card, name and address for that postal box they linked to Maryn in Cortez. That lunatic has been right in our backyard the entire time. Not only that, a new missing persons case has just been filed in Cortez. Damian hands out a file. Franka Mellis, a home-care nurse and single mother of two, did not come home last night. Her twelve-year-old daughter contacted the Cortez PD first thing this morning. The children's father was contacted in Norfolk where he is stationed and is apparently on a flight to Durango. The last person to have seen her is an elderly man with early onset Alzheimer's. Apparently, during the first five minutes of the interview with him, he was clear as a bell, yet in the next moment, he didn't even remember where he was. From what they could deduce, Ms. Mellis received an urgent text about her daughter, which is why she had to leave before her replacement came in ten minutes later. The daughter claims she never sent a text.

"Okay, let's work from the premise that this is the same guy who dropped off the map at Kendra's," Damian suggests. "If he actually has Franka Mellis, all we can hope for is that he's keeping her restrained somewhere. Jasper is looking for any other places, aside from the old farmhouse off of County Road D, that might be in his name. We're getting ready to hit the farmhouse as soon as my warrant gets here. If she's there, they'll find her." The agent puts his hand on his neck and stretches. "The other thing is, we haven't been able to find a regular source of income for Maryn, aside from the sale of some of his art through the Farmington gallery. Not enough to live off, so we know he must have money coming in from somewhere. We're in the process of getting access to his bank records—only one account with Bank of America in Durango found to date—but the paperwork is taking forever on that."

While Damian's been talking, I've been able to find a profile for Franka on MatureDatingOnly. Her handle was easy to spot, Franka not being a common name and FrankaMom2 was easy enough to pick out as hers. Especially since I'd already pulled up her picture from the DMV site and it was a match with the one on her dating profile. Fuck. It's becoming more and more frustrating to see how many people don't properly protect themselves when surfing the net. Some of this stuff can be hacked by a high school kid with half a brain. The woman's password is a combination of her daughter's name and her son's birthdate.

"What have you got?" Gus asks me.

"She has a profile on MatureDatingOnly. I just got in her account and am checking the profiles she's been in touch with… Son of a fucking bitch!" A sick feeling settles in the pit of my stomach when I spot the tag name for one of the profiles she's been conversing with up to last Friday.

"What?" Damian comes around the table and leans over my shoulder. "Goddamn motherfucker. Lucifer? The bastard's named himself Lucifer this time? What the fuck does that mean?"

"The fallen one," Gus mutters. "Also known as fallen star, or morning star. The ultimate dark angel." Looking up at Damian, he leans back in his chair. "I'm coming with you."

"So am I," I add, but both older men turn their attention back on me.

"Yeah?" Gus looks at me questioningly. "And what about Kendra?"

Kendra

This is not awkward at all.

I self-consciously sit down on the kitchen stool Kara waves me to while she starts pulling mugs from a cupboard and pouring coffee.

"Sorry, I didn't ask. I just assumed you'd want some? Coffee I mean?" she asks belatedly, wincing. Looks like I might not be the only one who is a little uncomfortable.

"Coffee is great, thanks." I smile at her, hoping to break the obvious tension. "And I wouldn't mind one of those scones you were talking about."

"Of course!" She busies herself putting sugar and creamer on the counter and presents me with a pastry that is almost bigger than the plate it's on.

"Holy shizzle—those are huge!" comes falling out of my mouth. A snort has me look up to see Kara with her hand covering her mouth, trying to hold back laughter.

"Mom tells me all the time to mind my size, but I can't help it, bigger just seems better to me," she says with a wink, before her eyes turn serious. "Look, I know its weird and this must be uncomfortable, but I want to tell you how happy I am about you giving Neil a chance. He's really a fantastic guy. He's kept me sane over the past few years."

Okay. That's nice I guess, but what the fudge do I say to that? "I'm glad," I try with a little smile, feeling utterly out of my depth.

"I should've asked—I'm so sorry—but how are you doing?" She points at the bandage I still have covering the cut on my head. Instinctively my hand reaches up to touch it. "Neil mentioned you got hurt."

Wait. Neil mentioned? I feel the ugly beast of jealousy taking a huge bite out of my stomach. "I'm fine," I manage, but apparently none too convincing because Kara winces once again.

"I'm so fucking this up," she sighs, oddly checking the hallway behind her and the door before leaning over the counter toward me. "I'd like to explain. Back when Mom came to live in Cedar Tree and I met Neil, I was really struggling. I mean, Mom is great, and I was happy that she was happy, but there was so much shit going on in her life that I didn't want to add on to it. All these new friends she was making... It just seemed easier to leave things as they were. I didn't want to mess anything up for her." Kara looks down at her hands, where she's been picking apart the scone on her plate into a pile of crumbs. "Neil seemed more of my generation, and he was certainly more in tune. I know he hasn't told you because he always says it's my story to tell, but sometimes I wish he'd just spill the beans for me." Taking a deep breath, she looks me straight in the eyes, tears filling in hers. Without thinking, I reach out and squeeze her hand lightly. "Neil clued in right away that I wasn't interested in him that way," she continues. "He's convinced it wouldn't make one lick of difference to Mom or Gus if they knew. Or to anyone else for that matter. But I just don't know. Things are good like this." She hesitates for a moment, turning her head to look out the back window. "Or at least they were."

She seems to have a hard time just coming out with it, but she doesn't have to say the words for me to understand. So I say them for her. "You're gay."

Surprised, her head swings around. "You guessed?"

I can't help the chuckle from slipping out. "Honey, you may not have said the words, but it's pretty obvious."

"It's so silly." Kara blushes a little. "You know how when you postpone things, they only get harder?" When I nod my encouragement, she goes on. "Well, when I met Marisa, I thought I would wait a bit until I felt more secure in our relationship and then I would tell. But life happened, and every time I would visit Cedar Tree, time was so short and I didn't want to spoil it. So I wouldn't say anything. Then I'd come back home and Marisa would get upset. I've met her family and they're wonderful, and yet I'm keeping her from mine, and that pisses her off. I just never realized how much until she broke up with me on the phone last week."

Now the tears are streaming and there's nothing I can do but round the counter and pull the crying younger woman into my arms. "You know?" I begin carefully. "From what I can tell about your mom and Gus, they don't have a judgmental bone in their bodies. I think you're underestimating them. Sure, it may be a shock at first, but honey, that's not judgement, that's simply concern and a need to adjust their expectations."

The sniffling against my shoulder slows down and then she lifts her head. "Neil says the same thing. I was a basket case last week, but he talked me through. Really, he's such a good guy."

Her eyes on me are willing me to hear her. Oh, I hear her, all right. Here I was, pissing away an entire weekend on anger over him being a good guy. I'm such a dumbass. "I know he's a good guy, Kara," I tell her with a little smile as I sit back down on my stool. "And he's also right. You're a grown woman and you can't even say it out loud. I've heard enough about you to know that you're smart as a whip, have a fantastic personality and are a kick-ass social worker. Come on, Kara, you've been living it for years. You're a social worker for crying out loud."

Her mouth opens and closes a few times before she finally swallows hard. "You're right. I don't have a problem at home in Boston, but here in small-town Colorado, I have trouble admitting I'm a lesbian."

"Well, it's about fucking time, girl!"

Both our heads swing to the hall where Gus is leaning casually against the doorway. Oops.

"You knew?" Kara's voice is no more than a whisper as she watches Gus approach her.

Folding his stepdaughter in his arms, he mumbles in her hair, "What kind of investigator would I be if I hadn't figured it out by now, sweetie?"

"What about Mom?" Kara asks him.

"What about Mom?" Emma echoes as she comes in from the front, having apparently just heard Kara's question.

Oh boy. Seems I'm caught right in the middle of a family drama. With slightly panicked eyes, I look for an escape but instead find Neil walking in. He doesn't stop, just walks up to Emma, divests her of the grocery bags on her walker and comes into the kitchen, quietly sorting and putting the stuff away. A quick glance my way, with a wink, makes it clear he's fully aware of the bombshell about to drop.

"Well?" Emma prods, not having moved from her spot, but looking directly at her daughter who is facing her, with Gus's arm now around her shoulders.

"I'm gay," Kara blurts out.

Emma frowns, biting off between tight lips, "How long have you known?" For added emphasis, she puts her hands on her hips, swaying back and forth.

Kara rolls her eyes. "Mom, I'm a lesbian. I love girls. Well, really only one girl, but I messed that up. I—"

"I get that, but what I'd like to know is how long since you realized you were gay?" Emma cuts off Kara's mumbling and Gus seems to find it all very amusing.

"Uhm, eighth grade?" Kara answers, her words laced with confusion.

"Right," Emma states. "And as your mother, did you really think I was clueless? I'm pissed at you, Kara. But not for the reasons you think I am. I'm angry because it took you this damn long to tell me yourself!"

I've already slipped off the stool and am edging toward the door. Really, I shouldn't be witness to this, but Neil is now leaning with his back against counter, arms crossed over his chest, watching it unfold like real life TV. Not for long, though, because Emma makes her way into the kitchen and gives him a hard shove in the shoulder.

"Hey…easy," he says with a smile, rubbing his shoulder, but moving out of the way nonetheless as Emma takes over sorting the groceries with much noise.

"You know what? She's been miserable here since she apparently messed up with her girl back home. You knew this. I've seen you over at the guesthouse, Neil. You should have told me. I'm her mother." Emma pokes her finger at Neil.

"And I'm her friend," he fires back. "And what kind of friend would I be if she couldn't trust me?"

That seems to hit home.

Emma stills before swinging around to face Gus. "And you don't seem surprised." It sounds more as an accusation than it does a conclusion. Gus seems impervious.

"Love this girl too, Peach. Wasn't hard to figure out." He stalks over to Emma, bracketing her against the counter and leaning in. "Now get over your snit, because we all know you're dying to start fixing your girl's broken heart, and I have a killer to go catch. Kiss me."

"Ugh," Kara exclaims, turning her back. "Too much PDA in this house. All over the damn house!"

Neil chuckles and hooks her around the neck, giving her head a good rub, but he's watching me the whole time. Letting Kara go, he holds his hand out to me, and with my head still spinning from the laser speed turnarounds in these last twenty minutes, I grab hold and let him pull me out the door.

"What just happened?" I ask still a bit stunned when he has me tucked in the passenger seat.

"Family, Cedar Tree style. That's what just happened."

CHAPTER SEVENTEEN

Neil

"How long will you be gone?"

I've got Kendra pressed up against the wall in the bathroom. Joe is outside in the living room, taking over Kendra's security for a couple of hours. I have a few errands I have to run in Cortez. For two days, we've been holed up in the apartment with only the occasional trip down to the diner for a bite. I've been busy running some searches for Jasper, but the FBI is firmly in charge. GFI now officially has been assigned to keep Kendra safe, and even though she thinks it's only me, there is always a second monitoring the outside of the building. Often Joe, but sometimes Caleb or Mal. It's tedious, but necessary, because despite all the information that we are uncovering, Casal Maryn is still in the wind. No trace of him and despite the copies of his driver's license they had on file at the bank in Cortez, there is nothing registered with the DMV. No records at all. The man is a ghost. One with a farmhouse and a bank account with apparently not much in it.

So with Maryn on the loose, there is no way in hell I'll leave Kendra on her own, which is why Joe is here.

"Couple of hours at most. Is there anything I can bring you back?" I ask her, nibbling on her neck. God I can't get enough of her. Two days—and nights—of being able to touch her, to love on her, hasn't even put a dent in my craving. Fucking insatiable when it comes to Kendra.

"Mmmmm," she hums under my ministrations. "A latte and a cinnamon bun would give me something to look forward to," she mumbles.

I lift my head and stare in her slightly veiled eyes. "Coffee and a treat you look forward to? What about your man?" I ask her with one eyebrow lifted. Immediately, her arms tighten around me and a smile pulls at her mouth.

"My *man*? That what you are?" she teases. "I guess you give me a few things to look forward to as well."

"Damn right I do."

With a smile she stands on her toes and offers me her mouth. Not going to say no to an offer like that. Almost instantly, the feel of her soft lips and dainty tongue, along with the fresh minty taste of her, have me reconsider leaving. Good friend that Joe is, he loudly reminds us when he starts banging on the bathroom door.

"You guys about done in there? I'm about to piss in your potted plants."

Reluctantly pulling away from Kendra with a last kiss on her nose, I open the door finding Joe on the other side. "Don't have any potted plants, asshole," I tell him, only making him smile bigger.

I pull Kendra out behind me to the door. "So latte and cinnamon bun."

"Yes please."

First stop is the Cortez PD, where Damian has been set up in an office. I want to drop off some files with him and find out how the search for Franka Mellis is coming along. Just as I'm sure everyone else is, I'm afraid she's already dead. Still, he seems to have kept that other woman Tracy Poole alive for a while. From what had been done to her, I'm not sure *alive* would be the better option.

I pull into the parking lot while stifling a yawn. Haven't had a lot of sleep. Some of that is as a result of a year's worth of sexual frustration being worked out by Kendra and me. But mostly, when she finally fell asleep in my arms, I slipped out of bed and ended on the couch, which is way too fucking short for my six-foot-three frame, and lumpy to boot. Not sure if she'd noticed. She didn't say anything and I tried to make sure that I was up and about by the time she came out of the bedroom. I saw her look, though, and the fucking thing of it is, I'd like nothing more than to wake up to her in my bed—in my damn arms. One battle at a time. Got to get this sick fuck off the streets first.

Damian is bent over a pile of files on his desk, and Luna is sitting on the far side of the office, pounding out a two-fingered staccato beat on a computer. Neither of them look up when I walk in.

"Morning."

Both heads turn towards me.

"Neil," Damian simply says, while Luna just waves her hand before turning back to whatever it is she's doing. "Have a seat."

I toss the thick file containing the detailed timeline for Franka Mellis, which I've been working on, on his desk and sit down. It's taken me a while to sort the information collected from her telephone records, the task force's interviews with colleagues, friends and family and the results of my online digging through her accounts. "It's all I have to date, starting as recent as the day she disappeared and going back three months. I can go back further if you like, but given that this *Lucifer* first contacted her only two weeks ago, I thought it was enough to start," I tell Damian as he starts flipping through my file.

"I see you've managed to dig up the name on his account. Clay Rasman? Looks like another anagram."

"Yup. And I looked, only record close enough I could find was for a Clay Rasmin, who is an African American trial lawyer in Denver."

"Not our guy," Damian says, stating the obvious.

"Nope. Not our guy. No properties, no bank accounts, not a license, nothing. I did do a bit of digging on the last name Maryn, hoping to come up with a family connection somewhere. Needle in a haystack. More hits on that name in Canada than the US and none at all in this neck of the woods." I'd hoped to have more to bring to the table, but on Casal Maryn, I've hit a dead end.

"Somebody has to have seen something, *goddammit.*" Damian hits a frustrated fist on the surface of his desk. "No witnesses whatsoever have come forward and the brass doesn't want to put out a public call for fear of panic. At least that's the official word. The *real* reason for holding back, I suspect, is the fact that this guy has obviously been operating for a while, and we've only now caught on. They're scared they'll end up with massive public and political pressure to get this case resolved, and that's why they're trying to keep it under wraps as long as possible. Getting fucking sick and tired having to tow these politically correct bureau lines."

It's ironic to hear those words coming from the man who, on previous collaborations with GFI, showed himself to be a stickler for those same bureau rules.

"This woman is out there—possibly still alive—and we don't even know where to start looking. We don't even fucking know for sure how Cayman is wrapped up in this. Could be they are one and the same, could be some ridiculous coincidence, but I don't really believe in those. Sure, we've put agents on the main entrances to as many parks and conservation areas in the region as possible, but you and I both know there's no way in hell we can cover all of them, and besides, that is a crap shoot anyway." His vexation is evident from his body language; the haunted look in his eyes and the way his hand keeps running through his overly long hair. Even the way he dresses is an affirmation of his mental state. Instead of his normal immaculate appearance, his old T-shirt and ratty jeans are an unusual sight.

"What about the stuff you hauled from the farmhouse? The map that was left on Kendra's porch? We get anything from forensics?"

"Luna?" Damian turns to his agent.

She straightens up, setting down her coffee mug and flipping through the papers on her desk. "We're waiting for the lab to get back to us on the skin we found glued to the drawings. There were twenty-two shadow boxes in total. Twenty-two pieces of skin, some of which were fairly fresh, but most of them were almost mummified. He sealed those boxes with epoxy glue, making it impossible for air or moisture to get in. Hope is that he left a print somewhere on the inside or on the actual drawings itself, but we won't know until the lab opens the boxes. Exterior didn't show any prints." Luna takes a breath and even on her face, the strain is visible. I can understand why. Twenty-two frames would imply the same number of victims. Far more than we'd originally come up with as a possible number. "Other than that, the house was kept immaculate. Looks like he didn't spend a whole lot of time there, and if he did, he cleaned up after himself. Even the paintbrushes were devoid of any prints or smudges," she concludes.

I know they had found a very spartan interior when they went in, Gus in tow. He's the one who told me about the boxes along the wall, like some sort of trophy gallery. They found one room turned into a studio with two more paintings of wings. One sitting on the floor against the wall, and the other sitting on an easel, unfinished. There was another room, a bedroom, that had been turned into a virtual prison cell. The one single window was boarded up and screwed down on the outside, and the door fitted with two deadlocks. The simple steel bar with brackets mounted on both sides of the door seemed like overkill. The door apparently had been left open, showing a simple double bed, a chemical toilet in one corner. If the reinforced door and window weren't clear enough, the chain and shackles bolted into the floor would have made it clear this was not your run-of-the-mill bedroom. But no Franka.

With little new information and nothing more to add, I head out to my next, and decidedly more pleasurable errand. Kara is already waiting for me in the parking lot, a big smile on her face and hopping from foot to foot with excitement. She's leaving for Boston tomorrow, back to the job and life waiting there. I guess talking about things in the open with Emma and Gus these past few days has given her the kick in the ass she needed to tackle real life again.

"I can't believe you are doing this!" she squeals as I get out of the truck. I just shake my head at her antics. When I called her earlier when Kendra was blow drying her hair, she almost blew my eardrum with her excited scream.

"It's not a big deal, Kara," I point out, but she doesn't agree.

"Like hell it's not," she says, hooking her arm in mine while we cross the parking lot. "This is a *huge* fucking deal, lover boy," she teases.

"Your momma heard you use that language, she'd take a rolling pin to you."

"Pffft, my momma uses worse than that, and you know it. Besides, she's so busy plotting ways to fix my relationship with Marisa, she wouldn't even notice."

Despite the rough patch Kara is going through, she keeps her chin up and her good nature shining. I squeeze her arm with mine. "You okay?" I ask, casting a sideways glance, catching her eye.

"Better, much better," she smiles. "I don't know if it's too little, too late when it comes to Marisa, but I'm going to fight for her. It sure feels good not hiding."

The last makes me chuckle, because really, it turns out she hadn't been hiding a damn thing. I push the door open and let Kara walk in before me. She lets out another excited squeal.

"Oh my God! Look at all of them, so pretty!"

Kendra

Not sure what's worse, knowing someone out there may be trying to harm you or knowing that confined to this apartment for much longer, you'll certainly go nuts.

I know it's only been a few days, but I like my freedom. I like my hikes. I like my life. Granted, some things are a definite benefit, namely Neil and *all* he brings to the table, but I've been marching to my own drum for so long, it sucks having to give up control. Even if it is for the best reasons, and with a virtual smorgasbord of fringe benefits.

My mind drifts to last night when, for the second night in a row, what started as a pleasant night on the couch watching Game of Thrones, ended up a hot sweaty tangled mess in bed. I'm discovering a whole new appreciation for the merits of youth. Stamina, regeneration, endurance, and an agility of lips and fingers that should be patented. The boy's got serious skills.

The guy also has serious issues, because last night, for the second night in a row, he disappeared halfway through the night and I could hear him moving about the living room. I know he doesn't want me to ask questions, which is why he pretends he's been at my side all night. And I don't want to pry into something that is clearly distressing and deep-rooted, so I pretend along with him. But it bothers me. A lot. Because I don't believe he would hurt me. Not even in the clutches of a nightmare.

It's not really the point, though, is it? Neil looks to be such an open and outgoing guy, when all that is only skin deep. Funny thing is, all those deeper cracks and crevices are what make him even more attractive to me.

The ringing of my phone breaks through my thoughts. Karly, the display says, and I take my phone into the bedroom so I don't disturb Joe, who is working on a laptop at the dining table.

"So, how was it?" is the first thing out of my mouth when I answer. I hadn't heard from her since she got back, although Mom mentioned she'd been in touch with her. I probably could've called myself, but I'd been a little preoccupied.

"Oh my God! It was awesome. I had so much fun, Kenny. You should've come."

I probably should've, in hindsight. I don't say that, though. "So glad you had a good time, honey. Meet any nice guys?"

"Well…" Karly hesitates, which tells me enough.

"You did, didn't you?"

A happy chuckle sounds over the phone before she gives me details. Way too many details, but that's my sister's way. The lucky guy turns out to be a thirty-five-year-old investment broker from San Antonio. Divorced, no children and has a *fabulous* condo with a view of the Alamo. When I ask how she knows it's *fabulous*, Karly admits to having gone home with him for a few days before returning to Durango, which is why she hasn't contacted me before.

"You don't think that's moving a little fast?" I ask her, painfully aware of how hypocritical that is, given that my own love life went from zero to a hundred in about the same length of time.

"Maybe," she surprisingly admits. "But when something feels right, you just know."

I find myself agreeing, albeit in silence. Despite all my misgivings about Neil, I have to admit this…connection we have feels more right than anything else. I just hope that when the intense situation we find ourselves in now is behind us, that feeling is still true.

I listen to my sister wax poetic over David, her new guy, and even smile when hearing how gaga she is over him. I'm happy for her and I hope this one can stand the test of time.

"Oh, and I wanted to come see your new place soon," she announces just as we're saying our goodbyes.

"I'd love for you too, but…" There is no way I want my sister anywhere near Cedar Tree right now, so I'm scrambling for excuses without letting her in on what is going on. "Give me a week or two to get the spare bedroom sorted and I'd love for you to come spend the weekend. Life's been a little hectic," I add by way of explanation.

"You know you don't have worry on my account, I'm fine sleeping on the couch," she responds. "Oops. Gotta go. I have another call coming in. It's David," she gushes, and before I have a chance to say anything, she's already hung up.

I'm bored out of my mind.

Joe hasn't moved since he got here this morning. His head is bent over a stack of files and his laptop. There's nothing on TV that can hold my attention and I'm flipping until I hit on the Food Network. Nigella Lawson is making brownies from scratch. Chocolate—exactly what I'm craving right now. Boredom is a dangerous thing. Thank goodness for Neil's state of the art PVR that allows me to pause and rewind the programming. I set it up at the beginning of the segment and then go on a hunt for the requisite ingredients. I'm surprised at how well stocked Neil's apartment is. Flour, butter, eggs, even a bag of semi-sweet chocolate chips in the back of a cupboard. The only thing missing is pure cocoa powder, but I have an idea who might have some.

"Joe?" I call out, waiting for him to lift his head from his work. "Do you think I can run down and get something from the kitchen? I need cocoa powder for this recipe and Neil doesn't have any."

"What are you making?" Joe pushes back from the table and approaches, curiously looking at the ingredients on the counter. "I'm liking the looks of those chocolate chips," he says on a smile.

"Brownies. Nigella Lawson's brownies," I enlighten him.

"She that gorgeous, stacked British chick? The one who makes cooking look and sound like foreplay?" His eyes light up with interest as he turns to look at her paused image on the TV screen.

"Better not let Naomi hear that lust in your voice," I caution him with a smile. Guys are all the same.

"You kidding? Naomi's the one who turned me on to her. Watching Nigella make trifle is better foreplay than porn." The smirk on his face tells me he *knows* what he's talking about.

"TMI!" I lift my hands defensively, just in case he wants to share any more. "I did not need that visual." Joe just chuckles.

"Give the diner a call. See if they have any, and I'll run down to get it."

I'm a little disappointed I can't run down there myself, and hang in the diner for a bit, but I'm not going to give him any trouble. I'm not a fool.

The moment I lock the door behind Joe—he insisted, waiting outside until he heard it engage—my phone rings again.

"Hey, honey," I say with a smile when I see Neil's number.

"I like that," his voice rumbles over the line. "You calling me *honey*. I'm just checking to see how you're doing?"

"A bit bored, but I just found something to do to kill some time."

"Yeah? What's that?" He wants to know, but I don't want to tell him in case my baking experiment fails.

"A surprise."

"I like the sound of that too." His voice goes husky, like it does when he gets turned on. Which is a lot. "Is Joe there?"

"Actually, he's just run down to the diner for a minute," I mention. It's met with silence. "Neil?"

"Is the door locked?" he bites off, sounding angry.

"Yes, I locked it behind him. Neil, he's just—"

"Stay away from the windows and only open the door when you recognize his voice," he snaps, cutting me off mid-sentence."

"All righty, Sergeant Major," I scoff. Another pregnant silence, and then I hear a deep sigh.

"Sorry, Pup. I'm just worried." He sounds tired, and I immediately feel myself softening. I know he feels the pressure and the frustration. Not being able to find this lunatic or the woman who's just gone missing, as well as the responsibility for protecting me. Add to that the fact that he's barely sleeping and I get why he snaps.

"I know. And I didn't mean to be flippant. I know you have cause to worry."

"Guess we're all stretched a little thin. I'll be another hour or so. I'll make it up to you then," he promises, his voice much warmer now.

Twenty minutes later, I have my pan of brownies ready to go in the oven. Joe has been sitting at the counter the entire time, following the process. Really, I think it was just an excuse to watch Nigella, but whatever. The moment I drop the bowl and spatula in the sink, he leans over the counter and snatches them back out.

"You're throwing out all the good stuff," he mutters, before scooping the minute traces of batter from the inside of the bowl with his finger and licking it off.

It doesn't take long for the warm, mouth-watering scent of chocolate to waft through the apartment. I take yet another peek at the timer to see if it's ready to come out when I hear steps coming up the outside stairs. Joe is up and out of his chair in a flash and steps cautiously up to the entrance.

"Just me," Neil's familiar voice sounds outside, and Joe opens the door.

"Damn, what smells so good?" he says, marching in with bags in his hands. And before I have a chance for a closer look, he drops them and stalks toward me. Without taking his eyes off me, he turns his head slightly, saying to Joe over his shoulder, "There are a few more things in my truck if you don't mind, Joe."

Joe just chuckles and disappears out the door.

"You know, babe," Neil says when he has me cornered against the counter. "Every time I come home and find you still there, I can't quite believe my luck." His nose rubs along mine and his eyes are seething with emotions.

"Neil, honey…"

"When I was growing up," he continues undeterred, "there was one thing I wished for every birthday and every damn Christmas but never got, because according to my parents, it would make a mess. Until I met you. Then you became all I wanted, but it felt like I'd never have that wish either. I'm smarter now, though. I know if there's something you want bad enough, you find a way to make it happen."

My hands have come to rest on his chest where I feel his heart pounding under my palm.

"Do you know that's why I call you Pup?" he asks with a bashful little smile, and I shake my head. "You're my unattainable wish, and yet, here you are," he says pulling me close with one arm at the small of my back and his other hand curling around my neck, his thumb stroking my jaw.

I'm lost in his gaze, my own blurring with emotion, when a voice sounds right outside the door. "Is it time yet?"

Neil's eyes roll up to the ceiling. "A minute!" he yells before looking down at me again. "I figured since I was successful once, I'd see if I could make another dream come true. For both of us."

"Sorry!" I hear from outside, "He got away!"

I shift to look around Neil's body just in time to see a dark whimpering mass barrel toward us, almost knocking both of us over.

"Chaos…"

CHAPTER EIGHTEEN

Neil

It had taken me much longer than anticipated at the animal shelter. If it hadn't been for the sheriff who happened to walk in with a stray cat he picked up on his rounds, I may not have been able to take the dog home. Drew can be a charming bastard when he wants to be and in no time had the two older ladies manning the place, eating from his hand.

"You owe me." He smirked at me when he passed me on his way to his patrol car. Yeah, I do.

I don't think I could've given Kendra anything that would've had more impact. The tears running down her face when she dropped to her knees and hugged the big dog were happy ones.

Chaos. Weird name for probably the most docile dog I've ever met, but when one of the ladies told me he was retired from the DEA, it piqued my interest. He was sitting upright in the passenger seat of my truck, looking straight ahead, his tongue lolling, looking eager to get wherever I was taking him. I'd had to stop at Kendra's house to pick up the dog stuff she'd already bought for him. It was enough to tide him over for a day or two.

I'm lying on my back on the bed recapping the day in my head. Kendra is curled up against me while the dog is snoring on the floor beside me, and I'm wondering how the hell I'm going to get to the couch without waking everyone. Hadn't quite thought that through when I followed Kendra into the bedroom earlier. The rhythmic sounds of Kendra's breathing and the dog's snores are quickly lulling me to sleep.

"James, movement at two o'clock. What can you see?"

I can barely hear the voice of Fitz through my headpiece. He's down there somewhere trying to get the drop on a group of insurgents who've been targeting our supply transports the past two weeks. Yesterday's attack that killed a UN worker hitching a ride woke up the brass. As of last night, our objective is to find, identify and neutralize. It's a nice way of saying hunt them down and eliminate them. For some reason, this order gives me a sense of impending doom.

I'm lying on what remains of a roof after last night's bombing, peering through the sight on my rifle, scanning the area Fitz indicated. I don't see any movement there, but from the corner of my eye I see the glint off a rifle sticking out a blown out window to the left.

"Fitz," I hiss, but only the crackle of static comes back. "Jesus, Fitz. Ten o'clock sniper."

Suddenly the rubble littered street down below comes alive with gunfire. Four of my buddies are on the street below, carefully making their way from building to building, including Fitz. Dirt flies up, partially obscuring my view of the scene below and I focus on the window where the rifle I spotted earlier is laying heavy fire into the street. I slow my breathing down, reset my sight and wait for the right moment. The instant the barrel of the rifle reappears, I take my shot and watch as a body comes tumbling out the window. The fabric of the thawb he's wearing floating behind him like wings.

When I get down, I find only three of my guys standing. Fitz is down, the blood pooling around his body and half his face gone. The pain in my chest at seeing my best friend dead at my feet turns into a burning anger, and in long strides, I walk toward where the body had fallen from the window. I find him among a pile of rubble. He looks small, lying in a crumpled heap. In my anger, I kick his body over. A boy, no more than twelve years old, with a face innocent and still in death, stares up with unseeing eyes.

Wet. My face is wet, and an unfamiliar whining hits my ears. Cracking open my eyes against early morning sunlight sneaking in through the blinds, the first thing I see is the dog's nose just inches from mine on the mattress. He's the one whining, but as my hand comes up to stroke his big head, I can hear the staccato of his tail against the floor. *Shit.* I fell asleep. Slowly I turn the other way, hoping the dog or I didn't wake Kendra. No such luck. She's sitting cross-legged on the bed beside me, her eyes sad but her mouth smiling.

"Hey," she murmurs, her hand reaching out to brush the hair from my forehead.

"Hey back," I respond, my voice more of a croak.

I look at her, wondering what I've done to wake both her and the dog. Did I hurt her? As if I've wondered out loud, she leans in and gives me a soft kiss on the lips. "You didn't touch me." Her words are reassuring, but at the same time they concern me. How much does this woman see? How much have I given away?

"You know," she starts, leaning over me to pat Chaos on the head. "I'm thinking the dog has more qualities than he shows at first glance."

"How so?" I ask, folding my arms behind my head.

"It's his whining that woke me up. You were muttering in your sleep, obviously dreaming, and he was sitting beside you licking your face. I think he senses your distress."

Slightly uncomfortable, I pull myself up to sitting, patting the mattress beside me. Kendra crawls up and settles in against me, her hand on my stomach. A pathetic little whimper draws my attention back to the dog, whose tail hasn't stopped thumping the floor, looking at me eagerly. "Oh fine," I grumble. "Get up here you big lug." All it takes is one tap of my hand on the mattress, and the heavy dog jumps up, crawling over me and lying down between our legs, his head resting on my thigh. His warm brown eyes never leave my face.

Despite the nightmare that is forcing me to relive the one thing I'd love to forget, I feel content—even happy—in this moment. I let Kendra's hair, which is floating loose around her face, run through my fingers and consider telling her everything. Before I can even stop myself, the words are coming. Slowly at first, but soon tumbling out of my mouth, racing to the end. The end; where I shot and killed a boy no more than half my age. Just a child.

Kendra's hand flexes on my stomach but surprisingly she doesn't move. There's no exclamation of shock, nor are there platitudes, neither of which I would've handled very well. There's just the dog, his eyes full of adoration on me, and the softly crying woman warm against my side. And for the first time in the last eight years, my heart feels as light as a feather.

***

Kendra

"Want more coffee?"

Arlene walks up to the table lifting the thermos. We'd been late finally getting out of bed. After Neil's early morning nightmare and subsequent confession, we didn't say much. Not in words anyway. Mal had come to the door, and Neil was able to convince him to take Chaos for a brisk walk before relieving Joe outside. The moment he closed the door on Mal, he was back in bed, and we let our bodies do all the talking.

"Please." I smile at her, pushing the leftovers of my breakfast to the center of the table and handing her my mug. Neil is already shoveling my leftovers in his mouth and Arlene just shakes her head at him.

"Bottomless pit, that one," she observes as she pours the coffee. "Never known him to say no to any kind of food offered. Growing boys and all that." Neil doesn't react, but somehow the reference to him as *boy* doesn't sit well with me. Even though I called him that quite often, up until just over a month ago.

"Actually, I hardly think Neil can be considered a boy, Arlene." Perhaps it came out a little too sharp, because suddenly I feel both Arlene's and Neil's surprised eyes on me. Avoiding Neil, I focus instead on Arlene, trying to soften my earlier tone with a smile. Arlene smiles back, a calculating glint in her eyes.

"Glad to see your eyes open and alert this morning, honey," she says with a wink, before picking up the now empty plates and heading back to the kitchen.

"Me too," Neil agrees, keeping his voice low and reaching for my hand across the table. "Very glad. Thank you, Pup, for earlier and for coming to my defense now." His tone is soft but slightly teasing, and I simply shrug my shoulder in response. I figure he probably wouldn't feel comfortable discussing the first and I *know* I don't want to discuss the latter.

His eyes turn away from me, and when I turn in that direction, I see Mal standing in the doorway with a phone to his ear. His chin lift is almost imperceptible, but Neil seems to understand what it conveys, because he immediately stands, takes out his wallet and throws some bills on the table.

"We've gotta go," he says, pulling me up from my seat.

The guys exchange a few words that I can't quite distinguish since Arlene is yelling goodbye. Before I know it, I find myself hustled up the stairs with Neil in front and Mal behind me. Once inside the apartment, Neil immediately pulls out his phone while Mal stands beside the window, peering outside. Not quite sure what the hell is going on, I can feel the tension in the room is thick. I sink down on the couch, listening to Neil's side of a conversation.

"Where?" I hear him bite off to someone on the other side.

"What time was that?—And it took you 'til now to notify us? What the fuck, Drew? Have you contacted Gomez?—Well, thank God for that, at least. No, I don't want any more attention drawn here than necessary. We're fine here. You just find that bastard." With that, he ends the call, throws his phone on the counter and pulls at the hair on his head. *"Fuck. Son of a whore. Motherfucking idiots!"* His voice booms so loud in the small space that I'm sure the patrons downstairs in the diner can hear the curses flying out of his mouth. Poor Chaos, who was sleeping on his bed in the corner, crawls almost on his belly over the ground to sit beside Neil, leaning his big body against his legs.

"Chill," Mal admonishes from his spot by the window, and I just pull my knees up on the couch, silently freaking out. Things just got really scary and I have no clue why.

Some of what I'm thinking must've shown on my face, because Neil is beside me on the couch in a flash, Chaos close on his heels. The arm he puts around me is only partly reassuring, given the tension radiating off him. "What's happening?" I manage, a bit wobbly.

A meaningful look is exchanged between the two men, but before I have a chance to work up a head of steam over that, Neil explains, "Your neighbor across the street, the old lady, called the sheriff's office. She says she saw someone slip from between your house and the house next door, getting into a car she claims having seen before, early this morning. Says it looked like the same guy she saw sneaking on the porch last week. That and the car he got in this morning was the same one parked down the street last week."

He's here. He's watching my house. Fear crawls up my throat in the form of bitter bile and I struggle to keep my breakfast where it is. Suddenly, being cooped up in this apartment with Neil indefinitely doesn't seem like such a bad option.

Neil squeezes my shoulder, demanding my attention. "The deputy Drew who had been keeping an eye on the place, was called away on a domestic disturbance call close by. Apparently, he never got back to your house. Doesn't look like whoever was there tried to get in. The grass on the side of the house was trampled a bit but he could've been looking for exterior wiring for the alarm system. What it means, Pup," he says, now holding both my shoulders with his hands, "is that he's still around. He was close enough that if a half-decent law enforcement officer had been on the job, he might've been off the streets."

"Knowing he's close is not a bad thing," Mal points out. "It also means we can tighten the circle. Especially now that we have a description of what he's driving."

"I don't understand," I wonder out loud. "What does he want with me? I don't get this focus."

"You messed up his pattern. He's a psychopath who seems to be working from a script. From what we can tell, you were supposed to be the seventh in his cycle, but you slipped through his fingers," Mal answers me straight, and a cold realization comes over me.

"But he took an eighth woman, didn't he? Last week?" Neither Neil nor Mal look me in the eye and the stark truth of what this means settles in my bones. "She's dead, isn't she? That's why he's come back, because she's dead."

"We don't know that, Pup. We can't know that for sure," Neil mumbles as he hooks me behind my neck and pulls me to his chest.

The rest of the day I spend trying to read a book and watch some TV, while the guys spend most of their time keeping watch and talking on the phone. Gus and Joe both popped in and had muted conversations over the dining room table, which apparently has become security central. I'm pretty sure if I asked, they would tell me what is going on, but frankly, my head hurts from everything I already know. So instead of trying to listen in, I try not listening, often disappearing into the bedroom. Neil occasionally checks in with a touch or a kiss, a soft-spoken question from time to time, but I don't want to distract him from what he needs to do.

I've just cleared away the dishes of the simple stir-fry I threw together and fed Chaos, who's been happy with the attention lavished on him. Mal offered to get something from downstairs, but I wanted something to do. Pulling mugs down from the cupboard for the coffee that is almost done brewing, I almost drop them when I hear the distinct ring of my phone. Setting the mugs down, I scramble for my purse and the phone located somewhere in its dark depths.

"Hello?" I sound out of breath and a familiar snicker sounds on the other side.

"Please tell me I interrupted you schtumpfing the hot hunky guy Mom tells me you hooked up with." My sister giggles. "Now that would be a true reversal of roles, wouldn't it?"

"Karly... I... it's nothing like that. I just had to run to find my phone." I turn to Neil, who is observing me from his perch at the table, a smile slowly stretching over his face. In response, I roll my eyes and turn away from him. My sister—always getting me in embarrassing situations.

"Oh, you had to burst my bubble, didn't you? Well, wherever you are, you're not home, because I'm standing on the porch and there're no lights on anywhere."

"You're... Wait, what? My house? Karly, what are you doing at my house?" I can't hold back the panic in my voice and my sister doesn't miss it.

"What the blazes is going on, Kenny?" she demands as I feel Neil stepping up behind me. Mal already has his phone out and is furiously punching numbers.

"Honey, get in your car right away and find the diner. It's only three blocks west from where you are. Just head back out to the main road, and—" A rustling and the sound of something hitting a dull surface stops me mid-sentence.

"NO!" I hear Karly scream in the background before the phone goes dead.

"Neil..." I whisper, turning and holding out the dead phone in my hand.

He doesn't say anything but lifts me up in his arms, just as I feel my knees folding. With Mal leading the way, he runs down the stairs with me, as if I were weightless. Mal already has the diner's kitchen door open and hustles us inside. Seb looks up from the grill and takes in the three of us.

"Shit's going down. Right now, she's safer here in a crowd," Mal directs at Seb, who nods in apparent understanding. Part of my brain is trying to figure out how it is all these guys can communicate barely using any words, while the other part is still hearing my sister's scream.

Before I know it, I'm planted on a stool at the counter and Neil is leaning in to me. "I will find her," he says through gritted teeth.

"Please," I whimper, not able to stop the tears from rolling.

"I will fucking find her," he repeats before turning to Seb and pointing a finger at him. "With your life," he snarls.

"You've got it, brother," Seb calmly says as Arlene wraps her arms around me and we watch the two of them sprint outside. A second later, they tear out of the parking lot, tires squealing.

I'm not one to pray, but I'm praying now.

CHAPTER NINETEEN

Neil

"Gus is on his way. He's calling Gomez," Mal says as we peel away from the diner.

He's driving, so I have my hands free to make a call of my own and save some time.

"Drew," I say when he answers his phone. "Where the fuck is your detail on Kendra's house?"

"What do you mean? I put my best guy on it. I don't make mistakes twice," he says defensively.

"That right? Well just so you fucking know, Kendra just listened to her sister being attacked on her own fucking doorstep. Where was your best guy then, huh?"

"Fuck! Hang on," he shouts, and I can hear him put a call out on his radio. "No fucking response," he says when he gets back on the line. "I'm on my way."

The line goes dead just as a loud explosion rattles the car. *Jesus Christ.* "Hustle!" I yell at Mal, who's already flooring it.

"On it," is his gritted response.

The moment we round the corner onto Kendra's street, chaos hits us. Debris litters the street and people are running out of their houses, panicked and scared. We ditch the car and start hoofing it only vaguely registering the patrol car parked halfway down the street. The front of what was once Kendra's house is a jagged pile of rubble. The front porch and most of the front of the house is gone. The only recognizable feature is the stairway going up toward the bedrooms. I don't think, I run up the drive, avoiding large chunks of the house, and start pulling on debris where I think the front door might have been. Although with the blast, anyone standing there would've been blown to pieces. *Jesus.* The scene is eerily familiar to ones from a time in my life I have no wish to revisit, but I can't stop the shaking that takes over my body. Nevertheless, I forge on, surprised to find Gus coming up beside me, helping to pull the rubble out of the way.

"Is she under here?" he questions as he helps me pull a large chunk of roof out of the way.

"I don't know, man, I don't know."

We don't stop working, not when Joe, Mal and some of the neighbors join us on either side. After what feels like hours, but was likely only minutes, we finally hear sirens in the distance. Gus steps back. "Fire and rescue are here, boys. Let them do their job." His voice sounds as dejected as I feel, and from the look on the other guys' faces, they are no more optimistic. Either he has her, or she was killed in the explosion, and I don't know which would be the better outcome for her.

Kendra. I know the phone ringing in my pocket is her, or possibly Seb. They surely heard the explosion. What do I tell her? Leaving Gus to explain things to the first responders, I walk away to find a quieter spot to take the call. The diner's number shows up on the screen.

"Seb?" I'm guessing.

"He's okay," I hear him shout out. "Brother. We've been going nuts here since that explosion. Good to hear your voice." His relief is evident. Then he continues on an almost whisper. "Don't know what happened, but we've had to almost physically restrain your girl from flying out the door. Better talk to her."

"Put her on."

There's the sound of movement and some rustling before I hear her panicked voice. "Neil? Oh God. What was that? Are you hurt? Did you find Karly? Where are you?"

The barrage of questions pierces my chest. I don't want to do this over the phone. "Pup." I get her attention in as calm a tone as I can manage. "I haven't found your sister yet, and I didn't get hurt, but there's some damage to your house." That's got to be the understatement of the century, but first concern is Karly.

"The explosion? It was an explosion we heard, right? I'm coming right now." The thought of her leaving the relative safety of the diner when we have no fucking clue what's going on has my hair stand on end.

"No. Baby, listen to me; this is the last place you should be, there is confusion, panic, people from the area milling about. It's not safe. Please stay where you are," I plead with her.

"But Karly—"

"Listen to me. That's exactly why you should stay there. We have to focus on finding your sister and the best way to help us do that is to stay safe." It breaks my heart hearing her cry on the other end of the line.

"Please tell me she wasn't in the house…"

She's killing me. I have to swallow down hard before I can reply. "Kendra, baby, we've looked, but nothing we found indicates she was there. We'll keep looking, I promise. Now can you put Seb back on the line?"

"Okay…"

"Love you, Pup."

"Yeah…" I don't know if she heard me because next thing I know Seb's on the line. I don't know if it was the right thing to say, but I needed to say it.

"…is about empty."

I just pick up the last of what Seb said so I ask him to repeat.

"I said, after the explosion, most of the crowd ran outside and the place is about empty. I'm keeping the girls close to me in the kitchen."

"Sounds good. I better go," I tell him, as I watch Kendra's neighbor, the white-haired nosey neighbor, wave to me from her front yard. Ending the call, I walk across the street.

"I saw him," she says when I'm near her. "Didn't have the same car, though. That's why it took me a while, but I know it was him. Tossed that girl in the back of the truck and took off. I was just about to call for help when the house blew up."

"Did you get the make and color of the truck?" I snap impatiently, earning me a huff.

"Well now, it looked like it might be an older one, beige looking. But it could've just been dirty white. I don't know much about brands. They're all big noise makers to me. But I did notice a trailer hitch when I was memorizing the license plate." I could rattle the old woman when she smirks at me.

"You have the number?"

"Yes, that's what I was trying to tell you. Reason I was taking a moment before calling 911 was because I wanted to make sure"—she shows me a piece of paper before continuing—"I wrote down the number before I for—Hey!" she yells after me as I snatch the paper from her hand and take off, running to where my team is standing.

"He's got at least a fifteen-minute head start," I call out when I get close. "Older truck, no known make, beige or white in color. I've got the plate." Gus takes the paper from my hand and starts dialing, just as Damian and Luna jog up from down the street.

"Hey, you know you've got an unconscious cop in that patrol car back there?" he says rather casually. I'd forgotten about the patrol car. "He's breathing, just has a sizable gash on his head. Fire department's EMT is looking him over now." His eyes focus on Gus. "What've we got?"

Gus calmly explains the sequence of events before handing over the scribbled license plate number. Damian immediately passes it off to Luna, who steps away with her phone in hand.

"Assuming he has Karly, they've got about a twenty-minute lead, at least, by now," I point out impatiently. An eerily familiar feeling of doom weighs heavy on my heart and I force myself to focus. Mal shoots me an understanding glance. The all too observant bastard probably noticed the lingering tremors in my hands. I tuck them deep into my pockets, away from prying eyes before turning my attention back to Damian.

"We alerted the state patrol. They're setting up roadblocks north and south of Cortez on the 491 at the junction with the 160. Another one…" I walk away as my phone starts to vibrate in my pocket and don't hear the last bit. A quick glance shows me the diner's number again.

"Yeah?"

"It's Kendra," I hear Arlene's voice. "Seb's taken off after her."

"What happened?" I quickly walk back to the huddle, set the call to speakerphone and hold up my hand to silence everyone.

"I don't know. She was upset after talking to you and went to the restrooms. I followed her in, but she said she wanted to be alone, so I left her. Next thing I know, I'm cleaning off tables, look outside and see her running across the parking lot. I yelled for Seb who took off after her. I'm sorry, I didn't hear a thing."

No. My heart is pounding so hard, I swear it's going to explode in my chest. Gus is the first one to speak up as he takes the phone from my shaking hand and starts talking to Arlene. "You stay right there, girl. Any patrons left?"

"Julie's still here and just two booths. The rest are gone." If I wasn't numbed with fear, I'd probably be shocked to hear Arlene crying. It's not something you see every day.

"Buck up, Arlene. I need you to lock the doors. Explain to whoever is there that there's a massive manhunt underway outside and that they should stay put until law enforcement clears you. They give you trouble, let me know right away. We can't have them get in the way. Help is coming, honey. Hang tough." He ends the call and immediately starts dialing again.

"Caleb, I need you at the diner ASAP. Make sure Katie locks up tight behind you. We've got a serious situation here."

The diner. Without thinking, my feet start moving in that general direction, no thought other than the need to get Kendra on my mind. A firm hand on my shoulder pulls me to a stop.

"Stop. Think." Gus's voice barely penetrates, but it seems to be stuck on repeat in my head as I accept my phone back. Mal steps up on the other side of me. I hear more sirens approaching and detachedly watch as Drew's duty vehicle pulls in behind the fire truck. Not in any shape to deal with him, I turn my back and face my teammates.

"What?" I force out through my tightly held control.

"Let Mal take you to the diner. We're setting up shop there. Grab your computer, get Jasper on the line. Let me sort things out here and I'll bring the feds over there. Anything happens on either end—notify immediately. Got it?" I nod once. "I'll text you the license plate number in a minute. You know what to do."

Mal claps his hand and on my shoulder and steers me to his car. The moment I sit down, my phone buzzes in my pocket again and I scramble to fish it out. A message reminder. I must've missed it earlier. It's from Kendra's phone.

My finger hovers over the screen hesitantly for a minute before sliding it across, and my breath hitches in my throat.

Kendra: Sorry xox

Kendra

"Please, just give me a minute," I plead with Arlene as she follows me into the bathroom.

"I'm right out here if you need me," she says as she pulls the door shut behind her.

I pull my phone out of my pocket, sit on the toilet seat and check the message again that had just come in while Arlene was cashing someone out. I'd been so eager when I saw it was from Karly…until I saw the message. I need to think.

> ***Karly:*** 5 minutes. SW corner parking lot. Crossroad. Hide in brush. White F150 westbound.
>
> Get in back, cover with tarp. ALONE or first cut will be your sister's face.

The second time reading it has more impact than the first, and I have a hard time getting my head around the instructions— my entire focus is on his last line. Karly. My wild, crazy, bighearted little sister. I drop my head between my knees when the room starts fading out. I can't pass out now. Making sure I breathe in and out in a deep, steady rhythm, the panic slowly eases. Then another alert sounds on my phone, and this time, it's an image of my sister, curled up under the dashboard on the floorboard of a truck. Her eyes are closed, and I gasp when I see a trickle of blood at her hairline.

I have to get out of here. Looking up at the tiny window, I dismiss it outright. Even if I could get my ass up there, I would run the risk of getting stuck. No. Out the front door, it'll have to be. I tuck my phone in my pocket with the sound turned off, after typing out a quick message to Neil. I don't want to give up my only connection with him. Then I get up, pull on the door, which *thank God,* doesn't make any noise and peek out. Arlene is wiping down tables, and there are only two booths full at the back. I can't see Seb or the other waitress. I wait until I see Arlene turn her back to me completely when she turns her attention to the next table against the far window.

Now, now, now. I slip through the door and move as fast and as quiet as I can toward the front where I push the door open and start running. Thank God my legs are in decent shape. If only I can get to the shelter of the trees here before someone…

"KENDRA!"

I hear Seb yelling just as I break through the tree line and head onto the road. I hope he hasn't seen me. With no traffic coming, I fly across to the other side and duck down behind some bushes. I can still hear Seb calling my name. Then I hear an engine start and within seconds, Seb's truck pulls onto the road. And stops.

I hold my breath waiting to see which way he'll turn and let it all out when I see him swinging right. Toward town.

Only moments later, I can see a dirty, old, light-colored pick-up truck coming from the direction Seb just disappeared in. My body seizes up in fear and I squeeze my eyes shut.

Oh God, Karly, I don't know if I can.

The crunch of tires on the gravel shoulder is loud in my ears. I take in a few deep breaths and look up. Even though I'm still ducked down, the figure in the cab of the truck seems to be looking straight at me. His body is shadowed, but then he leans toward the passenger side and slowly extends his arm through the open window, crooking his finger at me torturously slow before cocking his thumb to the truck bed.

Even at this distance I can clearly hear his voice. "Get under the tarp."

Karly is in there with him.

I'm instantly on my feet and run toward the back of the truck, climb in the bed and pull the bright blue tarp over myself, exactly as he said. I can feel the truck pulling away just as there's the sound of another car passing toward town. We are driving the opposite way, and I'm scared. There's little that way… A few places here and there along the county road but no towns, no city limits. No safety. Just the Ute reservation on one side and the Canyons of the Ancients on the other, with the Utah border looming beyond.

My hands restlessly explore the surface I'm lying on while trying to force my mind away from the panicked paralysis it wants to give in to. I will myself to breathe deeply through the nauseatingly sweet smell of rot and decay under the tarp. *Don't think about what was under here before.* I brush against something sharp, and I tentatively explore it with my fingertips. A sliver of wood, about the size of my palm. With shaking fingers I manage to slip it up the sleeve of my shirt and thank God for not wearing one of my regular T-shirts or tanks today. Not sure what I can accomplish with it, but feeling the rough texture against the inside of my forearm gives me a sense of control. It's better than nothing. Still, my hands keep roaming the surface, but unfortunately, there's nothing else but dirt.

The temptation to pull my phone out and call Neil is almost unbearable, but I know if I do, I will be putting Karly in danger. I need to get her safe first.

I can feel the surface we are driving on changing as the truck makes a left turn. Where before it was a relatively smooth ride, I'm now being bounced around in the back. A dirt road more than likely, or a trail. I can't be sure and I'm too afraid to move, so I just brace myself the best I can. When the truck finally slows down, my breathing becomes erratic again as panic grabs hold of me. A door slams and I hear the dull thud of footsteps coming around the truck. My fingers close protectively around the sleeve of my shirt, feeling the outline of the wood. I scream when a hand closes around my ankle and yanks me clear from the back of the truck. Landing hard on the packed ground, I get the air knocked out of me. The instant I manage to suck in a breath, I start scrambling backward to get away from the large man looming over me. A large boot comes down on my ankle, pinning me down, and slowly he leans his weight on it. I scream when the pain becomes excruciating, but it only brings a smile to his face. Grinning, he lifts all the weight off his other foot and the sound of a loud snap breaks my bones. The contents of my stomach spew out of my screaming mouth.

My world fades into gray and just as I'm about to give in, I hear someone yell.

"Stop! Stop it! Let her go!" My sister comes hobbling around the side of the truck, with what looks to be a flashlight in her hands, waving it around. The man chuckles as he lifts his foot off my ankle, causing a fresh surge of pain. Barely able to focus on the figure of my sister, I try to warn her away.

"Go…" My voice is barely audible. "Go…run!" I try again, this time a little louder. Harsh hands yank me off the ground and on my feet. But the pressure on my ankle has me scream out in pain. A large arm folds around my neck in a chokehold and his laugh in my ear sounds almost maniacal. With my air supply nearly cut off, I force myself to focus on Karly, who is swaying from side to side in front of us. Her eyes are wild, almost disoriented. "Karly," I try, my voice now faint and hoarse. Still, she hears me and locks her eyes with mine. "*Run,*" I mouth and simultaneously I twist in his hold, swinging my arm at his head and feel the wood sliver I slipped into my hand sink deep.

His hands cover his face as he howls in pain. Now free, I turn to run but my ankle collapses under my weight and drops me to the ground.

This time the pain is too much, and the last thing I see before my world turns dark is my sister running into the trees.

CHAPTER TWENTY

Neil

"Anything?" I ask Arlene, who's standing just inside the diner's front door.

She shakes her head, her eyes red rimmed, and my stomach does another lurch. Mal walks in behind me after pulling the car into a parking spot. I'd jumped out while we were still rolling. I'd been trying Kendra's phone continuously on the way, but there was no answer. Either she doesn't have it with her or she's not in a position where she can pick up. Neither answer is good.

Looking around the diner, I spot Caleb coming out of the kitchen. He must've just arrived before us. There are only two tables occupied: one by a young family I've seen around from time to time, and the other by two of the older regulars. One of Arlene's waitresses Julie is busy refilling cups.

"Seb take his phone?" Mal asks Arlene, and I turn around just in time to see her shake her head again. *Dammit.*

"I tried calling but heard it ring in the kitchen. He just ran out yelling for Kendra and then hopped in his truck and peeled out of here." Her voice wobbles a little when she turns to me. "I'm so sorry. I didn't think she—"

"Not your fault. Don't even go there," I cut her off. And it isn't her fault. It's mine. I promised her nothing would happen to her. I left her behind when I should never have left her side. That's on me, not on anyone else. I try not to think about the fact that based on the time she left me her last text, she's been gone close to forty-five minutes.

"Did she leave her phone? Kendra?"

"I don't know," Arlene says, starting to move toward the restroom. Caleb walks up and puts his arm around Arlene.

"I already checked," he says. "Nothing."

"What direction did you see her go?" I ask, and Arlene points to the west side of the parking lot. I immediately head outside in that direction. I go as far as the road, scanning the ground as I walk, but can't find a trace. Not surprising, since this side of the parking lot is poorly lit, and the night is clouded, so I don't even have the faint moonlight for help.

By the time I turn back to the diner, Gus's Yukon is pulling in with Joe right behind him. Inside, four tables have been pulled together, and Mal comes in from the kitchen with my laptop. *Fuck yes.* I'm going to go nuts if I can't do something. I don't say anything, just sit down at the table and boot up. I barely notice chairs scraping as some of the others sit down around me, talking to each other or on the phone.

"Seb!" I hear Arlene shouting out and I look up to see him walking in, his face grim. His eyes find mine as Arlene throws her arms around his neck. He doesn't have to say it, I already know.

"Fuck, brother," he says as he walks over to where we're sitting. "She was there one minute and gone the next. Didn't see anything on the road either. It's a ghost town."

"Yeah, that's because half the population is at the site of the explosion," Joe points out.

"Only damn truck on the road was that old rust bucket Bill Krutcher drives," Seb says scratching his head, referring to one of the local farmers. "Must be pissed or something, because he didn't honk his damn horn the way he usually does."

I turn my eyes back to the computer and pull up a the software that's supposed to track the app I installed on Kendra's phone a while back, but I'm not getting a signal.

"What are you looking at?" Gus asks, leaning over my shoulder.

"Kendra's tracker. It's not working."

"I thought you said those things work even if the phone is switched off?"

"They do," I slam the lid of the laptop shut. "Unless someone takes out the battery entirely. *Son of a motherfucking bitch!*" Swinging around I clear the table behind me with one swipe of my arm, sending condiments, cutlery and napkins flying.

The diner is dead silent, or at least I thought it was, until I hear a child crying. My eyes flick to the two tables at the far end, where the young mother is cradling her scared little boy in her lap while her husband shoots daggers in my direction. The door opens and Damian walks in, Luna in tow. "Drew's right behind us," he announces sardonically, taking in the puddle of ketchup at my feet. Arlene bends down and starts wiping the mess off the floor, but I immediately pull her up by her arm.

"I'll do it."

Without argument she hands over the rag. The time it takes me to clean up my mess is enough to get control of my frustration, and after handing the dirty rag back to Arlene, who awards me with a small smile, I prepare to eat crow.

The father is still glaring at me when I approach, but I try to focus on the little boy, no more than maybe three or four, still cowering against his mom's shoulder. "Hey buddy," I start tentatively before dropping down on my haunches so I am at eye level with him. "I'm really sorry I yelled and got mad. I didn't mean to scare you." When the kid still doesn't show his face, I stand up and face his parents. "I'm sorry. I..." I stop there, shake my head and turn around. I have a woman to find.

I walk back just in time to hear Damian instruct Luna to see the remaining patrons home. Joe offers his help. They no sooner leave and Drew's SUV pulls up.

"What've we got?" he says as he comes in, directing his question at Damian.

"Not much. Seb went after her, but was too late. Only thing he saw was some old geezer in a truck."

"Who was it?" Drew wants to know.

"Bill Krutcher," Seb answers. "Well at least it looked like it, but he didn't honk like he usually does."

Drew goes rigid when he hears Bill's name. "Krutcher reported his truck stolen earlier today. He said he was sure it was those Vandenbeek kids down the road. I was on my way there when the call went out over the radio about the explosion." His mouth snaps shut and immediately gets on his radio, barking orders. The rest of us suddenly become a flurry of activity.

Gus points out the truck was heading west, toward the Utah border. Damian is barking in his phone to make sure the trooper stationed at the state border was in place and I'm already scanning Google maps for close up satellite images of any abandoned structures along County Road G.

"Mal, grab my printer upstairs," I yell out over the diner. There are a few turn offs between here and the state border and I want to document them all. Within minutes, Mal is hooking up my printer on the table. I take screen shots of every lonely structure I can find and print several copies off.

"I'm going," I announce as I see Drew and Damian head for the door, my printouts in hand. There's no fucking way in hell I'm going to hang around here and wait while Kendra is out there somewhere. Been out there for well over an hour and a half. I'm already moving to the door with my own set of copies, when I hear Gus behind me. "Mal, go with him. Take the Yukon, just in case." I hear the clang of keys and Mal catches up with me by the door. The Yukon is parked right out front. I know why Gus suggests the Yukon. The seats in the back can fold down. He wants to make sure we can accommodate anyone who might be injured and needs quick transportation. I can't even go there.

"We'll find her," Mal says quietly as we pull out.

"I'm gonna rip him in two if he's hurt her, Mal." My voice cracks. "I love her."

I feel Mal's hand squeeze my neck as I try to get ahold of my emotions. "I know, buddy. I know."

Up ahead, Drew's Durango turns right, into the first cut off. We keep going, following Damian, who takes the next exit we see. Mal continues on to the next one, a narrow dirt road off to the north that, according to my map, has what looks to be an old barn or shed at the end. Just as we pull up to the building, my phone buzzes in my pocket. It's Drew.

"Yeah."

"Nothing here. Did you guys grab the third exit?"

"Checking it out right now."

"I'm taking the next."

Mal slowly drives the Yukon towards the dilapidated wooden structure. Probably once a barn, but now nothing more than a stone foundation and a collapsed frame. Still, we get out of the car, armed with Gus's giant Maglite to take a closer look. It doesn't take long to figure out nothing or no one is here. Doesn't even look like anyone's been on this trail in recent days. Only our tracks are visible.

We're almost back to the car when my phone goes off once more. Drew again. "Get down here." Is all he says before hanging up.

"Next exit. Drew's got something," I yell at Mal as I run the last few steps to the truck. Mal's ass barely hits the seat and we're turning a donut on the loose dirt, leaving billowing clouds of dust behind us as we barrel toward the road. I manage to shoot a quick message to Damian who ends up right behind us on the road.

Drew's duty vehicle is just off to the side of a small clearing on the side of an old dead end dirt road that cuts south of the county road, about six miles west of town. It crosses over McElmo's Creek before suddenly stopping. The only things there are some old storage sheds that were once used by Sutcliffe Vineyards north of here to store their equipment. They've long since built a large storage barn north of the road.

Mal pulls the Yukon in behind Drew's wheels and we quietly get out and walk to where Drew is shining a flashlight on the ground.

"Cell phone. Crushed," he says in a soft voice.

It's Kendra's, the remnants of the shiny red case as unique as its owner.

Kendra

The first thing I notice is the smell.

It's earthy, like wet soil and compost, but there's a faint trace of yeast too. Just a hint, but enough to tingle the inside of my nose. The second thing, immediately following, is a hot pain radiating up my leg. It's like something is chewing on my ankle.

I crack open my eyes, but I can't see much of my surroundings, it's too dark. It isn't until I try to move my head that I notice the rough texture against my skin. And when I try to move my hand, I realize I'm tied facedown on something. Something curved and rough against my skin. I'm buck naked.

I can't hold back the whimper that stays trapped behind the duct tape I can feel pulling across my mouth. Struggling against the ropes around my ankles and my wrists only causes pain and I soon stop, recognizing the futility of fighting. With tears running down my face, and snot clotting my nostrils, I gasp for breath, managing only to make myself lightheaded.

Karly. Did she manage to get away? I remember seeing her disappear into the trees, but I have no recollection of what happened after. I stabbed him. Didn't I? I can't think straight, my head is so fuzzy. And Neil. Oh my God, Neil. I should've said it back. I had one chance, and I blew it. I don't think I'll survive this.

Pain and the gentle touch of fingers along my back wake me up. And I blink my eyes against a soft glow around me. Candles. No longer completely dark. For a moment, I think I may have been dreaming earlier, but then I feel a searing hot pain right along my spine and a scream crawls up my throat with nowhere to go. I try to roll my body away, but all that does is pull on my restraints. I stop fighting when I feel hot breath against my ear.

"1 Cor. 11:7. Woman is the Glory of man. For the man is not of the woman; but the woman of the man. Neither was the man created for the woman; but the woman for the man."

I can't make heads or tails of what he's whispering, over and over again. Corinthians, he said, so a Bible verse, but the words all blend together as he slices my back again and a fresh wave of agony washes over me. I can hardly produce a sound when my mouth opens in a scream. This is hell.

My eyes focus on the licking flames of the candles as I welcome the dark slowly edging in.

Cold water washes over my head and my back and a low chuckle greets my sharp intake of breath.

"Raphael. My travel guardian. My healing God. My angel of mercy." Each reverently whispered statement is followed by a new splash of water, that feel oddly soothing on my burning body. The pain is hot, searing, and so overwhelming, I can't even feel the source.

"The Lord's holy angel, said he, go with you on your journey and bring you home without scathe…"

I scream when a fresh piercing pain slices my back. I can no longer make out the words he mumbles, one simply drifting into the next as I welcome the darkness closing in on me.

The last thing I feel are his lips brushing the shell of my ear as he whispers to me. "You. It was you all along. My trial…my ultimate test. You will be the crown on my work. My masterpiece. My victory. My perfection."

CHAPTER TWENTY-ONE

Neil

Mal is already walking up the road a bit farther, shining his light down. He and Caleb are both excellent trackers. Thinking of Caleb, I send him a quick text. Figure two are better than one.

Drew and Damian are both talking on their phones, calling in reinforcements, I guess. I just stand there. Breathing in and out, trying desperately to connect with Kendra somehow while hanging on to my sanity. Every minute she is in that depraved cocksucker's hands is one too many. I close my eyes for a moment, praying to God or Allah or the Great Spirit—fuck, to whoever the hell will listen—that my Pup is still alive.

"Tracks," Mal says in a low voice as he joins us. "Tracks continue up."

"All right," Damian says, taking charge. "You and Neil…"

He doesn't get a chance to finish his instructions because from the edge of the woods, on the far side of the clearing, a figure tentatively approaches.

"Kendra?"

My feet are moving before my brain is fully engaged, and before I know it, I'm running at the woman who has stopped in her tracks, shielding her head with her arms. Not Kendra. Her sister. Realizing my mistake, since the woman doesn't know me from Adam, I instantly slow down my pace and call her by name.

"Karly?"

Slowly her arms fall away to her sides and through a curtain of tangled hair, she eyes me with trepidation.

"My name is Neil. Has Kendra mentioned me?" I ask her in as soft a voice as I can manage. She nods her head, wiping impatiently at her hair and in doing so, reveals her face, which is bloodied.

"He's got her," she whispers, and I tentatively take a step closer when she suddenly reaches out and grabs my shirt. "He hurt her. She attacked him, told me to run and he hurt her. I was running away when I heard her scream. I was running away..." Her words are stringed together as if she has to force them out before she collapses, keening in my arms.

"I'll find her. I promise I'll find her," I say over the top of her head.

I recognize the irony, since no more than maybe two hours before, I had told Kendra the exact same thing about the trembling woman in my arms. I should never have left her.

A heavy hand falls on my shoulder. "Let me have a look at her," Mal says from behind me. "Karly? Can you look at me, honey?" When she lifts her head, I carefully let go of her and leave her in Mal's capable hands. Drew is already on the phone calling in an ambulance but tells them to head to the diner.

"What did she say?" Damian asks, looking past me at the girl.

"Kendra's injured. I didn't get much more out of her. I have to find her." I try to move past Damian toward the tracks that lead up the hill, but he grabs my arm.

"We've got to be smart, Neil. Plan this thing. You run in there and we'll lose the element of surprise."

I pull against his hold, but it's firm. He doesn't budge. *"Kendra is hurt!"* I hiss at him, beyond reason now.

Headlights coming up the road illuminate the clearing. The cavalry has arrived.

With Karly loaded in Drew's unit and on her way to the diner where hopefully he'll be able to get some more information from her, Damian outlines our plan of action. I have a hard time concentrating because my entire being wants to run up that trail and yell her name at the top of my lungs. Years of military training is the only thing holding me back. I *know* Kendra's best chance is us going in prepared, but I can feel every fucking second that ticks away. And she's been at this guy's mercy for over two hours now. Two hours for him to… I can't even allow myself to think it.

Joe and Gus arrived with Caleb, who apparently made a run to the GFI office at some point, because the back of his truck is stuffed with any tactical equipment or firepower we might need. It might be a while yet before other reinforcements arrive, but Damian doesn't want to wait. Caleb and Mal, both outfitted with radio earpieces and weapons are to go ahead and scout for the location of the truck. Joe and I, along with Damian, will follow them at a distance, while Gus stays behind and takes care of communication.

We're only a few minutes up the trail when my earpiece crackles to life and Caleb comes through, keeping his voice low. "Found the truck. Up ahead the trail splits, truck is just over the rise on the left side of the fork. Following boot prints heading through the trees to the path on the other side of the split."

We move on opposite sides of the track, just inside the tree line. When we get to the split, I can see the other two going left, but on Damian's instruction, I continue along the path on the right side. My breathing slows down as I find myself slipping into focus. Pushing panic far down, I focus on the assignment.

"On your two," Mal whispers in my ear and my eyes immediately turn in that direction. It's damn near pitch black out here under the trees, so the double blink of a penlight to the right, just up ahead, is easy to spot. With Mal's location marked, I look farther ahead and see an old building up ahead. Not too big, maybe the size of a two-car garage. Made of old wood planks, it looks like it's on its last legs, the roof starting to drop on one side. When I crouch down beside Mal, I notice faint light coming from between the boards.

"Caleb went around, checking for entrance and exit points." He keeps his voice so low. All I pick up are the consonants, but it's enough for me to get the message.

I scan what is visible of the structure from our vantage point. There are no windows, just a door that seems to be hanging off its hinges. I'm working out the right approach when the sound of soft chanting drifts my way. My eyes find Mal's in the dark, who lifts his index finger to his lips. *Prayer,* he mouths. Seconds later, a soul-shattering scream pierces the night sky and stops my heart dead in my chest. *Kendra.*

Blood roaring in my ears and red filtering my vision, I'm up and running full speed with every next scream cutting into my soul. I don't register any sound or see anything other than the door, behind which my heart is suffering. Another scream. I don't stop. I plow down the door and zoom in on the scene before me.

Kendra

I want to die.

I'm already in hell. It can't be any worse than this.

The one thought I hold on to is the hope that Karly managed to make it to safety. Any thought of Neil hurts and carries sharp regret. Regret that I wasted years pushing away this unbelievable man who has made me soar from the moment he forced his way into my life. Treasured, protected, cared for and loved. *My God.* He makes me feel loved. There isn't a doubt in my mind about the way he feels for me. Time gone I can never get back. I could've had a head start on happiness but was too much of a coward—too scared.

It's the chanting that first penetrates my awareness. Low, melodic and completely indecipherable. Next is a hand, trailing my body all the way around, from my toes up the side of my leg, along my ribs and down to my stretched out arm, only to return on the other side of me doing the same in reverse. I try to hold my breath, to feign sleep, but I know he's aware I'm awake. He likes it to hurt when I can feel it. "Not long now," he whispers. "Soon I'll bring you to sun dance as well."

I barely listen to his ramblings. My body is one burning, throbbing mess and I don't know how much more I can withstand. A vague hope of Neil finding me still lingers until he suddenly rips the tape from my mouth.

"Sing, my angel."

I feel the almost familiar pain of the knife piercing my back, and I can't hold back the involuntary screams that burst free. Once again, I'm grateful to feel myself slipping into oblivion against the backdrop of his eerie mumbles. But when I feel his body lean over mine, chest rubbing against the open wounds on my back and his hips pressing between my spread legs, I scream again.

Neil

Candles everywhere. Sitting on the old wine barrels that haphazardly fill the space. The dark shape of a man leaning down over one of them. And skin. The brief flash of an expanse of bared skin beneath him. Blind with something animalistic, I pull the man off, and give myself over to the darkest rage. My focus narrows like a pinpoint on the sick fuck in my hands. His face is not just one, it is many. A target for impotent fury directed at an invisible enemy responsible for brothers fallen in battle. The center of my anger for the poor innocent women who've fallen victim. My fists pummel into his face for the light he has taken from Kendra and for the lifetime I will spend attempting to give it back to her. I'm no longer aware of anything but my boiling blood and the pounding of my fists.

"Enough," a voice growls in my ear as two pairs of hands pull me back. My vision is blurred by the tears I find tracking down my face. It takes me a second to recognize that the bloody pulp I'm looking at was once a man. "We'll take care of him. You take care of her." I now recognize the voice to be Caleb's and immediately turn to find Kendra. Her naked body, bloodied and spread facedown over one of the barrels, sears itself in my brain. Pulling my arms free, I'm by her side in three strides, the knife from my boot in hand, sawing at the ropes restraining her.

"Pup." My voice cracks as I cut the final rope and see her fingers move. My relief at the sign of life is overwhelming. "I'm here. Baby, I'm here." I mumble incoherent words at her as I finally get a good look at her condition. The skin on her wrists is scraped open and she's bleeding. Her right foot sticks out at an odd angle, bone showing through the skin. But the most devastating are the deep grooves carved along her spine, from her neck to the curve of her bottom. Shallow cuts, in the shape of feathers, go up the left side of her back, reaching almost to her shoulder blades. Behind me, I hear a sharp intake of breath followed by a furious curse.

I reach for her, wanting to lift her in my arms when Mal holds me back. "Don't move her, brother. Leave her as she is until the ambulance gets here. Just talk to her, let her hear you."

I sink down on my knees by her head, vaguely registering Caleb pulling his shirt over his head and covering as much of her as he can without touching her back. Her face is swollen and wet from crying and her eyes stare almost unseeingly in mine. Gently, I stroke the hair away from her face, murmuring nonsensical words of comfort in her ear.

Not sure how long I've sat here, while around us more reinforcements arrive, the low curses audible as they see Kendra. I don't care. I only care about the woman whose eyes are focused on mine.

Focused but still completely unreadable.

"Buddy, wake up."

I lift my leaden eyelids to find Gus hovering over me. I'm a little disoriented when my eyes scan my surroundings and I find just familiar faces staring back at me. Seb and Arlene, Mal, Joe and Emma. Naomi is standing right behind Gus, her hand on his shoulder.

"She's out of surgery," Naomi says. "She's going to be all right."

The last hours start coming back to me and I can't stop the full body shiver at the memory. *Fuck.* The blank look in her eyes will haunt me 'til the day I die.

The sirens, the ambulance-ride. I almost decked one of the EMTs when he tried to stop me from getting into the ambulance with her. Luckily, Gus was there to intervene. They hadn't been able to pry me from her side, not even when they tended to her upon our arrival in the emergency department. Those eyes stayed open, just staring at mine, and there was no way I was going to let go of that connection, albeit a thin one. Even through the prodding and prying to her ankle and her back, those eyes barely flinched. The memory almost makes me want to go back and beat the guy to shit. Again.

Then they took her in for surgery, saying she had an open fracture that required immediate cleaning and repair. That was hours ago, before I was forced to watch her eyes disappear through the automatic doors leading to the OR. And the adrenaline I'd been doped up on earlier left a hangover of intense fatigue. Bone-tired. So wrung out that I hadn't even protested when a nurse led me into a waiting room I'd become all too familiar with over the past few years. That's where I must've crashed. Until now.

I can't believe I slept through all these people arriving, but here they are. Looking back at Naomi, I see her eyes are red rimmed. Kendra is her friend, her colleague. "Where is she?" I ask, finding my voice rough.

"I couldn't get into the OR, surgery had already started, but I waited right outside the door and walked with her as they brought her to recovery. They had to place a few pins in her ankle—the damage was quite extensive. Her back—" Naomi's voice hitches. "They did the best they could on her back, but she'll carry the scars for life."

I don't know when the tears started rolling down my face, but Gus surreptitiously slips a tissue in my hands. I stare at it for a moment before lifting it to my face. "I want to see her," I tell Naomi as I wipe at my eyes. "I *need* to see her."

Naomi takes a seat beside me. "And you will, just as soon as she wakes up."

"Jasper is picking up Elsa and driving her down. They'll be here any minute," Gus says, taking over. "Kendra's sister is on the other side of the hall."

Karly, I'd forgotten about her. "How is she doing?" I ask with no small measure of guilt.

"They stitched her up and are holding her at least overnight for observation. Damian is in there questioning her now."

My eyes snap up at this bit of news. "Now? Can't it wait?" I surprise myself with the snap in my voice. Guess my instincts to protect Kendra automatically include her sister.

"Easy, Neil. She wanted to talk to someone. She was en route to the hospital already when the second ambulance was called out. Arlene rode with her, and she and Emma have been looking after her. She's aware her sister is here and offered to speak to law enforcement. Drew is handling things at the scene and Damian got here as soon as he could get away." Gus finally gets up and pats me on the back. "She's in good hands. Damian will be gentle with her."

For some reason, that makes me think of the poor dog who has been locked up in my apartment the entire night. "Chaos," I blurt out, drawing some curious looks, but Seb answers right away.

"Mal called. Suggested we bring him to his house. Poor dog was about to explode. I swear I had no idea a dog's bladder could hold that much," he says with a chuckle. "He must've pissed for a straight five minutes before he'd let us load him into the truck. Boo gave him a good sniff down and apparently approved because when we left Kim, the two were playing tug of war. By the way, I think you'll have a hard time getting Kim to give him back to you. She looked like she was in love." Seb chuckles again as Mal rolls his eyes heavenward. Boo is Kim's

Great Dane and although a bit bigger, is as much of a lug as Chaos seems to be.

"He's Kendra's," I clarify. "I'm thinking she's gonna need him." My words instantly weigh down the room.

"Dr. Waters?" A nurse stands in the doorway, looking at Naomi. "You asked me to let you know? She's in three."

"Thanks, Amy." Naomi smiles at her before turning to me. "Come with me."

I have to hold myself from barreling over her to get to the door. About fucking time. Outside of a door just down the hall, she holds me back. "She's gonna be groggy and probably starting to feel pain. People aren't always themselves when they wake up from anesthesia."

"I'm aware, Naomi, and for your information, she wasn't exactly herself after that monster carved into her," I say a bit too sharply, making her wince, but she doesn't seem to take it personal and steps aside to let me by.

A contraption over the bed with a chain elevating her right leg makes her look even smaller. The head of the bed is raised, so she is almost sitting, I guess to keep pressure off the injuries to her back. Her face is turned away from the door and angled toward the window. In the reflection, I can see her staring into the ink black night. I walk up to the bed. I know she can hear me when her shoulders draw up to her ears. Defensive mode. Leaving that space she seems to need, I stay on this side of the bed and pull up a chair. Her hand, the wrist bandaged, is lying on top of the bedding and her fingers don't stop moving. I cover her hand with mine and lightly stroke my thumb over her skin. The sound of her voice shocks me.

"Is he dead?" She sounds hoarse, the tone is ice cold.

"Baby…" I manage before she turns to face me. Now her eyes aren't empty—they are full of anger.

"Tell me. Did you kill him?" she insists, and I drop my head against her shoulder, needing her touch.

"I don't know." My voice is muffled. "I wanted to. I couldn't think, couldn't feel anything but rage. They stopped me. Mal. And Caleb. They pulled me off him and then I came to you."

Her face is blank, but with eyes holding fire, she just stares at me for a moment. "I hope you did," she says, turning her head back to the window. "And I hope he rots in hell."

CHAPTER TWENTY-TWO

Kendra

I hurt.

I can feel the effects of the drugs fading and the pain invades my senses. But I won't push the button the nurse handed me. You can self-administer, she'd said. But I want to feel the pain. I want it to overwhelm me so I have no room in my head to think of him. Instead I find myself thinking of the man sitting on the other side of the bed. Neil. He almost made me believe I could have him. Hold him. But I can't. He's young, God he's still so young, he'll find someone better suited. Someone who still believes in the possibility of a happy life. I... I can't. I no longer believe it's possible.

"Let's try and get you something to eat."

A nurse with a gentle smile stands beside my bed when I open my eyes to her voice. I must've been sleeping, because it was dark again outside. I can't even get my head around what day it is. I blink my eyes against the diffused light in the room and notice it is empty. He's gone. Resigned, I close my eyes. "Not hungry," I manage on a croak.

"Nonsense," the girl says matter-of-factly and examines the read out on the IV pump beside the bed, before turning to me with concern in her eyes. "Why haven't you used your pump?"

I haven't because the pain is almost welcome. I can *feel* it, whereas I can't seem to feel much else. It shields me from reality, which is much more terrifying now than the pain. As long as I have the pain to hold on to, perhaps my mind won't break apart the way I'm afraid it will, given the chance.

"There, I've given you a dose so you can eat. I'll bring you some toast and broth in a minute. Something in your stomach will do you good," she says as she turns toward the door.

"Where is…?" The unfinished question slips from my lips before I can check it. Unfortunately the nurse seems to know who I'm talking about and she smiles.

"Your young man said he'd be back. He left his number in case you needed him. Dr. Waters came in this afternoon and sent him off. Said he needed a shower, food and sleep, in that order. You're a lucky woman; he hasn't left your side in two days."

Wait, two days?

"Two days?" I question out loud. "I've been out of it for two days?"

Her face softens as she approaches the bed again. "It's not that unusual. You were mostly drifting in and out. General anesthetic can do that to some people. So can shock. Sometimes the body and mind go on hiatus for a bit. Give you time to heal. You've been through considerable trauma both physically and mentally and sometimes it takes time to process that."

"I don't remember…" I admit, feeling a little lost. I've lost two days. They're just gone.

"Let me get someone to sit with you while I grab you a tray," she says before walking out. I don't even have a chance to tell her I don't want anyone.

Maybe a minute later, my mother walks in. "Hey, my girl." She bends down to give me a kiss and sits down on the chair beside the bed. "So glad both my girls are going to be okay," she says with a sniff.

"Karly… how's Karly? Is she okay?" *My sister*. I forgot. I can't believe I forgot. Yet another layer of guilt is added as I listen to my mother talk.

"She'll be right as rain, just as you will. A few stitches to close the cut on her head and she stayed one night for observation. You have wonderful friends, Kenny. We were looking for a hotel to stay here in Cortez and your friend Emma offered us her guesthouse."

I don't know why it makes me cry, but it does. It makes me cry hard and suddenly those pieces I was hoping the pain would help keep together, are falling apart. I'm literally coming undone at the thought of my mother and sister sticking around. For me. I'm ashamed that my initial reaction is surprise when Mom says she and Karly are staying. I would for either of them, so why would I even question they'd do the same for me? Was I that judgmental? Or insecure? Am I a bad person? Is that why this happened to me? My head is spinning with a cesspool of emotions. Self-recrimination, guilt, regret, doubt, fear and anger. Holy schnikes, the anger. At that *man* and at myself. And I feel so sad. So, so very sad for those women who suffered in a way I unfortunately am now familiar with. I can't help but think their death must've come as a relief when it finally did. It would've for me. I wished it. Round and round in my head it churns and I can feel pieces of my sanity breaking apart as hysteria creeps up. I don't notice Mom calling for help, I just know she has when the smiling nurse from earlier walks in with Naomi. The next thing I know I'm falling, tumbling down a rabbit hole toward darkness.

◆

Neil

I hated leaving Kendra, but between Naomi's motherly concern and Damian's incessant texts to contact him, I finally caved and left her side. For the past few days, she's been mostly out of it, except for the few times when her eyes would open. The blank look was there again and each time she'd tell me to leave. To leave her be. Then she'd drift off again. I feel fucking helpless, sitting there not being able to comfort or ease her. Useless. Two days to give every memory of that night the time to become engraved in my mind. Torture for years to come. Her surgeon came in this morning to check the wounds on her back and asked me if I was sure I wanted to stay. Fuck no, I'm not sure, but I'm not leaving either. Cleaned and mostly stitched up, the sight of her back was almost worse, more gruesome, than it had been that night. With horrifying precision, he had carved the beginnings of wings in her flesh. The doctor commented that she would likely be left with substantial scarring, but that they would refer her to a good plastic surgeon. I didn't bother responding. He must've thought I was or would be repulsed at the condition of her back, at least that's what it sounded like. Nothing could be further from the truth. Oh, I'm repulsed alright, but by the butcher who was able to do this to her. There isn't anything that would change the way I see Kendra. Not a damn thing.

During the entire examination, Kendra only made the occasional sound of discomfort, but never quite woke up. I was glad for that. By the time the doctor left and Elsa came in with Naomi, I was wrung out. I guess that's why I finally gave in and headed home for a quick shower and a bite at the diner.

"How is she doing?" Arlene asks the moment I sit down at the counter. It's quiet, being that it's seven thirty on a Sunday night and most folks have already come and gone.

"I don't know," I admit. And I don't. Sure, physically she'll heal, although she might be left with a slight limp, and have difficulty running. The wounds on her back will heal as well, but there will be constant reminders of the ordeal she survived and there is no way to gauge the emotional impact this all will leave behind. That's what worries me most.

"She'll get through it," Arlene says, putting her hand on my arm. "She's strong. It'll take some time, but she'll get there." Arlene would know, a victim of a brutally violent crime herself. She may not have outward scars to identify her, but she has some deep emotional ones she's had to deal with.

"Thanks." I smile at her, trying to communicate how well aware I am that she knows what she's talking about. She's worn those shoes.

"Let me feed you. Special is chili today. Are you game?"

I nod. I'm not really hungry but recognize the need to eat. Unusual for me, since I always seem to be hungry, but the last few days have taken their toll. I'm sick with worry. Scared that the tentative progress I made before Friday night will not be enough to bind her to me. Afraid that if she persists her repeated pleas for me to leave her, it will eventually be too painful for me to resist. A reminder she put her trust in me and I failed her. I told her I'd keep her safe and I didn't. Another mark on my soul.

When Arlene puts a steaming bowl and a cold bottle of beer in front of me, I notice Seb standing behind her in the kitchen doorway.

"Hey." I'm surprised to see the strained look on his face as he bites off the greeting. It also doesn't escape me that Arlene shoots some furtive glances his way.

"Good chilli," I try, lifting a bite on my spoon before shoving it in my mouth. It is good. Wholesome and spicy, with just the right amount of heat, and loaded with meat, beans and vegetables. From under my eyebrows I see him slowly approaching.

"She gonna be okay? Kendra?"

And suddenly it hits me. Guilt. I might as well be looking in the mirror, because now it's clear as day what I'm seeing on his face. "Look," I start, putting my spoon down, "she'll be fine. She'll heal."

Seb busies himself with the glasses on the shelves against the wall before turning back to me. "I'm—"

I don't even let him start, let alone finish as I shove my bowl out of the way and lean forward on the counter. "No. None of this is on you. It's on me. I promised I'd protect her and I didn't. It's—"

"Oh, for crying out loud!" Arlene suddenly blows up. "Would you two knock it off? Are we having a piss-off on who is the guiltiest here? Shall I weigh in? I'm the one who let her go to the bathroom and didn't see her slip out." She wards off any protest with her hands up. "Enough already. Yes, she got hurt. And yes, it'll leave its mark, but you have to realize she made the choice to use herself to save her sister. And I can fucking guarantee you she would do it again. In a goddamn heartbeat. So stop taking ownership of something that is not even yours to own!" She tosses her towel in our general direction when she stomps by toward the kitchen. "Men are so stupid," I can hear her mumble as she disappears.

Seb shrugs and takes off after her, leaving me to myself, but not for long.

"Thought I might find you here," Gus says as he walks in and sits down beside me. "Emma mentioned you'd taken a break when she called me from the hospital. I thought you might like an update."

I lower the bottle of beer I just lifted to my lips. "Tell me." I turn on my stool to face him. For two days I've avoided everything by being plastered to Kendra's bedside, but now I want to know.

"First off, Beth and Clint dropped in on Saturday. They'd gone over to the house with an insurance claim adjuster and had a look at the damage. Good news is, whatever Kendra had in the bedrooms or bathroom is salvageable. Bad news is, whatever wasn't in there is toast. Clint says he can get his brother down here and between the two of them and their crews, they can have it fixed in a month, maybe two. He doesn't suspect any problems with the insurance company, but apparently Beth has decided it is finally time to sell. Doesn't look like her son will be coming back to live in Cedar Tree and—"

"I'm buying it." I'm not sure where that came from, but now that I've put it out there, I like the idea. I've always liked the house, and I know Kendra loves it. So I'm buying it. I can see Gus isn't so sure.

"Are you sure you can afford to? I mean, I'll help—"

"Gus," I cut him off. "Spent years in the military with nothing to spend my money on. And since coming to work for GFI, have you ever seen me spend more than is absolutely necessary? I've got savings, investments. Substantial ones."

A small smile spreads on Gus's face. "You've got investments?"

"What can I say?" I shrug my shoulders. "I've got mad skills."

"You do it yourself? Fuck, should've had you have a look at my portfolio instead of that slick suit at the bank."

"Anytime."

"Take you up on that. And as for the house, you'd better give Beth or Clint a call. I'm sure she'll be thrilled if it stays in *the family,* so to speak."

"Who's the guy? Was it Maryn?" I prompt Gus to get back to business.

"Yes and no. First of all, he's alive, although I can safely say he'll never look the same again. You did a fine number on him," Gus says, one eyebrow raised.

"Should've killed him."

Gus doesn't say anything, just gives me a long hard stare before continuing as if I'd never spoken. "The shack was winery property, but had been unused for years. It used to be a workshop where they'd repair the old barrels. No one's been in there for decades. Owners had plumb near forgotten it was there. There was evidence someone had been bunking there. Theory is Maryn used it as shelter after the FBI raided the farmhouse."

I could've figured all that out myself. "What about the guy? And the last victim, Franka?"

"No sign on Franka. No evidence she was ever there. As for him, you know there was little history to be found on Maryn. Nothing that could be traced very far. On Saturday morning, the FBI was able to collect his fingerprints and some DNA. Fingerprints match a print found on the inside of one of the shadow boxes in the farmhouse on County Road D. Same guy, Casal Maryn. But here's where it gets interesting… the prints had a second match."

"I call bullshit," I blurt out. "No two sets of fingerprints are alike. None. Doesn't happen."

Gus lifts his hand. "Hear me out. The second set were fingerprints taken a couple of weeks ago by the Gallup PD as a standard procedure when bringing in suspects. Suspect in question at the time was one Lars Cayman."

Sonofabitch.

"Say what? How the fuck is that possible?" I know I'm yelling when Seb and Arlene's heads poke out of the kitchen.

"Calm the fuck down and I'll tell ya!" Gus barks, staring me down. Clenching my jaw, I manage a mere barely-there nod. Angry thoughts swirling through my mind. They'd had him. Had him in Gallup and let him go. Let him disappear.

"He seems to have meticulously planned this before he ever even met face to face with Kendra. The conference was obviously part of his cover as was the police report he filed in Grand Junction for the supposed theft from his car. He was carefully building sufficient bits and pieces of alibis so that if ever attention came his way, he'd be ready. This guy's had a head start on us from the get-go. His bad luck that he picked Kendra for his next victim. No way he would've known her circle of friends included the same people who were investigating his case. Only odd thing is that he approached her under his own name and not another alias."

"She was special," I mutter to myself.

"How do you figure?" Gus obviously heard.

"I read his e-mails. He seemed genuinely interested in Kendra. Spent a lot of time just getting to know her. With the others, he exchanged just a handful of e-mails before moving quickly into pushing for a face-to-face meet. He didn't do that with Kendra until four months after they started talking. Almost like whatever he'd been looking for, he'd found in her." I'm rolling with that theory now and the pieces start falling into place bit by bit. "He never used the Sux on her. Not the first time he took her from the hospital parking lot and not this time. He used a Taser on her sister, and as far as we know, the Sux on the other victims we know of, but nothing on Kendra. The shed—it looked like some kind of freaky church with candles everywhere, him chanting what sounded like Latin and Ken…Kendra was like the altar he worshipped."

I see comprehension coming over Gus's face. "Son of a bitch…the map. He left her Tracy Poole as an offering."

"Yes," I agree, a sick feeling in my stomach. "And when she didn't respond the way he thought she should, he left her the rest of the map as a reminder. That's when he got impatient." I grab Gus by the shoulder. "Kendra can't know this. She's barely coping. If she finds any of this out, it'll push her over."

"She's a grown woman, Neil. You can't keep everything from her."

"You didn't see what I saw in her eyes, Boss. I know I can damn well try," I spit right back at him.

Gus shakes his head, obviously not agreeing, but that's his problem. Seeing I won't budge on that, he changes the subject. "Damian went down this morning to search his place in Gallup himself with an FBI forensic team. Cayman called in sick the last few days of the school year apparently. Went to a walk-in clinic to get some antibiotics and from what the Gallup PD keeping an occasional eye on the place could see, he never left the house. They never even realized he had flown the coop until after we discovered the possible connection. They'd forced their way in, only to find the house empty, as it appeared to have been for quite a while. Last time any of the patrols had an actual visual on Cayman was last week and no one bothered to update the FBI. Major fuck up. Damian is livid and is ripping the place apart. Let's hope we get some more clarity tomorrow."

Yeah, let's hope. Although I'm not so sure clarity is going to help Kendra much.

CHAPTER TWENTY-THREE

Kendra

I try not to look at the man sitting beside me.

I've sent him away from my bedside this past week as many times as he returned to it.

I cracked. Crumbled. I'm alone in my bubble and wish to stay there. The pain has gone dull, unfortunately, and the rest of me has dulled, too. I'm no longer sure how to feel, how to react. I don't trust my read on other people's feelings or thoughts. I'm drifting.

But Neil won't leave me alone. The rest of them leave when I tell them to, but not him. He keeps coming back. Just like he came back today, making sure I have somewhere to go now that I've officially been released. Mom offered to take me to Durango but the thought alone gives me hives. People have been impacted enough by my actions.

"What's going on in that pretty head of yours, Pup," Neil asks, not appearing put off at all by my silence.

I push down the tingle I feel when he calls me that name. My mind can't seem to keep still, flitting from one thought to the next and I just can't seem to grab ahold of just one. No focus. Not since they started me on the sedatives last weekend. If it hadn't been for Naomi and Neil promising to keep a close eye on me, I don't think I would've been allowed to leave the hospital.

I still haven't answered Neil.

He reaches over and covers my fidgeting hands with his big one. The warmth is like magic. Stillness seems to spread through my body from that touch alone. He does that. Every time he touches me.

I vaguely register that we are not heading to the apartment over the diner, where I expected him to take me, but turn off toward Gus and Emma's place. Yet even when he parks the car and comes around to help me out, I don't say anything. I just let him carry me around the house and straight to the guesthouse in their backyard. I can't help but wince when his arm comes around my back. Even with most of the stitches gone, it's still sensitive.

"Sorry," he mumbles as he carries me inside and sits me on the couch, elevating my cast and piling the rest of the pillows behind me. "Stay here, I'll be right back."

Almost detached, I take a good look around. I don't remember if I've ever been in here before but it's a decent-sized place. Outside, I hear voices approaching. By the sounds of it, Neil and Naomi, who said she'd be following behind. But it's Chaos who rounds the doorway first and, without stopping, jumps on the couch beside me and lays his big head on my leg. My Chaos. I don't even notice my hand gently stroking his head, or the tears that start rolling down my face. Nor do I catch the meaningful look that Neil and Naomi exchange. I just feel the unconditional acceptance of the dog on my lap as I close my eyes and let my feelings wash me away.

***

Neil

Jesus.

This is the first real emotion I've seen from Kendra since that night. Naomi told me about the violent breakdown she'd had in the hospital, which was the reason they had her drugged out of her brain when I got back. She's been like a robot the entire week. Someone I don't recognize—emotionless, cold, uncaring. Not my Kendra. She didn't even react the first time her tearful sister came to see her. She was quick to dismiss her family when her mom told her to come back to Durango with them and instead told them to go home without her. They'd eventually done so reluctantly, after reassurances from Naomi and myself that we would look after her.

I had, or as much as she allowed, which wasn't much. And I was planning to continue doing it as long as necessary.

"Step outside with me." Naomi tugs on my arm, and I hesitantly follow her out.

"You called it," I told her, seeing as getting the dog in to see Kendra was something Naomi had been trying to accomplish all week. The hospital wouldn't budge, since he wasn't registered as a service dog and although that is something that can be done online, we'd still have to wait for the paperwork to come in. Besides that, she'd had Chaos for less than a week at the time of her attack. I have to admit, I didn't think his presence would have any impact, but Naomi was determined to try. She said she'd seen amazing results from her residency days in Phoenix, whenever animals were introduced to patients who had all but *checked out*. After a week of staring into blank eyes, I'd been ready to see something there. Anything.

"Lucky. Key is now to try and capitalize on the little cracks. Get her to talk. She refused to speak to the social worker. Kendra is normally a very controlled person, doesn't easily share much about herself in the best of circumstances. Doesn't trust easily either, but she trusts you. I think you stand the best chance of getting somewhere." Naomi looks at me earnestly and I know she wants the best for her friend, but I can't help wonder if someone so adept at hiding his own monsters is really equipped to deal with someone else's. Seeing the doubt in my face, Naomi steps closer and puts her hand on my arm. "You love her?" she asks softly and my eyes find hers.

"Yes," I tell her with conviction, making her smile.

"Then you are the right person to bring her back." She goes up on her toes and presses a kiss on my cheek. "I'm a phone call away at the clinic, and Emma is inside the house, cooking for an army. You'll be all right. *She'll* be all right." With that, she leaves.

Fuck.

A little hesitant, I step back inside only to find Kendra on her side on the couch, the big lug of a dog stretched out in front of her on the couch, her arm holding him close. She's sleeping. Good. I grab my laptop and facing the couch, I sit down at the kitchen table.

Three hours later, after having sorted through my e-mails, most of which are from Jasper and Damian, I am up to date on the case. I'd had a hard time focusing on anything while sitting in a hospital room, especially since every time I tried, the rage for what was done to my girl threatened to overtake me. No place for that when I was sitting next to her bed. Now, with her home and safe, it seems easier to process.

So when Kendra finally opens her eyes, looking around a little dazed, I feel sufficiently prepared to deal with whatever comes my way.

"Hey, babe." Her startled eyes come up to meet mine.

"Hey." She seems almost as surprised at the sound of her own voice as I am.

Quickly capitalizing on that small victory, I walk over and sit on the edge of the coffee table. "You hungry? Emma brought over some food. A ton of food, actually. I stuck it all in the fridge for you to sort through." I grab the crutches Naomi brought with her and offer them to Kendra, who is trying to sit up. "While you do that, I'm gonna take this guy for a walk." I indicate Chaos who jumped off the couch the moment Kendra removed her arm from around him, and made a beeline to the door. Without waiting for a response, I grab the dog leash and clip it on. "Be right back," I say over my shoulder as I push open the door.

I don't know if she's scared that I'm leaving her alone, but I'm hoping she still trusts me enough to know that I wouldn't leave her by herself if I thought for one minute there was any danger. There isn't. As of this morning, Maryn is still in a coma. I know I did substantial damage and I don't feel the least bit guilty about that. Looks like there is little interest in investigating the circumstances, given the man is linked to the now confirmed death of eleven women and suspected of more. Apparently, the search of Maryn/Cayman's house in Gallup, FBI style, netted quite a bit of interesting information over this past week. Searches went out and the bodies of two of the women, Shirley Haig and Jenny Weber, were found near Perins Peak. Two more bodies of missing women turned up near Aztec, New Mexico, and three in total in Canyonlands National Park in Utah. There were still more expected to turn up. But there'd been no sign or mention of Franka Mellis.

Lars Cayman, which turns out to be the name on his birth certificate, which was discovered along with some journals, was one sick and twisted puppy. From what Jasper was able to piece together, he grew up the only child of a single mother. Sarah Cayman, a recent nursing school graduate at the time, was the daughter of a Mormon priest who grew up near Monticello, Utah. When she became pregnant out of wedlock at the age of twenty-two, the young nurse was expelled from the family and their strict congregation by her father. She ended up finding work and living a rather reclusive life in New Mexico with her young child. She committed suicide when Lars was only sixteen. Police reports from that time showed Lars as the person to find his mother hanging from a tree in their backyard. A coroner's report indicated open wounds on her back along with substantial scarring. Wounds he did not believe could have been self-inflicted. According to the journals the FBI found in Cayman's house, Sarah Cayman was convinced since Lars was the reason she was cast out of the *fold*, he should be responsible for her redemption. So from around the age of six, he had been made to believe that it was up to him to give his mother the wings she had lost.

I can't help but feel sickened at what the boy grew up around and was genetically burdened with. But other than giving me a better grasp on why, the information doesn't change the hate I feel toward the man he became. Deranged, predatory, calculating and narcissistic in his view of himself as some kind of savior. Part of me hopes he succumbs to the injuries he sustained at my hands.

Soon I have the house back in view. As the dog and I make our way to the guesthouse in the back, I'm thinking it's not reasonable for me to believe this can all be kept secret from her. She'll find out. Maybe not immediately but there is no way this kind of twisted tale won't become fodder for the media. I'd rather she hear it from me than the hyped up, mangled versions the networks and newspapers will likely come up with.

I don't see her when I walk in the door, but I can hear water running in the bathroom. The moment I unclip the dog's leash, he heads to the bathroom door and lies down in front of it.

"Come here, boy. Let me get you dinner." I try to coax him into the kitchen and out of the way of the door. Don't want

Kendra to trip over him. It isn't until I put his food bowl down that he leaves his guard duty. While he eats, I go listen at the bathroom door. The water is still running as it was before but I don't hear anything else. I try the doorknob and to my surprise it turns freely in my hand. I push the door open, but what I see almost brings me to my knees.

Kendra

Why does it feel like my skin is crawling? When I woke up, I wasn't sure where I was, until Neil spoke and my eyes found him. A sense of calm came over me and for a moment, everything seemed to settle in place. My voice sounded like a stranger's when I spoke, yet oddly…right. I watched his lips move as he said something about taking the dog. Then they were gone, both Neil and Chaos. And I feel like my world is tilting on its axis as I look at the closed door.

I don't know how long I've been sitting there, staring at the door when I lean forward and suddenly feel something shift against me. Right. My crutches. And I need to pee. Gritting my teeth against the discomfort and fighting through the fear of suddenly finding myself alone, I manage to get on my feet and wobble unsteadily on my crutches to the bathroom. After taking care of business, I notice the big tub which is looking very inviting. I haven't had more than sponge baths for over a week and had my hair washed at the sink two days ago. Without thinking, I start running the water. I strip off the shirt and sweats Naomi had brought over, but when I stand up again, I catch a glimpse of myself in the mirror, something I'd managed to avoid so far. It's like looking at someone else. My face is gaunt, my eyes dull, set deep and circled dark. My hair is flat on one side and sticking out all over on the other. Lips chapped and bruised on the side of my face. Before I can stop myself, my eyes trail lower, but other than some faint bruising, I can't see anything remarkable, other than the old scars under my breasts. Then I slightly turn my back to the mirror and thick ridges of red, swollen skin rise up in an unidentifiable pattern where he cut me. I'd felt them when the stitches had been removed yesterday, but I hadn't seen them. I'd made sure nobody else did either and had sent Neil from the room. Again.

Mesmerized at the sight and the size of my injuries, I try to twist my torso to have a better look when the door opens.

"Baby," Neil's tortured voice sounds from behind me, and I swing around. I almost lose my balance when strong arms slip around me. "Steady now. I've got you." The deep rumble of his voice settles warmly under my skin. I haven't been able to *feel* much this past week, both because of the medication and because I've been afraid to. But I feel this. His warmth behind me, his arms safely around me, and the press of his lips against my shoulder. It's as close as I've let him come, but now that he's here, I don't want him to ever let go.

"Don't let go," I whisper, giving voice to my thoughts.

"Never," he softly but firmly returns. When his arms loosen around me, leaving one hand on my hip to steady me, I'm suddenly cold. It's got to be close to 85 degrees out there, and still goosebumps rise on my skin. Neil reaches around me, turning off the tap. The bath is full and I hadn't even noticed. "Sit down on the toilet and let me get a bag to tie around your ankle. Don't want it to get wet."

I hold on to the edge of the counter and look at myself again. Nothing has changed from earlier, except my eyes. They looked flat just a few minutes ago—now I can see life there. "Neil!" I call out, my voice still a bit rusty. Heavy footsteps sound before he appears in the door, alarm on his face. "I'm okay," I quickly tell him. "Do you have your phone on you?"

His expression changes from concerned to puzzled. "It's on the counter, do you need someone?"

"No. I don't need anyone else. Just the phone please."

He's back in a flash, holding out his phone to me. I scroll through the menu until I find what I want. "Here," I hand the phone back to him. "I want you to take a picture of my back." I watch his eyes change through a range of emotions in the mirror. Worry, fear, pride—but they settle on tender.

"You sure, Pup?" he asks, in a voice that matches the look on his face.

I am sure. Positive in fact. This has not been me—I have not been myself—but it's been enough. I look at myself in the mirror. I've already given that son of a bitch more than enough of me. He doesn't get any more. I'm taking it all back.

"Absolutely." I find his eyes again in the mirror, showing him my conviction.

I hear the shutter sounds as he snaps pictures, but I don't take my eyes off him, hardly believing that whatever age difference between us once meant so much to me. It means nothing. Any other man young or old would likely have faltered at any time during or after this ordeal, but not Neil. He's been steady and consistent from the start. I'm the one who's been all over the place, who's been irrational and unpredictable. Time to let him in all the way.

He's put down the phone and is on his knees, taping a bag over my foot. "Join me?" I ask him and this time, he doesn't ask if I'm sure. With his eyes locked on mine, he gets up and strips down where he stands. "Bring the phone," I remind him as he helps me settle in the tub, my plastic-wrapped leg hanging over the side. He slides in behind me, keeping distance between his chest and my back, leaving it to me to make myself comfortable against him. The hair on his chest rubs slightly against the cuts on my back, just painful enough to remind me I'm alive, and I settle against him with a deep sigh. "I'm ready," I tell him, indicating the phone he is holding in one hand, while the other settles around my waist on my stomach.

One-thumbed, he flicks over the screen until I see the image on my back. A deep outline of wings in my skin with an intricate network of cuts and slices, making up what look to be the feathers. He made it all the way up the left side of my back, from the top of my butt cheek almost to my shoulder blade. I wince remembering the fiery pain each of these cuts caused. It's brutally beautiful and shocking at the same time. My skin—my body—permanently altered. And I realize that, at some point in time, when I can get my head around it, I will have to take that back too.

"Are you okay?" Neil puts the phone down on the toilet lid and wraps his other arm around me.

"No," I tell him honestly. "But I'm starting to think maybe I will be."

CHAPTER TWENTY-FOUR

Neil

Maybe I will be.

Kendra's skin against mine, her body wrapped in my arms, her scent in my nostrils and those words from her lips, and all is right in the world. I'd like to freeze this moment and bring it back from time to time to savor.

"I'm sorry."

Last thing I expected was to hear those words from her and my body seizes up. "What do you have to be sorry for?" I ask her, an edge to my voice I can't disguise. "It's me who should be sorry for leaving you. I should never have left you. Never."

Kendra twists sideways, so both legs are now over the side of the tub, and she tilts her head back to look at me. Cupping my face in her hand she slowly shakes her head. "No. You're wrong. I would never have forgiven you if you hadn't gone after my sister. It's what I wanted—what I *needed* from you. I'm saying I'm sorry I scared you. That I hurt you by leaving, but I had no choice; he had Karly. I would do it again, even knowing what was waiting for me. I wouldn't hesitate for a second. Crazy, right?"

Now it's my turn to shake my head. "No. Not crazy at all." I bend down and lightly touch my lips to hers. She tucks her head in my neck and leans her body against me. And then she speaks.

"I was so scared. Felt so helpless. He told me to get into the truck bed, and for a minute, I thought that maybe I could do something from there. I was looking for weapons, for anything, but all I could find was a large wood sliver." A shiver runs through her body before she lifts her head. "I stabbed him with it, you know?"

I drop my head so our foreheads touch. "Good for you," I say quietly. Knowing from what Damian has told me that Maryn/Cayman had a large open gash in his cheek, and they'd found the bloodied piece of wood on the side of the trail. Karly had apparently been witness to most of that encounter. That is, until her sister yelled at her to run. I don't know what Kendra thought my reaction would be, but it's obviously not what she expected to hear. That's why when she looks at me slightly confused, I lay it out for her. "You were saving Karly. Even when you were hurt yourself, you took care of her first. You weren't helpless. You were courageous and incredibly brave to do what you did. So baby, *good for you.*" I emphasize my words with a light press of my lips against hers.

"The pain was so bad, Neil. I've never felt anything like it." She snuggles back under my chin and I have to make a concerted effort to keep my breathing regular, even though the rage I feel at what he did to her is almost blinding. "The guilt and the pain, his constant chanting, it was getting to me. I could feel myself slipping away and kept hoping it would be the last time. That I wouldn't wake up again. I'm so sorry." I can feel her soft sobs against my chest and they about rip my heart out. Still, I can't say the trust she is showing me right now doesn't feel pretty fucking good.

"Nothing to be sorry for," I reassure her. Guilt has no place in the emotions she's living through.

"He called me his angel. Told me I was his masterpiece, his ultimate test. I didn't understand any of what he was saying.

He even said something about going to a *sun dance*. None of it made sense to me. I never saw his face, but he was familiar."

I know I won't be able to keep it from her much longer and perhaps while having her relaxed in my arms would be a good time. "Probably because he was familiar to you," I say hesitantly, and she immediately lifts her head, her eyes searching mine. "Babe, it's been Lars Cayman all along and the only reason he focused on you is because, according to Gomez, you bear an uncanny similarity to his mother." Her body goes stiff in my arms and I quickly tell her what I just recently learned about the man, hoping that it may help her realize that his obsession with her was something entirely out of her control.

"I noticed this time," she cryptically states.

"What?"

"His gait. I could hear the uneven steps on the dirt every time he'd walk toward me. I started focussing on it. That's what must have made him seem familiar because it sure as hell wasn't his voice. From what I remember he had a much higher-pitched voice. This guy's voice was very deep and gravelly. They don't even sound alike, but his odd gait was familiar."

"Given what we know about him now, it's clear he lived two completely separate lives, one as Lars Cayman, respectable high school teacher, and the other as reclusive artist Casal Maryn. Same person but two apparently different personalities. Gomez never felt good about having to let the guy go after interviewing him in Gallup. He always had suspicions, but we were likely dealing with two separate personalities. His appearance, especially his limp, was not so easy to hide."

Kendra goes silent after that and I give her a chance to process while grabbing the shampoo. With soft hands, I wash her hair, and then as much of her body as I can, before noticing another shiver running over Kendra's skin. Whether it is the topic or the cooling water of the tub, it's time to get out. I carefully slide her away from me before standing up and helping her out. Then I wrap her gently in a large bath towel, making sure not to chafe the wounds on her back, and sit her down on the toilet seat. Doesn't take long for me to dry off and lift her in my arms before carrying her to bed, where she curls on her side.

"I'm going to give Chaos a quick walk before grabbing us something to eat. I'll be right back." I step in the bathroom to pull on my clothes and get my boots on, before returning to the bed and handing the remote for the flatscreen hanging over the dresser to Kendra. "Find us a movie to watch," I tell her, leaning down to kiss her softly. I can feel her eyes following me toward the door, and just as I reach for the door, she pipes up from the bed.

"Can you tell me again?"

I turn around to face her. She has a slight blush on her cheeks and her eyes look a little freaked out. Not sure what she's referring to, I wait her out. "What you said on the phone," she continues hesitantly, "I'd like to hear it again."

It takes me a minute, but then a knowing smile spreads over my face as I stalk back to the bed and sink on my knees beside the mattress so we're eye to eye. With my right hand, I stroke back a few wet strands from her face as she looks at me with big eyes. Leaving my hand to cup her cheek, I lean in and deepen our eye contact. "I love you, Pup. I hope you believe me when—"

"Me too," she says, barely making a sound. "Love you."

⁂

Kendra

I can't believe I said that.

A quick glance at the clock confirms that it is after midnight. I fell asleep watching some silly movie that apparently tickled Neil's funny bone because the last I remember when closing my eyes was the soft chuckle reverberating in his chest. He'd come back to bed, as promised, after walking the dog and he came bearing food. A selection of containers—no doubt Emma's work—filled with chili, peach pie, roasted vegetables and some hummus. Chaos followed him closely and settled on my side of the bed probably hoping for spillage. Fat chance of that, I went for the peach pie. Funny how I had barely eaten as far as I can remember this past week and yet the thought of Emma's pie made my mouth water. In my defense, I had roasted veggies with hummus for dessert. Neil, of course, finished off what I left in record time, and although he hadn't said anything, I know he heard my words. If possible, he was even more gentle and attentive with me than before, never without a little smile teasing his lips whenever he looked at me. And those eyes…I could completely forget myself when looking into them. But at some time during the evening, I drifted off and apparently so did Neil although he did manage to turn off the TV at some point.

It's dark in the room now, and I'm watching the deep rise and fall of Neil's substantial chest where my head was resting. Slowly the insecurities and fears start crowding my mind. The man's chants, his warped words, are humming in my ears making me want to press my hands against my head to block the sound. But then Neil's voice crowds them out, telling me he loves me. Washing the grimy residue of Lars Cayman's deranged ramblings away. And then my own declaration, something I never have said to anyone except my mom and sister. The look on his face when I formed them with my lips without really moving air. An irrational fear that somehow giving voice to them would change everything. Ridiculous, because everything had already changed. The feelings were there long before the words formed. Although if our lives had not been thrown into turmoil, I'm not sure when I would've been ready to say them out loud. But they had, and it had felt good to be able to release some of my emotions out loud. It's crowded in my mind and in my heart and I know I will likely need some help processing, not only the mental impact of what happened to me, but also the physical reminders he left behind.

"Go back to sleep, Pup."

I lift my head to see Neil's warm eyes on me. Thick-lidded and slightly glazed, the emotion in them unmistakable. Without warning, my eyes fill, and immediately his hand reaches to catch the first tear falling. "You're safe, baby," he mumbles, gently stroking his thumb to wipe at the wetness on my cheeks.

"I know," I tell him. "That's why I'm crying. Because I'm safe, but the other women…"

"Shhh, don't. They're doing everything they can to find them. To bring them home to their families."

"But Neil, those poor kids, Franka's kids." I sniff, thinking about the one woman I feel most responsible for. The one he took after I ditched him at the coffee shop. The only one here in this area who had not yet been found. I couldn't let my mind rest. Couldn't allow myself the luxury of sleep if she was still out there somewhere. My mind started running through everything I saw and everything I heard during what seemed like an endless time, and suddenly I freeze. *Soon I'll bring you to sun dance as well.*

"What is it?" Neil immediately reacts.

"What if he wasn't talking about an event but a place? He didn't say 'I'll bring to *a* sun dance as well, he said 'I'll bring you to Sundance as well' as if he was talking about a place instead of an event. And Neil, *as well*? What if…" Before I have a chance to finish that sentence, Neil is up and stalks out of the bedroom, coming back seconds later with his laptop in hand. He settles back beside me as he enters Sundance in a search engine and pages of companies or restaurants with that name pop up. Then he refines the search by geographic location.

"What are you looking for?"

"Not sure," Neil admits. "I guess anything by that name that would be a location where he'd be able to take you to. Something off the beaten path. Secluded even."

I nod at him in understanding and settle in against his shoulder, staring intently alongside him at the screen. He scrolls through an amazingly long and diverse list of businesses by that name when my eyes catch something. "Hold up," I tell him when he gets ready to scroll to the next page. "What's that?" I point at a name that for some reason pops out at me. "What is that? Sundance Rentals?" Neil doesn't answer, but his fingers type a staccato rhythm on the keyboard, and in seconds, a map pops up with a little flag indicating a spot just north of the 184 between Mancos and Dolores. Another click of his finger and a website appears advertising rustic, secluded hunting cabins.

"Bingo," he whispers and immediately bends down to retrieve his phone from his jeans. While dialing, he leans in and gives me a resounding kiss on my lips. "Well done, baby. Hang tight." He peeks closely at the screen of his laptop when someone on the other end picks up. "Drew. You in the office?— What do you know about Sundance Rentals?—How long since it was shut down? I think the place needs to be checked out, but let me call Damian real quick. He may want in on this." With a snap, and apparently without waiting for an answer, Neil ends the call before dialing again. "Gomez," he says and my mind starts wandering as he curtly relays information to Damian. I'm not sure what this might mean, if anything, but a small seed of hope takes hold. Then I hear Neil say something that catches my attention. "No. I'm not. Not leaving her. I'll call Gus. I'm sure he'll be there. Yes, I hear you; thirty minutes at the sheriff's office in Mancos. Gotcha." Once again, he ends the call before immediately dialing again. When I open my mouth to say something, he holds up his finger to hush me. "*One minute,*" he mouths at me before turning his attention to the phone. This conversation is even shorter than the previous two, and I can't imagine how anyone could've made any sense out of the cryptic message Neil relays, but true to his word, not much more than a minute later, he turns to me. "Damian and his team and Gus and whoever he can dig up, are going up to the rental place with the sheriff. Drew says it's been empty for a year, basically abandoned when the owners just walked away. From what he remembers, there are sixteen cabins spread out over a couple of acres. That's why we need every hand on deck, it's a lot of ground to cover. If by some miracle, Franka is there somewhere and should she be alive, then every second counts. We can't wait for daylight."

"So why aren't you going?" I finally ask, having sat on that for a bit.

"Not leaving you. I promised you and I'm good with that." He sets his jaw, and I can tell he means every word.

"I'm not," I say, surprising the heck out of him. "If there is any chance that woman is still with us, you said yourself you'll need every spare body. I want you to go. Dammit Neil, I know you *want* to go and I can't live with any more guilt. If she dies because…" I don't have a chance to finish that sentence because his mouth is on mine.

"God, I love you," he mumbles against my lips. "I'm going to get Emma."

"No! Don't wake her up," I admonish him, but all he does is laugh.

"Are you kidding me? Emma is probably in the kitchen already, baking up a storm. She always holds vigil when Gus gets called out," he clarifies.

"Well, in that case, help me get dressed and over there. I'm not gonna get in between Emma and her stove. I'll wait there for you." I'm already off the bed, wobbling on one foot when he comes around and helps me get dressed in record time. With my crutches in hand and Neil's firm hand on my back, he walks me down the garden path, Chaos lumbering half asleep beside us. Sure enough, the house lights are blazing and Emma's red mop of hair can be seen through the kitchen window. Neil knocks on the back door and a startled Emma shuffles over to unlock it.

"You guys al lright?" she asks, looking mainly at me.

"We're fine. I just wanted to stay with you while Neil goes looking." Emma is obviously surprised when I'm the one answering, given that I've barely spoken since the attack, but she recovers quickly.

"Of course, come in. To be honest, I could've sworn Gus said you were going to stay with Kendra," she says half accusingly to Neil, who in turn lifts his eyebrow at me.

"I need him to go. For me. I asked him to go," I ramble a bit as I quickly explain.

"Better head out, Pup. You'll be safe here. I'll have my phone on my body and you call me for anything, okay? Anything," he presses that point.

"Okay."

"C'mere," he says, completely ignoring Emma and taking my face in his hands before kissing me breathless.

"Careful," I mutter, still half-dazed from that short but intense tongue action. "I love you."

A big smile spreads over Neil's face. "I will and I know you do. Me too." A quick hard kiss and he's gone. Emma closes and locks the door behind him before she turns, smiling from ear to ear.

"He calls you Pup," Emma observes with humor in her eyes. "Swear to God, I don't know where these men get their pet names from, but that's a novel one."

I shrug my shoulders not quite able to keep my own smile to myself. I'm not going to admit that every time he calls me that, my insides melt a little, knowing the meaning behind it. There's no way I'm going to share that. It's mine.

"You look better," she says, tilting her head to one side. "You've been like a zombie and frankly had us worried for a while there. Looks like the clouds have lifted some. Of course, love has a way of doing that." She passes by me on the way to the kitchen where she pulls out a large mixing bowl. "Love. Mmmm, I'm thinking red velvet cake for the occasion."

Emma is a great listener and two and a half hours later, she sets a mug of tea and a slice of her freshly baked cake in front of me as she surreptitiously wipes at her eyes.

"You know, those scars, just like this whole experience, will become part of who you are. Claim them. Make them yours. He may have put you through hell, put those marks on you, but it's in your control how much more of *you* you'll let him have."

I let her words settle in my heart. I've been a control freak all my life, tightly guarding my actions and my feelings. This past week—hell, even before that, since the time Neil accosted me in the clinic kitchen—I've felt the ground shifting under my feet. Control slowly slipping from my hands and where before my head would rule, my heart started taking over. Neil had shown me over and over again that I am in safe hands with him, but it's Emma's words that point out the power I still hold. The power to choose what I carry along in my life. Lars Cayman was just a bump in my road. Granted, a pretty damn scary and significant one, but a bump nonetheless, and I'm not about to let it stop me in my tracks, *dagnabbit*. I stick my fork in the slice of red velvet cake and take a good-sized bite. Emma sits back in her chair, her hands around her mug of tea, and simply smiles at me.

That's when the house phone rings.

CHAPTER TWENTY-FIVE

Neil

"Thought you were staying with Kendra?"

Damian is standing in the doorway to Drew's office, a coffee in his hand. Courageous man to try the coffee Carol, the ancient woman who's been waving the scepter over the sheriff's office for many decades, insists on brewing to resemble tar. "Puts hair on your chest," she always says. Carol never seems to go home, because she was in her usual perch behind the front desk when I walked in. At two o'clock in the morning. Still, no one seemed to think it strange. Joe once told me he suspected she had a tracer on his car, because she always knew where to find him when he was still sheriff.

"She's with Emma. Insisted I go," I admit to Damian, shrugging as I walk behind him into the office which is already crowded with Gus, Caleb, Malachi, Joe, Luna and, of course, Drew, as well as a handful of his deputies. Twelve of us packed in there like sardines.

"Let's get this show on the road," Damian announces, wincing as he takes his first sip. Without hesitation, he tosses the full cup in the wastebasket by the desk, drawing a chuckle from most of us. We've been there and done exactly that. "What have we got?"

Drew stands by a whiteboard on the wall, on which a schematic layout of what I assume is Sundance Rentals is drawn. "It's just a dirt road going north off the 184 toward Dolores. Last time I was up there, the sign had been taken down, so you'll have to start looking for the entrance near six miles from Mancos. The main building is at the end of the dirt road, about three miles up. You can't miss it. Carol printed off resort maps that show each of the cabins. We should probably divide them between us." Drew looks to Damian for guidance.

"Teams of two. Each team starts in with an odd numbered cabin. It appears that although the cabins are spread out, they're numbered in some order of proximity, so that seems easiest. Clear one cabin and move on. Got six radios?" He directs the last at Drew, who nods at one of his deputies. The moment the guy comes back in, his hands full, Damian continues, "Pick a partner, grab a radio and let's go."

Mal elbows me in the side. "Coming?"

"Yup," is my response as I grab us a radio and a map and head out the door.

As we pass the front desk, Carol leans over. "Got ambulance on standby. Just in case."

"You're the best, Carol," Joe pipes up behind me.

"Tell me something I don't know," she says on a snort. The woman may look a little past it, but nothing gets past *her*. How she knows the shit she does is a mystery.

Once outside, I follow Mal to his SUV which makes more sense than my truck in case we have to transport someone. I try not to think about the possibility of what we might find, if anything, but I can't stop the persistent nugget of hope that this is not a wild goose chase. Despite the fact there seems to be sufficient evidence to hang Cayman by the balls if he ever recovers enough to stand trial, there is a sense of unfinished business with Franka Mellis still unaccounted for. For the sake of everyone, I hope we find her alive, but at the very least, for her family, even a body would bring some closure. I've learned that indefinite doubt is much harder to live with than the certainty of bad news, in the long run.

It doesn't take long for us to get to the turn onto the dirt road, and I keep my eyes peeled for anything that might help us. Being the first to team up, I picked cabin seven. So once we pass the main lodge, we park the vehicle as close to the foot trail going into the forest as possible. Seven is one of the cabins farthest away from the lodge and it takes us just shy of ten minutes to get there on foot. ATVs would have been helpful, but our feet would have to do. The only equipment we have with us is the radio, our weapons and a big Maglite Mal pulled from behind his seat. "Why seven?" Mal wants to know.

I shrug my shoulders, not sure myself. "Don't really know. Other than the fact that the guy likes to follow patterns. Seven archangels. I don't know."

"Right, but wasn't Kendra the seventh? This should be the eighth then. Lucifer. The fallen angel."

"You may be right," I tell Mal. "Good thing that's our next stop." I look at the cabin in front of us and note the storm door hanging half off the hinges. The general condition of the old log structure is decrepit at best, with tree shoots growing from the damn roof and the half collapsed deck on the front. It's a wonder it still has some windows intact.

We split up and each go around a side. There's one window on my side but I can't see much with my little penlight when I look in. Doesn't take long for the beam from Mal's Maglite to come bobbing around the back of the cabin. "Nothing round the other side and two small windows up high on the back. Lemme see." I step aside to give him better access to the window. "I don't see anything," he says as he moves along the side back to the front. "Let's get inside."

All it takes is a shoulder thrown against the door for the lock to break right through the rotting post on the inside. The sound of scurrying comes from one of the bedrooms in the back, and while Malachi gives the kitchen and living area a good once over, I move to the first of the three doors along the back wall. The first room still has bedding on the bed, but by the looks of it, a family of rodents or something have pulled stuffing out of the pillows or bedspread to make a nest of sorts in the middle of the mattress. Doesn't look like this place has been touch by anything with opposable thumbs. As I open the door to the second bedroom, Mal slips into the third door, which I suspect is a bathroom. Just seconds later, both of us come back out, empty-handed.

"Doesn't look like anyone has been here in a fuck of a long time," I tell Mal, who simply nods in agreement. Looks like cabin eight is next.

Mal clicks on the radio he is holding. "Cabin seven clear, moving to eight."

"Ten-four," Damian's voice crackles in response.

The walk to eight, which is one of the most northern of the cabins, doesn't take quite as long. I'm jolted in my steps when Mal puts his arm out to stop me just as we get a visual. "Something's off," he says, aiming his light at the ground in front of him. I don't question Mal. He's proven himself time and again with his tracking ability. He's got some kind of sixth sense and the nose of a bloodhound.

"There," he points with his light. "I'm guessing ATV." The area he's lighting up shows the distinct ridging of heavy-duty off-roading tires. Immediately, my eyes go back to the cabin in front of us and I start moving. I don't even bother with the windows first. The closer I get, the clearer it becomes that someone has most definitely been here. The old storm door on this one has been carefully removed and propped up against the side of the house and the windows look like they've been cleaned. Before I have a chance to try the door, Mal busts through. The stench inside is overwhelming and doesn't bode well. As Mal mumbles into the radio, I head for the bedrooms.

I find her in the second bedroom rolled up in a fetal position on the floor beside the bed, a dirty pot filled with brackish water that must've come from the hole in the roof above beside her. Naked, bloody and with her back carved up, I don't think she's alive, but I have to check. The woman looks emaciated when I get closer and my heart clenches in my chest. With a tentative hand, I lift the dirty strands of her hair off her face and neck and almost jump back when I see her eyes open. She is very much alive, judging by the rapid blinking of her eyelids. "Franka?" I ask her softly as I hear Mal come in the room behind me. The nod of her head is slight, but it's there. "You're okay, honey. We're going to get you out of here. He's not gonna hurt you again." With quick movements, I pull the shirt from my back and use it to cover her body, trying to avoid the mess on her back. "You're a fighter, aren't you? Good for you for hanging in there." I'm mumbling nonsense, trying hard to contain my own emotions at the knowledge that this woman not only has seen hell up close, but she's been alone for almost nine days. That must have been a curse and a blessing all at the same time. Starving was a painful business and someone with her injuries should not have been able to survive. Judging from the blood pooling under her body, those injuries extend beyond the now morbidly familiar pattern carved in her back.

"K…kids?" The word is no more than a sigh from her cracked lips but the desperation in her eyes is loud enough.

"They're good. Your daughter reported you missing. She's a smart girl. Strong too, just like her momma." I carefully stroke the back of my hand over one of hers, hoping the human contact will bring her some warmth. As I watch a thick tear rolling down her face, I wish I could at least fucking hold her to give her comfort, but I'm afraid to move her. Then I see Kendra's face superimposed on hers and for the second time in so many weeks, my emotions overwhelm me. This woman had hung on for the sake of her kids. Kendra had sacrificed herself for the sake of her sister. Both of them the epitome of courage and selflessness.

It humbles me. It also heals something in me. They did what they had to do for theirs. I did what I had to do for mine. My team, my men, my friends.

Perhaps killing that boy was my sacrifice to make.

Kendra

"Gus is coming to pick us up."

Emma turns to me and grabs my hands, her eyes wet with unshed tears. "She alive, honey. Those poor babies are getting their momma back."

I pull one of my hands from hers and slap it over my mouth in disbelief and overwhelming relief. "How?" I manage.

"I didn't get much detail but I know Neil and Mal found her, badly injured, dehydrated and starving but with a heart that apparently beats strong. Your man is going with her in the ambulance and asked Gus to bring you if it's not too much."

"Good," I cry. "Neil will be gentle with her. I'm so relieved…yes, of course I'll come." When the floodgates burst, Emma is right there, holding me in her arms.

Gus gets there twenty minutes later with a smile on his face and doesn't hesitate to kiss his wife soundly before turning to me. "Girl," he rumbles, his voice rough with emotion. "Don't think that woman would've survived another day. *Fuck me.*" He shakes his head before cupping my wet cheeks in his hands. "Saved her life, you did. No doubt in my mind."

I do a face plant in his shirt, which smells of outside air and sweaty man, as his arms close gently around me. "C'mon," he rumbles. "Your man needs you."

"Such a Neanderthal," I hear Emma mutter as she grabs for her walker, and I can't help but chuckle through my tears.

Neil is rushing to Gus's big Yukon before the thing has come to a full stop, and pulls my door open. Instead of helping me out, he climbs in the back seat with me and buries his head in my neck, holding on tight. I hear the soft click of the doors, suggesting Gus and Emma are giving us a private moment. My hands rub his back as I try to distinguish his mumbles against my skin.

"Honey," I try, but his face stays buried in my neck. "Neil?"

Finally, after I hear him take a deep breath in and let it out slowly, he lifts his head, resting his forehead against mine. The anguish in his red-rimmed eyes rips at my heart. One of my hands comes up to touch his face and he tilts his head to kiss my palm. "Talk to me, baby," I whisper, watching his eyes turn to me.

"I don't think you've ever called me that. I like it," he says, his voice gruff with emotion.

"Talk to me," I urge him again.

"I kept seeing your face. She was so frail, so broken, and yet her eyes were still so full of life. For her kids. She survived for her kids." His disjointed words are a testament to the horror she must've endured. "I couldn't leave her. I'm sorry I didn't come get you myself. I needed you, but she…"

"Shhh," I hush him, covering his mouth with my fingers. "I'm glad you were there. Glad it was you who stayed with her.

Remember, I experienced firsthand what an amazing comfort you are. I love you so much."

His face dives back down in my neck and I hold the back of his head while the other hand softly rubs his heaving back. Instinctively, I know this is about more than what he experienced out there. This is something that runs so much deeper. I don't say anything, I just hold him the same way he's held me through my struggles. Without questions, without judgement, but with overwhelming love in my heart. What a fool I've been.

What could've been hours later, but was likely only a few minutes, Neil lifts his face from my shoulder and kisses me softly. "Thank you," he says simply, unashamed of the tears streaking his face. That, more than anything, shows me the depth of his trust in me and I feel honored. I don't insult him with a response, the situation doesn't require one. I gently smile at him instead. "I'm pretty sure she was violated, and I feel guilty for saying this, but I'm so grateful he never got that far with you. If I could have another go at him, I'd finish him off." I can hear the anger in his voice and shudder to think what the woman's had to endure. "But I just found out from Damian that Cayman died earlier tonight." I see him clench his jaw before he bites off, " Too easy. He should've suffered."

I swallow as I lift my hand and soothe it along his jaw. "Well, I'm glad. Seems like sweet justice to me. Franka is found alive, just when he gets sent into the flames of hell. Let's go in."

Gus and Emma are standing beside the car, Gus holding a wheelchair he must've picked up inside. Without argument, I sit down and let Neil drive. He seems to need to take care of me right now, and I'll gladly let him. The only ones in the waiting room are Luna and Damian when we enter the waiting room. The other guys all went home to their wives and kids. Only Drew is still at the cabin, keeping an eye out until Jasper and the forensics' crew get there. No one is in a hurry anymore, now that Franka is found and Cayman is dead. There won't be a trial which, I have to admit, gives me no small measure of relief. But, of course, the case still has to be closed out properly. There are many jurisdictions involved and everyone will want to be assured Cayman was the man involved.

For a minute, I worry about the effect this would have on Neil, being responsible for a man's death, but he doesn't seem fazed. Damian assures me there will be no charges against him.

It's close to daybreak when a nurse comes in with a tired-looking, forty-ish, familiar-looking man in tow. The nurse whispers something to him and points him in Neil's direction, who lifts his arm from my shoulder before standing up.

"Neil?" the man asks as he approaches, his hand stretched in front of him. "My name is Ben Bridges, I'm Franka's brother." The moment he grabs Neil's hand, he pulls him forward into a hug, complete with manly backslaps. "Thank you for looking after my sister. She says…" The poor guy can barely get his words out. "Franka says you stayed by her side."

"I did. Your sister is an amazingly strong woman," Neil says gruffly.

"She wouldn't have made it if…if you hadn't kept looking for her," Ben says.

"Actually, you have my girlfriend to thank for that. Kendra is the one who didn't give up. She's also the one who pointed us in the right direction, so she deserves that credit." I'm still a little stuck on the *girlfriend* title and the rest of his words register only when I find myself drawn up from my chair. Ben pulls me in a bone-crushing hug that has me yelp out in pain. Shocked, he releases me immediately.

"What did I do? I'm sorry…I…"

Still trying to catch my breath, it's Neil who answers. "Kendra was one of his victims, or perhaps I should say one of his survivors. Her back…I don't know if you are aware of your sister's injuries, but *he* would carve wings in their backs. Kendra has—"

"My back is healing, it's just a bit tender still," I say, interrupting Neil, finally able to speak.

I smile at him, hoping to make him feel a little better.

"Wait, you're Kendra?" Ben asks incredulously. "You're Kendra the PT? I didn't realize…my son—"

"Ben," I fill in, finally figuring out why he seemed familiar. "You're Toms's dad."

Neil's arm pulls me close. "In that case," he says to the man. "No thanks necessary at all. Your son saved Kendra and I will never be able to thank him enough for that."

"Small fucking world," Damian mutters behind me and I can't hold back my words.

"No shit, Sherlock."

CHAPTER TWENTY-SIX

Neil

Surreal.

This whole ordeal has been mind-boggling from beginning to end.

I'm standing in the doorway, watching Kendra reach over and stroke the hair away from Franka's face and it about does me in. These women have come through the other end of a nightmare of epic proportions, and yet for each of them the focus is on someone else.

"This is good." Naomi walks up and leans against my side, sliding her arm around my waist. "These two won't need to explain to each other how they feel. They'll know. They can talk about what happened without shame. They won't need to be concerned about their injuries or their emotions. Their connection will likely be as non-judgmental as is possible."

Her words carry an underlying message and I hear it. "How do you know?" I ask her softly, and I feel her shoulders shrug under the arm I've loosely draped around her.

"Women have a natural inclination to share. Sharing their burdens with others who have lived through similar experiences only makes it easier. Ironically that makes them mentally tougher, generally better equipped to deal with the unexpected. Men on the other hand have a tendency to avoid. They seem to feel the best way to deal with struggles is to pretend they don't exist. They don't process properly, and as a result, it can leave them crippled. Less resilient." When I look down at her upturned face, I see no judgement, only friendly concern. "I've seen the struggle in you from the beginning. Don't know why it's always been clear to me, it just has. Maybe the way you always worked hard at being exactly what everyone expected of you. Too hard. But I think you'll find most of us here see right through that facade."

"I told Kendra. I never told anyone, but I told her," I say to her quietly as my eyes are unwittingly drawn back to the woman in the wheelchair.

"Good. I'm glad, but maybe you should also consider looking into a group. Check in with Veteran's Affairs to see what there is on offer."

I don't say anything when she gives me a quick squeeze before letting me go, but that doesn't mean I didn't listen.

Kendra is very quiet when we finally leave the hospital around lunchtime. Other than a coffee and muffin from the cafeteria, we haven't eaten since last night's picnic in bed.

"You hungry, Pup? You've gotta be hurting by now." I put my hand on her leg to get her attention. When she turns her face to me, I can see the exhaustion in her eyes.

"Not really, but I guess we should eat."

"Gus took Emma home earlier. I bet she's already back in the kitchen whipping something up. Or we can stop at the diner if you like? We could pick something up from there and bring it home." When I don't get an answer, I look over to find her chewing her bottom lip. "What's up?"

"Where's home?"

"For now, the guesthouse. Clint and his brother are going to start work on your house this coming week. I'm not sure how long it'll be before they have all the repairs done, but it sounds

like Clint means business. He's pulled in his brother's entire
crew from Durango as well. My guess, a couple of weeks?
You'll be back in your house before you know it." I don't tell
her that I've already made arrangements to buy the house as-is
from Beth and am footing the bill for the repairs. Beth's
insurance is dragging their feet, which is why I agreed to a
reduced price. That way, when her insurance finally pays out,
Beth can pocket that money as part of the proceeds of the sale.
And with Clint and Jed doing the renos, they're offering a
friendly price, so I benefit in the long run. It just doesn't seem
like the right time to talk about the fact that I've bought my way
into being her landlord, or rather, her roommate. For now—I'm
planning on changing that status as soon as I can.

Kendra

"Thank you for coming."

The woman's soft voice and brittle smile brought tears to
my eyes.

When her brother Ben, Tom's father, told me Franka
wanted to see me, I wasn't sure what to expect. It certainly
wasn't this frail looking woman with steel in her eyes, greeting
me politely like we were just introduced at a social event.

"Of course," I manage inadequately.

"You have his scars?" I nod, knowing she's talking about
the wings.

"He didn't get a chance to finish. I assume yours are?" It
feels odd to talk about this in an almost matter of fact way, but
it's not with her.

"Yes," she says, squeezing her eyes shut. Probably remembering, just as I am, the hot pain of the cuts in already inflamed skin. "He talked about you. You were his Raphael. He called you his angel of mercy."

"I'm sorry."

"Don't be. You hold no responsibility. In fact, from what I understand, you're the reason I was found at all. I was so close to giving up…" Her voice trails off.

"I'll leave you to get some rest," I tell her softly, reaching to swipe the hair back off her face. "You need it so your body can recover."

"Please give Ben your number; I'd like to stay in touch."

I smile at her. "I can do you one better, your nephew Tom already has it. He's my favorite patient." Her eyes open wide in surprise.

"Well, I'll be…" I see how the weird connections are starting to come together for her just by watching the expressions on her face. "It looks like somehow our paths were destined to cross. I'll be in touch." She grabs my hand and squeezes, her emotions getting the best of her.

It seems like the most natural thing in the world to lean forward and kiss her cheek. "Unless I beat you to it," I tell her with a wobbly smile.

Somehow I feel that in that short visit, a lifelong friendship was forged.

It isn't until I'm sitting next to Neil in his truck that it hits me. It's over. The monster is dead, and three of us survived, counting my sister. But what happens now?

With my mind trying to find some traction on all the thoughts randomly floating around, I'm almost catatonic when Neil asks about food. Maybe that's not such a bad idea. I'm surprised at how little of an opinion I have about anything right now. When Neil brings up going home, it startles me. I hadn't thought about that. Of course, I haven't thought about anything remotely practical or concrete in recent days, but I literally have not once paid mind to the house and my possessions. Now I do and can't help wonder if the fact I don't have a place to call mine is part of what is making me feel a bit disjointed. Unattached. Something I worked hard to maintain for years, but that suddenly seems to have lost all its appeal. I don't want to be unattached. I want to be part of something…someone. Neil.

By the time we pull up to Gus and Emma's house, I'm half asleep, and Neil comes around to help me from the car.

"I have my crutches, you know. I can walk," I point out when he lifts me out of the car and carries me toward the house.

"First of all, in your current state, you're likely to land on your face. You can barely keep your eyes open. And secondly, I happen to like holding you. So just let me."

All right then. I'm too tired to argue, and besides, it is not exactly a hardship to be carried around, snuggled against his comfy chest. Instead, I settle my forehead against his jaw and loop my arms around his neck. Not bad at all.

Before we get to the door, it's already pulled open by Emma. "She okay?" she asks Neil, but I answer.

"I'm good, Em. Just really tired, and this behemoth here insisted on carrying me." Emma's giggle precedes us into the house where Neil unceremoniously deposits me on the couch.

"Stay," he growls at me. "Gonna get some food."

I've settled with my foot elevated on the coffee table when he comes walking in from the kitchen with a tray. "Thank you," I manage while already shoveling the first spoon full of stew in my mouth. I wasn't hungry earlier, but the scent of bay leaf and garlic permeating the air had my stomach rumbling in seconds. The fresh chunk of cornbread is gone in three bites before I look up and catch Neil watching me. "What?"

"Nothing. Just enjoying watching you eat," he says prior to diverting his attention to his own bowl.

Emma walks in with a glass of wine in her hand which she deposits on the tray in front of me. "You're not on painkillers or anything, are you?"

"Not anymore," I inform her. Neil pretend coughs and my eyes shoot daggers at him. He seems to find this amusing since he shakes his head grinning. "Well, I'm not."

"Babe, you never took any. I checked. Only reason you'd occasionally get a dose is because you got them intravenously at first, and the nurses caught you trying to go without when you were obviously in agony. Stubborn," he mumbles.

"I hate how they make me feel," I admit grudgingly. "All loopy like."

"I know," Emma says, taking a seat beside me. "I hate pain meds. Avoid them like the plague." Happy with the unexpected support, I gloat at Neil, who just continues to eat while shaking his head. Ugh.

When we're done eating—and surprisingly I finished every last bite—Neil gets up and brings his bowl and my tray to the kitchen. He sticks his head back inside and looks at Emma. "Is Gus in the office?"

"Yup, just go on through," she answers.

"Be right back," he directs at me. I give him a thumbs up. I'm sure there's a ton of work waiting for him, since he's spent the best of the past week by my bedside. I already feel bad enough.

When I turn back to Emma, she's looking at me through slitted eyes. "How was she?" I don't need much more clarification. She's worried that seeing Franka may have made me regress back into zombie mode, but it hasn't. "So fucking strong, I'm in absolute awe," I tell Emma honestly. "He had her for a long time. Did unspeakable things to her and yet she hung in there. Even when she was left for dead, she didn't give up. It makes me almost ashamed there were moments in the short time I was with him that I wanted to die. She didn't. Her focus on her children needing her is what kept her going, collecting water where she could, keeping herself hydrated as best as possible." Emma's hand settles warmly on my arm.

"It's amazing the strengths we discover in ourselves during a lifetime. Having kids is one way to find a core of steel. But honey, you've been no less strong. She had her connection with her kids to pull her through, whereas you were ready to sacrifice your own life for your sister's safety. There's no real measurement for strength, nor should there be. The same goes for pain, and happiness as well, those can only be measured against your own experience, not ever someone else's."

***

Neil

"Hey, do you have a minute?"

Gus's back is to the door of his office, and he's pecking away at his keyboard with two fingers.

"Yup," he says, turning around and indicating one of the visitor's chairs. He rests his elbows on the desk, folds his hands under his chin, waiting for me to spill.

"You looked into my background when you hired me," I state and Gus grunts his affirmation. "How much do you know?"

"Enough to know you'd be an asset to GFI. That's all I was interested in." He leans back in his chair and scrutinizes me.

"But I have a feeling that's not what you're after." His eyes never waver from mine, and I end up being the one to lower mine first. I came in here to talk to him. To clear the air, to ask for advice. Now that I have his attention, the words seem to get stuck in my throat.

"Fine," he says, filling in the heavy silence. "I know your unit was called out to take out a group of rebels that were attacking supply convoys. I know you were a sniper. And I also know that this particular mission went wrong when you were ambushed by said rebels who took your best friend down. I know you took out the shooter." He leans forward again, looking at me hard. "Look, I understand the kind of damage that can do to a person. The survivor's guilt. The what ifs, the questions, the regrets. I get it. And I know it can ruin a person's life if they let it, but bud…you've got—"

"It was a young boy," I interrupt him and watch confusion hit him. "The shooter I took down was just a boy." I'm waiting for a reaction, for the shock, the horror, but instead, Gus reaches over and grabs my forearm.

"In that case, I hope the adult that indoctrinated that child, put a gun in his hand and trained him how to use it is burning in hell for all eternity, because that boy's death is on his hands. Not. Fucking. Yours." He bites out word for word. His hold on my arm is painful and his eyes burn a hole in mine. "Not yours, son," he repeats quietly.

I swallow hard before I can talk again. "I love Kendra."

"Not a surprise." He smiles.

"I mean; I love her. I want a future with her. The whole package. I already bought the house. We have the dog. I'll put a ring on her as soon as I know for sure she'll have me, and I want a family, Gus. I need to be right to have a family. I don't want any of this touching them. Ever."

Letting my arm go, Gus pulls open a drawer in his desk and pulls out an address book and a piece of paper before looking at me. "You're afraid if you'll have kids…" He lets his words trail off and all I can do is nod my head. "Okay, I get that, but you've been around Beth's grandkid, Max, and Caleb and Katie's little guy Mattias worships the ground you walk on. Has being around them ever triggered anything for you?"

"I don't think so," I admit.

"Still, I'm going to call a buddy of mine who runs a veterans' clinic in Durango. I know they offer some services. Might be a good place to start?"

"Naomi mentioned something along those lines," I mumble.

"Naomi's always been sharp as a tack. What about Kendra? She know?"

"Told her everything."

"Proud of you. That can't have been easy, although I'm sure it didn't make one lick of difference to her," Gus says and the lump shoots back up my throat.

"She cried, but I think it was as much for me as for that boy," I admit. "I'm surprised she didn't judge me."

"Is this why you don't see your family? Mormons, right? I'm guessing they weren't too supportive when they found out you were a sniper. That you had killed."

"Got it in one."

"Their loss, son. Don't know whether you've noticed, but there are a lot of people with fucked-up backgrounds here in Cedar Tree. All different kinds of fucked up, but we make up the best family a man can have. Now," he says, resolutely sitting back and picking up his phone. "Let's get you sorted out."

CHAPTER TWENTY-SEVEN

Neil

"Please, Neil."

Kendra's good leg slides between mine and her hand is snaking into my boxers. She already has a good grip on my painfully hard cock by the time I can grab her wrist.

"Babe…" I warn her. "We said we'd wait." I can barely get the words out, because although I can now control the movement of her hand, I don't have any control over her thumb, which is rubbing the blood-engorged head of my Johnson. This is week three of abstinence, one and a half weeks since Kendra was released, and I'm about to explode just from the feel of her skin against mine.

Since finding Franka, Kendra has been on an emotional roller coaster, one that I have a hard time keeping up with. The two of them have talked on the phone, and I've brought her to visit Franka in the hospital, but every time they've had contact, it's like Kendra has a little setback. Naomi assures me it's actually good that some of those emotions brought on when they are together are coming out, but the result is either withdrawal or tears. Neither of those I want to see from her. And her emotional outbursts usually end in a search for affection. We tried once last week, and when I accidentally ran my hand under her shirt and touched the skin of her back, she burst out crying. I told her then, until she was one hundred percent ready, we weren't even going to go there. But here she is again, for the second time in as many days, with her hands all over me. It takes everything out of me not to roll her on her back and sink into her, but I'm afraid I won't be able to be gentle. And that's what she should have—gentle.

"I need you," she whimpers in my neck, letting me pull her hand from my underwear. "I'm not kidding, Neil. I'm about to spontaneously combust if I have to wake up next to you, feeling your morning wood against my ass. Please…"

I don't know whether it's what she's saying or the fact that her leg is still rubbing suggestively between mine, that has me roll on top of her. She's assured me the past few days that her back doesn't hurt anymore, and to demonstrate she willingly drops her legs open, allowing my hips to sink between them.

"Yessss…" she hisses, lifting her hips to rub her pussy against my cock. Instead of letting her get off like that, I lift my hips. Lowering my head, I capture her lips between mine and rub my tongue along the crease so she opens for me. I kiss her long and deep until her body is squirming under mine. Then I pull away from her mouth and plant kisses along her jaw, down her neck and along the edge of her T-shirt.

"Need to see you, Pup," I mumble against the swell of her breast and she willingly allows me to shift up her shirt to expose her gorgeous tits. I close my mouth over her breast, sucking the perky nipple and surrounding creamy flesh in my mouth.

"Gahhh…Jesus. Yes."

Switching sides, I slide one hand down her soft belly and into the top of her panties. Her body instantly freezes and I stop with only the tips of my fingers under the elastic. "Babe?"

"I'm sorry. I wasn't thinking. I haven't…I didn't…" she mutters incoherently.

"What?"

"Since…well, I haven't bothered *grooming*." She whispers the last word like it's the dirtiest thing to ever have come out of her mouth, and I fight to keep the chuckle that bubbles up contained. Mostly. "Don't laugh. It's probably a jungle down there." This time, I don't bother holding back and I belt out a laugh. That earns me a punch to my shoulder which only serves to make me laugh harder. "It's not funny," she hisses.

"I don't care. I don't," I repeat when she lifts an eyebrow in disbelief. "But because I see you do, we're going to solve this problem." In one move, I'm up and off the bed, pulling Kendra along with me.

"What are you doing?" she squeals as I lift her up with my hands under her ass, and her legs instinctively wrap around me. Marching her into the bathroom, I sit her on the edge of the tub.

"Stay put," I tell her when she makes a move to get up. Grabbing a bar of soap and my razor, a wet washcloth and a clean towel, I drop to my knees in front of her and set it all on the toilet-seat lid. "Lift your butt," I tell her, slipping my fingers in the elastic of her panties.

"Neil!" she protests. "I can do it myself."

"I want to."

She rolls her eyes and doesn't budge. One very determined look her way and she finally complies as I slowly slide her panties down and wrestle them over her cast.

"Spread for me," I tell her when she clenches her knees together. "Pup, we're going to do this. You may as well open up." Leaning in, I plant a soft kiss against her lips and mumble, "I promise to make it worth your while later."

"Oh, fine," she sputters, trying to mask the heated blush on her cheeks as she spreads her legs wide.

Trying not to react to those pretty swollen lips peeking through the negligible pubic hair she finds so offensive, I wet the area before gently soaping her up. "How do you like it?" I ask, the razor ready in my hand.

"Uhhh, shouldn't I ask you that?"

"Like I said before, I don't care. You're beautiful any way you come. But I want you to be comfortable, so what stays and what goes?"

"Erm, well…I usually leave a landing strip. You know? Just a bit of—"

"I know what a landing strip is, Pup. Seen one or two of those." I chuckle, but from the look on Kendra's face, she didn't find it that amusing. *Not a good time to fuck up, dumbass.* "All right, ready?"

I'm a little nervous, since I've never done this before, but I've been able to do my face without too much damage for a few years now. As gently as I can, I slide the razor along one side of her labia, noting the strong scent of arousal. *Fuck*, she likes this, the minx.

It only takes a few strokes to get her smooth. "Gotta stand up for the next part. Hold on to the counter." I help her up and have her lean her butt against the counter. "Spread your legs a little." This time, there is no protest, and I kiss her belly right above her mound.

When I'm done and have wiped away the soap with the washcloth, I lift my eyes to find hers half-lidded and looking down at me. "That okay?" I ask, and she slowly nods, not even looking at my handiwork. Without taking my eyes off her, I lean in and nudge at the top of her crease with my nose. Her mouth falls open, and her chest rises. Dropping whatever I still had in my hands, I place my hands on the back of her knees and slide them all the way up to her ass, forcing her legs open a little more. Just enough to slip my tongue over her soft folds. Her taste is rich and unique, and I'm suddenly hungry. "Bed," I manage, before standing up and helping her into the bedroom.

"Come here." I lie back on the mattress and have her straddle me. "Now hold on to the headboard." The moment her hands reach over me, I slide my body down between her legs, giving me a perfect view of that plump pussy. With my hands on her hips, I guide her down until I feel her thighs against my ears and her arousal against my lips. Fucking heaven. Gently, I lick and prod her, at times running the flat of my tongue up to flick her clit. When she starts rocking her hips, I give her the friction she's looking for. "Ride my face, baby," I mutter, my voice muffled against her pussy. With a cry, she grinds herself down while I feast on her. When I feel her legs shaking with her impending release, I quickly slide out from under her and push my boxers down. Moving behind her, I take all of her in. Arms stretched out in front of her and her upper body leaning over so that her ass is gloriously tilted up in the air.

"Beautiful. My beautiful girl."

Kendra moans in response, lifting her ass higher when I gently push her shirt up and her shoulders down at the same time. So needy, she doesn't even notice that her shirt is now up around her neck, exposing her back completely. Not even when I slide my rock hard cock inside her from behind and thrust balls deep into her heat. Already her pussy is clenching, she's that close, and having saved up for three weeks, I'm not far behind. I lean over with one hand in the mattress and the other slipping around her hip to find her clit. Pinching it between two fingers, I pound inside her once, and again, until I hear my name cried from her lips and feel her body shudder her release beneath me.

Then I let go with an explosive roar.

Kendra

I vaguely notice my ears ringing from Neil's bellow.

Still catching my breath from my own mind-numbing orgasm, it takes me a minute to realize my shirt is around my shoulders, leaving my back exposed. But before I can wiggle out from under his weight, I feel his lips against my skin, leaving a trail of kisses down along my spine and up my side. I can't breathe. His touch is so slight, so tender. I feel treasured and the lingering worries that the markings on my body might turn him off simply drain away.

"Breathe, babe," he mumbles against my skin and I do as he says, taking a lungful of air in and slowly releasing it—letting all my reservations go. "That's my girl."

I try to roll over with him still on top, but my cast hampers my movements. Instead, Neil rolls off me and lies on his side, head perched up on his hand. I turn to face him and put my hand on his chest. His face is soft, relaxed, and his eyes show everything that I'm feeling reflected back at me. It's one of those moments where no words are needed. Still, my mouth wants to form them. "Thank you for not giving up on me. For following your heart and letting me find mine. For the way you force me to feel everything instead of letting me retreat. I wish I hadn't been so blinded by my own misconception and had given you half a chance from the start. You are so much more than I ever allowed myself to believe of you."

"Shut up." His deep voice sounds rough as he pulls me close, pressing his chin to the crown of my head. "I have what I always wanted and never thought I was going to get. Don't fucking thank me. I don't deserve you, but I have you, and there's no way in hell I'll let go of my dream."

"Anyone want to share?"

The no-nonsense therapist manning the therapy group both Franka and I joined looks around the room at every individual. This is our second time. The first session just three days ago had been branded in my mind. I was shocked not only that both men and women were in attendance, but at the diversity and depth of cruelty people inflict on each other. These are all victims of violent crime, and although I initially balked at the fact there were men present as well, Franka insisted I give it a chance. So I did, and the few men that spoke up when this same question was asked in the first session, made it painfully obvious that my preconceived idea of women as victims was archaic. Some of the stories shared, by both men and women, were horrifying, but what struck me hardest was that the feelings—the emotions—experienced during and after the events described, were heartbreakingly similar.

Which is why, only the second session in, I don't flinch when Dr. Marten's eyes land on me. Instead, I give Franka's hand a squeeze and take a deep breath. "I'll share," I say, my voice a little shaky.

"Then so will I," Franka surprises me by saying in a much stronger voice beside me.

There are a few tears, and not just ours, some horrified looks but much less than I'd have expected, and finally there is a sense of acceptance expressed in looks and softly murmured words of encouragement by the other twelve members of the group. It's also harder than I thought it would be to expose myself to strangers like that, but I'm trying. For someone who's always been carefully contained, sharing simply doesn't come naturally. What makes it possible is the knowledge that the emotional aftermath is very similar for everyone here, regardless of what they were victim to or even of gender. Guilt, self-doubt, regret, anger; those seem to be common themes.

I'm exhausted by the end of the session and I'm surprised, when we walk out of the hospital—me still on those blasted crutches—to find Neil leaning against the grill of his truck, talking with Tom Bridges.

"Guess Ben has a double shift tonight," Franka explains. "He's taking on as much extra work as he can. His medical insurance isn't the best and he really wants to give Tom his dream of going to college, but the expenses for his surgery and treatments, plus the fact that there are three more kids waiting in line, have really drained them. I'm lucky I have the insurance I do through work, or I'd be screwed too."

When we reach the two men, my mind is preoccupied with Franka's words. I give Tom a quick hug and tell him I hope to be back at work next week, which earns me an eye-roll from Neil. A cheek kiss for Franka and the promise we'll see each other next week and then they are off.

Neil helps me into the truck cab and leans in for a kiss. "How was it?" He wants to know.

I wait until he is buckling up in the driver's seat. "I shared," I tell him, noting the surprise on his face.

"Already? Fuck me, Pup. I'm so proud of you. Can't have been easy."

"She shared right after me. It made it easier having her there."

"Naomi was so right," he mumbles under his voice.

"Naomi?"

"The first time you two met in the hospital, Naomi told me to watch, that you'd be good for each other. She's right," Neil explains. I turn to look at him and see him watching me from the corner of his eyes, obviously chewing on something. But rather than question him, I wait him out. I know it pays off when he blows out a breath he's clearly been holding and closes his eyes. "I don't know how she figured this one, but she also told me to contact Veteran's Affairs and see about handling my own shit." I reach over and slip my hand upside down under the one he holds clenched on his thigh, lacing my fingers with his. I know this is big. This is something he's carried around for many years and from what I gather I'm the only one he's told, which is why what he says next surprises me. "I talked to Gus the other day. Told him." He snorts his disbelief. "His reaction surprised me about as much as yours did. He put in a call to a buddy of his running a veterans' clinic in Durango in his typical no-nonsense way. Guy told him to give me his number but that I'd have to make that first step myself. Been hanging on to that piece of paper not sure if I'd call or not." He twists in his seat, turning his body toward me, his eyes serious. "I'm gonna call. Figure if my girl can find the courage to stand up and tell her story, then dammit, so can I. Or I'm not worthy of her."

"I love you so much." My hand strokes his jaw and I try to convey with my eyes how deep my feelings run. "I'll always be proud of you, of what you do, but more so of who you are. Call him, by all means, but don't do it for me. I don't need it to know how much courage you carry in your heart. Do it for you. Because you deserve to put your own monster to rest." His face turns into my palm as he sucks in a deep breath.

Sitting up, he pulls his phone and a piece of paper out of his pocket. And right there, sitting in the Cortez Memorial Hospital parking lot, he makes the call that will hopefully, finally, free his soul.

CHAPTER TWENTY-EIGHT

Neil

"I told you already. Fuck me, you're a pain in my ass. It'll be done."

I chuckle as I end the call. I'm sure I've been a pain in his ass these past weeks. Since closing on the house, the work has gone into overdrive. Especially since I hit Clint's Mason Brothers up with a few additional requests. Maybe I should call them requirements. Both Kendra and I have become quite attached to the sizable bathtub in the guesthouse and can appreciate the benefits of a separate shower, which is why I'm having the guys renovate the bathroom as well. It was intact after the explosion, but since work was already being done… Same with the kitchen. That needed to be redone anyway, but I put in some requests, hoping Kendra would be pleased with them. Instead of a closed off kitchen, it would now be an open-concept to the living/dining room so that we'd never have to lose sight of each other.

I glance at the clock on my dashboard, hoping like hell I won't run into any traffic on my way back from Durango. Naomi was supposed to drive Kendra to Cortez to get her cast removed, and I'm rushing to meet them. I'd wanted to take her, but Kendra wasn't about to let me skip a session at the veterans' clinic. Probably because after the last one, I told her I thought I might be ready to share my story. Today was my third time going and the things some of the others had shared before, as well as the group's reaction to them, showed me it was safe for me to open up. Veterans of all ages, from all backgrounds, none of whom had been able to leave combat behind completely for a variety of reasons. It was the common monster in the room. It had taken two individual sessions to be deemed ready for the group and by that time I felt wrung out. But now, after sitting through two, just observing and listening, I was ready to jump in. And I did. Although it wasn't any easier than the previous times I've had to recount the story, it sure felt fucking great to only see nods of understanding around the room. So by the time I got to my truck, my shoulders felt lighter, and I was anxious to get to my girl.

The quick call to Clint was only to make sure that by the time I bring Kendra home after her appointment, the house will be ready. She still doesn't know I bought the place, let alone am making some changes, but I hope she'll love it. I know the dog will be happy to have his fenced yard again. Malachi and Gus are bringing over the dog and our belongings, which Emma was going to pack up after Naomi picked Kendra up. This way, by the time we head back for Cedar Tree, we'll be all moved in.

Three weeks ago, Kendra had slowly started taking some of her patients back. Tom Bridges had been first in line. She told me she was waving her fee for him, feeling it was the least she could do. Little does she know that I'm working on my own plans to make sure Tom will not forget how grateful we are.

The parking lot is full, and it takes me ten minutes of driving around to find a spot. I'm frustrated, because I was already cutting it thin and now I'm most definitely late.

But when I make a beeline for the reception, I hear my name called, and I turn to find Kendra and Naomi still sitting in the waiting area.

"He's a little late," Kendra informs me after I kiss her hello. "He had to check out an emergency that was brought in." I settle in beside her on the couch when Naomi announces she has a patient to check on before heading back.

"Unless you want me to stay," she asks Kendra, who shakes her head.

"No, go on. We're not expecting any complications, right?"

"Nope. As of the last look they had a few weeks ago, it seemed to be healing okay. He'll suggest PT to help maximize mobility of that joint, but that's your specialty, not mine." She smiles and waves before heading off down the hall.

Kendra puts her head on my shoulder and her hand in the middle of my chest. "How did it go?" she asks carefully. I could tell she was on pins and needles this morning, knowing I was planning to share today, so I quickly reassure her.

"Well. Surprisingly well." I press a kiss on her head.

"Good. That's really good."

I can hear the smile in her voice and feel some of the tension drain from her shoulders.

There isn't much of a chance to say much more, because Kendra gets called in. Grabbing my hand, she pulls me up. "You're coming with."

-

A little over an hour later, I take the turn off to our new house.

"Hey, you're taking the wrong turn," Kendra, both her feet now in her preferred rubber flip-flops, points out.

"I just want to have a look to see how the house is coming along." I point at her cast-less foot. "I'm sure now that you are a free woman, you'll want to move back in as soon as possible."

She doesn't say anything else, but quietly stares out the window until we pull up in the driveway. "Holy shiznit! Look at it!" She unsnaps her seatbelt and is about to jump out of the cab when I manage to grab her arm.

"Easy, Pup. Doesn't seem like a good idea to jump on that ankle just yet," I comment dryly. Kendra turns to me and sticks her tongue out, clearly not in the mood for teasing. "Let me give you a hand."

⬥

Kendra

The new porch is beautiful. A brand new swing is hanging from the beams and instead of the old wooden railing, a gorgeous new wrought iron one is mounted on the extra wide deck boards. New, larger windows have been put in, and I can only imagine how much lighter it would make the living room. The yard is still a bit barren but I'm sure I'll be able to plant some things now, and the rest maybe October. I'll check with Katie, who has the green thumb.

I have to admit, when Neil pointed out I was moving back soon, it took me by surprise. We've spent almost the entire past eight weeks together. We certainly had shared the same bed each night. It would be weird going back to each of us living in our own place. I hadn't even thought about it before now, and honestly, it makes me a bit sad. I think mostly because of the matter of fact way he said it. Guess I'd assumed we'd live together even after life settled back down. Maybe he's not in that place yet.

"Want to go in?" he asks, pulling me from my thoughts.

"Are you sure that's okay? I mean, I don't see any work trucks here but perhaps—"

"Kendra, it's fine. Come on."

Still on my crutches for another week, I hobble up the three steps to the porch and find Neil already has the door open. With a grand gesture, he waves me in and although the stairs to my right don't appear to have changed, to my left it is a completely new house. I slap my hands over my mouth when I see how bright, with windows on all three sides. The kitchen is visible from the front door and a beautiful gleaming L-shaped bar where the wall used to be, separates the workspace from the living space. Some of the kitchen cabinets have frosted panels and are lit from inside showing glassware and china. To my surprise, Neil's furniture from his apartment fills the living space, and there is even a big bouquet of flowers sitting on his dining room table. I'm stunned. This place is ready for us to move in.

I turn to Neil and see him watching me intently, a nervous little smile on his lips that I can't quite place. "This is amazing. Just beautiful. I don't understand. Your stuff…it's here. I thought when you said I'd be moving in, you meant alone."

He takes a few steps closer and puts his hands on either side of my neck, leaning down to look me straight in the eyes. "You thought I'd just move back into my apartment? Alone? Not gonna happen, babe. You're stuck with me." I drop my forehead to his chest and feel the rumble in his chest as he chuckles. "There's more," he says.

"More? But I thought the rest was not damaged."

"Well no, but Clint did some improvements while he was at it. Upstairs."

I'm glad the stairs only have five steps because I'm not feeling too stable with my crutches. Luckily he's right behind me to catch me if I fall. It's only a small landing upstairs, with the bedrooms on both sides, and the bathroom straight ahead, but something seems a little off on the configuration. I turn to Neil, who just nods in the direction of the bathroom door.

"Oh my God," I exclaim when I take in the completely new layout of what seems to be a much bigger bathroom than before. A lush corner tub is installed in the far left corner and straight ahead is a glass enclosed shower stall. To my right is the connecting door to the master and immediately on my left, against the wall, a new vanity with two sinks and mirrors. "How?" I manage, a little confused at the decidedly larger bathroom.

"Moved the door a little and took out the small closet in the spare. Come look," he says, putting his arm around my shoulders. The spare bedroom only holds a small desk, what looks to be my double bed, and in front of where the closet used to be stands a shelving unit. "There's room for a dresser," Neil assures me before turning us around and heading for the master bedroom. The only thing that's changed in here is the bed. Neil's bigger, and admittedly more comfortable one sits against the far wall. But when he opens the walk-in closet, I'm surprised to see both our clothes hanging neatly on hangers. A million questions run through my head but before I can formulate even one, Neil sinks on his knees in front of me. "Emma packed," he explains. "And the guys moved everything over." Suddenly he's on his feet, swearing under his breath as he stalks to the door. "Stay put, I forgot something," he says before disappearing downstairs.

I hear the opening and closing of a door and then very familiar nails clicking up the stairs. "Chaos!" I call the big black lug of a dog who comes barreling through the doorway. With one, rather uncoordinated leap, he lands on the bed with his legs up in the air for a belly rub. Neil follows slower and watches us from the doorway, a small smile on his face as I indulge our dog and scratch his belly.

"Forgot Gus left him outside," he says as he walks toward the bed and sits down on the edge. "Now where was I?"

"You were about to tell me how you pulled off this amazing surprise," I tell him, abandoning the dog and sneaking up behind Neil, draping myself over his shoulders, my arms around his neck. He twists in the bed so his back can lean against the headboard before pulling me onto his lap.

"Just a bit of help from our friends and some planning."

"Uh-huh. And what about the bathroom? The downstairs, my God…why would they go to such lengths for a rental place?" I see a small muscle twitch in his cheek. "Neil?"

"It's not exactly a rental place anymore," he confesses and it doesn't take long for me to clue in.

"You didn't," I whisper, pushing myself off his lap.

"There's room for us to build further to the back, and we have the basement we can utilize," he continues as if I hadn't spoken.

Neil

Oh man.

I'm pretty sure I fucked the toaster on this one. Her face is a mask of disbelief and I don't know what else to do but to push ahead and lay it all out.

"I was looking for something anyway, Pup, when you moved here. And I loved this house so much. Then I finally had my shot with you… It seemed perfect. If you don't like it, I can—"

"Shut up," she says softly and repeats louder. "Shut up."

Taken aback, I sit back and wait for the blow out. I watch her bend her head and release a few deep breaths before she looks up again, tears pooling in her eyes.

"It's perfect," she whispers as she climbs back on my lap. "I've run the gamut of emotions today, honey. Nervous about my appointment, nervous about how you were doing. I was worried you might not be at the hospital in time and I really wanted you there, except I didn't want you to miss your session. I've been all over the place. Then thinking you were wanting to slow us down, just as I started catching up and then the house. My God, Neil, the house… It's perfect."

I hold her as I feel all the pieces of my life sliding home.

Not sure how long we've been sitting like this, Kendra cuddled against my chest and the dog—who crawled closer to us on the bed, with his head on my leg—when I hear a knock and the front door opening.

"Hello! Anybody home?"

"Mom?" Kendra mumbles as she sits up and Chaos jumps down to check out the visitor.

"Surprise!" That's Emma's voice, and I remember she'd mentioned something about coming by after we've had a chance to settle in. Make that *visitors* then.

"Told you they'd prefer to celebrate by themselves, Peach." Gus's deep voice can be heard scolding his wife.

"Nonsense," Elsa pipes up, and I feel Kendra's body shaking in my lap. She's laughing.

"Fuck me," I mutter, shaking my head.

"Why's everyone standing in the doorway? The rest of us would like to come in too. Move!" And that is Arlene. By the sound of it, Emma has rounded up just about the entire population of Cedar Tree and beyond. Kendra just sits in my lap, giggling her ass off.

"We should go downstairs." She hiccups. "Before they send Arlene up as reconnaissance. Or worse, my mother."

I groan getting off the bed. "Fine. Sooner we get this shindig over with, the sooner we can crawl back in our peaceful bubble."

Still on her knees on the bed, Kendra reaches up and pulls me down by the neck. "Don't be grumpy. I promise to make it up to you later," she says, her lips brushing mine.

"Gonna keep you to that," I mumble, my mouth already slanting to fit over hers. My tongue slides between her lips and instantly the kiss turns heated with Kendra's hands slipping under my shirt and clawing at my back. My girl is needy.

"They're up here!" Arlene hollers down from the bedroom door before turning just her eyes on us. "And they're getting a head start on christening their new home!"

"Arlene!" Seb's voice sounds from the bottom of the stairs. "Get your ass back down here, Spot. They'll show up when they're good and ready."

Arlene huffs loudly but turns around and stomps down the stairs. We can just hear her say, *"party-pooper"* sending both Kendra and I into fits of laughter.

Instead of letting Kendra struggle down the steps, I end up carrying her down, her crutches in her hand. The place is packed with people. Clint is showing Beth around the kitchen, getting shoved out of the way when Emma and Seb start spreading out food on the new kitchen bar. Fox and Joe come walking in carrying crates of beer, and Naomi follows behind with a potted plant.

"You knew too?" Kendra accuses her when she spots the plant. Naomi just smiles and shrugs walking to the coffee table and setting the plant in the middle.

I set Kendra on the couch next to Kim, and she's instantly absorbed by the baby bundle Mal's wife places in her arms. Elsa slips beside Kendra on her other side, shoving me out of the way. Dismissed. I just shake my head and accept the beer Malachi hands me with a big smile on his face.

"What did you think?" he asks with an eyebrow raised. "Saying okay to any of these women when they propose briefly *popping in,* is like consenting to a mosh pit in your living room."

"I heard that," Kim's head pops up from the baby-huddle on the couch.

"You know I'm not lying, *Nizhóní,*" her husband shoots back. Kim just rolls her eyes and dives back into the cluster of women around Kendra.

"I've got the meat," Caleb's voice sounds from the door. He's behind Katie who is trying to hang on to their son Mattias. The little guy has spotted his favorite two people in the universe next to his parents: his uncles.

"Uncanee!!" The kid produces a volume that such a little body shouldn't be able to produce, as he yanks his arm free from his mom's grasp and toddles in high gear toward me.

"Hey, little guy." I smile as I bend down and pick him up, setting him on my hip. "Did you see the dog yet?"

"Doggie?" the little tyke bellows when his mom walks up.

"Matty, use your inside voice, baby," Katie says gently.

"Shhhh," is the toddler's response, accompanied by a little index finger pressed to his lips and a gush of spittle spraying me.

"Sorry." Katie winces.

A soft chuckle catches my attention, and when I turn I see Kendra's eyes sparkling with amusement at my expense. Her face is soft and she looks as relaxed as I've ever seen her. My heart does a little flip in my chest until a certain pint-sized town cryer slaps his little hands on my face.

"Doggie!" he yells in my face.

"Yes, kid. Doggie. Let's go find him." I swing Mattias up and onto my shoulders. Instinctively, his little fists clutch in my hair, and with one last look at a laughing Kendra, I take the boy to see a dog.

Kendra

Best night ever.

I look over at the alarm clock to see it's almost midnight. Seb finally managed to coax Arlene to go home after Emma and Gus had taken Mom home. She's apparently staying in the guesthouse for the weekend. Neil laughed at that, said that that guesthouse had never been vacant. Not since they had it built many moons ago.

Chaos is snoring beside the bed, tired from trying to avoid a hyperactive little boy all night, and Neil is brushing his teeth in the bathroom. At his own sink. A smile steals over my face as I let my eyes wander around the room. I can't quite believe I'm living in this gorgeous house. For keeps.

"What are you smiling at, Pup?" Neil's warm voice comes from the bathroom doorway where he is leaning against the post, his arms crossed over his naked chest.

"This," I confess, waving my arms to include everything. "Tonight. Our friends. This house. Everything."

Neil smiles as he stalks the bed and climbs up from the bottom, stopping at my ankle which he strokes lightly with a finger. "How's the foot?"

"Good." I smile back as that finger slowly travels up my calf to the back of my knee.

"Happy?" he asks, his lips following the path of his finger, lightly kissing the inside of my leg.

"Blissfully. You?"

"Sweetheart, I was happy from the first time I got to taste your lips, and you went from a distant dream to a perfect reality. I had a head start."

Kendra

"Are you ready?"

I grab her outstretched hand. Both of us are facedown on tables side by side in Durango's best-rated tattoo shop. I had some skin grafts done two years ago, taking care of the raised patches on my back. The feathers. The deeper grooves along my spine and marking the outlines had filled in but had been too deep to attempt to fix. Franka had opted to do the same, but started a year later, and hers took several surgeries. Our markings were eerily similar. I don't know how we got onto the subject of tattoos, but Franka showed me one she had on her thigh which was intricate like a henna painting. She mentioned always having wanted more, but visible tattoos were still often frowned upon in her line of work, dealing with mostly an older generation, so she never got any more. Then something Emma once told me about claiming those marks, making them mine, popped in my head. Franka had loved the idea but at the time was still healing from her final surgery.

Now, six months after that conversation, the two of us are ready to reclaim what was ours to begin with.

The sensation of the needles piercing the mangled flesh on my back feels like a purging of sorts. Out with the bad and in with the good. The cherry blossoms to me have always symbolized spring—the start of a new growing season. Spring is also when I started falling for Neil, finally letting down my guard and entering a new phase in my life. It has taken me a long time to learn not to allow the dark side of that spring to overshadow or even dull the beauty of my life right now. Another reason for the cherry blossoms is that they are the most beautiful things I can imagine. The dual hum of the tattoo needles is the white noise that allows my mind to drift, even as my scars disappear under the intricate artwork that is being applied to my back.

I turn my eyes to look at Franka who is looking back at me and we both smile.

"How was Durango?" Neil asks as he walks in the door later that night. All he knows is that I was going for a girl's day, maybe to visit a spa with Franka, who had relocated to Durango for work this past year.

"Good. We had a good time," I tell him, stirring the soup made with vegetables from our own garden.

His arms slip around my waist and I have to swallow the yelp that wants to break free when he presses against my rather tender back.

"What are you cooking?"

"Veggie soup and I have a ham and cheese loaf baking in the oven." I put down the spoon and gingerly turn in his arms. "Hey, baby." I smile as I slip my arms around his neck. My handsome husband.

He'd asked me to marry him the first night we spent in our new house. I'd managed to evade answering for two months before he'd had enough. I'd just slowly started hiking again, an activity that luckily Neil and Chaos seemed to enjoy as well. Although my ankle was healing, I'd likely always have a slight limp. That's when I started thinking about fixing my back, and Neil was able to convince me that his medical insurance would allow for broader choices. More options. It's not like I wasn't going to say yes eventually anyway, I just wanted to settle first. Get my feet under me, so to speak. So I told him yes, but made it clear it had nothing to do with his insurance, but rather with the fact that I love him to distraction and can't see my life without him permanently in it. The insurance bit was just an added benefit. We were married four months after that. Caleb and Katie had generously offered up their beautiful barn house, and we had kept things simple. Neil had even spoken to his parents for the first time in many years and asked them if they wanted to come. When they'd discovered his future wife was not part of the Church of the Latter Day Saints, they'd declined. I'd been furious, but Neil just shrugged his shoulders. "I can't control how they act. I can only control how I allow myself to react," he said sagely.

The wedding was simple and glorious. Kara flew out from Boston with her girlfriend, who she had reconciled with, and with Neil's best friend there and his brothers, my best Cedar Tree girls, my mom, Karly and even Franka, we had all the family we needed.

"Where is your mind?" Neil whispers against the shell of my ear sending a shiver down my spine.

"I was thinking about our wedding. Our friends. How lucky we are."

"I'd have to agree on that. How long does that bread still need in the oven?" I can tell from the smirk on his face that he has some ideas on appetizers.

"Fifteen minutes," I tell him, laughing at the pout he sports. "Not enough for what you have in mind, honey."

"I can be quick," he tries, but I shake my head.

"First we eat, then you get to play. Why don't you give the dog a quick walk while I finish up here?"

He grudgingly complies and the moment the door closes behind him, I rush upstairs. The tattoo artist had said to leave the dressing on for four hours and it had only been three and a half, but I figured those thirty minutes wouldn't be a big deal. I don't want him to find a big patch of plastic on my back. I want to surprise him. I know my man, once he has his mind set on getting in my panties, he won't waste any time. Nothing has changed in that respect.

I stand in front of the mirror and carefully peel away the plastic. It's hard to see the whole thing, looking over my shoulder but what I can see is stunning. With a few acrobatics, I manage to get most of the tattoo covered with the ointment they gave me. Grabbing a clean T-shirt, I quickly pull it on and rush downstairs just in time for the bread to come out of the oven.

⯈⯇

Neil

I have to force myself to take Chaos for his usual constitutional. My instinct is to rush home, but I may as well give him his due now, since it looks like I may not get around to walking him again before bedtime. I'm planning to have my hands full.

The moment I turn from the trail onto the street our nosy neighbor is hanging over her fence, waving me over. I'm barely within speaking distance when she starts. "This morning, there was a strange car that pulled into your driveway."

Every so often the old lady would spot something she deemed suspicious. Having discovered I work for a security company, she seemed to think I was the appropriate person to share this with. "Are you sure it wasn't the mailman?" I ask. A valid question, since she twice had called 911 last winter when she wasn't able to recognize him during a snowfall.

"Of course I'm sure," she huffs insulted. "I may be old but I'm not senile. The mailman is nearing his retirement, but when he got out of his car, I could clearly see this was a young man. Even younger than you."

"Okay. Do you remember what kind of vehicle he drove? A truck? A regular car? What color?"

"Of course I do. A hunter green crew cab F-150. My guess'd be no later than 2007," she says proudly. I have to bite my tongue not to chuckle at her. Since the explosion at our house a few years ago, she'd made it a point to study every make and distinguishing branding of any vehicle out there. She was determined to be able to give complete reports and descriptions just in case she was called up as a witness. Poor thing had been the only one disappointed when she discovered there would be no trial for Lars Cayman. The prospect of pointing her finger at the accused and saying that is the man when asked to identify him, had been something she'd only dreamed of before.

"I'll ask around," I tell her.

"You do that, and let me know if anything comes from it," she says, waving her gnarly finger in my face.

"Sure thing. Best get inside now, it's getting chilly."

Reluctantly she shuffles back to her porch where she defiantly sits down again, pulling an afghan over her lap. Shaking my head, I walk back across the street, wondering when Tom got back to town, since he's the only person I know with a hunter green Ford F-150. She was right about the age too. The truck is a 2006. I know, because I bought it for him when he went to college in Denver.

"Did you know Tom was back in town?" I ask as I close the door behind me and take the dog's leash off.

"I did. Forgot to tell you. He must've dropped by sometime today. He'd left a note on the front door. I called him," she says, turning around and setting bowls and a cutting board with a steaming loaf of cheesy bread on the counter. I take off my boots and sit down on one of the stools.

"Yeah? How's he doing?"

"Great. He says. His marks are awesome and he got a summer job as gopher with Mason Brothers."

"Clint hired him? That's great."

"Says he needs the job to pay back whoever is paying for his tuition, if ever he finds out," she says, smiling at me.

"I don't know anything about that," I tell her with a straight face.

"Well, of course you don't."

Smartass. She knows, even though I've never told her. I can tell from the smirk on her face as she cuts a chunk off the bread and hands it to me. It was the only way I knew to pay him back for what he did for my Pup back then. It hadn't been hard to set up a one-time anonymous scholarship. The trickiest part had been to find out what places he'd set his mind to, but that's where his old high school coach had come in handy.

"Soup's great, babe. But I think I'll save some room for later." I push aside my now empty bowl and watch Kendra eat hers torturously slow. Minx. The instant she puts her spoon down, I grab her hand and pull her toward the stairs.

"Neil! Let me at least put away the bread before Chaos climbs up on the counter again."

I reluctantly let her go to take care of that. The dog, although not the sharpest knife in the block, has the uncanny ability to steal our food from the oddest places. We've even had to put a lock on the fridge after discovering he knows how to open the damn thing. As soon as Kendra joins me at the bottom of the stairs, I bend down, put my shoulder in her stomach and carry her, fireman style, up the stairs.

"Neanderthal," she grumbles, but I know she secretly enjoys when I toss her around a bit.

"You love it." I slap her luscious ass for emphasis.

Once in the bedroom, I unceremoniously drop her on the mattress, catching her wince when she lands. "Did I hurt you?" I ask, sitting on the edge of the bed beside her.

"Wasn't anything you did," she says with a smile.

"So someone did?" I feel the hair on my neck stand on end. If someone as much as laid a hand on her, I swear I'll fucking lose it.

"You tell me." She crawls off the bed and steps in between my legs, grabbing the bottom of her shirt and slowly pulling it over her head. No bra. Nice. My hands automatically come up and cup her breasts in my hands, flicking lightly at her pebbling nipples. I bring one to my mouth, but before I can close my lips over it, she pulls back. "Wait." Taking a step back, she pushes her jeans down and steps out of them, leaving her in a cute pair of pink boy-shorts. I immediately pull her back with my hands on her hips, but she turns around in my hold. And then my hands drop away. Along her spine, up over her shoulder blades and down her sides, her familiar scars have been transformed into blossoming branches. I know my mouth hangs open as my eyes look at the intricately shaped flowers, covering almost every one of her scars. Deep, rich browns for the branches and a delicate pink for the blossoms.

Kendra looks over her shoulder at me, her face insecure. "Do you like it?"

"Do I like it? You have spring on your back."

She slowly nods her head, still waiting for an answer. There's only one answer I can give her.

"Gorgeous," I grunt as I stand, push her face down on the bed and yank down her panties. Fucking gorgeous. In two seconds, my shirt is on the floor and my jeans and boxers are around my ankles as I lean down over her and whisper in her ear. "Perfect."

I slide the head of my engorged cock down her slit once, to test her and she is slick already. In one surge, I implant myself balls deep. Kendra groans and lifts her head from the mattress and tilts it to the side, finding my eyes with hers.

"Holy tater tits…"

Kendra

"What's with the hand over my eyes?" I want to know as Neil shuffles me up the stairs. The moment I walked in the door, he had taken my purse from my hand, dropped it on the hall table and covered my eyes.

"Just bear with me," he mumbles in my ear as he guides me into the bedroom.

I can sense we're standing at the foot of the bed and the only thing I can think of is that my husband is planning a kinky afternoon. Something I would not think to object to. So when he whispers, "Are you ready?" in my ear and pulls his hand away, I'm not prepared.

Over our bed, covering most of the empty expanse of wall, is a giant canvass. I blink furiously to clear my vision, since it is an image I haven't been able to see yet in its entirety. I don't recall him taking a picture, he must've done so while I was sleeping, because before me, larger than life, is an image of the beautiful cherry branches, permanently tattooed on the skin of my back.

My throat is thick with emotion when I turn to him to find his eyes on me. Tender and soft, they convey everything he feels for me. His hand comes up to wipe the tears from my cheeks and I turn my face into his palm.

"I love you," I manage to tell him. This man is my everything.

THE END

ACKNOWLEDGEMENTS:

Once again I have to thank my editor, Vanessa of PREMA
Editing. She and her partner Manda manage to correct and tweak
my work without even once making me feel bad about it. They
continually challenge and encourage me to hone and refine my
writing skills with each book I write. Thank you so much for
helping me grow!

I'm actually blessed with a few fantastic editors who alternate to
facilitate my writing schedule. Karen Hrdlicka is involved in all
my books. Both editing and alpha-reading. She was pivotal in
working out some of the nuances in the plot for Head Start, as
was my good friend and fabulous blogger, Pam Buchanan. They
both had hands and eyes on Head Start when it was still in its
raw form. I owe these ladies a lot and I love them dearly.

I would be nowhere without my awesome, no-nonsense, always
available, brutally honest beta-readers; Catherine, Lena, Deb,
Kerry-Ann, Sam, Debbie, Chris, and last but not least, Nancy.
With each book I finish, I receive a resounding YES, when I ask
if they are available to beta for me. I cannot tell you how blessed
I feel with such an amazing team at my back. They are my
trusted friends who are not afraid to let me know when
something doesn't sit well with them. And I welcome it, each
and every time, because without these girls I wouldn't know if I
was on the right track.
All of you are so very valuable to me. I love you hard!

The woman who carries me day by day. Who patiently listens to
me when I cry and moan when things aren't going my way. And
who never rests to find creative ways to promote my books,
which she does so well with the help of Leanne Hawkes!
Francessca Webster, you are a fabulous friend, the hardest

worker I know and an absolute treasure I've been so lucky to find. I absolutely adore you!

My man. I can't ever leave him out because most of the time he puts up with my one syllable answers (when I'm ducked down behind my laptop) or watching me walk out the door when I leave with my suitcase for yet another signing somewhere. He takes care the dog is taken care of, the house is kept up and the fridge is stocked. I'm so lucky to have him.

I have a few very close friends. Friends who will always be there for me, whether I've spoken with them five minutes or five weeks ago. It just doesn't matter. They have my back and I have theirs—always. They are the fabric against which I forge the fictional connections and friendships in my stories. Linda, Dana, Barb, Aimee—I love you!!

I come from a long line of strong, down to earth women. Women who are able to pick themselves up and start over. Sometimes time and again. I want thank each of them for what I've learned about being a strong and resilient woman. Mom, Maaike, Sanne, Kyra, Mariette, Louise and Holly, thank you for keeping it real and in balance. Lord knows I need that sometimes. I love you more than I can say.

And finally (yes….I'm almost done), I need to put the focus on the incredible support shown by my readers, who embraced my Cedar Tree stories from the very first one—you are what makes me able to live a dream. The bloggers and reviewers who took a chance on that first book and fell in love. And my fellow authors and friends who don't ever seem to tire of showing their support. Thank you all so much for everything you do!

ABOUT THE AUTHOR

Freya Barker inspires with her stories about 'real' people, perhaps less than perfect, each struggling to find their own slice of happy, but just as deserving of romance, thrills and chills, and some hot, sizzling sex in their lives.

Recipient of the RomCon "Reader's Choice" Award for best first book, "Slim To None," Freya has hit the ground running. She loves nothing more than to meet and mingle with her readers, whether it be online or in person at one of the signings she attends.

Freya spins story after story with an endless supply of bruised and dented characters, vying for attention!

Freya

https://www.freyabarker.com

http://bit.ly/FreyaAmazon

https://www.goodreads.com/FreyaBarker

https://www.facebook.com/FreyaBarkerWrites

https://tsu.co/FreyaB

https://twitter.com/freya_barker

or mailto:freyabarker.writes@gmail.com

ALSO BY THIS AUTHOR

CEDAR TREE SERIES:

SLIM TO NONE

HUNDRED TO ONE

AGAINST ME

CLEAN LINES

UPPER HAND

LIKE ARROWS

HEAD START

PORTLAND, ME, NOVELS:

FROM DUST

CRUEL WATER

THROUGH FIRE

STILL AIR

NORTHERN LIGHTS COLLECTION:

A CHANGE OF TIDE

A CHANGE OF VIEW

A CHANGE OF PACE
(Coming soon!)

ROCK POINT SERIES:

KEEPING 6
CABIN 12
(Coming soon!)

SNAPSHOT SERIES:

SHUTTER SPEED
FREEZE FRAME
IDEAL IMAGE
PICTURE PERFECT
(coming soon!)